ONCE UPON A HIGHLAND AUTUMN

Also by Lecia Cornwall

Once Upon a Highland Summer
What a Lady Most Desires
The Secret Life of Lady Julia
How to Deceive a Duke
All the Pleasures of the Season
The Price of Temptation
Secrets of a Proper Countess

ONCE UPON
A HIGHLAND
AUTUMN

LECIA CORNWALL

AVONIMPULSE
An Imprint of HarperCollinsPublishers

Excerpt from *Once upon a Highland Summer* © 2013 by Lecia Cotton Cornwall.

Excerpt from *What a Lady Most Desires* copyright © 2014 by Lecia Cotton Cornwall.

Excerpt from *Catching Cameron* copyright © 2014 by Julie Revell Benjamin.

Excerpt from *Daring Miss Danvers* copyright © 2014 by Vivienne Lorret.

Excerpt from *Woo'd in Haste* copyright © 2014 by Sabrina Darby.

Excerpt from *Bad Girls Don't Marry Marines* copyright © 2014 by Codi Gary.

Excerpt from *Various States of Undress: Carolina* copyright © 2014 by Laura Simcox.

Excerpt from *Wed at Leisure* copyright © 2014 by Sabrina Darby.

EPub Edition June 2014 ISBN: 9780062328458

Print Edition ISBN: 9780062328465

JV 10 9 8 7 6 5 4

For my aunt, Mary Hayes-Sheen, with love

Glen Dorian, 1817

"Is that a true story?"

Duncan MacIntosh let his gaze bore into the child from across the fire.

"It's as true as any tale ever was, lad. 'Tisn't a story—it's the history of your own clan. Do you doubt my word?"

"But how can a dragon eat a whole village?" the boy asked, not half as frightened of the aged clansman's scowl as Duncan would have liked. So he raised his hands over his head, spreading his plaid above himself like wings. He leaned away from the fire, letting the shadows transform him until his eyes gleamed, and the crags and valleys of his wrinkled skin deepened in the firelight. "He *is* a dragon!" the boy cried out in terror, and clutched his mother's skirt.

The *seannachaidh* of Clan MacIntosh sat down, coming back into the light, his face benign now. He set a gnarled hand on the boy's shoulder. "Och, don't be afraid, lad. 'Tis all for fun, that tale. It's a *seannachaidh*'s job to keep the tales of the clan, and tell them—even the almost-true ones about dragons. Shall I tell you a truly true one?"

The boy stuck his lip out mutinously. "Are there dragons in it?"

"No. There's a pretty lass called Mairi MacIntosh, her brave laird, and a soldier in this tale, but no dragons—well, unless you count the fearsome Duke of Cumberland."

"Who's he?" the boy asked.

"He was the wicked son of a king. He came to vanquish the MacIntosh clan, and all the rest of the Highlanders."

The boy's eyes widened. "Is there blood and swords and killing in this tale?"

Duncan's brow crumpled. "Too much of that, I fear. Are you afraid?"

The lad shook his head. "Is there kissing?"

The old man's brow smoothed as he laughed. "Aye, some—though not nearly enough."

"How does the story end?"

"I don't know. It hasn't got an ending yet."

"Haven't you made one up?" the child demanded.

Duncan pursed his lips. "As I said, this is a true tale, not a made-up one. True tales are long in the unfolding, lad. You can't just conjure the ending out of the air. Something happens to begin the story—a dreadful thing sometimes—and then we must wait for the outcome. D'you understand that lad?"

"I think so."

"Good. Then you must listen closely, and learn this story, so one day you can tell it. There have been a great many MacIntoshes in this glen before you and me, and I intend to see to it that you know all about every one of them before I leave this earth. Someday it will be you sitting here by the fire, lad, telling the tales to your sons or your grandsons, and they will do the same in their turn."

The boy glanced over his shoulder at the loch of Glen Dorian, named for the otters that had always lived there. The water shimmered in the moonlight, black and deep. "Will I find the ending of this story?" the boy asked, stepping away from his mother to set his hand on Duncan's knee.

"I hope you will. But for now you should know how it started." The old *seannachaidh* took the boy onto his lap, kissed the top of his dark head, and looked out at the rest of his audience, a half-dozen MacIntosh clansmen, women, and children who sat around the blazing fire on this summer evening, listening to stories under the stars, just as other MacIntoshes had done before them.

Duncan stared into the fire as if he could see faces and events written there, and the others leaned nearer too, as he began to speak.

"This is the story of love, and hatred, and war—and of kindness, too. It all began many years ago, during the forty-five, when the clans rose to fight for Bonnie Prince Charlie Stuart, and in the choosing of sides, many things happened— terrible, sorrowful things that still hover over this glen— including a powerful curse."

"Mairi's curse," someone whispered fearfully, and a murmur rose with the smoke of the fire.

"Aye," Duncan said. "Mairi's curse. Listen now. I will tell you all I know, but that curse remains upon our glen, waiting for the day when someone will come at last and break it, and bring love and happiness back to Glen Dorian."

"And kissing?" the boy asked.

"And kissing, too," Duncan said, and began to tell the tale.

Chapter One

Glenlorne, summer 1817

Lady Megan McNabb stood beside the old tower of Glenlorne and looked out across the valley. Summer was at its
height, hovering on the pinnacle between lush green perfection and the graceful slide into the golden glory of autumn.
Megan drank in every detail—the old tower behind her,
the new castle in the valley below, the loch, and the way the
clouds rested on the peaks of the highest hills that sheltered
the glen, and sighed. She would miss autumn here, but she'd
be back again by spring, and then she would never, ever leave
home again, no matter what anyone else expected of her.

She looked down at Glenlorne Castle, and her defiance was
nudged aside by guilt. She should be packing. She and her sisters
were leaving in a few short hours. They would board the coach
and travel to Dundrummie Castle to stay with their mother.
The Dowager Countess of Glenlorne had retired to live with her
widowed sister-in-law now that her stepson Alec had taken his
place as Earl of Glenlorne. Alec was newly married, and it had
been decided that his sisters would spend a few months with
their mother, to give the newlyweds time to enjoy a honeymoon.

Megan understood *why* they must go—really she did, being in love herself. But she could not help but envy her brother's happiness. Megan's love was far away, and they could not marry. Not yet at least, and that made it seem most unfair indeed.

Oh, Eachann, lovely Eachann! She had kissed him good-bye on this very spot, in the shadow of the old tower, pledged to wait for him, to keep their love a secret until he returned and could honorably offer for her. She put a finger to her lips, lips he'd kissed scarcely a month before, and felt her heart twist with yearning.

Surely the time would pass faster if she went away, didn't face reminders of Eachann everywhere she looked. It was hard to hide her sighs of longing, but she must. Her mother would forbid the match as unworthy of an earl's daughter. Alec would tell her she was too young to know her own mind. Alec's new wife, Caroline, would tell her gently that she should see more of the world, spend a Season in London, before she made her choice and settled into wedded bliss. Her sisters would tease her for falling in love with the penniless son of Glenlorne's gamekeeper. No, better it remain a secret that only she and her true love knew. She took the tiny promise ring out of her pocket and slid it onto her finger and stared at it with a smile. Soon, very soon, Eachann would come home, rich, a man of the world, and no one would tell them no then.

But now, Megan was to go to Dundrummie, then on to London in the spring for the Season. Her mother expected her to charm a rich English lord, wed him before summer came again, and live forever in England. Lady Devorguilla

McNabb had spent all the nineteen years of Megan's life, and the seventeen years of her sister Alanna's life, and every moment of Sorcha's twelve years planning to marry her daughters to Englishmen, whom she considered superior in every way to Scottish men, plain or noble, poor or rich.

Megan frowned. Her mother was going to be very disappointed with her eldest daughter, but a lady could not help falling in love, and Megan's heart had been given. She loved Eachann Rennie, gamekeeper's son, and she was certainly old enough to know her own mind. The very idea of marrying an English lord of her mother's choosing—a complete stranger—and never seeing her homeland again made her shudder.

Megan scanned the glen again without seeing it. Her heart was sailing the high seas with Eachann as he strove to make his fortune. Not even her mother could object to him then, surely, with gold and a fine wedding ring in his pocket. They would be married in Glenlorne's chapel, build a grand house here in the glen, and live happily ever after.

"Megan!" she turned as Sorcha, her youngest sister, struggled up the hill, her braids coming undone, russet curls askew around her flushed and freckled face. Her gown was stained with grass and tucked into her belt, her bare feet muddy. She wondered just how her mother was ever going to make an Englishman's bride out of Sorcha. But then, her little sister was only twelve, and by the time Devorguilla frog-marched Sorcha to London for her debut, she would be the perfect lady, fit to wed a duke. Perhaps. She wished her mother—and the unknown lord—the best of luck with Sorcha.

Her sister panted like a hound as she tried to catch her breath. "I've been looking for you for nearly an hour. Muira says it's nearly time to go, and you're not even half-packed. You won't have a thing to wear when we get to Dundrummie."

Megan scanned the valley once more and ignored her sister. "I'm just saying good-bye to Glenlorne. At least for now."

"Better to say farewell to people than places," Sorcha said. "I've already been to the village, telling folk I'll be back come spring." She grinned mischievously at her sister. "You won't though—you'll be in London, bothered by the attentions of all those daft English lairds at your first Season."

Megan felt a rush of irritation. "Lords, Sorcha, not lairds—and stop teasing," she commanded, and flounced down the steep path that led back to the castle.

Sorcha picked a flower and skipped beside her sister like a mountain goat. One by one, she plucked at the petals. "How many English *lords* will Megan McNabb kiss?" she asked, dancing around her sister. "One . . . two . . . three . . ."

"Stop it," Megan said, and snatched the flower away. She wouldn't kiss anyone but Eachann. But her sister picked another flower.

"How many English lords will come and ask Alec for Meggy's hand in marriage?" she sang, but Megan snatched that blossom too, before Sorcha could begin counting again.

"I shan't go to London, and I will never marry an English lord," she said fiercely.

"We'll see what Mama says to that," Sorcha said. "And Muira would say never is a very long time indeed."

Megan stopped. "What exactly did Muira say?" Old Muira had the sight, or so it was said.

Sorcha grinned like a pirate, and rubbed a dusty hand over her face, leaving a dark smudge. "I thought you didn't believe in the old ways."

Megan rolled her eyes, let her gaze travel up the smooth green slopes of the hills to their rocky crests and thought of the legends and tales, the old stories, the belief that magic made its home in the glen.

Of course she believed.

She believed so much that she had decided to become the keeper of the clan's tales when Glenlorne's ancient *seanna-chaidh* had died last winter without leaving a successor. She loved to hear the old stories, and she planned to write them down so they'd never be lost. But for now, in Sorcha's annoying company, she raised her chin. Now was hardly the time to be fanciful. "Of course I don't believe in magic. I think being sensible is far more useful to get you what you want, not counting flower petals or relying on the seeings of an old woman."

"Muira foresaw an Englishman, and a treasure," Sorcha said, not deterred one whit by talk of sense. "Right there in the smoke of the fire, clear as day."

Megan felt her mouth dry. "For me?" she asked through stiff lips.

"She didn't know that. For one of us, surely."

Megan let out a sigh of relief. Perhaps she was safe. If only Muira had seen Eachann, riding home, his heart light, his purse heavy, with that fine gold ring in his pocket. "That's the trouble with Muira's premonitions. She sees things, but can't say what they mean."

"Still, a treasure would be nice," Sorcha chirped. "A chest of gold, or a cache of pearls and rubies—"

"Not if it comes with an Englishman attached," Megan muttered.

"Och, I'm not worried. I'm only twelve. He won't be coming for me, that's certain. But you're nearly twenty. According to Muira, it's far past time you were wed. Muira says you should have a dozen bairns by now."

Megan felt her cheeks heat. "Muira says," she grumbled. She and Eachann had spoken of the babes they would have—four or five strong lads to take after their father, and two or three pretty little lasses. She felt her heart quicken with longing. Perhaps she could ask Muira to look again, be sure— They'd reached the path beside the loch, a cool and shady haven out of the sun. Megan stopped and stared out at the dark water, and wondered if Eachann was staring out across a very different body of water, and likewise longing for her.

"D'you suppose we have time for a swim?" Sorcha asked, dabbling her toes in the water. "'Tis uncommonly hot today."

Megan looked at her sister's flushed face, took note of the smudges of dirt. Tomorrow they'd be at Dundrummie, and Mama would expect—insist—that they behave like ladies. There'd be no swimming, no running free in the hills. Sorcha would be kept indoors learning English, and Megan and Alanna would be given long hours of instruction in dancing and deportment, and be fitted for a grand wardrobe of stiff, horrid English gowns for their upcoming London Season—and corsets, tied tight enough to cut a lass in two.

The loch beckoned, and Megan grinned at her sister as she kicked off her shoes and pulled her gown over her head.

"Aye, why not?" she said. "I'll race you to the black rock." She dove into the chill of the water, came up gasping, the hills wavering through the drops on her lashes. Pleasure, pure sweet pleasure.

She grinned and dove again. Whatever the future might hold, there was still joy to be had today.

Chapter Two

Bellemont Park, Derbyshire, England, June 1817

Lord Christopher Linwood paced the drawing room of Bellemont Park, his favorite and most elegant manor, and the home he would soon be forced to vacate.

"Am I not the Earl of Rossington, and head of this family?" he demanded of his mother, who sat placidly by the window, embroidering.

She glanced up as she drew the thread through the fine linen. "Of course you are, dear. No one is in any doubt of that."

He swept a hand around him to indicate the magnificent room, the gilded plasterwork, the fine paintings, the expensive carpets, clocks, and furnishings. "And is a man's home not his castle, his sanctuary, his inviolable right?"

The countess took another stitch. "Indeed, but alas, you are a bachelor, Kit."

"What has that got to do with it?"

"I'm simply saying that if you were married, your wife would not countenance your siblings pushing in on you as they've done. You could have said no—your wife, if you had one—most certainly would have. But as a bachelor, your home—or homes, in this case—are wide open. What need has a single gentleman for an entire castle to himself, let alone five?"

Kit frowned at her, but she had turned her attention to a delicate stitch and didn't notice. "They belong to me," he said, knowing he sounded peevish, but it was too late to put his foot down now, as he should have done weeks ago—a year and a half ago, in fact, when he'd inherited the title, and the mess that went with it. "I pay the bills and give my siblings generous allowances besides. Arabella is married with a home of her own, if I might point out, and—"

The countess looked up at her son in surprise, and let her embroidery hoop fall into her lap. "Now really, Kit, be reasonable. How can you expect your sister to remain with Collingwood after such an insult? He must be taught a lesson, and doing without his wife for a few weeks will do him a great deal of good. In fact, it will do them both good."

"Every day there's a new and unforgiveable insult between them, but it's never clear just what the insult is. This time she's vowing never to return to him at all, threatening to remain here at Bellemont for good," Kit said.

"Nonsense," the countess muttered. "As soon as Collingwood makes a proper apology, she'll fall back into his arms like a ripe plum. You needn't fear—it won't take long. By Christmas, at the worst."

Kit's brows shot upward, and he stopped pacing to gape at his mother. "I'm to be locked out of my home until Christmas?"

Her eyes slid away from his. "Well, I'm sure Arabella will

not let it go beyond the start of the Season next spring under any circumstances."

Christopher felt his chest cave in. "Next spring? That's hardly a few weeks—it's nearly a year."

The countess forced a smile. "Be a dear and ring for tea, will you? The weather is hot today, even for July." She watched as he did as she asked, and frowned when he gave the bell a killing yank. "I still say this is your own fault. You could have offered to make peace between them, or you might stay here at Bellemont and convince your sister to return to her husband sooner. You *are* the head of the family."

Kit frowned. Head of the family—he was his father's second-born son, meant for the army, not the title, until nearly two years ago. There'd been an accident, and both his father and his brother were killed, leaving Kit as the new Earl of Rossington. He remembered his sister pointing at him with stunned surprise. "*Kit* is going to be the earl?" she'd crowed, and dissolved into laughter at the idea. "What a disaster!"

A disaster indeed. Quite suddenly he'd gone from the son no one paid much attention to, to the man expected to provide leadership, guidance, and all the necessities of life to his family. The army career for which he'd been groomed had been out of the question—he had *responsibilities*. It had become one of his least favorite words. It wasn't that he was weak—he may not have been raised to be the earl, but he knew what he liked and what he wanted. It was just that standing up to his powerful mother, his loud sister, and his needy younger brother was rather like telling a high wind not to blow—it would blow whether you wanted it or not, and the only recourse was to hang on and weather each gale as it came.

It was well and good for his mother to suggest he step in, but just how was he supposed to solve Arabella's problems? Her marital spats were legendary, and she and her husband had the hottest tempers, and the most stubborn dispositions in the entire English aristocracy. He could, he supposed, *order* her to go back to her husband, but any further unhappiness between the Collingwoods would then become his fault, and he would rather thrust his hand into a hornet's nest than put himself in the middle of their feud. There was no point.

"As you said, Mother, I'm a bachelor. What advice could I possibly give her?"

His mother smiled. "Then go to Shearwater, and enjoy a few weeks there."

His second house—a jewel box by the sea. "Can't. Alan is spending his honeymoon there. He's renovating his own house, and it won't be ready until November."

"Yes, that would be awkward, squatting in the middle of your brother's wedding trip that way. Well what about Linwood House?" she asked.

"Go to London? At this time of year?" Kit said. "It's too hot and too dull to be in town at the height of summer." He crossed to the fireplace, gazed up at the painting above it, a lovely oil of Coalfax Castle, his fourth estate. "There's always—"

His mother shot to her feet. "Don't say it! Coalfax is mine until Christmas as it is every year. I've already made all my arrangements."

"But the dower house at Coalfax was lavishly done over

just last year. I remember the bills. Surely you'd be quite comfortable there."

She sent him a baleful look. "It was two years ago, and it's too small. My cousin Winnifred is coming to stay as usual, and we will need enough space to house us both, each with a wing of our own, just in case."

"In case? The same thing happens every year—Winnifred arrives, and there are tears of joy and several days of gossip, companionship, and peace. Then, the small things begin to irritate you both. Before long, you are not speaking at all, and you live in separate wings for the rest of her visit. Why do you insist on spending half the year together? You fight like cats. Would an exchange of letters not suffice? In fact there's still time to write to her now, and tell her she can't come this year."

His mother's chin jutted stubbornly. "How unfeeling you are, Kit. She's my cousin, and we are both lonely widows. Of course we must see each other. Your company would not be welcome. You'd find us dull in the extreme. What about Turnstone Abbey?"

Turnstone was Kit's last property, in the north of England, tucked away in the Cheviot Hills. He loved the place, but it was currently undergoing extensive and much needed renovations, and was therefore uninhabitable at the moment.

That left nowhere at all for him to live.

He considered his options as Swift, the faithful butler who had been with the family since Kit's father had been earl, brought in the tea tray. Swift was a fixture, as much as the fountain in the rose garden was, or the stone temple of Apollo on the hill, or the family portraits in the gallery—he'd been here long enough to warrant having his own face immortalized with the rest of the family. Swift ensured everything was in order, knew the family's habits and preferences, and kept every nuance of life at Bellemont Park running smoothly. Kit adored the old fellow.

"Perhaps I could simply remain here," Kit ventured, his eyes on the butler's calm, sober, reassuringly bland face.

His mother poured out. "Perhaps you could indeed—it wouldn't be so bad with Arabella's company, now would it? She's bringing the girls, and she's bound to invite company. Perhaps even a potential bride for you."

Kit felt jittery dread creep up his spine. Since the day he had inherited the title, his sister had been tossing her unwed friends at him, or their unwed friends, or even the eligible daughters of vague acquaintances, with horrifying regularity.

"I shall forbid her to have guests," he said.

His mother's lips pinched at that. "It's your house, Kit," she said again. "You may set whatever rules you like, I suppose, but Arabella won't like it."

Of course she wouldn't. She'd make it sheer and unending hell.

He pounded his fist into his palm. "If she's going to stay here, then I will be the one to decide the rules this time." He ignored his mother's smirk.

Perhaps it *wouldn't* be so bad. Bellemont was an exceedingly large house, and it was summer. With the windows open, and his own space, he would hardly know his sister and her five children were even here. He would refuse to allow unmarried female guests to set one hopeful toe over his doorstep. He was resilient—he could make it work for a few weeks. It wouldn't be any worse than it would have been if he had joined the army and marched away to fight in Spain, been forced to share a billet. Not that his sister's opinions weren't as sharp as bayonets, and as cruelly thrust upon her victims.

Kit settled into the elegant side chair and sipped his tea, and reached for a cherry tart from the tray the butler proffered—Swift knew they were his favorites. He chewed thoughtfully, and enjoyed the genteel peace and comfort of his home. His home was indeed his castle, and he would not allow himself to be put out of it. Just a few firm rules, and he could rub along well with his sister. He began to imagine companionable walks by the lake, picnics, quiet games of chess in the evening.

The door burst open and a whirlwind flew into the room. Shrieks ripped at the sultry air, and barking, and Swift was overrun and knocked down, taking the tarts with him.

A small bundle landed on Kit's lap, and he dropped his teacup in order to catch it, and heard the delicate china smash.

A pair of blue eyes gazed up at him. "Hello, Uncle Kit," said his six-year-old niece with a gap-toothed smile, batting her eyelashes like a seasoned coquette.

"Hello, Molly," he managed.

Another small pair of hands grasped Molly's blond curls and tugged. "My turn to sit on Uncle Kit!" Rebecca said.

Molly let out a shriek that made Kit's eyeballs ache, and dug her fists into the first thing that came to hand, his cravat, in order to keep her seat, not noticing or caring that she was strangling him. Rebecca threw a punch at her sister and missed, her seven-year-old fist connecting with Kit's jaw instead. His teeth rattled. If little Rebecca failed to grow up and marry well, she might make her fortune as a prizefighter, he thought.

Then Rebecca's twin sister Rose joined the fray, trying to dislodge Molly by climbing over her. Rose's elbow caught Kit's nose, and a small knee went somewhere far more painful than that. Too late, he heard the chair crack beneath him, and he barely had time to throw protective arms around the squirming gaggle of infant harridans before the chair collapsed beneath them. His mother cried out—her concern all for the girls, of course, ignoring the fact that they were bouncing on his lungs and crushing his vital organs. Kit shut his eyes and hoped that his younger brother would prove to be a better earl than himself, and would not find his wedding trip too terribly inconvenienced by Kit's untimely death.

"Is that a dignified way to greet your nieces?" Arabella asked, and he opened his eyes, forced air into his lungs, and glared up at his sister, who stood over him. "Really, Kit, you do need to grow up. It's far past time you did. This game is too rough for young ladies." She clapped her hands. "Girls, go to the nursery at once."

He wasn't surprised when his sister's offspring did not obey. Instead, they began to devour the contents of the tea tray as Swift got slowly to his feet, brushing the worst of the crumbs and crushed cherries from his clothing.

"Swift, perhaps you could bring more tea?" his mother asked. She glanced at the remains of the cherry tarts, covering the butler like bloodstains after a battle. "Once you have changed your clothing, of course."

Swift merely bowed. "Of course, my lady," he said with

plummy dignity before he picked up the ravaged tea tray and limped toward the door.

"Aren't the boys with you?" the countess asked her daughter.

Arabella tossed her head. "They're with Collingwood. He insists they must spend the summer with their tutor, under his supervision—as if I could not supervise them here, or have Kit oversee their lessons. Who better to direct the education of a future earl than another earl?"

"Me?" Kit asked, looking up from his inspection of the remains of the broken chair. No one else took any notice of the splintered wood, or his own dishevelment. He poked gently at his bruised jaw. "I agree with Collingwood. The earl in question should be the boy's father, not his uncle," he said, and saw too late the dangerous spark in Arabella's eyes.

"When you have sons of your own, Christopher Linwood, you will understand."

There was a crash in the corner, and Kit looked up to see his nieces climbing a shelf of rare books and Chinese porcelain. He wondered if Arabella had come simply because her offspring had demolished her own house, rendering it uninhabitable. He pitied her butler.

As his mother scooped her embroidery supplies out of harm's way, Kit considered ringing the bell once again, demanding to know where the girls' nurse was hiding. He pictured the poor woman jabbering incoherently under a stairwell somewhere, overwhelmed by her charges, reduced to a shivering wreck.

"Perhaps their nurse should take them upstairs—" he began diplomatically.

"We're between nurses," Arabella interrupted. "My maid has taken charge of them for the time being, but she is unpacking my trunks at present."

She seemed completely oblivious to the fact that her children were now climbing out the window and escaping into the garden, where there were bees and thorny roses, and a deep pond full of curmudgeonly eels.

He crossed and rang the bell himself. "I shall summon one of the maids," he said.

"As you will, Kit. It is your home, after all," Arabella said, and Kit swallowed a moment of deep sympathy for his sister's husband.

Swift cautiously opened the door and carried in the tea tray once again, his shirt perfect, his hair combed, and the girls squealed. The gracious servant's eye twitched.

Kit made a silent vow. He would not marry until he had no choice in the matter, and an heir was required. When the time came, he'd select a meek and quiet female, and as a wedding present, he would purchase a sixth property, and house her there, and think of her only when absolutely necessary—and how often could that possibly be?

He beckoned to the butler. "Swift, have my trunks brought down from the attic, and ask my valet to meet me upstairs at once," he whispered.

He left the next morning for Turnstone Abbey.

CHAPTER THREE

Dundrummie Castle, July 1817

Megan bit back an oath as yet another pin pricked her skin through the seamstress's muslin. She sent the woman a sharp look and got down from the stool she was perched on. "It's too hot for this!" she said. How she'd love to be swimming in the loch at Glenlorne now.

"You must be prepared, Megan," her mother told her, sitting placidly in her chair, watching the proceedings. Her own gown was perfect, pink and ruffled and cut in the first stare of French fashion. "You have a great deal to learn before we go to London next spring, and you'll need dozens of gowns."

"Dozens?" Sorcha gasped, and Megan tried to imagine just how long it might take to be fitted for so many garments.

"Morning gowns, tea gowns, walking dresses, evening gowns, pelisses, bonnets, nightgowns—" the seamstress recited, mumbling over the pins from her mouth.

"First impressions can never be made a second time," her mother said.

Megan sighed and stood still. She'd promised to spend an hour in the village, visiting the local folk, taking note of their tales, adding them to her growing collection. Not that her mother would understand or approve, of course. Megan told her she was visiting the sick and elderly, taking baskets of food to those in need. That was admirable—English, even— in her mother's opinion, while collecting clan stories was a pointless pursuit.

"Stand up straight, Margaret," her mother commanded, using the English name that was just one of the changes she had insisted upon in preparation for going to England. Sorcha and Alanna—Sarah and Alice—looked at her sympathetically, as they waited miserably for their turn for torture by muslin and pins. At least Alanna, just a year younger than Megan, would be right by her older sister's side come spring, at the same English balls and parties.

"I know you've only just arrived, but we must begin as we mean to proceed," Devorguilla insisted. "There will be a strict schedule. In the mornings, you will meet with the seamstress for fittings. You will, of course, be fitted for a *full* wardrobe when you get to London, but for now a dozen or so new gowns for each of you will do." She pursed her lips. "I daresay Miss Carruthers, your new companion, and the lady's maid she's brought with her, will ensure your hair is properly dressed, and remains that way from now on."

Megan put a carful hand to her upswept hair, carefully curled and pinned and primped until she felt like screaming. Sorcha clutched her braids as she cast a horrified glance at her sisters' coiffures. "For the rest of their lives?" she asked. "It takes hours!"

Devorguilla squinted at her youngest daughter, and Megan wished she were still Sorcha's age. Megan looked out the window wistfully, at the purple heather on the hillside, and the blue sky, and watched an eagle coasting on the warm wind. He could probably see all the way to the sea, to the islands shining in the sunlit waves, to Eacha—

"Margaret McNabb, are you listening?" her mother demanded.

"Of course. We were speaking of hair," Megan murmured. She thought of the old tale Arran McNabb had told her about the lassie with the lovely hair, and how she used it as a silken snare to capture her true love and rescue him from the arms of a false lass.

"We've gone on to dancing," Alanna murmured.

"Monsieur Le Valle arrived yesterday," Devorguilla said. "He will teach you to dance. Miss Carruthers will ensure you speak proper English, and know English manners."

"But surely Caroline can teach us that," Megan said.

Devorguilla frowned. "I would prefer to oversee your instruction myself. Caroline is married to your brother now, and busy with Glenlorne."

"She made me promise to write to her every day—I'm to write in English, and she will reply in Gaelic, so we both learn," Sorcha said, but Devorguilla ignored her.

"Are there other rules, Mama?" Alanna asked.

"We will speak together in English," Devorguilla said. "And we will dine on English food. I have hired an English cook, and an English butler. Your future English husbands will want to know you can rule over their household with proper grace and dignity."

English. Megan had grown to hate the very word in the two days they'd been at Dundrummie.

Would a Scottish husband not expect the same dignity and grace in his wife? Megan knew better than to ask the question aloud. She glanced out the window again, watched the clouds crest the hills and disappear over the other side. Her heart was here, in the Highlands, and no English lord would ever win her away.

Of that, Lady Megan McNabb was very certain.

Chapter Four

Kit woke with a start as something heavy was dropped on the floor above his bed, and a trickle of dust fell on his face. Well, not his *bed*—he'd made do with the aged settee in the study of Turnstone Abbey. The rest of the house was uninhabitable, in various stages of being torn down or built up, plastered, painted, or bricked over. He could not walk from one room to another without ducking under scaffolding and Holland cloth.

He wiped a hand over his face and glared up at the ceiling. He hoped his mother, brother, and sister were all quite comfortable in his homes. He hunched deeper into the blanket, rescued from his coach late last night.

"Mornin' milord," said a cheerful worker as he carried a box past the settee, as if it was not an extraordinary thing to find an earl sleeping rough. He hadn't bothered to knock, but then the doors had been removed to facilitate moving the furniture into this part of the house, and there was nothing to knock on.

"What's that?" Kit asked, his eyes on the man's burden.

He was about to place the box on the floor, amid the rest of the abbey's displaced treasures. Paintings leaned against the walls, statues huddled in corners, and tables and cabinets and desks from all over the house were piled high with books and trays, barrels and boxes.

Those boxes were inlaid with ivory, silver, and mother-of-pearl. This one was plain battered leather.

The workman looked down at it. "This? We found it upstairs in the attic, my lord. In the suite of rooms that overlooks the garden. We're taking the ceiling down today. It had to be moved."

Kit rose and came forward, wearing the blanket like a custom tailored coat, or so he hoped. The man stared at him anyway. They both looked down at the battered trunk, and Kit bent to read the engraved brass plate on the front, just above the hasp that held the box closed. *Captain Nathaniel Linwood, Cobham's Dragoons.*

"Ancestor of mine," Kit murmured. He bent and tried to open the hasp but it was rusted fast, or locked.

"I'd best be getting back to work," the man said, and tugged his forelock and departed back the way he'd come, neither interested nor curious about the old trunk.

"My great-uncle," Kit informed the portrait that hung above the fireplace, and recalled that the man in the painting would already know that, of course, being Nathaniel's nephew. He glared down at the mayhem balefully.

Kit had no recollection of Nathaniel Linwood, as he'd died the very year Kit had been born. In fact, Kit bore his great-uncle's name as his own middle name by way of tribute to the man's passing. Nathaniel had never married, or left a child, or a fortune, or anything at all as far as Kit knew. He'd been a soldier, the second son of the fourth Earl of Rossington. His name was merely a notation in the family Bible—born 1709, died 1785, soldier.

But here was Nathaniel's trunk, a scuffed military footlocker that had seen much hard wear. It called up tales of bold adventures, battles, skirmishes, and campaigns in distant lands.

Kit felt a tug of regret. He would have liked to have gone on campaign, if things had been different and he had not inherited the title. He might have gone exploring when his military days were done, had adventures, and traveled. He'd read of such things—sea voyages to strange islands, travelers who crossed deserts with caravans of silk, riding on camels, explorers who dug for ancient treasure in Egypt. He ran his hand over the scarred leather and wondered what adventures Nathaniel might have had, and what he'd left inside the trunk.

Kit tugged at the hasp again, but it refused to budge, and the box remained tight-lipped about whatever secrets it held.

Kit wondered where the key might be. Had old Nathaniel taken it to his grave? He was buried here at Turnstone where he'd lived the last years of his life.

A loud thump shook the plaster above his head, and Kit flinched and glanced up at the ceiling. He had arrived late last night, and the local inn was filled to capacity with the men working on the renovations. He had had no choice but to spend the night in his coach, or to make the best of it and find shelter amid the drop cloths and scaffolding inside the abbey. He'd chosen the latter, taken the blanket, and sent his coachman and valet off to search for a more pleasant place to stay.

Kit wondered how often Nathaniel had found himself sleeping rough, waiting for battle to begin, or exhausted after the fighting ended. He shut his eyes. The pounding of hammers could easily have been the pounding of drums. The calls of the workmen might have been officers bellowing orders. That—the army, not the renovations—might have been his life . . .

Kit tilted his head and studied the box from the side, then the back. The chances of finding the key, even if it was exactly where Nathaniel had last left it, were remote indeed. Kit had never broken into anything before, or picked a lock. He'd never had reason to, though he had read of such things. It took something sharp—or so he understood—and thin.

He opened the drawer in the nearest sideboard, searching for something narrow and pointed, such as a letter opener. Only a candlesnuffer came to hand. He put it back and turned to the desk—the most logical place to find a letter opener—but the drawers were barricaded by a pile of other things, including a painting of a small angel, who gazed at him with parsimonious horror at Kit the would-be lockpick. He found a box filled with lady's cloaks, crumpled and musty, and several bonnets, their once-proud feathers limp. He tossed them aside, but a forgotten hatpin, long and sharp as a dagger, caught his hand, and despite the beads of blood that welled up along the stinging scratch, he drew it out of the bonnet in triumph, and turned back to the trunk.

He fidgeted with the lock as the sun rose and filled the room with summer heat. He wiped the sweat from his brow, felt the grit of plaster and dust on his skin. He jiggled the hatpin one last time, and with a click, the lock gave at last.

Kit opened the lid.

The first thing he saw was a long dagger with a thin blade and a jeweled handle. Now that, Kit thought as he held it up, would have made short work of the lock. He set it aside.

Under the knife was a uniform coat, carefully folded, scarlet wool faced with blue, the brass buttons black for want of polish. The cuffs showed hard wear, a few battle scars, and a black-edged bullet hole in the sleeve. Kit poked his finger through it. If it had been inches to the left, Nathaniel would have died on the field, instead of here, in a comfortable bed. The box also contained a few other ordinary remnants of the captain's life—a leather-bound book as scuffed as the foot-locker itself, a silver flask engraved with the Linwood family crest, and a small bag containing a few coins, some cuff links and a watch chain.

He picked up the book, and looked at it. It was bound shut with a length of pale blue ribbon.

Kit untied the ribbon, and several items fell into his lap. There was a pressed flower—a sprig of heather, if he guessed aright—and a tattered bit of plaid too, orange-red, blue, and green. There was also a letter, yellowed by age, still sealed, the address blurred with damp, but still readable. "Connor Mac-Intosh, Inverness Gaol," Kit read aloud. He frowned. Now why would Nathaniel have kept a letter addressed to another man, a Scot by the looks of it, yet never read it?

After a moment's hesitation, Kit broke the seal, and un-folded it. The ink was smeared in places, perhaps by tears, or age, and the script shook a little, as if the writer had been overwhelmed by emotion. He read the name at the end—Mairi—and frowned. There was no Mairi in family lore, he was sure of that. He took the letter back to the settee and began to read.

Glen Dorian, May 1746

My love,

I pray this finds you well, and you will be home soon again. Captain Linwood was able to learn that you were taken to Inverness Gaol with the other prisoners after the battle at Culloden Moor. Ruairidh is with me, safe. The captain brought him back to me, regretful that he could save only one of you in the terrible moments after the battle. They would not tell me how you were captured, or what you are enduring in prison, so I can only imagine and fear. I hear there are many wounded men dying for lack of care—word of that has reached us even here in Glen Dorian. Linwood has promised me that he will see you are freed, and bring you home again to me, since you are innocent, and he will willingly attest that you took no part in the battle.

I hope you will forgive Ruairidh—my brother is a foolish child. He thought it would be a grand adventure to watch a battle. He knows now he was wrong, and knows that if not for him, you would not have been near Culloden Moor, but here with me at Glen Dorian, safe. I do not know what Ruairidh saw as he lay on the edge of the battlefield, for he will not or cannot speak of it, or perhaps the captain warned him not to tell me, but to spare me. It makes it worse, not knowing. Nor will Linwood give me details of the battle, except to say the Jacobites lost, and will not rise again. Charles Stuart has fled, and they will hunt him down if they can. The government

*soldiers are coming into the villages and the glens, searching
everywhere for him, or for any Highlander, to punish us.*

*Captain Linwood has come to say that we must flee. We
are in danger, even here in Glen Dorian. I will take what
kin will follow me and hide. Linwood says I dare not name
the place here, but you will know it well enough.*

*The captain is waiting while I write this letter to you,
and promises to see it delivered. How I wish I could place
it in your hands myself, kiss those hands, and see you and
know that you are well.*

*I know you will come home to me, Connor. You must. I
have our treasure safe, hidden where the English thieves will
not think to look for it. Again, you will know the place.*

*I will wait for you, watch for you to come back to me
every day, and keep safe all that you and I hold dear until
you are in my arms again.*

> *Mairi*

Kit stared at the letter. Nathaniel had obviously not delivered it. Kit frowned. Had Connor MacIntosh returned to
Mairi? If not, there was a treasure hidden at Glen Dorian,
a place Kit had never heard of. Mairi—whomever she had
been, had done as women did after a losing battle—hidden
the family valuables and fled. Had Nathaniel known about
the treasure? He obviously hadn't read the letter, but he'd
been waiting as she wrote it, and he pictured his great-uncle
standing behind her, reading over her shoulder, hurrying her
along. "But you were a cavalry officer, and English. Why were
you delivering letters for a Scotswoman, addressed to a Jacobite prisoner?" he murmured to the air. He wondered if old

Nathaniel had been a traitor. Would he have been welcomed home, been allowed to live here at Turnstone if he were?

Kit turned to the journal, looked at the scrap of plaid and the dried sprig of heather, held it to his nose, smelled paper and age, and the faintest, sweetest echo of the flower itself.

"Did she get away?" he murmured to the book.

"Pardon, my lord?" Kit looked up to see his valet, Leslie, in the doorway, a hamper in his hands. "Forgive me, there is no door upon which to knock. Were you speaking to me?" Leslie set the hamper down and opened it to reveal a flask of ale, a loaf of bread, and some cheese and fruit.

Kit folded the letter and put it back into the book and rose. "Ah, Leslie, just in time. I feared I would starve in the ruins of this place. What news have you? Is there another inn nearby, or a house I can rent?"

"I came as soon as I could, but I'm afraid the news is not good, sir. I have been unable to find suitable lodgings in the neighborhood. Everyone is here in the country for the summer months, and there is nothing left to rent. I can search farther afield, but—" He looked dubiously at the disheveled surroundings. "Is there a bedroom in order, a kitchen, water, any servants in residence?" he asked.

Kit got to his feet and brushed at the plaster dust on his breeches and grinned. Leslie's jaw dropped in horror at his master's filthy state. Kit could imagine what the valet saw— the Earl of Rossington, as he'd never been seen before, disheveled, needing a shave, a bath, and clean clothes. His hair was probably standing up in unruly, sleep-raddled spikes. He grinned at his manservant. "It doesn't matter, Leslie. We're going to Scotland."

The valet's hands faltered and the ale he was pouring out spilled, soaking into the dust on the floor. "*Scotland*, my lord?" he squeaked.

"Yes, Scotland. A place called Glen Dorian, somewhere in the Highlands. I believe it is near Inverness." He watched as his valet's merely worried expression dissolved into a look of horror. Kit crossed and broke off a chunk of cheese and bit into it.

"You needn't look so grim. It's an adventure." A treasure hunt, to be precise.

Leslie ran a nervous finger under his cravat. "I've never had an adventure, my lord. I'm not the adventurous sort. I had hoped to grow old and die in a comfortable bed, right here in England, with my limbs intact."

Kit picked up Nathaniel's journal and put it back into the box and shut the lid. "I understand Scotland is very pleasant—and it's bound to be cooler than London. Think of the tales you'll have to tell your grandchildren." He strode toward the door with Nathaniel's footlocker under his arm.

Leslie blinked after him for a moment, then hurried to catch up. "Grandchildren, my lord? But I'm not even married!"

CHAPTER FIVE

Megan climbed the crest of a hill, and felt the wind lift her hair and her cloak, and for an instant she felt as if she were flying. The air was sweet with the scent of heather, and she shut her eyes, glad to escape the endless fittings and lectures and lessons. She'd slipped out after breakfast, while the seamstress was busy with Alanna, and Sorcha was having her English lesson, and Mama was still abed.

Megan was certain even if she did go to England she would not remember half of what had been crammed into her head in the past week, nor would she recall which dress she was expected to wear at each time of day, or how she was to address a baroness as opposed to a bishop's wife. What if she got it all wrong? Isn't that what her mother feared most, that her girls would make themselves—and her—look foolish by using the wrong fork at dinner, or failing to be pretty or witty enough amid their English competition?

Megan was certain they'd laugh at her, the fine lords and ladies of England, make fun of the Scottish burr in her voice, the awkward way she walked, as if she'd spent her life roaming over hills and glens. Which she had. She looked down at her feet now, clad in sturdy boots made for walking over rough ground, knowing her stride was too long, her pace too rapid. Would she ever get used to taking the dainty steps of an English lady?

She reached the top of the sheep path, and overlooked Glen Dorian, the vale of the otters, and she let the wind buffet her, blow away the fear and uncertainty. She lifted her arms, felt the wind fill her lungs, and imagined flying away over the hills and mountains. What would she seek? Eachann, or something bigger still?

"Och, ye gave me a turn, lass," a voice said, and she opened her eyes and saw an elderly man reclining in the heather, smoking a pipe.

Megan came to earth with a jolt, and wrapped her cloak around her body. "I'm sorry. I didn't see you there," she said, regaining her composure. "It's a fine day, is it not?"

He squinted at the sky. "We'll have rain before the afternoon is out. There are clouds on the horizon. I've been watching them move up the glen."

Megan set a hand to her eyes and stared out across the landscape, watching the placid white clouds scudding toward them. They looked harmless to her.

"What brings you out? Shouldn't you be home helping your mother?" he asked sharply. "Is there no wool to card or bannocks to bake?"

Megan lifted her chin at his presumption, but felt instant guilt as well. She was supposed to be enduring a lesson in English conversation. Alanna was probably finished with the seamstress, and Sorcha was no doubt simmering with annoyance that Megan had had managed to slip away to walk in the hills while she was kept prisoner indoors. The old man's sharp gaze reminded her that she was shirking her duty, even if that duty was far more complicated than carding wool.

She raised her chin and gave the old man what she hoped was a proper English lady-of-the-manor look. "My mother has servants to do that."

He wasn't impressed. He simply puffed his pipe, held her gaze, and waited. Megan lowered her eyes. "I came out for a walk, if you must know. Can a body not enjoy the hills on a fine afternoon?"

He squinted at the clouds once again. "What are you hoping to find here? True love, four leaf clovers, gems, treasure?" he asked. "You have the look of a lass who's searching for something."

Megan sat down beside him on the hillside. "I suppose I am. I collect tales—write them down to keep them from being lost. Have you one to tell?"

The white eyebrow shot upward. "Tales? Aye, I know a lot of tales. What kind do you want?"

She scanned the valley, noted the ruined castle below. It stood on a rocky island in the loch, held from floating away by the tenuous scrap of a causeway, a narrow path of rock and rubble. "True ones—the history of places and people. Like that castle—what can you tell me of it?"

He regarded her sharply. "Glen Dorian? 'Tis cursed, or so they say. I could tell you a dozen tales about it. Heroes once roamed those halls, ladies sang as they wove, and the MacIntoshes of Glen Dorian were a mighty clan."

"Are you a MacIntosh?" she asked.

"Aye. One of the last of the MacIntoshes of Glen Dorian."

"What happened to the rest of the clan?" Megan asked, looking at the castle's crumbling walls, gray and cold against the verdant green and purple of the valley.

"Culloden, first off, then what came after. Some died, some left to find a better life. The laird of Glen Dorian was a good man who swore he'd take no part in the fighting for either side, but other MacIntoshes took up arms, sided with Prince Charlie. The English troops took the laird away in chains, they say, and left his young wife to grieve his loss. They burned the castle, drove away the cattle, and left nothing. Mairi MacIntosh was a brave lass, and she led the few folk who were left up into to the high hills, and kept them safe, and that's why I'm sitting here now, able to tell you stories about this place." He pointed to a hill that overlooked the loch and the castle. "After her man was taken, Mairi came here every day for the rest of her life, and stood on that ridge, and waited for him to come home. She grew old waiting, longing for him."

Megan held her breath and waited, but the man scratched his bearded chin, puffed on his pipe, and let the blue smoke swirl around him and said no more.

"What happened to him?" Megan asked eagerly.

"No one knows. Executed as a rebel perhaps, somewhere in England with some of the prisoners they took, or transported across the sea, or dead."

He tapped the ash out of the pipe onto a rock, and rose to his feet. "Good day to ye, then," he said.

She hurried after him, heading down the slope. "Wait, there must be more."

He glanced at her and kept walking. "More? What more could there be, lass?"

"Well, who lives there now?"

He let his eyes go to the castle in surprise. "In the ruins? No one," he said. "The English burned it so no one could ever live there again. Och, a few have tried to make a life there, but the castle sends them out again. 'Tis said Lady Mairi MacIntosh laid a curse on the place before she died, that the castle would suffer no one to live within the walls until true love returns to Glen Dorian, and it becomes a home again. Until that happens, it's fit for none but otters, birds, and badgers and whatever folk travel the hills and dare to spend a night there. They don't stay long."

"Are there ghosts? Does Mairi's shade walk the halls?" Megan asked, made as breathless by the man's swift pace as by the actual story.

He chuckled. "You're a fanciful wee thing, aren't you?" he said. "I've not heard tell of ghosts, but there's a feeling you get within those walls—a terrible creeping of your skin, a sadness. Go in yourself if you don't believe what I say. You never know—it might be you that finds true love here. Not sure I believe the curse is anything more than a tale to keep the bairns away from the old place, myself." He turned, his blue eyes bright upon her. "But it makes no difference what I think. What do you believe, lass?"

"I already have a true love," Megan said, trying to picture Eachann's face. He'd been gone less than two months and already she was forgetting little details about him. She frowned, and stopped, trying to force herself to remember.

"What is it? Are you unsure about it after all?" the man

asked, pausing as well, and Megan wondered which he meant—entering the castle or her love for Eachann.

She realized they had reached the causeway that led across to the castle. The gray stones stood with battered dignity, and the empty windows regarded her solemnly, waiting for her decision to continue on or draw back. She swallowed, felt her palms itch.

"Is it safe?" she asked.

"There's no roof to fall in on you," he said. "But I wouldn't climb the walls. Go on—it's a wee adventure, if nothing else."

She hesitated for a moment, and the wind whistled through the cracks and holes as if the castle itself was calling to her.

"Come now—you said you wanted a tale about the place. I daresay you'll tell find a better tale on your own than any I can tell," he coaxed, and stepped back.

Megan looked at him. "Aren't you coming?"

"Me? Och, no. I've things to do, and I must be on my way. Go if you wish, lass, or go back home, but I'd decide before the weather changes if I were you." His gaze dared her to walk away, and she glanced at the castle again. It was a bonnie old place really, with the sun shining on the stone and wildflowers growing in the crevices. Birds flew over the tiny island, no doubt nesting inside the broken walls. An otter pulled itself out of the water onto a rock by the old tower and regarded her with a curious black gaze. Megan couldn't resist.

"I'll wish you good day, then," she said, and stepped onto the causeway. The shadow of the castle loomed over her as she crossed the narrow bridge, and the wind hummed. When she reached the black and twisted iron of the open gate, she turned and looked back, but the old man was gone.

She went through, found herself in a courtyard, and crossed to the heavy oak door, scarred by fearsome blows and age. She imagined angry soldiers pounding it open with rifle butts, rushing inside . . . She set her hand on the cold iron of the latch and hesitated a moment before she pushed it open.

The hinges groaned an objection—or a warning. She ignored the chill that raced up her spine and shoved the heavy panel open enough for her to slip through.

The humming stopped. Just a trick of the breeze, she told herself, and stepped across the threshold.

"Hello?" she called, her voice a tentative quaver. She flinched as a flock of birds shot out of the shadows and fled for the open sky. Megan stared up at the hole above her. Charred timbers bristled around the edges like jagged teeth, and she drew a sharp breath. It was damp and musty inside, the old stones radiating wintery cold even in the heat of summer. She wrapped her cloak around her thin gown, felt a sense of loss and sorrow seep into her very bones that was almost overwhelming. She put a hand to her chest, and felt the rapid thump of her heart.

She forced herself to step away from the door, into what had surely once been the laird's hall. It must have been a magnificent home once. Two great fireplaces hugged the walls, but their hearths were dark and empty mouths. The room was filled with rubble—broken stones, shattered roof slates, charred wood, rotting beams and planks in forlorn piles. A stone staircase wound upward in one corner, guarded and unreachable amid the destruction. She moved forward, her footsteps chattering on the gritty floor. The stone walls whispered back, a thread of sound that might have been her imagination, or perhaps it was just some small animal, hiding in one of the dark corners. She didn't dare look.

This end of the room was close and dark, the floor above intact, the air thick with dust. She felt something brush against her face, and she flinched and cried out, heard the sound echo. Her fingers shook as she swiped at the cobweb that clung to her cheek.

Faint fingers of daylight poked tentatively through charred shutters, and she hurried across, and forced one open. Light poured in, and Megan drew a deep breath of air, stared out at the hills that surrounded the glen—was that the place Mairi MacIntosh had stood and waited for her lost love? Megan felt another deep wave of sadness pass over her, and the wind keened, sending dust swirling through the air like ghosts.

The lives lived here, the happiness, the joy, had ended the day the castle had burned, when the family was driven out. Seventy years later, it stood empty, bereft of life, but longing to be filled. She could feel that, too—the old stones pleading for mercy, for love. She felt a moment's anticipation and she turned to glance at the door, her heart rising in her throat.

But the doorway was empty, the hall silent, and she felt her heart sink, her knees weaken under the crushing weight of despair. The open shutter rattled, and she gasped and spun again. Under that sound she heard the faint echo of laughter, a snatch of a pibroch played on bagpipes, the clatter of boots on the stone. She crossed to the door, looked into the courtyard.

"Hello?" she called again, but it was empty, and she was

alone. The cold crept up from the floor, wound around her legs, pulled at her.

Megan felt her skin creep, just as the old fellow had said it would. She picked up her skirts and hurried out, rushing across the courtyard. She felt eyes on her back like a touch as she crossed the causeway, but she was too afraid to look back. She didn't stop until her feet touched the shore.

Only then did she turn. The movement of the shutter caught her eye, and she felt her heart kick into a gallop.

But the wind brushed over her cheeks, and a cloud passed to let the sun through, and the light warmed her icy skin. She let her shoulders drop. "Just the wind," she whispered. "Just the wind."

Chapter Six

Monsieur LaValle clapped his hands, and the sharp staccato sound rang though Dundrummie's music room. "Young ladies, form a line, if you please."

The dancing instructor stood primly before his charges and waited. Megan sighed as Alanna firmly clasped her arm and nudged her into position between herself and Sorcha. There would be no escape today. Megan did not want to dance. She'd slept badly, her rest fraught with dreams of standing in the hall of Glen Dorian, waiting, hoping, her stomach aching with terror. There was a pounding at the door, and she watched the oak panels shiver, saw them crack, begin to give way. Then strong hands gripped her shoulders, pulled her away, and she fought, tried to free herself, but he would not be deterred. She turned and looked up into his face, met a pair of fierce gray eyes . . . and that's when she woke up.

She furrowed her brow, trying to remember, hoping to see his face in her mind's eye, but like most dreams, it had disappeared in the harsh light of day, leaving only smoke to torment her daylight hours.

Monsieur tapped his foot impatiently.

"We are ready, Monsieur," Alanna said in French.

Monsieur's eyebrows flew into his pin-curled hairline. "Ready? How can that be? There are only three of you—how are we to dance with three?"

Megan regarded the dancing master. He was as trim and light on his feet as a bird on a branch, and just as nervous. He looked about with his lips pursed into a pointed beak, and fluttered. "Are there no gentlemen? Boys even?"

"Our—um, companion—will be joining us shortly I believe. She is with Mama—the Dowager Countess of Glenlorne—at present," Megan said in careful English. Monsieur LaValle may understand French and English, but he spoke not a word of Gaelic. Megan wondered if "companion" was the right word to describe the formidable Miss Carruthers. She was not a ladies' maid exactly, or a governess, nor was she a nursemaid. She had been hired to teach English language, English etiquette, English dress, and the kind of dull, witless conversation that apparently was actually enjoyed in English drawing rooms, and to guard her charges against all things Scottish. Sorcha called Miss Carruthers The Torturer, and Alanna called her The Dragon. She was ever present, ever vigilant, and never, ever tolerant of "un-Englishness" in her three charges. They all missed Caroline, their previous governess, a gentle and lovely lady who had fallen in love with their brother, Alec, and married him.

How dull the English must be, they decided. Miss Carruthers seemed incapable—or unwilling—to teach the fine points of flattery and flirting, or to countenance a longed-for lesson on gossip. Megan and her sisters could politely ask for scones, or for cream and sugar for their tea, or even request a glass of orange squash, whatever that might be. She could comment on the weather, be it cloudy or bright, warm or cold.

Miss Carruthers warned that they must never, ever stray from the banal list of discussion topics she considered safe and polite. "One never knows when one is speaking to a duchess or an earl. One must guard one's tongue, and never give the impression of a less than perfect upbringing."

An upbringing like hers, Megan was given to understand, a happy time of running barefoot in the hills, consorting with village children and gamekeepers' sons. What would a duchess say to that? What would an earl think if he knew Megan loved a ceilidh beyond all things, a chance to dance to the skirl of the pipes, and drink ale and whisky with the folk of Glenlorne village, with nary a single drop of orange squash to be had?

She wriggled her toes in the uncomfortable English dancing slippers Miss Carruthers had insisted upon. It wouldn't matter—Eachann would be home again before she ever had to set a single toe across the border, and it wasn't as if any eligible English gentlemen were likely to come calling here at Dundrummie. She smiled. No, she would never need to know how to waltz, or find a reason to ask for orange squash.

Monsieur flapped his arms and rose up and down on his toes. "Companion? We do not need another female. We require gentlemen."

Sorcha giggled. Alanna blushed, and Megan straightened her spine. "My mother will not allow Scottish lads into the castle, Monsieur, and I daresay there isn't an English gentleman to be found between here and Inverness. We are as a convent at Dundrummie Castle—save for yourself and Mister Graves, of course."

Sorcha tittered again, but Monsieur clapped his hands once more. "Summon him."

Megan raised her brows. "Mister Graves?"

"*Oui*. At once, if you please, so we may begin the lesson. We must have male partners, and if, as you say, he is the only one—"

"But he's the butler!" Alanna said, and clapped her hand over her mouth, surprised at her own outburst. "I don't think he knows how to dance."

He probably did not even bend in the middle, Megan thought.

But Sorcha crossed the room and tugged the bell. "I doubt it, too, but I can't wait to see his face when he's asked," she said in Gaelic.

"In English, if you please," Monsieur said, fluffing his feathers again.

"*Oui, Monsieur*," Megan replied tartly in French.

Mr. Graves appeared in the doorway, his expression as stiff as his spine. "Do you require tea?" he asked Megan, as the senior lady in the room.

"We require dancing partners. You will dance," Monsieur LaValle chirped.

"I beg your pardon?" Graves asked, looking down the hump of his nose at the tiny Frenchman.

"Do you dance, Monsieur?"

"I do not," Graves said, drawing his dignity around himself like a cloak. Megan noted the impish delight in Sorcha's eyes, and hid her own smile.

"But there are not enough partners for the young ladies. You must," the Frenchman insisted, bounding across the room to Mr. Graves. He stood facing the English butler, his nose barely reaching the middle button on Graves's shirt. Alanna was holding her breath, waiting for the argument to come to blows as the two stared at each other.

"What sort of dancing?" Graves asked at last. "The Scottish Reel, the Highland Fling?"

Monsieur LaValle's face crumpled. "*Mais non!* These ladies are going to England. I am teaching them the classics every young lady must know—the quadrille, the polonaise, the waltz."

"What of English country dances?" Graves demanded. "There will be country dances at every social affair, and being such pretty young ladies, they will most certainly be invited to dance every set at every party. They must be prepared. When I was a footman to the Duchess of—"

Monsieur LaValle snapped his fingers. "And I suppose you are an expert on these country dances?"

Graves flushed slightly and straightened his cravat. "Quite so."

"Truly?" Sorcha asked, her eyes popping. "Where on earth did you learn?"

Graves sent her the quelling glance butlers and dignified gentlemen reserve for puppies and children. "As I was about to say, I was once a footman in the employ of the Duchess of Kelledge. That good lady loved to dance, and held balls and parties often. It was a matter of observing. The staff would practice the steps in their off hours when the lady was out of the house—with her full permission of course. We knew all the very latest dances."

Monsieur LaValle bounced on the balls of his feet once again, and folded his arms over his chest. "Oh really? Do you know the Cat In Pattens, or Miss Mary's Frolick? What of the Duchess of Devonshire's Reel?" he demanded.

Mr. Graves smirked, if a mere quirk of his cheek could truly be considered a smirk. Megan noted the rest of his face remained impassive. "I know them indeed, but those are very old dances. No one in fashionable society has performed the Cat In Pattens in some thirty years. Her Grace kept to the very latest dances."

"Such as?" Monsieur demanded, his dark eyes darting over the butler.

"The New Dash, or Prince Edward's Fancy, and the Brighton Waltz—the *very* newest dances, the ones that young ladies in England are learning this very moment, in order to be able to execute them flawlessly during the next Season."

Megan could have sworn that Monsieur LaValle's nose quivered like a mouse's. He snapped his heels together and held out his arms. "Show me," he commanded.

Graves drew back. "Show you?"

"Dem-on-strate," LaValle annunciated.

"With you?" Graves let a disdainful glare tar the Frenchman from head to toe and back again.

Monsieur ignored it. "At once, if you please. I must know this Brighton Waltz and this New Dash."

Mr. Graves sighed and pulled his white cotton gloves out of his pocket and drew them on. "Very well, but I will lead."

"We shall see," Monsieur said tartly.

The countess's lady's maid—hired for her skill with hair and her ability to play the piano—sat down to begin an accompaniment. "Ready," she said, and Mr. Graves gave a crisp nod and took Monsieur LaValle in his arms.

As the waltz music filled the room, Megan watched as the dour English butler whirled the French dancing master around the floor in a room that had seen far more drunken Highland reels than waltzes. Mr. Graves's gloved hands were placed just so on his partner's waist, and he kept his head high and his knees flexed as he carried Monsieur through the steps with elegant grace. Monsieur played the role of the perfect debutante, his head turned like a flower on a delicate stem, his smile placid.

"It looks like fun," Sorcha whispered to Megan. "If I could dance like this every day, I wouldn't mind going to England so much."

It did look like fun—Megan pursed her kips, trying to imagine Eachann waltzing in his heavy boots and his plaid. She frowned at her sister. "Surely they don't waltz *every* day."

Sorcha gasped as Miss Carruthers appeared in the doorway. The Dragon's yellow eyes popped in surprise and her hand flew to the high neck of her gown as her vast bosom heaved with horror at the sight before her.

"What's the meaning of this?" she said, coming into the room like an ill wind. The music and the dancing died at once, and Graves stepped back, standing at attention, his expression inscrutable.

"It is a demonstration of dancing for the young ladies," Monsieur said breathlessly. "It is always best to have a male partner."

Miss Carruthers squinted at him. "Better for whom?" she demanded.

Monsieur LaValle blushed to the tips of his elfin ears. "For the young ladies, of course. In London, they will *not* be dancing with other young ladies." Miss Carruthers looked confused. "*Cher Madam*, if there are other suitable fellows to serve as dancing partners—and Lady Megan assures me there are none to be found this far north— then bring them. Otherwise, I must teach as I see fit." He clapped his hands and turned to his pupils. "Lady Megan, you will partner with myself. Lady Alanna, you will permit Monsieur Graves to lead you out."

"Wait," Miss Carruthers said. "I will try it myself first." She stepped up to the butler and made a deep curtsy. "Like this, young ladies. She rose and allowed the butler to place his hand upon her thick waist. "Do not allow the gentleman to hold you too close if by chance you *are* given permission to waltz—and you *must* have *express* permission, mind you, and even then, *do not* give in to the perils of moonlight and music and a handsome face."

"Thank you, Miss Carruthers. I shall observe every propriety," Graves said dryly, maintaining a very proper distance indeed as he took her hand in his.

The Dragon blushed. Actually, she turned nearly purple. "Oh, I didn't mean that! I mean, I thought—" Graves offered what Megan had come to think of as the English imitation of a smile. Was it characteristic of butlers only, or did all Englishmen smile with such cold hauteur? Why bother to smile at all if you didn't mean it? Graves twirled Miss Carruthers, and she stifled a surprised whoop as he released her. He turned to Sorcha and bowed.

"Shall we waltz, Lady Sorcha?" he asked, holding out his hand. "With Miss Carruthers's *express* permission, of course."

Megan stifled a fit of laughter. She stumbled, crushing Monsieur's toes. He winced and glared at her.

"It is all well and good here with me, Lady Megan. I am paid well to suffer the breaking of my toes, but what if I was a duke or an earl? *Non, mademoiselle*—you must not crush *his* feet. Your full attention, if you please."

"But I won't—" Megan began, but she was interrupted when her mother rushed into the room.

There were tears in her eyes, and she crossed to Megan at once, ignoring the unusual dance whirling around her. Monsieur stepped back as the countess took her daughter's hands.

Megan gripped her mother's icy fingers, her throat drying with dread. "Good heavens, Mama, what's wrong?" A dozen possibilities whirled through her mind—Alec killed, Caroline hurt, Eachann shipwrecked and given up for lost in some foreign land.

"Oh my dearest girl. All our dreams have come true. An English lord has come to us! A *single* English lord, unmarried, and an earl!" she gushed. "It's an answer to a prayer!"

Or a curse. Megan felt her skin go cold. "He just— appeared?"

"Shall we have a proper dancing partner for our lessons at last, then?" Monsieur interrupted brightly.

"How is that possible?" Megan asked. "An *English* earl? Here?" She imagined him sitting in the salon, waiting for her to arrive, so he could snatch her up and carry her south. She felt her stomach clench, her heart draw in. She might have fled if her mother wasn't still holding her hands in a deadly grip.

The countess blinked at the dancing master through happy tears. "Oh, he's not here to be part of our lessons, Monsieur."

"What a pity," Monsieur said, deflated.

"Then why has he come?" Megan asked. "Why now?"

But her mother was still beaming at the Frenchman. "It's not a pity at all, Monsieur! He shall be my daughter's husband before the year is out." She turned to her daughter at last. "Oh, my dearest Margaret, you'll be a countess!"

Megan's stomach fell to her feet like a dead bird. Sorcha's jaw dropped in surprise, and Alanna stared at her sister, her face blanching. No doubt she was afraid she'd have to go to London alone if Megan married. Miss Carruthers turned purple yet again.

"Countess of where?" Sorcha asked.

"Does it matter?" her mother asked. "He's a bachelor, so he must want a wife. Peers must have heirs, and for heirs, they must have wives."

"Why not an English wife?" Megan asked.

"I have heard the daughters of English peers are often horse-faced. Perhaps he has not found a lady to his taste, and has widened his search. How fortunate you are that he has," the countess said, grinning like a horse herself.

"Is he here? I mean *here* in the castle?" Megan croaked, looking anxiously at the empty doorway.

"He is presently staying in Dundrummie village, I believe, at the inn. Everyone is talking of it. He's said to be looking for a more permanent place to stay. Your aunt had word that he was seen in Glen Dorian only yesterday, poking around that dreadful old castle. I had your Aunt Eleanor send an invitation to him at once, of course, and I am pleased to say that he shall be here for supper tonight."

"Yesterday? But I was at—" Megan snapped her lips shut.

Had he been there, hidden in the rubble, or standing high on a hill, watching her? Hot blood flooded into her cheeks. She'd fled from the castle like a ninny, at a dead run, her skirts high. "Tonight?" She realized the horror of that, too.

"You must go upstairs and make ready at once," the countess said, looking at her daughter's plain dress. "Her hair—Miss Carruthers, it must be done in an English style, and her gown must be in the first stare of London fashion."

Miss Carruthers drew herself up to her full height, looking proud. "I shall see to it at once, my lady. It will take a great deal of work indeed, but Lady Margaret shall be quite up to snuff by the time his lordship arrives. What time is that, pray?"

"Eight o'clock, which I understand is a very fashionable hour indeed," the countess gushed.

"But it isn't even time for luncheon yet!" Sorcha piped, but no one paid any attention, save Megan, who glanced at the clock. Nine hours.

"We'll need every minute," Miss Carruthers predicted.

"Mister Graves, I shall wish to confer with cook and yourself about tonight's meal," Devorguilla said.

Mr. Graves bowed.

The countess turned back to Megan. "We'll plan a fall wedding," she cried, and squeezed her daughter's hands, which were now even icier than her mother's. "It will probably need to be in England of course, at his estate, wherever that might be. There are so very many preparations to be made! Should we start packing?"

She glanced at the maid, still sitting at the piano, watching the proceedings with interest. "For heaven sake, don't sit there—go and fetch the seamstress and the pattern books at once. We will need a completely different type of wardrobe if we're to go south now! What does one wear to a wedding in England, Miss Carruthers?"

Miss Carruthers's eyes glowed as if lit by a fiery furnace inside, and she smiled like a dragon as she set off with the countess to make plans.

She'd been forgotten, Megan noted, and wondered if she could slip out the door unnoticed, and flee into the hills and not come back until after the English earl had come, had his dinner, and left again.

But Miss Carruthers returned, rolling up her sleeves as she crossed the room, and took Megan firmly by the arm and marched her upstairs.

CHAPTER SEVEN

News traveled quickly in the Highlands. Kit had been in residence at the Glen Lyon Inn in the market town of Dundrummie for scarcely two days before invitations began to arrive. The dour-faced landlord had dutifully carried the first five missives up the winding stairs to the suite of rooms he had assured Kit were the best in the house, but after that he had turned the seemingly endless task of their delivery over to a pair of younger legs, his daughter Catriona's.

"There's another letter for you, Your Majesty," the inn-keeper's pretty daughter said, dipping a curtsy when Kit opened the door to her knock.

"Thank you, Miss Fraser, but I am simply your lord, not Your Majesty." He watched her freckled face flush with pleasure.

"*My* lord? Oh, my. Then you must call me *your* Catriona."

Kit felt a frisson of fear climb his spine at the gleam in her eye. "Not your personal lord, Miss Fra—"

"Catriona," she reminded him.

"Catriona," he repeated gallantly. "I am not *your* lord, Catriona. Nor am I Your Majesty. I am, *my* lord."

"Your very own?" she asked, her fair brow furrowing.

"I am an earl," he said patiently. "What do they call earls here in Scotland?"

"The Earl of Bothwell is called Jamie, I think," Catriona replied.

Kit swallowed his aggravation. "What's written as the address on the letter you've brought me?"

"Oh!" she said, her face lighting. "I canna read."

"Perhaps just call me Rossington, then," he sighed.

"Or Ross, mayhap. There's a Ross in the village one beyond this one. Ross MacIntosh. He's a smith."

Kit held back a sigh. "Would you bring up some hot water, Catriona?"

"For tea?" she asked, twining a dark curl around her finger.

"For bathing. I'm expected at Dundrummie Castle for supper."

Catriona grinned. "Och, how grand. Lady Eleanor is kindness itself."

"I know," he said patiently. "It was she who invited me, and if it's all the same Miss—Catriona—I'd like to be on time, so I'll need that hot water anon."

"Anon?" Catriona asked.

"It means now," Kit said. He reached out and plucked the letter from her hand, and Catriona headed for the stairs at last.

"Then I'll just go and put the kettle on." She turned and gave him a slow-eyed smile. "D'you need someone to scrub your back?"

"I have a valet for that," Kit said, and shut the door before she could ask about Mr. Leslie's title, or his marital status.

"The young lady seems quite smitten, my lord," Leslie teased as he laid out Kit's evening clothes.

"With you, I hope," Kit said, peeling off his shirt and tossing it to the valet.

"Oh, not at all," Leslie said blithely. "You must be growing used to it. I have seen that look on the faces of countless other young ladies, many times, where you are concerned. I daresay you shall not lack for feminine company even here in the wilds of Scotland.

Kit frowned. "That's the one thing I do not want. I came here to spend time alone." When the hot water arrived, Kit got into the tub, and Leslie added the kettle of hot water. "If any female asks after me while we are here, you are to say nothing, is that clear?"

"Oh, perfectly clear, my lord," Leslie replied. "It's just that—well, I didn't really need to say much at all. The innkeeper's daughter seemed to have the whole story about you."

Kit looked up from the hot water. "Oh? What did she say?"

"Apparently, there are a number of unmarried women—lassies, I think they call them hereabouts—who are intrigued to meet you. Miss Catriona said that if you do not go to them, they will come to you. I do believe they have started arriving. There is quite a congregation downstairs. The innkeeper is taking wagers as to which lady you will marry. The smith has already been alerted, in case it's a hasty match, and so has the local churchman, if it's to be a more formal affair. They've put the lassies in the tearoom for your perusal. There were six of them when I last looked in."

Kit felt his balls shrivel in utter dread. He looked at the door of his room, wondered if the lock was strong enough.

"Can it not be put about just as easily that I have no wish to marry?"

"Would they believe that, my lord?" Leslie asked. "The ladies in England do not."

"We'll move tomorrow," Kit said.

"Very good, my lord. I'll start packing. Will we be returning to England?"

Kit considered. "No." He soaped his chest, rinsed it, then dipped his head. "We shall simply find other lodgings. Inquire if there's a reliable man of affairs in Inverness. In fact, if there is, I'll see him at once."

"This evening?" Leslie asked, his face falling. "But Lady Fraser—"

"Tomorrow is soon enough." Or was it? Kit had a moment of horror. "Leslie, is Lady Eleanor Fraser a young woman?" He had accepted the invitation because Dundrummie was very near to Glen Dorian, and he had questions.

"I'm afraid not, my lord. I understand she is quite an elderly lady."

Kit relaxed. "Good." He would face no surprises tonight, then, and the old lady would certainly be as sweet and benign as his own grandmother had been. Old ladies knew all the local stories, the history of a place. Why, Lady Fraser might even remember Culloden, and Nathaniel, and Mairi MacIntosh, if she was very old indeed. The chance of that was slim, of course, but perhaps her mother had told her tales, or her grandmother.

He rose from the tub and took the towel Leslie held out, and considered how to ask as diplomatically about the possibility of hidden treasure at Glen Dorian.

An hour later, Kit was dressed and ready to go. "You look

very well, if I do say so, my lord," Leslie said, as he always did, admiring his handiwork.

Kit cast a last glance at the flyblown looking glass. "I am no doubt overdressed for these parts."

"The innkeeper suggested you might wear a plaid, my lord, but I could not imagine that. Better to appear as you would at home, I think."

"Quite right, Leslie." He picked up his hat and gloves. "I shall be back before midnight." Elderly ladies retired early, he recalled, and he wanted to make an early start tomorrow.

"I'll be waiting, my lord. Shall I peruse the rest of the invitations we have received thus far and determine what might be needed in the way of proper dress? If there's a shooting party, or a ball, or a picnic, then—"

"We're not here for that, Leslie. This is an adventure, remember? Adventures don't require proper dress. Quite the opposite." He liked that idea, of working in shirtsleeves, without a cravat or a coat, but Leslie looked horrified. "The shooting season is a fortnight away yet, so there's plenty of time," he said to placate his valet. "There's a list on the table by the window of things that I'll require. Be so good as to ask our host where they can be obtained, will you?"

Kit left the room. The sound of doves on the staircase made him pause. No doubt the birds made their home under the eaves of the old inn. How quaint, he thought, until one of the creatures let out a squeal that tightened his chest.

It wasn't doves—it was Miss Catriona Fraser, the innkeeper's lovely daughter, standing at the bottom of the steps with a dozen other young girls—lassies—with all of them cooing or squealing besottedly at the sight of him.

It's not that Kit wasn't used to such attention. Sadly, he was. Women had regarded him thus since he inherited his title. He was handsome, rich, and eligible—a marriage prize. He wished he could go back to the days when he was all but invisible to females who wanted anything beyond a mere flirtation, but he was an earl now, and infinitely more desirable as a husband than anything else. Even a simple conversation might be misconstrued. Of course he appreciated a pretty face and a lush female body as much as any man. He just didn't want to find himself as unhappily wed as Arabella. Try as he might, it seemed an impossible thing to convince the world that he was not looking for a wife—or a casual tumble in the innkeeper's hayloft, for that matter.

He was here to search for a treasure, and solve a mystery.

"Good evening," he said as he passed the gaggle, being careful not to make eye contact with any of them. He hurried into his coach and lowered the blinds, and did not open them again until they had left the village.

Dundrummie Castle was square, solid, and brown—a sensible, sturdy place. Kit felt a moment's disappointment. He had expected—hoped, rather—for something wild, barbarous, and ancient, a clan seat, or a warrior's fortress, but this castle looked as bland as what it was—the home of an elderly lady, right down to the roses that grew in manicured beds beside the door.

Ah, but the door—that at least was a thing to fire the imagination. It was ancient, scarred by weather and fire. It did not offer a welcome. The black iron studs warned away visitors and invaders alike—especially English ones, he imagined.

He was equally surprised to be welcomed by a proper English butler, in proper plummy English tones. He had expected a Scottish servant, squint-eyed and suspicious of any Sassenach who still had the temerity to knock after setting eyes on the forbidding portal.

Instead, Kit was welcomed inside, and escorted to the drawing room—a very English drawing room, with the kind of décor his mother would have found tasteful. It was hardly the ancient Highland hall Kit had hoped for.

"The Earl of Rossington," the butler intoned.

Two females rose at once from a pair of chairs that would have been very much at home in the Prince Regent's own drawing room.

"Good evening, my lord. How kind of you to come," the younger of the two women gushed, a lady past the blush of youth, yet not yet old. She rushed across the room to grip his hands, as if he were a long lost and much missed relation.

It was then that he saw the all-too-familiar look of speculation in her eyes, the quick assessment of his worth based on his looks, his bearing, and the expensive cut of his clothing, from cravat pin to evening shoes.

He'd seen that look often enough to recognize it for what it was—a matchmaking mama appraising an eligible bachelor. His spine prickled. Somewhere about, tucked away and ready to be sprung upon him, this woman had a daughter in need of a husband. Now Kit wondered if the formidable door was meant to keep men in, rather than out. He had the urge to call the butler back again, take his hat, and flee.

"I'm the Countess of Glenlorne, Lady Devorguilla McNabb.

My daughters will be down in a few minutes," she said, her voice honey sweet.

Daughters. His shoulders tensed. There was more than one. How many? He wished he'd come armed.

"Devorguilla's the *Dowager* Countess of Glenlorne," the older lady said with a devil's grin, and a very English accent. Still, she proudly adjusted the tartan shawl over her shoulders as she came forward. "She's in exile. Her stepson is the Earl of Glenlorne, and they cannot stand the sight of one another, so she's come to stay with me. I'm Lady Eleanor Fraser, Devorguilla's sister-in-law, and mistress of this castle."

"Eleanor, what will he think?" Devorguilla admonished in a light tone, though her gaze was hard enough to kill a lesser woman than Eleanor Fraser.

Lady Eleanor swept a glance over him from head to foot. "He'll think as he wishes, I suppose. Do come and sit down, Lord Rossington, and allow me to bid you a proper welcome. Will you take a dram of whisky?"

"Thank you, I will. Dundrummie is—" He couldn't bring himself to say charming, or elegant, or evocative. It was homey.

Eleanor grinned like a pirate. "Yes, isn't it?" She turned to the dowager countess. "He's fair of face, and his manners are good."

Kit could almost smell the danger he was in. Lady Devorguilla looked anxiously at the door. No doubt awaiting the young ladies upstairs primping for him. He imagined the gaggle of lassies at the inn, wondered if he faced worse yet here. Upstairs, a score of marriageable chits were even now dreaming of the moment when he would be struck dumb by the breathtaking sight of one or another of them in the doorway, so much so that he would fall to his knees and propose to one, or even all of them. Was that legal in Scotland? He shifted uncomfortably, and gratefully accepted the tumbler of whisky the butler presented to him on a silver tray, tempted to ask the man to leave the decanter within reach.

The clock on the mantel ticked. Lady Devorguilla sipped from a small glass of sherry, and stared at him. He was beginning to wonder if she ever blinked. Lady Eleanor studied him, too, with the air of one expecting a wondrous piece of theater to be enacted here tonight. Kit's sense of dread deepened.

Given the countess's title, the young lady was obviously the daughter and sister of an earl, and judging by her mother's gown, she had been brought up to marry well. She was, of course, the perfect bride, schooled in flirtation, social niceties, and the proper duties of a wife, mother, and countess. She would be utterly charming, and within the course of the evening, she—or her mother—would work the size of her dowry into the conversation, along with any particular talents the young lady might have. His lips rippled, and he resisted the urge to tug his ear, fearing it would shortly be abused by a ghastly display of singing by yet another tone-deaf debutant. He looked miserably at the piano in the corner, ready and waiting, like a rack in a medieval torture chamber.

Worst of all, he would quite likely leave without any information at all about Glen Dorian.

"She has sisters, as well, you know, our Megan," Eleanor Fraser offered unbidden. "Have you any unwed brothers or cousins?" The hair on the back of Kit's neck rose. Was his whole family in danger of being hunted down and wed against their will?

"My only brother wed just two months past, my lady."

"Pity. If he'd waited, it might have made Devorguilla's task a great deal simpler," Lady Eleanor said.

Devorguilla's cheeks reddened. "Margaret—her name is Margaret," the countess insisted. "Megan's that is. She is called Margaret. What part of England are you from, my lord?"

Here it was. "My principal seat is in Derbyshire," he said, sipping his whisky. Whisky truly was a delightful tipple— quite relaxing.

Her eyes lit. "How wonderful."

"Yes, it's quite pleasant at this time of year," he said, and wished himself there, with Arabella, her unruly children, and all.

"Is it—large?" She ran her eyes over him as she asked, and her cheeks pinked slightly.

The whisky made him giddy. He gave her a roguish smile. "Very." He cast a quick glance at the amber liquid in his glass, and wondered if it was drugged.

But it seemed he could say nothing wrong in the countess's eyes. She laid a hand on her heart and smiled. "Now where could Meg—*Margaret*—be?" she mused and rose to her feet. "I think I'll go and see."

Kit watched as she hurried out of the room.

"I understand you've been asking about Glen Dorian," Lady Eleanor said when her sister-in-law left.

"I am hoping to rent it," he confirmed.

"Rent it?" Eleanor asked. "Why on earth would you want

to do that?" He noted the sharp light in the lady's eyes as she waited for his reply.

"My great-uncle spent a few months here, many years ago. He mentioned Glen Dorian."

Her gray brows rose. "I see. Soldier then, was he?"

He tightened his grip on the glass in his hand. "He was."

"Do you know about the curse?"

"Curse?" he said, keeping his tone even.

Lady Eleanor leaned forward. "Aye—they say that Mairi MacIntosh put a curse on the glen. She left her heart buried in the rubble of the old castle, and swore that none would ever remain within those walls unless they are pure of heart, and loved truly. The old stories say there are great rewards waiting for those folk, and terrible trouble for anyone else who sets foot there. Do you believe in legends and curses and the like, Lord Rossington?"

He met the amusement in her eyes, and for a moment, he did believe, felt the power of unseen hands, heard a whisper in his mind, a soft sigh, drawing him in. "Of course not," he said, giving her a charming smile.

She sat back. "Another pity. Glen Dorian Castle won't welcome you, being English. It was English troops that burned it after Culloden. The MacIntoshes fled, went into hiding, disappeared one by one, all save Mairi. She died in the glen, waiting, hoping. No one has lived there since." She raised her glass to him. "I wish you luck if you plan to stay."

He leaned forward to hear more, but there was a commotion in the hall, the unmistakable whisper of silk gowns, the soft rush of satin evening slippers on stone as they hurried toward him. Kit rose to his feet, steeled himself for the onslaught of simpering smiles, batted lashes, and breathless and boring conversation, designed to draw him closer—and close the snare. He took a step back as a young woman was shoved into the room.

She wasn't smiling—she was scowling mutinously—and Kit met a pair of fierce dark eyes before a whispered word from her mother—and a sharp pinch judging by the way she leaped forward—brought her eyelashes down.

She didn't simper. Her curtsy was brief, sharp, and resentful.

She did not gush when she was introduced as Lady Margaret McNabb. She said nothing at all. Her gaze moved over him once, then flicked away, and Kit had the feeling he'd been found wanting and dismissed. She kept her eyes firmly fixed in the center of his cravat.

She did not rush to him, and hold out a trembling hand for his kiss, or raise adoring eyes to his. The countess was grinning with hopeful delight, rattling off a list of her daughter's accomplishments. He watched as Lady Margaret's cheeks pinkened, then turned a deep shade of rose, then scarlet.

Lady Devorguilla should be proud indeed, he decided. She had created the perfect debutante from the top of Margaret's elegant and rather alarming coiffure, to the demure pearls at her throat and the expensive cut of her fashionable gown. The gown was a ruffled abomination, vivid pink with lavender flounces at the hem and shoulders. Her complexion was now nearly the same color as the dress—the lavender part—and her jaw was tight with irritation. Her dark hair was perched on the top of her head, rigidly held there by an army of pins. It was bedecked with a riotous array of roses, ribbons and jeweled clips. It didn't suit her.

"Good evening, Lady Margaret," he said, and she raised her eyes to his. He read a warning there, as clear as the one given by Dundrummie's formidable front door. It took him aback a moment. She tossed her chin, and looked him straight in the eye. There was nary a single bat of her long, thick lashes.

"I'm Lady *Megan*. Margaret is a kind of pet name my mother has for me. And you are Lord Rossington, from England. May I ask why—how—you came to be here in Scotland?" She made no attempt to hide her Scottish burr. It was like being rubbed with silk. Her eyes, too, were remarkable—a cauldron of color, gold and russet and green, like the Scottish hills.

Beautiful, he thought, and checked himself at once, and clasped his hands behind his back.

"A holiday," he said vaguely. She attempted to nod, and remembered her coiffure and raised a steadying hand to it. Rose petals scattered at her feet.

"He's here to visit Glen Dorian Castle," Eleanor said, and Kit watched Margaret's—Megan's—eyes widen at that, and saw her cheeks flush a much more becoming shade of pink. Then she picked up her skirt, manhandling the train, and crossed the room away from him.

Were she in London, he thought, Lady Margaret/Megan would fit in perfectly—until she spoke, or moved. Her bearing was proud, coltish, athletic, even, as if she was more used to running than walking. She went to the fireplace and stood beside it, and studied him from the shadows.

"Allow me to introduce my younger daughter," Devorguilla warbled, and he turned to look at the second girl. "This is Alice," she said, and the girl blushed as she curtsied. She, too, was fashionably dressed, but in green. She was demure and shy, her eyes downcast. Not his type at all, Kit decided— even if he *had* a type he preferred.

"Or Alanna, if you wish," Eleanor said.

"How did you come to hear of Glen Dorian, my lord?" Lady Margaret/Megan asked.

He met her eyes from across the room, felt her gaze like a touch. "My great-uncle wrote of it. His journal was recently found at a house I am renovating." He didn't mention Mairi's letter, but the slight narrowing of her eyes suggested she suspected there was more.

"Happy memories, then," she said acidly, and he sent her a sharp look, which she returned, steel clashing on steel.

"You found this journal in Derbyshire?" the countess asked.

"In Northumbria, my lady."

"You have two estates?" she warbled with delight.

Kit smiled blandly but did not elaborate. Still, he knew the added value of a second home must be ringing like a cash box in the countess's mind. He cast a sideways look at Lady Margaret/Megan, felt her eyes hard and bright upon him. She did not look away when he met her gaze. "I understand you are here on holiday as well, my lady," he said.

She raised her chin, a captivating, swanlike gesture. "My brother is newly married. My sisters and I came away to visit our mother and allow Alec and Caroline to spend their honeymoon alone," she replied.

"And are you enjoying your stay at Dundrummie Castle?"

"Of course," she said, but he read the opposite in her eyes—wariness and something akin to fear, perhaps. What color were her eyes exactly? She arched one shapely eyebrow disdainfully, and he realized he was staring. He looked at Lady Alice instead. She sat silently beside her mother, her expression curious, but reserved. He knew that look—he was not for her, but intended for her sister. He smiled at her and she blushed like a rose. The Dowager Countess of Glenlorne had graceful daughters. They would have no trouble at all in finding willing husbands—but not him.

"Dinner is late," Eleanor said peevishly.

"I asked Graves to delay the meal a little while," Devorguilla said. "I thought it might serve as a celebration of sorts after—" She sent Kit a glorious smile and rose to her feet and held out her hand to her eldest daughter.

Kit felt his chest tighten with sheer dread.

"I would like to propose—"

"Oh please do say a toast to his lordship's health, Devorguilla!" Eleanor interrupted. "You've only just met the man."

"Marriage," Devorguilla said, firmly, ignoring her sister-in-law. "Between Lord Rossington and Margaret." Kit felt the whisky roll in his belly like lava under a mountain. He stumbled to his feet and stared at the countess. She beamed anew, began to come toward him, since Megan had ignored her mother's outstretched hand and stayed where she was by the fireplace. He could not look at the girl. "The details will have to be finalized with Glenlorne, of course, but tonight—" the countess went on, but Kit wasn't listening.

"No!" His cry of horror came out at the same moment as Megan McNabb's own refusal.

The countess turned toward her daughter. "Don't be silly, Margaret. It takes only a single glance to see that you and his lordship are well suited. There is no reason why Alec should object, and a fall wedding would be lovely. If you are willing and his lordship is willing then why should there be an impediment to the match taking place at this very moment?"

This very moment? Kit heard warning bells, not wedding bells.

"I am most unwilling," he said. "I would never marry *her!*"

Megan's gaze turned from her mother and onto him. Her jaw dropped, and her complexion turned from pink to ashen white. He realized he could have said it more gently, but it was done now.

Margaret/Megan McNabb folded her arms over her chest and squinted at him. "And I would never marry *him.*"

Oddly, it felt like the unkindest insult he'd ever received. "You would never—?" he spluttered. "I expected this to be a quiet supper, not an ambush."

"Then go," she said. "We shall not detain you a moment longer." She reached up and began to pluck the pins out of her hair, dislodging the roses too, and the thick dark waves tumbled over her shoulders.

For an instant, Kit was speechless. He watched as she transformed from a passable debutant to a rare beauty. Her mother gasped. "What are you doing?" she asked. "Margaret, please—" But the pins scattered. Her color was high, her face radiant, her hair a glorious tangle. She looked like a woman who had just been bedded, or should be.

"Megan, Mother. My name is Megan." She said something more in Gaelic, something that made her mother and sister blush, and her aunt giggle. Kit had the feeling that he had just been insulted yet again. He felt his skin heat. He bowed stiffly.

"I shall bid you goodnight," he said. "It was a—" He paused. He could hardly say it had been a pleasure. "Thank you for inviting me, Lady Eleanor."

"Have you recalled a prior engagement, my lord?" Megan demanded tartly. "I wish her luck, poor lass."

He colored. "And here's to your future husband, my lady," he said, and drained his whisky in a single gulp. "I have no doubt he will need all the luck—and all the whisky—in the world."

He watched her jaw drop at the insult, wondered what had gotten into him. He had been brought up to be polite, solicitous, and chivalrous to women. An apology hovered on his lips, but the look of glittering fury on her face changed his mind. Lady Megan's pretty eyes were dark now, almost black. "Go," she said, and he read the word on her lips, even if he could not hear her over the countess's desperate protestations.

Kit turned on his heel and strode out. What right had she to be insulted? He was an earl, wealthy, handsome, and quite charming—usually. He waited for the sound of tears, or screams, but aside from the countess's strident lecture, Megan McNabb said nothing more, as if he'd been dismissed and forgotten. As he waited for the butler to bring his hat, she came out of the drawing room, sent him a single scathing glance and proceeded up the stairs, her chin high, her movements elegant, as if he didn't matter in the least. He watched the graceful sway of her hips until she disappeared, and winced as a distant door slammed.

He turned to see Lady Eleanor watching her niece as well. "Pity you couldn't stay for dinner, but understandable. I doubt I'll get any dinner myself. I daresay there'll be ruffled feathers to be soothed. I have qualms about breakfast, too."

"My apologies, Lady Fraser. I wasn't expecting—"

"Och, never mind. Hunting season is about to begin here in the Highlands. I have no doubt Devorguilla will find more biddable quarry to suit her purposes. Ah—here's Graves at last. Well, it's a small village, my lord. I daresay if you're still planning to stay we'll see you again before long," Eleanor said.

Graves's expression remained bland as he opened the door, as if dinner guests left before the meal all the time—but if this is the way every gentleman was received, Kit was hardly surprised. Outside, his coach had been brought round, and he climbed in, pounded on the roof, and set off at a fast trot.

He leaned back into the plush squabs as the castle disappeared from sight and the village lights twinkled in the distance. Once again, he had successfully avoided entanglement with a hopeful debutante and her scheming mama. Once again, he'd kept his freedom.

He looked out into the darkness and saw a pair of flashing eyes, the dark silken fall of her hair against flushed cheeks, and felt the thinnest wedge of regret.

CHAPTER EIGHT

Megan stared at the empty doorway for a long moment after he strode through it, unable to speak—they all did, for different reasons. He was the handsomest man she'd ever seen, Megan thought, and shook the idea right out of her mind. He was also the rudest.

Alanna stared at her with pity in her green eyes. It had been insulting, humiliating, and horrible. Megan put a hand against her tight belly, felt her knees shaking. How dare he? It wasn't as if she were a strumpet in the street—though her mother had acted as if she was, throwing her at him that way. Her mother had been certain the earl had come to the Highlands to find a wife. Was she so disagreeable? How mortifying. No doubt she could expect the same reaction from other gentlemen in London. Her chest tensed with dread.

Devorguilla stared at the doorway in disbelief, as if she expected him to come back. Slowly, as the seconds passed, her skin flushed an angry scarlet, and her mouth worked as she tried to find the words to express her disappointment, or perhaps it was outrage. Megan hoped it was outrage, but it wasn't directed at Lord Rossington's humiliating rejection of her. It was directed at her. "Go after him!" she hissed, but Megan stood her ground.

"I will not. How could you do such a thing, Mother?"

"Indeed. Most indelicate," Eleanor said calmly. "Someone ring the kitchen and see if dinner is ready. I wonder why he's really come to Glen Dorian."

"Not to find a wife, obviously," Devorguilla sniffed.

Alanna blinked, her eyes swinging from Megan, to her mother, then back to Megan, wondering where to offer comfort first, and just how to do that best. "But not Megan," she ventured, and Megan glared at her. Alanna shrank back.

Megan's cheeks burned. She had never been so humiliated in her entire life. He'd looked as if he'd been asked to kiss a toad. He could not have been more horrified. He might have laughed it off, made a joke of it, continued with the evening, but he had fled as if the devil—her—was chasing him. Was it the gown? The seamstress had assured her it fit to perfection, was cut in the latest style. She couldn't wait to take it off and burn it.

She headed for the door.

He was still standing in the hallway, but she did not stop. She kept on going, climbing the stairs, feeling his gaze on her backside—and that was also mortifying. She reached her bedroom, slammed her door, and leaned on it. She almost leaped out of her skin when someone knocked on the other side. She opened it just wide enough to peer through the crack with one eye. It was Eleanor.

"No need to be so upset, dear girl," Eleanor said. "Take a drop of whisky and calm yourself. Hunting season starts in just a few weeks." Devorguilla pushed in behind her sister-in-law, her handkerchief pressed to her eyes.

"Hunting season? What's that got to do with anything?" Megan demanded. "Do you suggest I go out and shoot him, bring him to ground that way?"

Devorguilla stopped crying and looked hopeful, and Megan rolled her eyes. "Really, Mother, I wouldn't marry him now if he fell on his knees and begged."

"No, not Rossington," Devorguilla said quickly. "Your Aunt Eleanor is quite right. There are other English lords. Dozens and dozens of them. You might shoot one of them— I mean, *with* one of them. That's what you meant, isn't it Eleanor? More amenable gentlemen, just as rich, just as handsome."

"Are you suggesting I go to London now?" Megan demanded.

"No, she means the ones coming here," Eleanor said.

Megan turned. "Have you invited *more* guests like Rossington, dozens and dozens of them? Mother, I don't want—"

"Don't be silly, Megan. Autumn in Scotland is hunting season—they'll come on their own," Devorguilla said, the look in her eyes cheerfully predatory once again. "You will simply be a pleasant surprise. A new quarry."

"The Earl of Marion has a shooting box not five miles away, and Lord Berry's is nearer still. There are always properties rented out for the hunting season by English lords." Eleanor chuckled. "And you, my pretty squab, will be fair game when they get a look at you. Don't fret."

"I'm not fretting," Megan said, but they ignored her.

"Of course she will," Devorguilla said. "I don't see how any gentleman worth the name could resist such a lovely girl. I expected that I'd be announcing your betrothal to Rossington, but we'll simply put it about that there is an earl's unmarried daughter, fair of face and well dowered, here at Dundrummie. I daresay we'll have to drive off hopeful suitors with a pike. Then won't Lord High and Mighty Rossington be sorry that he was so hasty? We'll stop at nothing short of a duke, with ten—no, twenty—thousand a year."

Megan stared at the canny look on her mother's face, and an uneasy feeling settled in her stomach. She'd be trapped. "What if the Earl of Berry and Lord Marion are already married?" she asked. Oh where was Eachann?

"It's the Earl of Marion, and Lord Berry," Eleanor corrected. "It doesn't matter. They always bring their sons, and cousins, and assorted aristocratic friends up for shooting parties."

"You make it sound like a seasonal migration," Megan said. "Don't Englishmen bring the females of the herd?" She imagined flocks of English lords flying into the windows of the castle, honking like geese, their feathers fine, their manners abysmal.

Eleanor chuckled. "Of course they do. Just be careful out in the hills, all of you, lest they mistake you in earnest for a grouse. Poor Bessie Fraser was grievously wounded that way one year."

Her mother's eyes were glowing. "It's all the better if they do bring their sisters and daughters. If you befriend the ladies, the gentlemen will follow."

"But I don't want to marry an Englishman!" Megan tried the truth, holding her breath.

Her mother waved her handkerchief. "Don't be silly Margaret. You saw Rossington," her mother sighed. "What a fine figure of a man, tall, handsome, elegant—"

"And completely uninterested in marrying me," Megan said. "If you liked him so much, why don't you marry him, Mother?"

Devorguilla smiled. "Perhaps I will."

"Mother!" Megan looked at the countess in surprise. Devorguilla crossed to the mirror and peered at herself, touching a hand to her cheek, still soft and smooth despite her years, and met her daughter's gaze in the glass.

"What? I'm still young enough to marry again. Would you have me sit and knit and grow roots like Eleanor? She is more oak tree than woman now."

Eleanor merely cackled at the description.

Devorguilla turned to her daughter. "But my first concern is seeing you married—and Alanna and eventually Sorcha after you. You are the eldest, and the match you make will set the standards for your sisters. They will see how very happy you are with your English lord, and wish to marry English lords themselves."

"But what if a Scot could make me happier still?" Megan asked.

"The heart obeys the head," Devorguilla quipped.

"Not if you're lucky," Eleanor murmured.

Megan put her hand in her pocket, touched the tiny ring that Eachann had given her the day he left. She dared not wear it. She tried to picture his face, remember how his kisses felt. But she saw only one face, one pair of horrified, disdainful gray eyes. She felt her skin heat all over again. Apparently beauty by Scottish standards was quite different from what was considered beautiful in England.

Eleanor squeezed her hand. "Never mind. We'd best take our supper before it's time for breakfast. I don't see any point in letting a fine roast of beef go to waste."

"I'm not hungry," Megan said. She wanted out of the creaking stays before they strangled her.

"Poor Margaret. It's understandable," Devorguilla sighed. "Your first broken heart. I remember my own. I didn't eat for three days."

"It's not—" Megan began, then paused. Why bother to explain? She wasn't hurt—she was furious. "It's just been a long day."

"I'll send up some tea and toast, then. Tomorrow we'll make a list of eligible English lords arriving to hunt, and prepare to bag ourselves a prize. I suppose we'd better have the seamstress make at least two or possibly three suitable outfits for hunting."

Megan watched them leave her room, almost numb with horror. If her mother had her way, she'd be married before the first snowflakes fell on the hills and glens.

She had to do something. She paced the floor and racked her brains, trying to think of a way to make herself the most unmarriageable lass in Scotland. But perhaps all English gentlemen would share Lord Rossington's opinion and find her hideous.

But the idea was not as comforting as she'd hoped it would be.

CHAPTER NINE

"Old Glen Dorian Castle needs to be pulled down, of course, and I daresay an English lord like yourself would want something more modern—a grand and glorious hunting lodge, perhaps, to spend a few weeks of the year visiting. The Highlands are grand indeed for hunting," Angus Grant, canny Inverness solicitor and man of affairs, said. "There's excellent game here in the glen with those woodlands there—" He pointed to a lush stand of deep green trees that filled half the glen. "Or the loch could be stocked with trout if you prefer to fish."

They sat in Kit's carriage on the hillside, looking across Glen Dorian at the castle on the island. The day was sunny and warm, and birds wheeled over the broken towers. The loch sparkled, the deepest blue he'd ever seen, and Kit wondered if there existed a finer view anywhere. If he climbed the hills on one side of the glen, he would have an endless view of other lochs, rolling green hills, and the narrow silver edge of the sea beyond. If he walked the other way, there'd be snow-capped peaks as far as he could see. Here in the glen itself, all was peaceful. There wasn't a single matchmaking mama, or one simpering debutante for miles and miles. He took a deep breath of the soft air pouring through the open window of the coach.

"I'd thought only of renting it for a few months," Kit said.

The man's expression turned sharp. "But there's no house to stay in, save that little cottage on the hillside, there—Mairi's Cottage, it's called—if it's still habitable after so many years." He pointed to a small stone house. "Glen Dorian was once a fine holding, but the castle has been unoccupied for some seventy years, the cottage for well over twenty."

"Why?" Kit asked. He doubted Angus Grant, a sensible man of cashboxes, leases, and bills of sale, would give him some foolish story about curses and legends.

The solicitor took off his beaver hat and scratched his head. "We-ell, living in the castle was banned after the Forty-five, to punish the Jacobite rebels. Lady MacIntosh stayed, so they say, and made her home in the glen in that very cottage, determined to hold the land for her husband's return." He paused, and withdrew a flask from his inner pocket and held it out to Kit, then sipped when Kit refused.

"And then?" Kit prompted.

"Then? Well, I suppose there's some that say she's waiting still," Grant whispered. A gust of wind buffeted the coach, and Grant frowned and sipped his whisky again. "Wild deer graze in the glen, my lord, and the otters and birds nest by the loch, but no one else has found a welcome here. There's no heir to claim it, and it wants a buyer. I daresay the government will gladly allow the purchase of it."

Kit considered. He could hardly look for the castle's

hidden treasure without some kind of legal right to do so, such as a lease, or a deed.

Angus Grant took out a pencil and scrawled a number on a scrap of paper, then passed it to Kit. "'Tis all it would take," he said.

Kit looked at the cottage. It stood patiently on the hillside, the small windows staring down at the old castle, like a hopeful wallflower at a ball, waiting to be asked . . .

It could serve as a home for a few short weeks, a place to stay as part of the adventure.

"Done." He took the paper and tucked it into his pocket. "I will write to my man in London at once, and you may conclude things with him."

High on the hillside, Megan McNabb stood with her hand shading her eyes, watching the coach. After a number of minutes, she saw the Earl of Rossington get out and begin the steep walk down the hill toward the causeway, and the coach trundled away, up and over the lip of the glen on the narrow track.

"Trespassing," she breathed, and the wind snatched the word away, dragged at her skirts.

She watched as he crossed to the castle, stopping to watch the otters playing in the water, and to look up at the hills that surrounded him. Megan ducked low.

Even from here, it was plain to see he loved the old place. She could see it in the way he took note of the details of Glen Dorian—the heather-covered hills, the loch, the hot sun on his back that made him take off his coat and sling it casually over his shoulder. It was exactly the same way her brother looked at Glenlorne—with pride and awe at the beauty of the land, down to the last rock, and the very grass.

But this Englishman did not belong here. Megan felt anger surge, and she pulled out a tuft of grass and threw it. She waited for the castle to throw him out, to frighten him away and send him back where he belonged, but after an hour, he still hadn't emerged.

With an oath, Megan picked up her skirts and hurried down the hillside.

Kit looked around the ruins of the great hall, noted the charred wood, the broken stones, the hideous scars war had left on the castle. Surely somewhere there was a clue to guide him to the treasure. He took Nathaniel's journal out of his pocket, found Mairi MacIntosh's letter and read it again. "*I have our treasure safe, hidden where the English thieves will not think to look for it. Again, you will know the place,*" she'd written. Now where would a lady hide her most valuable possessions? He could see three fireplaces. A secret space under a loose hearthstone made sense, but how could a lady lift such giant slabs of stone? The walls were three feet thick, and formidable, but the stones stood close together without any secret gaps that he could see. The room was filled with rubble, wood and roof slates, heat-shattered stone, and nothing else. The castle had obviously been looted before the English troops set fire to it. Had they found Mairi's treasure?

He looked across at the staircase, blocked by a mountain of debris. The floor above that part of the room was intact, the wood there barely scorched. Perhaps there was a bedchamber or a solar there. It might be a place to look, but the rubble between himself and the steps was twenty feet across, and too sharp and dangerous to climb over.

Kit sighed. He'd wanted an adventure. It seemed it couldn't begin until he'd moved the debris out of the way, one piece at a time. He tossed his coat aside and rolled up his sleeves. He grunted as he grasped a chunk of charred stone and tossed it aside. Under it lay three other pieces of stone, and he shifted those too, and considered what had happened here, and wondered how well his uncle might have known the people who lived here. "What's the secret, Nathaniel?" he murmured, and the whisper echoed back to him, sending a prickle up his spine.

CHAPTER TEN

Near Inverness, Scotland, February 1745

Captain Nathaniel Linwood sat in his tent, huddled beside a brazier that provided little warmth in the damp, frigid cold. In England, snowdrops were blooming. Here, the ink was frozen, and he held the bottle close to the glowing coals for a few moments to warm it enough to allow him to continue writing yet another report for the Duke of Cumberland. According to the spies, Charles Stuart's army was scattered across the Highlands, and there were rumors that there was no money and no weapons to continue the Jacobite fight to claim the thrones of England and Scotland from George II. The loyalty of the Highland clans was split between the King of England and the prince, who fought for his father James, whom the Jacobites called the King in Exile.

Nathaniel stared at the feathered end of his pen in the firelight and considered the next sentence. When would they come?

There was a scuffle outside his tent, and Nathaniel rose and threw back the flap. His sentries forced a man to his knees, a Highlander, his hands bound behind his back.

"He came into camp bold as you please, Captain, and armed to the teeth, demanding to see you, but he swears he's not a spy," the sergeant told him, his bayonet pointed at the Scot's throat.

The man tried to rise, his eyes on Nathaniel, defiant and angry, but the sergeant shoved him down again. The Highlander sighed and stayed where he was in the mud. "I'm not a spy. I care nothing for the concerns of Charles Stuart. I am simply here to find my wife's young brother." Despite the accent, his English was excellent. He wore a fine brooch, indicating his wealth the way his proud bearing—even on his knees—indicated authority. Nathaniel glanced at the weapons his sentry held—a fine sword with a jeweled hilt, a pair of Highland pistols, and a dirk.

"You came well armed for someone just looking for his brother," Nathaniel said.

"I haven't killed anyone," the man said calmly, as if he could easily have done so if he'd wished it. Judging by the size of the man's broad frame, Nathaniel was inclined to believe him.

"Who are you?"

"MacIntosh of Glen Dorian." He said it simply, as if Nathaniel should know the name. "My brother is Ruairidh MacIntosh, and he's a lad of just thirteen. If he's done aught wrong, I assure you he'll not be doing it again. I trust the English army doesn't kill children."

Nathaniel looked at the sentry. "Do you know anything about this?"

"We have a lad, aye, a Jacobite whelp. He was caught slipping into camp on his belly with a wicked-looking knife. He scared two men half to death when he leaped out at them. After a terrible fight they managed to subdue him and take the knife. He's in proper custody now, swearing like the devil himself, though no one can understand a word of what he's saying."

"He's speaking Gaelic. Is he hurt?" MacIntosh asked.

The sentry raised a hand to strike his prisoner, but the laird held his gaze, and the soldier dropped his fist and swallowed.

"I'll ask the questions, Sergeant. Bring him inside." Nathaniel stepped aside and waited while they hauled the Scot to his feet and led him into the tent. "Fetch the boy," he commanded.

MacIntosh filled the tent, and though Nathaniel was tall and broad himself, the Highlander made him feel puny by comparison. "Sit down," he said, indicating a campstool, but the prisoner held out his bound hands. Nathaniel picked up the knife he'd been using to sharpen his quill and cut the bonds. He moved to sit down himself, and hit the lantern hanging above the desk with his shoulder. The shadows swung, making the jeweled brooch at the man's shoulder glitter, and light flared over the signet ring on his hand.

"I'm Captain Nathaniel Linwood. *Are* you a spy?" Nathaniel asked him.

MacIntosh's lips quirked. "Why, because no one else would be fool enough to be out on a night like this? No, I'm not a spy. As I said, my family takes no side in this fight, though there are some of my clansmen who are on Charlie's side—and my wife's foolish young brother, of course. A friend dared him to steal an English soldier's hat. That's all he was after—just a silly prank."

Nathaniel opened his footlocker and took out a bottle of

brandy and two cups. "The lad should find better friends," he said as he poured. "Everyone is on edge. My men have orders to shoot the enemy on sight rather than risk having their throats cut. Your brother is lucky."

MacIntosh took the cup Nathaniel held out to him, but didn't drink. "We'll see how lucky he is when he gets here. His sister—my wife—will thrash him within an inch of his life, once she's sure he's safe and unharmed, of course. I hope you've saved her that pleasure. I trust he hasn't been hurt."

Nathaniel read the warning in the man's eyes, and took a sip of brandy, let it burn through the chill in his bones. His sword lay under the cot where he'd stowed it out of the way, directly under the Highlander's feet, out of reach if he needed it. "I hope so as well. I am not in the habit of injuring children. A good caning when deserved is another matter."

The Highlander nodded. "Agreed. But I'll be the one to do it if it comes to that."

"You speak very good English," Nathaniel observed.

The man smiled. "For a Scottish barbarian? I attended Oxford for a time."

"Ah. My family are Cambridge men," Nathaniel replied.

He heard the sound of footsteps approaching, accompanied by harsh commands in English and higher pitched curses in Gaelic. MacIntosh rose and threw back the tent flap, letting in the wind and rain.

"Bring the boy inside," Nathaniel ordered, and the sergeant picked the boy up by the scruff of the neck and tossed him at his brother's feet.

"The Jacobite puppy bit me," the redcoat snapped. "Like animals they are, all of 'em."

"That will do," Nathaniel said. "Return to your post."

He waited until the man trudged away, and turned. MacIntosh was speaking to the child in Gaelic in low tones, his expression serious. The boy looked up at him fiercely, his throat working as he tried not to cry. His relief at seeing his brother was evident. MacIntosh turned him to face Nathaniel, and he read hatred and fear in the lad's pinched face.

"Say it," MacIntosh warned him when he remained stubbornly silent.

"I apologize," the boy mumbled in English. "I meant no harm."

Nathaniel stood staring down at the child, in his muddy plaid, his small hand clenched in a fist. "Did you not? You hate the English, I assume. Who taught you to hate us? Not your brother."

His chin rose. "My mother's kin fights for the true prince. So do I."

"Ruairidh," MacIntosh warned him into silence with that single word, clamping a hand on the lad's shoulder. "I trust we are free to leave?" he asked Nathaniel.

Nathaniel hesitated a moment, then nodded. He did not imprison children, and there was no reason to detain the laird of Glen Dorian.

MacIntosh reached for his purse. "Is there a fine to pay?"

Or a bribe. Nathaniel watched the boy's lip curl, and waved his hand in dismissal. He opened the tent flap, and called for the nearest soldier to bring MacIntosh's weapons back.

It was a fine sword, basket-hilted, set with gems, Nathaniel noted as they handed it to MacIntosh, and he watched the Highlander slide it back into the sheath buckled to his waist.

"You seem to be a man of some wealth," he said, wondering if the man had any influence over his rebellious kin.

"He's the MacIntosh of Glen Dorian," the boy piped proudly.

"Let's go. Mairi's waiting for us" was the laird's only reply.

"I trust I won't see the boy here again," Nathaniel called after him.

"You won't," MacIntosh agreed, and the pair strode out into the night.

CHAPTER ELEVEN

It had been an hour, and still Lord Rossington had not emerged from the castle. Megan hurried down the slope to the causeway. He did not belong here. Why did the castle not frighten him away? If the castle would not send him off with a flea in his ear and fear in his heart, she most certainly would.

She paused halfway across and looked up at the empty windows. What if the place had *killed* him?

Even now, the earl could be lying on the stone floor, staring up through the broken roof, his gray eyes empty of life, rubble crushing his legs or his chest. Or he might be alive, in pain, his cries for help snatched away by a laughing wind, as he grew weaker and weaker, until—

She picked up her skirts and ran, silently admonishing the castle not to harm him.

Not that she cared, really, but he was young and handsome and alive. She did not believe in revenge—not for the wrongs of the *distant* past, at least. She hadn't forgotten how Rossington had insulted her with his cruel rejection.

Not that she wanted him. If he had shown the slightest

interest in her mother's ridiculous plan to marry them off, she would have been the one to refuse—he'd just said the word first, with sharp horror, as if marrying her was the worst thing that could happen to a man. She tasted the bitterness of that on her tongue as she hurried through the courtyard.

She reached the inner door she'd entered a few days earlier, and prayed the shutter would still be open, letting light and air and sanity into the room beyond. The door swung open as she approached, and she stepped back and swallowed a cry of surprise. The heavy oak panel shivered in the wind—it must be the wind, surely—and light poured through the portal. She forced herself to step forward. She was being foolish. It simply meant the shutters *were* open, and the wind had blown the door wide. No ghostly hand had opened it for her.

"Hello?" she called, slipping into the hall. There wasn't even an echo. "Lord Rossington?" She stepped farther inside, scanned the corners, looking for signs of fresh blood, or a broken body.

She took a step down, stood near the fireplace, heard the wind whistling down the chimney, crooning a sad, haunting tune.

"It's me, Megan McNabb," she said, and the whistling stopped a moment. The castle seemed to still, listening, considering. She felt the creep of eyes on her back, knew someone was watching her—someone she could not see. Unseen hands reached for her and she spun, but there was nothing behind her.

"Lord Rossington?" she called again, but her voice came out as an uncertain squeak. She cleared her throat. "My lord?" she said, making her tone firmer, more commanding.

She heard a grating sound, watched as a beam the size of a caber shifted on the far side of the room. There was a clatter of dust and debris, and a roar like a waterfall.

"Bloody hell!" she heard him bellow. It must be Rossington, since it was in English. It was followed by a string of words she didn't understand, but made her blush just the same. Curses, in any language, were clear enough.

"Hello!" she said, louder still, and the cursing stopped.

He came out from behind a pile of rubble. His face was dirty, and there was blood on his shirt.

"Dear God, you *are* hurt!" she said and rushed toward him, fumbling in her pocket for her handkerchief.

"There's a splinter of wood in my finger," he said. "Where on earth did you come from?"

She ignored the question and took his hand in hers, examining the injury.

A shard of blackened wood stuck out of his flesh. Blood dripped and pattered on the stone floor.

She flicked a fingernail over the protruding end of the splinter. He cried out and tried to pull his hand away. She held on tight.

"What on earth are you doing?" he demanded.

She looked into his eyes fiercely. "Hold still. It must come out."

"I can do it myself," he snapped, trying to pull away again.

She stepped back, and folded her arms across her chest and waited. She watched as he looked at the wound. "I think I'll need medical assistance," he said stiffly. "It's in very deep."

She tilted her head and looked at him smugly. "Suit yourself. The nearest doctor is in the village—that's a half-hour's walk, and he might be out. If you leave it, you might bleed to death, or it might become corrupted. That stick is dreadfully dirty."

"Nonsense. It's hardly a stick—it's a tiny splinter. I get them all the time." Still, he looked at it again, his brow furrowing. "Do you really think it's as bad as that?"

She tried to remember he was English, arrogant, and rude, and that she found him utterly detestable. But the light poured through a hole in the roof and illuminated his fair hair, and his eyes were soft now, uncertain. He looked like a lad, as sweet and kind and young as Eachann. Her breath caught in her throat. He was surely twice as handsome as he had been in the drawing room at Dundrummie.

She moved toward him carefully, her half boots crunching on the little stones that covered the floor. "Does it hurt?" she asked.

"Only very little," he said.

"Is it still bleeding?" She drew nearer still.

"No, it's almost stopped." She leaned over his hand, her forehead nearly touching his, and gazed at the wound. She touched his wrist, and still he didn't move. Instead he looked at her. She could feel his eyes on her face like a caress, and tried vainly to refrain from blushing.

She felt his pulse pick up under her fingertips. He didn't say anything, and she felt her skin tingle, heating where it touched his. She could feel his breath on her cheek, and for an instant she was powerless to move.

Then a bird took flight, flapping its wings as it rose, seeking a way out. He turned to look at it, and quick as she could, she brought his hand to her mouth, caught the end of the splinter between her teeth and pulled it out.

His roar shook more birds from their roosts, and for a moment the air shimmered around them, light and shadows whirling, ascending to the sky. She put her hands over her head, told herself that it was only birds and wing beats and dust.

"You bit me!" he cried, looking at the blood dripping from the injury.

"Have you a flask of whisky?" she asked him calmly.

He rummaged in his inside pocket with his good hand. "Why, do I taste bad?"

She smiled. "Dreadful. Pour a little over the wound."

He hesitated. "It's brandy."

Megan took the flask, and opened it. "It won't work as well, but it will probably do." He hissed as the spirit flowed over the cut, and looked away while she bound his finger with her handkerchief and tied the ends. "Are you one of those who can't bear the sight of blood?" she asked.

He glared at her. "Of course not. I was very nearly a soldier. I would have seen plenty of blood."

"Nearly? What happened? Was it too fearsome?" she said tartly, squeezing his hand to stop the bleeding faster.

"I inherited an earldom. I had responsibilities in England, and I could not leave."

She heard the very slight edge of regret in his tone, and felt guilty for teasing him. "I'm sorry," she murmured.

"For what? For biting me, or because I am an earl?"

She raised her eyes, found his face inches from her, and felt her breath hitch again. He really did have the most extraordinary effect on her. Standing close to Eachann never kept her from breathing properly.

"Because—" she began. Because she'd been the rude, saucy minx her family always accused her of being. Hadn't her mother warned Megan that her sharp tongue would get her into trouble one day? Perhaps today was the day. She told herself he'd been far ruder than she could ever have been, that he'd humiliated her, made her fear that if she did indeed go to England in search of a husband, she'd be laughed all the way back to Scotland.

She let go of his hand and moved away. "I meant I'm sorry you were injured. What on earth were you doing?"

He ignored the question. "You have a soft heart then. Or perhaps you are simply skilled at fixing small wounds. Is it a Highland tradition that women are healers?"

He was staring at her, his eyes intent. It stirred her belly. A soft heart? Not for him. "'Tis simply a matter of being practical. My sisters and I used to get hurt all the time—scraped knees, splinters, bruises . . . perhaps we are simply more resourceful here in the Highlands. I doubt you'll have a scar, if that's what worries you."

"I fell out of a tree when I was nine, and cut my leg. It took seventeen stitches to close the gash. Then there was the time I drove a fishhook through my thumb. I still have both those scars, and a few others besides. My horse threw me once, and I cut my chin, just here—" He tilted his head and showed her a small white line that traced the contours of his jaw. She had the oddest desire to reach out and touch it. She clasped her hands together and concentrated on glaring at him.

"You shouldn't be here," she said.

He raised his eyebrows, instantly looking every inch the haughty nobleman. "Oh? Why's that?"

She looked around. The castle was still now. Were the stones less forbidding, the air less oppressive than it was just minutes ago? "There's a curse," she murmured.

He grinned. "Yes, I've heard." He held up his hand, swathed in her handkerchief. "I don't usually, but this time I'm inclined to believe it's true."

"You're trespassing," she said. He really did have an incredible smile. Eachann had a broken tooth, but Rossington's smile was perfect. It made her feel like she was standing in the sun. It also made her unaccountably angry. "Is it common practice in England to go about breaking into houses and castles that don't belong to you?" she snapped.

He smiled again, and this time she saw something new in his eyes. Triumph. He reached into his pocket again, and pulled out a scrap of paper.

"But I do own Glen Dorian, Lady Megan—or is it Margaret today?" Her jaw dropped, and she felt her knees turn to water. "Have I succeeded in surprising you?"

"Yet again," she admitted, raising her chin.

She stared at him. His expression turned smug, and he was looking at her with the same haughty expression he'd had when he regarded her across the drawing room. But it appeared he had every right—she was the trespasser. She turned on her heel and went toward the door. "Then I should most certainly go. I'm expected back at Dundrummie, and I have . . ." She reached for the door latch and tugged.

It wouldn't budge.

She stared at it a moment. Hadn't it been wide open when she arrived? She tried again, jiggling it with all her strength. It refused to give.

"Here, let me," he said coming closer, reaching past her to grasp the rusted latch himself, the long length of his body inches behind her. Megan swallowed, and kept her eyes on the latch, and the strong, tanned hand upon it. "It's stuck fast," he muttered. "Odd, it opened easily enough before—" He yanked at it.

She looked around desperately, wanting to be out, away from his disturbing company. "Is there another way?"

"Not that I've seen. There's a staircase over there, but it's blocked with rubble. I was clearing it when you appeared, but it goes up, not down—or out."

"There's the window," she said breathlessly, hurrying over. She stepped up on a bit of fallen rubble and looked out. The ground was nearly fifteen feet below.

"It's too far," he said, and she started at the sound of his voice. He was right beside her yet again, leaning over the wide sill next to her. She could smell the warmth of his skin.

She dug her nails into the crumbling stone of the window-sill. "Nonsense. If you boost me up, I can find handholds in the stone and climb down to the ground."

"Have you done that before?" he asked.

"No," she admitted. "But I've heard tales of such things—lovers climbing up the sides of towers to rescue their lady-loves, prisoners escaping. There's a story about a man who tied bed sheets together to climb out of the dread Tower of London . . ." She realized she was babbling and he was staring at her, and fell silent. He really did have the most attractive gray eyes, keen and bright. They matched the color of the loch.

"I suspect it's different in real life," he said. "Far less romantic. No one in stories ever suffers broken bones or smashed skulls. If anyone is going to climb out, I think it must be me."

She gaped at him. "Then what?"

"I'll go around and open the door from the outside and let you out."

She wondered fleetingly if he'd ever come back, and shook the thought away.

"You don't agree with my plan?" he asked, mistaking her gesture. "May I remind you that you are a guest in my home—well, my castle—and it is my duty to rescue you?"

Were all Englishmen so gallant? Or perhaps he was merely stubborn, or horrified at being locked in with her, alone.

He climbed up on the wide windowsill, and slid one booted foot over the edge. She held her breath as he grinned and lowered himself. "Ah, I've found my first foothold, this isn't so difficult after all," he said. "Wish me luck."

"Better to be careful than lucky," she said, her heart cowering in her throat.

"That makes no sense at all, my dear Lady Margaret." He was groping with his left foot, the fingertips of one hand still clinging to the window's edge. Her handkerchief was tied around his finger, and the monogrammed edge fluttered in the breeze.

"It's Megan," she murmured, staring at the embroidered M.

He lowered himself again—and slipped. She watched in horror as his eyes widened, and he slid down the entire height of the wall. He landed at the bottom, flat on his back and didn't move.

"Lord Rossington?" she called.

"It's Kit," he said, without opening his eyes.

She frowned, and he forced his eyelids up and looked at her. "My name," he explained, getting slowly to his feet. His cheek had been grazed by the stone and was raw and bloody. His coat was torn, his hair mussed, and he looked as unlordly as it was possible for a man to look. He brushed the dust from his breeches and gazed up at her. "It's Christopher, actually, but they call me Kit."

"Kit," she murmured, testing it on her tongue. Odd, but it suited him well, and had a gentle dignity to it. "Are you unhurt?"

"I think so."

"Then please open the door."

She watched him disappear around the edge of the tower, then crossed to the door to wait, the sound of her steps loud in the lonely space. She ignored the shiver that crept up her spine, and tried the latch again. It still rebuffed her. She was stuck. Was it imagination, or were the shadows in the hall growing longer, reaching toward her? She leaped back in surprise when the latch rattled under her hand, but it was only Rossington—Kit—on the other side, shaking it. She put her hand to her pounding heart. "It won't budge on this side either," he said at last, his voice muffled. "Try again from your side."

She jiggled it desperately, tugged with all her might, but it held firm. The wind hummed though the hole in the roof. "Can you kick it in?" she called.

"Stand back," he ordered. She braced herself to one side, waiting for the door to splinter and crash to the floor. It seemed a pity to destroy one of the last whole things in the old castle, and she felt a moment's regret displace fear. The panel shuddered against the weight of his body, but remained stubbornly unscathed. Anger—and fear—instantly replaced regret.

"Can't you do better than that?" she demanded.

"It's solidly constructed. You'll notice that although most of the rest of the castle is rubble, this door is still here. I daresay it will stand forever."

"Should I wait that long, d'you think?" she asked sarcastically. She heard a sound behind her and spun, but there was nothing there. The wind stirred a cloud of dust in the middle of the floor, and it rose and danced, made the cobwebs shiver and sway. Was it getting dark? Surely it was too early. Perhaps a cloud had passed over the sun outside, but the shadows grew, crept closer, and Megan pressed her back against the wall next to the door, and felt her heart climb into her throat. Her eyes flicked around the dark edges of the room, but there was nothing there—at least nothing that she could see. Terror suddenly made her limbs shake. She did not want to stay here. She put her hand on the latch and tried again, pulling desperately, feeling tears sting her eyes.

Kit stared at the door from his side, considering how best to open it. If he had an axe, perhaps, or something to pry at the hinges, he'd be able to free her at once, but he hadn't thought to bring tools.

Suddenly, Megan was scratching at the door, and he could hear the sound of panic in her breathless cries.

"Are you all right?" he called out. "What's happening?"

"I—" She faltered, and he heard the thick sound of tears in her voice. "I want out!" She was afraid. He felt his gut tighten. Had the birds returned, was there an adder coiled amid the ruins, or a wolf?

"I'll get you out. Go back to the window if you can," he said, and he ran around the castle the way he'd come.

"Megan?" he called up to her, and she peered down at him, her eyes huge in her pale face. She had dust on her cheek. She looked young, terrified, and beautiful, Juliet to his Romeo. Or Lady Macbeth.

"Climb down, sweetheart," he said, as if he were speaking to a frightened child.

"I'll fall."

He shook his head. "No you won't."

"You did," she argued.

He swallowed an oath and held out his arms. "But I'll be here to catch you," he assured her.

She climbed over the sill. For a moment he saw a slim and tempting length of leg from ankle to knee. Then her foot slipped, and she shrieked. He watched her skirts swirl in the wind for an instant before she fell, twisting as the wind caught her, turning her around so her eyes were on his, big as saucers, and coming closer. He opened his arms and braced himself.

She hit him full in the chest, knocking him backward, and he closed his arms around her protectively as they tumbled into the thick grass.

The impact made his teeth rattle for the second time that day. Her knee slammed into his thigh, an inch from disaster, and her elbow met his ribs, knocking the wind out of him.

She lay still for a moment, and he held her tightly against his shoulder. Her hair was as soft as silk. "Megan?" he said dragging air back into his lungs. She wasn't moving. "Lady Megan?"

Slowly she raised her head, and looked down at him. Her eyes were wide, and inches from his own. They weren't green, or brown. They were a mesmerizing mix of colors, the shades of the heather, the hills, the setting sun, the glow of a fire. Her lips were parted in surprise, her cheeks flushed, and soft tendrils of her hair had escaped the tight braid to caress his cheeks. He was suddenly aware of the press of her body on his, the fact that her hip was resting against his groin, and her breasts were soft on his chest, and his arms were still wrapped around her. He gritted his teeth against the inevitable and quite natural reaction to holding a lovely woman, and closed his eyes, trying to think of anything but her, willing away his sudden arousal.

"Are you all right?" she asked. Her voice a husky purr that made the situation worse, not better.

"I think I'm supposed to ask you that," he managed.

"Oh," she said, her eyes scanning his face, her lips so close to his that his mouth watered. If she did not move, he would have to kiss her, and that might lead to—he swallowed a groan and lifted her aside as gently as he could, before his growing arousal became obvious, and got to his feet, gazing at the distant hills, counting to ten.

Then he held out a hand to help her up, felt the tingle of awareness rush through his body all over again as she set her fingers in his, and almost dropped her.

She mistook the reason for his sudden release of her. "Did I cause any injury?' she asked, advancing on him. "Is your hand—"

He looked down at the grubby, grass-stained handkerchief that bound his thumb, and laughed. No, it didn't hurt. Not as much as his ribs, or the damned inconvenient erection he was trying to hide, or his pride.

"I will come back tomorrow with some tools, fix the door, or remove the hinges and take it out altogether. Someone else might have gotten stuck in there, and not been able to get out."

She stared up at the window and bit her lush lower lip, catching it between sharp white teeth. It was an unconsciously sensual gesture, and he swallowed a groan. The wind blew her cloak back, pasted her gown to the contours of her body, the soft curve of her hip, the mounds of her breasts, the shape of her thigh. He looked away, and began to count again.

"There are tales of this place," she said. "They say there's a—"

He held up a hand. "I know—a curse."

"Not a curse, a legend. It's not the same thing at all," she said, her careful English pronunciation forgotten, the soft Highland lilt evident. It was enchanting.

"What's the difference?" he asked.

She looked up at the facade of the old castle. "A curse is . . . well, a bad thing. A legend is more like a blessing, a tale of the folk who lived here once, and a hope that a time like that will come again, that happy lives will be lived here once more, that love—" He watched a blush rise over her cheeks, like a rose coming into bloom. "I'm babbling like a ninny," she said, and her blush deepened further still. "I must look a terrible sight. No wonder you believe in curses."

"There's dust on your face, and cobwebs on your gown,"

he admitted. Not that they detracted from her beauty one whit. Her hands immediately flew to her cheeks, rubbed at them. She then noticed her hands were as grubby as her face. He smiled and held up his own hands, also covered with dust and blood and rust from the door latch. "I look just as bad."

"The loch," she said, pointing. "We can wash our hands at least."

He followed her down to the water's edge, and she knelt on a rock, dipped her hands into the clear water, and splashed her face.

Kit winced at the icy chill of the water. "Is the loch always this cold?" he asked. "It's late summer!"

"Of course," she said. "The water comes down from there—" She pointed to a snow-capped peak that peered over the end of the glen.

"Then I shan't swim," he said.

She sent him a sharp look. "Is that why you bought Glen Dorian?"

"To have a place to swim? Not at all," he assured her. "The river near my house in Derbyshire is warm and slow and pleasant for that," he said.

"There are shallower and warmer pools in the hills, higher up, and waterfalls." He watched her eyes scan the glen, saw her love for the land. It made his breath catch, and the hopeful edge of desire rose yet again.

"So why *did* you buy Glen Dorian?" she asked, fixing him with a sharp look. "You're not going to tear it down, are you?"

He slid his eyes away. He'd imagined this would be a simple adventure, a lark before he returned to London in the fall, to duty, responsibility, and sanity. He would solve the mystery of the treasure, follow the story laid out in Nathaniel's journal, and go home. He hadn't intended to buy a glen, complete with a ruined castle on an island in a loch. Now it was his, he could do as he pleased—even, if he wished, come back. The idea suddenly appealed to him very much.

"No, I won't tear it down. If I wish to build something, I'd put it there, perhaps, so there would be a view of the loch and the old castle."

"But that's Mairi's Hill!" she said. "It's part of the legend. For years she stood on that crag and waited for her true love to return to her."

"What happened to her?"

She shrugged. "Some say he came back and took her away from here, because they'd known as much unhappiness as happiness in this place. Others say she died waiting, and is waiting still."

He scanned the hill, looking for a lone woman watching the road that led into the glen, and the otters, and the castle. But there was nothing there. He felt an overwhelming rush of disappointment.

"What will you build?" she persisted. "A fine English hunting lodge?"

"I really just came to visit, a kind of grand tour. My great-uncle came here once, and wrote—"

Her eyes sharpened. "Yes?"

"He was a soldier," he began, then stopped again. Had Nathaniel had a hand in the burning of Glen Dorian? What if he was responsible for causing the terrible pain, the sadness that haunted the glen?

Her lips tightened. "After Culloden, you mean?" She said

the word as if it was poisonous, and it felt wrong to utter it here.

"Yes," he said, and she drew a sharp breath and got to her feet, and began to walk around the side of the castle, her chin high. He scrambled to catch up. She stopped and turned on him so suddenly he nearly crashed into her. He caught her arm to steady her, but she pulled away.

"Did *he* burn the castle?" she demanded. He read loathing in her eyes, suspicion, disgust. It made him angry that she would judge him by the actions of men long dead.

"Why I've come here is none of your business, my lady. If you must know, I wanted a little peace and quiet, away from chattering females. Need I remind you that you are the one trespassing? I own this land, and I will do as I please with it, is that clear?"

Her eyes glittered as she dipped a mocking curtsy. "Perfectly so, your lordship. There's no need to call your bailiff to arrest me. I shall bid you good day, and be on my way at once." She turned and flounced back to the causeway, and he leaned against the old tower and watched her cross, her cloak catching the wind, her tangled hair swirling around her head in a dark halo. She looked like an angel, or a spirit, he thought, watching her go. He glanced back up toward Mairi's Hill, scanned it again, but there was no one else watching Lady Megan McNabb flee the little island in high dudgeon. Still, the wind stuttered as it rushed through the broken stones and ruffled the dry grass, and it sounded like laughter.

Tomorrow he would bring tools and begin to search in earnest for the treasure hidden in the old castle. Tonight, he would return to the inn and spend the evening reading more of Nathaniel's journal. He had to know what had happened here. He would concentrate on that, and only that.

But watching Megan McNabb continue on her way, he hoped it wouldn't take too long to find the truth and the treasure. A pretty woman, a captivating, incredible woman, especially a marriageable one, was a complication he didn't need.

Chapter Twelve

Megan slipped through the kitchen door and up the back stairs to her room, making certain no one saw her. She was scrubbing her face raw, trying to cool the hot blood that filled her cheeks when Alanna arrived.

"Where on earth have you been? You missed tea," Alanna said, seating herself on Megan's bed. Megan ignored her sister and scrubbed all the harder. How many times would that man make her look foolish? Once again, he'd dismissed her sharply, made it perfectly clear he did not like her in the least.

Alanna caught sight of Megan's ruined gown and leaped to her feet, her jaw dropping in horror. She took in the mud, the grass stains, and the blood. "What happened?"

Megan tossed her chin. "Nothing at all." She went into the dressing room and took off the gown, bundled it angrily into a ball and tossed it into the corner. She would bury or burn it later. Even if it could be saved, she never wanted to see it again, have it remind her of *him*.

"Nothing?" Alanna said. She waited, and Megan knew

her sister was both patient and stubborn enough to wait forever if she had to, but she would have the truth.

Some explanation *was* required, Megan supposed. She offered the barest description she could—the door of the old castle had blown shut, and the Earl of Rossington had helped her climb out a window.

Alanna was scandalized enough at that. "Rossington? You were *alone* with *him?*"

"Yes," Megan said. The tale of tending to his splinter, of falling out the window and landing spread-eagled on top of him in the heather, with every inch of her pressed to every inch of him, died on her lips at the look of shock on her sister's face.

"You saw him again after he was so definite about not liking you?"

"I didn't intend to, Alanna. I wasn't looking for him. It just happened we were both in the same place at the same time, and the door just blew shut."

"So you said. But just how did you come to be at Glen Dorian? I thought you were going to the village to take a basket of scones to Granny Fraser and hear her tell tales."

Megan leaped at the change of subject. "And so I did— it was a wonderful visit—Granny knew Mairi MacIntosh, saw the destruction of the castle by the English soldiers after Culloden—"

"Why was his lordship at Glen Dorian?" Alanna asked.

Megan shrugged uneasily. "I don't know. Look, I just wanted to look at the old place on my way back here for tea."

"But you missed tea," Alanna pointed out again, her tone prim.

"I got locked in!" Megan insisted again, as if that explained everything. Or nothing at all.

"With the English earl who refused to marry you and left Dundrummie without even having his dinner," Alanna marveled, setting her hands on her hips.

Megan felt hot blood rush to her face, and she sat at the dressing table and began to undo the tattered ribbon that held what was left of her braid. "I had no idea he was inside," she lied. "Granny said the view from the battlements was magnificent. I went to see that, not him."

"Was it?" Alanna took over the comb, worked at the wind tangles in Megan's hair.

"The roof has fallen in. There's no way to climb up."

Alanna's eyes widened. "How dangerous! Perhaps it was a good thing the earl was there after all."

Megan lowered her eyes, hiding from her sister's questioning gaze. Alanna knew her better than anyone else, would know if she had feelings for the Englishman, which she most certainly did not. He was arrogant, rude, and . . . her heart flipped. He'd rescued her, caught her when she fell, protected her from coming to harm. She suppressed the sigh that bubbled up in her chest, and tossed her head instead and pasted on a ferocious scowl. "He had the audacity to accuse me of trespassing! Apparently he's bought the castle and the whole of the old MacIntosh holding. I was only too happy to come away."

"After he helped you climb out a window."

"I hope I'll never see him again," Megan said fervently. She saw the flash of his grin in her mind, roguish and charming, and blushed again.

"So exactly how did you happen to get blood on your gown if it was all so civilized?" Alanna asked.

Megan lowered her eyes. "It isn't my blood. I suppose he might have cut himself," she murmured. "There are sharp stones, and bits of broken timber everywhere."

"How unchivalrous of him to bleed on your gown."

"I hope I never set eyes on him again!" Megan repeated.

"So you said." Alanna set down the comb. "There. I have a fitting for a tea gown, whatever that might be, and Mama wants me to choose a pattern for a riding habit. No doubt a riding master will be coming here next. I hate horses. No doubt you'll want to commit the tales of the day—the ones Granny told you, of course—to paper, so I'll leave you to it. Of course, Mother will have questions about why you missed tea when you see her at dinner, so you'll want to be prepared."

"You won't tell her?" Megan said, horrified.

Alanna looked smug. "Miss Carruthers says that English manners require that if a lady is alone with a gentleman, even if the circumstances are quite innocent, the gentleman is expected to do the honorable thing and offer to marry her."

Megan felt her skin blanch. "Does Mother know this?"

"Of course she does. I can picture it: She'd drag you and Lord Rossington to the nearest anvil, and see you wed by the blacksmith, willing or not. No, I won't tell her—if you're sure you never want to see him again."

"Of course I am," Megan said, and Alanna smiled and left the room.

Megan stared at the closed door, her stomach churning. She'd never trick a man into marriage that way—or allow herself to be tricked. Especially not with a man like Kit—

Lord Rossington—who so clearly did not want her. She stared into the mirror, pictured his gray eyes inches from her own, remembered the scent of his skin, the feel of her hand in his, the sensation of lying on top of him with his arms around her . . . smoke curled through her belly and she pressed her fist there. She opened the trinket box on her dressing table and took out Eachann's promise ring, and gazed into the tiny golden-green chip of the cairngorm in the center.

She slipped the promise ring onto her finger, and sent up a prayer that her true love came home very, very soon.

Chapter Thirteen

"There's a caller for you downstairs," the maid said, interrupting the embroidery lesson. "An English gentleman."

"A caller?" Sorcha asked eagerly, tossing aside her stitchery, thrilled that something—anything—might interrupt the hated task.

Alanna looked up from her perfect work, met Megan's eyes with her brows raised. Alanna's embroidered silk rose bloomed on her linen sampler, the stitches so perfect that the dew looked wet, and it was possible to believe that if one pressed their nose to it, it would even smell like a rose.

Devorguilla shot to her feet. "An English gentleman? Is it Lord Rossington?"

Megan plunged the needle into her finger and let out a cry. She sucked the small injury, but that reminded her of extracting the splinter, and her stomach knotted as tightly as her tangled embroidery threads.

"Would it be such a great surprise?" Devorguilla asked, mistaking Megan's outburst. "He might have changed his

mind upon reflection. We shall make him sweat if he has."
She grinned unpleasantly.

Alanna's gaze was full of speculation, and Megan felt her
stomach turn to water. Did Rossington feel honor bound to
wed her now, having been alone with her?

But perhaps he'd come only to see if she was well after
their misadventure three days earlier—it *would* be the gentle-
manly, chivalrous thing to do.

And when her mother found out the dreadful details
of their encounter at Glen Dorian, she would insist that he
marry her, and Megan would be the one to sweat.

"It's not the gentleman who was here the other night, no.
It's a different one," the maid said.

Megan felt her spine melt with sheer relief, even as her
mouth dried with a certain measure of disappointment. Of
course he had not come—he made it plain on both the times
they'd met that he had no liking for her as a wife, as a neighbor, or even a friend, for that matter.

"A different gentleman! Girls, tidy yourselves at once,"
Devorguilla said, her smile instantly transforming to the one
she reserved for eligible gentlemen.

"And I'll say no if you propose to this one," Megan said,
raising her chin.

"You most certainly will not!" her mother said.

"Perhaps we'd best let this one have tea at least," Alanna
said with a twinkle in her eye, and Megan warned her with a
sharp glare.

"Jeannie, go and tell Graves to nail the man to the floor if
he has to, but to keep him in the salon until we've heard what
he has to say for himself," Devorguilla said, and took Megan

by one arm and Alanna by the other and hauled them both downstairs.

Megan braced herself to face this new English invader, schooled her features to what she hoped was haughty disinterest.

Her mother stopped outside the door to the salon, and pinched Megan's cheeks to pinken them, and smoothed back a wayward lock of hair before she opened the door and shoved her into the room.

A gentleman rose to his feet, and turned to regard Megan.

"Here's another one, Devorguilla," Eleanor piped up from her chair by the fire. "I do hope you'll be more gentle this time."

But if the visitor found anything curious in the old lady's remark, he said nothing. His eyes were on Megan. He bowed deeply, and his pate shone like the moon through his thin hair.

"Good afternoon, dear ladies. I'm the Marquess of Merridew." He smiled, and a spread of teeth filled his face.

"A *marquess?*" Devorguilla warbled. "I am Lady McNabb. Let me introduce my daughters. This is Lady Margaret McNabb, my eldest, and Lady Alice, and Sarah."

"A veritable rose garden of Highland beauties," the marquess said and snorted a laugh at his own wit.

"Won't you sit down? I see Eleanor has already ordered tea," Devorguilla said, looking the marquess over like a housewife considering a particular fish at the market stall. Megan half expected her to lean in and sniff him to see if he was fresh. "What brings you to Scotland?" she asked as they settled themselves.

"I have come for the grouse, of course. Nothing is more delicious than Scottish grouse, though there's nothing akin to English pheasant in juniper sauce. The bird shooting season doesn't open for a few days more, but I bagged a buck just yesterday, so I thought I'd come and pay my respects, since I was given to understand there are several lovely young ladies residing here," he chirped, and let his eyes take in the entirety of Megan's slim figure before coming back to ogle her breasts. She resisted the urge to fold her arms over them. "I see I have not been misinformed," he said.

"A different kind of hunting today, eh?" Eleanor said with light sarcasm. "The marquess's father is the Duke of Beresford, Devorguilla. Merridew is his son and heir, which makes him a much better catch than a mere earl."

Megan watched her mother's cheeks flush with excitement at that.

"Where exactly is your shooting box, my lord?" she asked her guest.

"At Loch Dun, Countess," He grinned. His keen stalker's eye scanned the room, as he assessed the value of the items in sight.

"You probably have antlers just like those," Eleanor said, watching his eyes fall on some fifty years of hunting trophies that graced the wall. "I made my late husband move most of his to the old hunting lodge on the edge of Dundrummie. He chose to hang them in the dining room, of all places. Where do you keep yours, my lord?"

"I believe he was looking at the clock on the mantle, Aunt," Megan said. "The one beside the silver candlesticks, right under the portrait of you painted by Mister Gainsborough."

"*Thomas* Gainsborough?" the marquess asked, his eyes popping.

"Indeed," Eleanor said, primping as she gazed up at the handsome woman in the portrait. "He and Joshua Reynolds nearly came to blows over which of them would have the honor of painting me," she said. "In the end, I decided based on price."

"Was Gainsborough cheaper?" the marquess asked, and Eleanor sent him a flirtatious smile.

"Why no, my lord—he was more expensive."

Megan hid a smile.

"Ah, it is so interesting to discuss family treasures. Where are your English estates located, my lord?" Devorguilla asked. "Do you collect art, or jewels, or gold, perhaps?"

They were like dogs circling one another, each trying to find out the other's value without actually asking.

"In Suffolk, my lady," he said. "My father's ducal seat is in Kent, however."

"How wonderful!" Devorguilla chirped. "Megan was just saying the other day that she hopes to have the opportunity to visit Kent while she's in London for the Season."

"I daresay the duke—and his heir—will be in London as well," Eleanor said.

"The two places are not close to each other, I'm afraid," the marquess said, before he turned to Megan. "I knew your brother in London, Lady Margaret—at least I heard the tales of his unexpected inheritance, and his wedding to Lady Caroline Forrester, the Earl of Somerson's sister.

"There is nothing like the scent of money to set the hunter on the trail, is there?" Eleanor said. "Devorguilla, did I not tell you suitors would come flocking just to get a look at Megan and Alanna?" Devorguilla sent her a quelling glare. Alanna blushed to the roots of her hair, and Sorcha giggled. Megan sent her little sister a narrow-eyed glare of your-turn-will-come.

"Have you many suitors?" Merridew asked, looking from Megan to Alanna, as if wondering if one would do as well as the other, should the competition become heated.

"Dozens," Alanna murmured. The marquess blanched slightly. "Do you by chance know the Earl of Rossington?"

"Why, yes. Or I should say I knew his brother."

Devorguilla interrupted quickly, steering the conversation back. "Do you know Countess Caroline's English kin, my lord, her half-brother, the Earl of Somerson, for instance?"

"I consider Charlotte—the Countess of Somerson—a very dear friend," Merridew said. Sorcha made a face behind her hand, recalling that lady's recent visit to Glenlorne. The countess had arrived in a huff, succumbed to fury, and left in high dudgeon.

"I understand her second daughter is to make her debut next spring," Megan said conversationally.

The marquess perked like a hunting dog on point. "Oh?"

There was no time to go into detail. Graves arrived to announce another visitor, a Mr. Edward Parkhill, and his sister, Miss Jane Parkhill. Devorguilla quickly discovered they were the cousins of an earl and a baronet, though they had no titles of their own.

The Parkhills had also come to Scotland to hunt grouse, and apparently to find a wife for Edward. The conversation skirted awkwardly around the issue of dowries, income, titles, and property, and Megan marveled at her mother's ability to juggle the conversation so expertly. Devorguilla clearly believed that Lord Merridew was the right suitor for Megan—unless someone better turned up, such as a duke, a royal prince, or the king himself. Mr. Parkhill and his gossipy sister knew everyone, it seemed, and Devorguilla mined them for information. If not a candidate for her daughters' hands, Edward Parkhill would at least serve to point the way to bigger, better fish. While the keen look in the marquess's eyes told Megan he was most certainly interested in her—when his eyes weren't on Eleanor's silver candlesticks, that is—Mr. Parkhill clearly admired Alanna. Both gentlemen were delighted to have found two pretty, unmarried ladies with good dowries and excellent English connections. If either girl was fortunate enough to inherit Dundrummie Castle when Lady Eleanor died, they would bring a prime bit of Scottish land to their marriage as well.

Megan glanced at Eleanor, saw the amusement in her face as she watched the melee. She winked, and leaned forward. "Shall I set the cat among the pigeons for a bit of fun?" she whispered. Then turned to her visitors.

"I do believe there's an heiress at Kinglossie looking for a husband," Eleanor said aloud.

The gentlemen's heads whipped around, their eyes alight.

"Do you mean Annie Fraser?" Devorguilla said without missing a beat. "The one with the crossed eyes and bad skin?"

"But has she any money?" Merridew murmured.

"A veritable fortune in sheep and cattle, I am given to understand," Eleanor said. "Perhaps poor Rossington has gone there. No doubt he would have enjoyed an excellent supper indeed."

Miss Parkhill lit up like a candle. "D'you mean the Earl of Rossington?" She set her teacup down and laid a hand on her heart. "Is he here, in Scotland, nearby?"

"Within walking distance, in fact," Alanna said, and Megan felt her jaw clench, willed her sister to silence, but she continued, oblivious to Megan. "I understand he's at Glen Dorian. Do you know the earl?"

"Isn't the weather lovely at the moment? We shall have a lovely autumn at this rate." Megan tried to change the subject. "We should be able to get outside every day, to walk in the hills or to hunt. I should be pleased to show you some of the—"

"Oh, I'm not here to hunt," Jane Parkhill said with a conspirator's smile. "Well not grouse, at any rate. If Kit Rossington is here, then I shall have far more important game to stalk," she said with a simper. "And I mean to bag him."

"There are fine gentlemen here at any time of year, Miss Parkhill," Megan said.

"Oh, but I mean *English* gentlemen. Lord Rossington's sister is a particular friend of mine. Dear Arabella has been trying to arrange a meeting between myself and Kit for an age, but he always seems to be out when I call."

Megan choked on her tea, and Alanna patted her on the back.

Miss Parkhill's eyes lit. "Now I will finally get my chance with him here in Scotland. I hoped to bring him to the point during last year's London Season, but he is devilishly difficult to find—always mobbed by eligible ladies when he does bother to appear at a social event, which is rare indeed. I daresay if one is to gain the advantage over Rossington, one must track him, like a fox, or lay a trap as for a coney, or corner him and shoot true, as if he were a stag." Her bright face grew sharp. "I daresay other young ladies of quality will soon be on Kit's scent, once it's known that he's here. He is the most eligible bachelor in the entire *ton*, and tops every debutante's list of desirable husbands." She glanced sideways at Alanna and Megan. "Are either of you . . ." she said, letting the question trail.

"Not at all," Megan said, looking away, out the window.

"Excellent!" Miss Parkhill chirped. "Do you know his direction?"

Megan felt queasy. Had Rossington not mentioned he had come to Scotland to get away from chattering females? Jane Parkhill's tongue had not stilled for more than ten seconds since she'd arrived.

But Rossington had been nothing but rude to Megan. She studied her tea, saw his gray eyes, inches from her own, felt his arms around her, his body beneath hers. She felt her skin heat, and opened her mouth to deny she knew anything about the earl's whereabouts.

Alanna spoke first. "I understand he's staying at an inn in Dundrummie village—the Glen Lyon." Megan set her cup down before she squeezed the delicate china to bits, and forced a smile, as if she didn't care one whit if Jane Parkhill wanted Kit Rossington, and she didn't, really she didn't.

Until Miss Parkhill grinned, her face triumphant, as if she'd already bagged her prey, and Megan felt her heart tighten in her breast, and felt a moment of regret. Perhaps it was sympathy for Rossington. Or jealousy. *Certainly not!*

Graves arrived, and yet another suitor entered the room, and descended upon her, and to her horror, Megan spent the next hour juggling questions, compliments, and the assessing gazes of hopeful gentlemen.

Kit sat on the bench in front of the cottage, and looked out across the loch. The sun was high, the breeze light, and a pair of otters frolicked in the shallow water. After casting a curious look at him, the creatures went about their game, glancing at him only occasionally, pretending to be oblivious to his presence entirely, like coquettes at a ball, flaunting their charms as if they had no idea that the gentleman they'd set their cap for was watching them. He smiled as they chased each other over the slippery rocks on the bank, dove into the water, then surfaced side by side in perfect unison.

He'd spent the morning in the cottage, doing what repairs he could to make the place habitable. He had decided to stay here in the glen, in part because he loved the surroundings, the quiet, and the fresh air—and also because he was hiding. He had arrived back at the inn after meeting Megan McNabb in the castle to find the whole place in an uproar.

A thick stack of notes and invitations had arrived for him, many of them scented with perfume. The innkeeper and his patrons scowled at him from a barroom that smelled like the parlor of a brothel. Leslie had turned away no less than six females—two English and four Scots—who had flouted propriety and come to call upon him. Thankfully, he'd been away in the glen, with Megan McNabb. Next time, he might not be as fortunate.

If he spent a polite fifteen minutes with each of the people who wanted the courtesy of a return call, he would spend his days doing nothing but drinking tea and fending off hopeful virgins and their scheming mamas. There would be no time for treasure hunting at all.

No, he would leave Leslie at the Glen Lyon Inn to manage things, with strict instructions to tell no one that he was staying at Glen Dorian. The cottage would do nicely, a quiet, private place to rest. He had enjoyed the work he'd done. He'd repaired the roof, made sure the windows were snug, and had stacked a good supply of peat for the fire. He would be entirely content simply to spend the remaining days of the summer and early autumn reading, working in the old castle, and watching the otters. He felt the warmth of the sun on his arms where he'd rolled up his sleeves, and his cravat and coat lay beside him on the bench he'd just finished hammering together. He put his hands behind his head and grinned with a deep sense of accomplishment. Perhaps he'd buy a kilt and a homespun shirt.

Suddenly, the otters gave a sharp whistle of warning, and slipped away into the depths of the loch, leaving only the barest of ripples. Kit felt his own hackles rise as he searched for the danger that had spooked the otters. He almost dove for the loch himself when he saw it.

There was a coach and four lurching up the narrow track that came over the lip of the glen—a London coach.

He wished again that he could follow the otters, but whoever his visitor was, they had no doubt spotted him by now, since the coach was making a beeline straight for the cottage, and him.

With a sigh, he rose and pulled his coat on, doing his best to make himself respectable.

Surely it wasn't his mother, or his sister. He felt his jaw tense at the very thought of that, but his crest wasn't on the door, and the vehicle's shining paint was green, not Rossington blue. The matched horses staggered over the bumpy goat track, used to far better roads.

A handkerchief fluttered at him from the window, and his gut tightened with dread.

His caller was female. Men did not wave lace handkerchiefs at other men.

Kit put his hand in his pocket, felt another handkerchief there, the square of sensible linen embroidered with Lady Megan McNabb's initials, the one she'd bandaged his hand with. He'd had Leslie launder it, and he had intended to go to Dundrummie and return it, but instead he'd been carrying it with him, half hoping she'd come to him and demand it back. But it had been four days since they'd met in the castle, and she had not returned to the glen.

When he'd returned to the castle with a stout axe and a sharp chisel the day after their misadventure, he'd found the inner door wide open. Not only that, it swung easily, and refused to remain shut at all. He'd spent a great deal of time staring at it, examining the hinges, and the latch. It was baffling, but when he was in the castle, he took the precaution of propping it open, and kept an eye on it. In truth, he wasn't only waiting to see if it would slam shut again—he was half hoping that Megan McNabb might come through it, demanding her handkerchief back, her remarkable hazel eyes aglow. The castle was a lonely place without her.

Now, looking at the coach coming over the hill, he felt a slight hope that maybe, perhaps, by some miracle, it might be Lady Megan waving to him.

"Hallo-o-o!" The hair on Kit's neck rose at the sound. It was the call of a female on a husband hunt. The cry had an unmistakable tone to it, filled with hope, determination, and giddy flirtation. Not Megan, then.

He looked around. It was too late to hide, and the little cottage had only two small rooms and a loft, and he was over six feet tall. He'd be easy to find if his visitor wished to hunt him down, and that would be most embarrassing indeed. No, he had no choice but to clasp his hands behind his back and wait.

She descended almost before the coach had come to a halt, and rushed toward him.

"Good afternoon, Lord Rossington!" she cried. Her eyes darted over his person, then returned to his face, her lips forming a hungry pout.

Kit recognized Miss Jane Parkhill, a friend of Arabella's, and forced himself not to wince at the high pitch of her voice. Arabella had been singing Jane Parkhill's praises for the past year, begging him to meet her, to court her, to marry her. In fact, his sister was so certain that Miss Parkhill would be the perfect bride for him that she encouraged him to skip the first two steps entirely, or simply perform all three at the altar to save time.

He marveled now that even if he had managed to avoid the matter of Miss Jane Parkhill in England, here she was, in the Highlands of Scotland of all places, coming at him. Her brother, Edward, whom Kit knew slightly, appeared next, grinning hopefully, without a hint of apology on his bland face.

Kit silently rebuked his sister as he bestowed a thin smile on the Parkhill siblings. He wondered if Edward might be here to arrange the marriage contract. One word, a single incautious glance, and Edward would no doubt pluck the prepared document from the pocket of his elegant coat.

Edward Parkhill was a goodly enough chap, but one who had inherited a mountain of debts along with the ancestral pile. He needed money, through a lucrative marriage of his own, or better still, by arranging one for his sister. Kit noted the disappointment on his face as he looked from the cottage to the castle and back again.

Jane was dressed in the first stare of fashion, looking more prepared for a carriage ride in Hyde Park or a stroll on Bond Street—or a marriage proposal—than a walk in the Highlands. She tottered on high-heeled boots, dyed rose pink to match the frill on her fashionable spencer, and the feathers that beckoned to him from the top of her straw bonnet.

Jane's sweetly expectant moue left Kit in no doubt that if he were to reach out and grab her hand and drag her inside the cottage to have his way with her in the hayloft, she'd not object beyond asking him not to crush the lace trim on her gown. Edward would happily guard the door, contract in hand.

Kit took a step backward, and felt marginally safer. He pictured Megan, sprawled across his chest, her face smudged, her eyes bright, her lips inviting a kiss, and wondered what she would look like in a hayloft, with straw in her hair. He shook the thought away and concentrated on his guests.

"What brings you to Scotland, Miss Parkhill?" he asked politely.

"We've come for tea," Jane replied, as if it was perfectly obvious, and not at all odd that a lady might travel over hard roads for a fortnight just to take tea.

"I'm afraid there isn't any," Kit said. He'd come armed with only a flask of ale, a loaf of bread, and a promise from Leslie to have a meal ready and waiting when Kit returned to the inn. He'd been considering dropping a line in the loch and catching a fish to roast over a campfire on the shore. He could not imagine offering the fashionable Miss Jane Parkhill a hunk of bread, a bit of fish skewered on a stick, and a cup of water dipped from the loch. Megan, though . . . He firmly shut the door on that thought. Jane cast a brief look of despair at the cottage, then tilted her head.

"Why, where is your manor, my lord? The Earl of Rossington is famous for the magnificence of his homes. Lead me to your estate and stop teasing. I swear I am quite parched," Jane said playfully. She cast her eyes around the glen, but found nothing to stop them until she reached the castle. Her nose wrinkled. "Goodness," she murmured.

"I wasn't expecting visitors," Kit said.

"You aren't staying *here*, are you, old chap?" Edward asked in horror. "Lady Megan made the place sound as if it was quite grand when she told us you were here. I see she has a rather biting sense of humor."

"Lady Megan?" Kit blurted. He felt a sense of betrayal that she had given away his direction so casually, and to Jane Parkhill of all people. His stomach slithered to his boots as he realized what that meant. The Parkhills had been at

Dundrummie, possibly had the supper he'd missed out on. He cast a sharp look at Edward. Had the dowager countess proposed to him, too? Edward simply regarded him with a bored smile, and Kit felt an irrational desire to punch him in the nose.

"I came for an—" He stopped at the word *adventure*. The Parkhills, with their identical sets of pale blue eyes, now gazing at him with identical expressions of horror, would hardly understand.

"I see," Jane murmured, suddenly looking awkward. "I had hoped . . ." She swallowed and looked at her brother. "Edward, I think we must invite Lord Rossington to come and stay with us in Inverness."

Kit stifled his own horror. "I am not homeless, Miss Parkhill. I am residing at a local inn. I am simply here to consider what might be done with the glen," he said, and instantly regretted it as Jane's eyes lit.

"Oh, you mean to *build* here! How wonderful. I see a fine manor house just there, in the Palladian style. If that monstrosity in the loch were torn down, imagine how fine the view would be, especially if a woodland garden was added." She came to his side, looped her arm through his and pointed. "Or, we could turn the castle into a kind of dovecote, or a menagerie, perhaps. I've always wanted to raise rabbits."

We? "Do you . . . hunt rabbits, Miss Parkhill?" Kit managed, feeling acutely uncomfortable. The lady's perfume was overwhelming, like flowers at a funeral.

Jane giggled. "Not for the meat, silly—for the *fur*."

"That waterfall at the end of the valley would be a good spot for a mill. Wool processing, you know," Edward suggested. "There are plenty who would invest in such a scheme, if you get rid of any peasants taking up space unnecessarily."

Kit was silent. He knew precisely what Edward Parkhill had in mind. Other Scottish landowners had thrown their tenants off the land to make room for advancements, little caring that the poor folk had lived there for generations and had nowhere else to go.

"There's Merridew, for instance," Edward continued. "He's looking for a new venture. I was just speaking with him yesterday—"

"Merridew is here?" He knew the man, of course.

"For the hunting he says, but I daresay he was as smitten as I was with the young ladies at Dundrummie. They have a connection by marriage to the Earl of Somerson, you know."

Kit felt a bolt of heat climb his spine.

"I understand you have already met Lady Margaret and Lady Alice," Jane said.

Megan and Alanna, Kit corrected silently. "I have," he replied evenly.

"Then you must know that Merridew is to host a dance in their honor at the assembly rooms in Dundrummie village a week from tomorrow," Jane said. "I doubt it's anything to rival London or Bath, but it will be a pleasant diversion. You will come, won't you?"

"I—" Kit stared at her. He would have refused the invitation at once, but Megan would be there. He shook himself yet again. Attending the dance, or at least putting in the briefest of appearances, would provide an opportunity to return her handkerchief, and put an end to any connection between them. "I will check my engagements." He used the excuse he usually gave in London, but it sounded ridiculous here in the Highlands. He had no engagements, no appointments, no obligations. He smiled, contented with that—no *happy*—for the first time in a very long while.

Jane mistook his smile for agreement. "You will come!" she said, clasping her hands together, regarding him with such delight that he feared for a moment that she might actually rush forward and kiss him.

"Come to us before the dance for dinner, my lord," she gushed. "We can arrive at the assembly together." Her smile was so sweet it made his teeth ache. Warning bells clamored in his brain, and he stepped back.

"Thank you, but I have other plans for dinner that evening, I'm afraid."

Jane cast a petulant look at her brother. "It's Katherine Fairchild, no doubt. She's staying at Castle Crief with her cousins. Or is it Lady Mary Lennox? And I heard rumors in London that Lord Underwood intended to bring his nieces north . . ."

Kit's chest clenched. Were there truly so many English debutantes in Scotland? He'd have been safer if he'd stayed in England. He remained silent, mostly because his tongue was stuck to the roof of his mouth. Jane and Edward regarded him curiously, as if waiting for a reply. Had he missed a question, or a comment that required a reply?

He bowed. "Thank you both for coming," he said, in what he hoped was a dismissive tone.

"You will come to the dance, won't you?" Jane pleaded, advancing toward him, staggering over the uneven ground in her ridiculous footwear. Megan had crossed the ground in graceful, confident strides, the wind in her hair, her eyes on the hills . . .

Kit avoided answering. Instead, he turned and picked up his wrinkled cravat from the bench, and pointed up the hill. "Must meet with my surveyor," he said. "Up there." Jane could not possibly follow him, and Edward would be a cad indeed to leave his sister here alone. "Good day, Miss Parkhill, Edward." He strode up the hill without looking back.

By the time the coach had lumbered back the way it had come, Kit was high on the ridge. He shut his eyes. It was the very thing he had left England to escape—women he had no interest in marrying. And yet they'd found him. Jane Parkhill, Katherine Fairchild, Mary Lennox, and God knew how many more—they were all here, all single, all having set their caps for him and failed during the London Season. He glanced at the empty road, wondered how many more London coaches he could expect to come trundling awkwardly over the lip of the glen. An otter poked its sleek head out of the water and stared at him in alarm.

And there was quite another problem. How could he search for treasure with a constant parade of females stalking him? He understood how the grouse felt during hunting season, a hundred guns pointed at them, beaters flushing them out, dogs baying.

And he had Megan McNabb to thank for all of it—she'd given Jane Parkhill his direction, told her exactly where she could find him. How many others had she told? How many would Jane tell? The numbers expanded in his brain.

He pictured Megan McNabb in his mind, standing in the wind, laughing at him. He clenched his fist on his knee. When he saw her again, he'd—

The warning bells in his brain sounded again, but they didn't dissolve the image of the lovely Lady Megan.

Kit felt a flare of terror. If he wasn't careful, he would indeed end up a married man before the year was out. He needed a distraction. He took Nathaniel's journal out of his pocket and began to read.

CHAPTER FOURTEEN

Glen Dorian, March 1746

Captain Nathaniel Linwood pulled the collar of his great-coat tighter, and tried to ignore the icy rain that found its way inside his clothing anyway. It was a miserable day, and the routine patrol had done little to inspire anything but a feeling of impending doom. He looked down into faces simmering with anger as he rode through village after village with naught but three men. Those same faces had been carefully blank at the sight of a red coat a few weeks earlier, but folk were bolder now, fiercer. The battle was coming. Cumberland was on the march from Aberdeen. He planned to stop at Nairn and await Charles Stuart's pleasure.

Nathaniel paused on the brow of a hill to get his bearings.

The troopers behind him broke their silence to grumble about the weather, declared it worse than England in the dead of winter, and remarked that the flowers were blooming at home by now. Nothing bloomed here save chilblains.

"Why would anyone choose to live here, Captain?" his sergeant asked, and Nathaniel pointed.

"That's why," he said.

This misty valley of Glen Dorian spread out before him, gray and grim in the rain, the loch black. But the castle stood on a rocky island in the loch, rising from the water with elegant grace, the lofty towers poking the low clouds. Golden light shone out from the windows, and flaming torches marked the way along the causeway to the gate. "Shall we go and pay our respects?" he asked.

"If there's a chance to warm ourselves, I'll take it," the sergeant said. "Are they rebels or loyalists?"

Nathaniel remembered the earnest face of the MacIntosh of Glen Dorian, his assurances that he intended to remain neutral in the fight. Would he still, even now, with battle imminent? Nathaniel was making this visit to find out.

He hadn't seen MacIntosh—or his young brother-by-marriage—since the night they'd met in Nairn. But if the laird was arming for war, he wanted to know.

They stopped at the foot of the causeway that led across the water, holding a moment, giving the laird a chance to ride out if he did not wish them to ride across. No one appeared, and the heavy iron gate at the other end stood open.

"Is it safe?" one of his men asked.

Was it? Nathaniel's gut was pressed against his spine, his hands tight on the sodden reins. He remembered MacIntosh's proud face, his intelligent eyes, his assurance that he wanted only peace. As he looked at the man's castle, Nathaniel felt a sharp tug of longing for the comforts of home—the welcome, the warmth, the company of family.

"I suppose we'll find out," he replied, and urged his horse onto the narrow strip of road. He heard his escort follow, but kept his eyes on the castle.

He rode into the courtyard and pulled up. A dozen men stood waiting, seemingly impervious to the weather. The torchlight gleamed in their eyes as they appraised him silently.

"I've come to see the MacIntosh. Is he here?" he asked.

"What for?" asked one of the Highlanders, his expression blank and wary.

Nathaniel forced a grin. "A neighborly visit, nothing more." Without waiting for an invitation, he dismounted, standing among the warriors, putting himself on the same level. They were bigger than he was, and he was a tall man himself. He raised his brows expectantly and held the gaze of the man who'd spoken. Highland hospitality was legendary. So were the stories of giving a guest a meal and a bed for the night only to cut his throat come morning.

The Highlander finally jerked his head toward the door. "This way. Your men can warm themselves in the smithy."

Nathaniel followed the clansman to the door and wondered what kind of welcome awaited him inside.

The room was presumably the great hall, but it was a fine wide, warm place, and though the floors and walls were solid stone, there were soft rugs laid down, and the walls were hung with colorful tapestries. A display of weapons fanned out over the fireplace—fierce Lochaber axes, shining swords and dirks, and studded targes. The furniture was fine, and the cupboards displayed gleaming pewter and fine china.

A group of women sat before the fireplace, sewing and chattering.

"Mairi, we've got a visitor," Nathaniel's escort called. "He wants to see Connor."

The chattering stopped at once, and there was a collective

feminine gasp of horror at the sight of his red coat. Nathaniel removed his hat and bowed. The women immediately began to whisper in Gaelic.

He almost gasped himself when the lady of the house rose to her feet, hushing her companions. She was the prettiest woman he'd ever seen. Her dark hair hung over her shoulder in a thick braid, and the firelight played over high cheeks, a long swan's neck, and a slim and elegant figure clad in work-a-day russet wool. It was her eyes that stopped his breath in his throat—clear and golden, fringed with thick lashes. He saw fear pass over her fine features as she scanned his uniform once again. She dropped her sewing on the bench, and hurried toward him.

"Is Connor—"

The clansman interrupted. "He says it's a neighborly visit," he said in English, then switched to Gaelic, no doubt telling the lady that Nathaniel had brought only three men, and they were lightly armed.

He saw the tension fall from her shoulders. "I'm Mairi MacIntosh, Connor's wife."

He bowed again. "I'm Captain Nathaniel Linwood," he said. "I met the MacIntosh—and your young brother—at Nairn a few weeks ago."

"Oh!" Her eyes widened. "Yes, my husband mentioned it to me." She smoothed her hands over her skirts and indicated the chairs by the fire, now vacated by the women. "Come and warm yourself by the fire. Connor is out hunting today, but he is expected back very soon. Will you take a cup of ale or a dram of whisky while you wait?"

"Whisky, if you please," he said, and remained standing

while she crossed to the cupboard and took down the cups. He had to remind himself to breathe. She moved with an unconscious grace, concentrating on her task. He unbuckled his sword before he sat down, and laid it aside, a show of good faith. She took a seat across from him, and the giant clansman took the last place, his eyes never leaving Nathaniel.

"The weather is cold," Nathaniel said to him in fledgling Gaelic.

The clansman's lips rippled, and one brow rose in sardonic amusement. "As a witch's teat," he replied in English, and Mairi blushed.

"Hush, Iain. Major Linwood will think we've no manners."

"He's a soldier, Mairi. He knows what I mean."

"He's a guest, and this is my home," she insisted, and he heard the steel wrapped in her soft tone.

"Aye, Mairi," the clansman said, cowed. Nathaniel felt a surge of admiration for her. She took a poker from the fire and put the hot end into the cup of whisky. It hissed furiously. "It's best warm on a cold day," she said. Nathaniel took it and smiled his thanks.

She handed a cup to Iain as well, with her eyes on Nathaniel. "Iain Fraser is my husband's cousin," she said by way of introduction.

Nathaniel sipped the hot whisky and felt it burn a trail not only down his throat, but also up into his head while stealing the breath from his lungs. "I've not had whisky warmed this way before, my lady, though I've grown to like the drink very well since I came to Scotland."

"What did you drink before?" Iain Fraser asked.

"Oh, brandy, wine, coffee . . ." Nathaniel said.

"I've heard the English drink nothing but lukewarm tea," Iain said.

Nathaniel forced a smile. He was not here to fight with anyone. "I don't touch tea myself. On a hot summer day, ale is best, or on a cold spring evening like this, brandy is preferable—or whisky." He held up his cup. "How do I wish you good health in Gaelic?"

"*Air do sláinte*," Mairi said. "On your health."

"Or *sláinte mhòr*," said Iain softly.

Nathaniel watched Mairi's eyes widen, and she pursed her lips and set her cup down, unsipped. He wondered what the clansman's toast meant, but before he could ask, the door opened, bringing a gust of cold into the warm room.

Connor MacIntosh strode in, carrying a brace of rabbits.

"Connor!" Nathaniel watched Mairi's face light up. If she was pretty before, the love in her eyes and the radiant smile on her face made her breathtakingly beautiful now. She hurried across the room, and Connor MacIntosh quickly deposited the rabbits on the table, put a powerful arm around his wife, and drew her in for a kiss.

Nathaniel felt his stomach knot with envy.

"What's *he* doing here?" He heard the boy's cry ring out. Ruairidh MacIntosh appeared behind his brother-in-law, carrying two bows slung over his narrow shoulders. Nathaniel rose and met the boy's fierce glare.

"Ruairidh MacIntosh, Captain Linwood is a guest in our home. You'll mind your manners," Mairi admonished. Nathaniel's eyes were on Connor. The laird kept his hold on his wife as he regarded his visitor, his jaw tight, a slight frown creasing the skin between his brows.

"What brings you to my door on such a dreadful day, Captain?" Connor asked.

"We were passing by," Nathaniel said, suddenly feeling like a trespasser.

"Were you?" Connor asked. "Then this has nothing to do with the capture of Fort Augustus this morning?"

Nathaniel felt a shock rush through him. He'd been out on patrol all day. He hadn't heard. Prince Charlie's forces were on the move then. He glanced at the sword he'd placed so politely out of reach, and wondered if he was in any danger, if the men in his charge were safe. Iain Fraser began to ask rapid questions in Gaelic, his eyes ablaze. Ruairidh, too, spoke up, and Nathaniel watched Mairi's face pale.

"We'll speak English," Connor commanded, putting them off with a wave of his hand. "Woman, I'm parched and half frozen. I'll join the captain in a dram, if you please."

Mairi hurried to obey, pouring a cup for her husband. "Ruairidh, take the rabbits into the kitchen and find some dry clothes," she ordered. Nathaniel stood where he was as the boy went away grumbling.

Iain Fraser went to sit at the table, where he checked over the bows and knives Connor had brought back.

Connor approached the fire and warmed his hands by the blaze.

"You've had no more trouble from Ruairidh, I trust? He gave me his word."

Nathaniel shook his head.

MacIntosh took the cup from his wife's hand, curling his fingers around hers for a moment before turning to regard his guest. "*Sláinte,*" Nathaniel said softly.

"*Sláinte*," MacIntosh repeated and drank.

"Terrible weather," Nathaniel said again.

"I trust you've found warmer quarters than a tent," Connor said. He sat at his ease, at home in his castle, yet Nathaniel knew by the hardness of the man's jaw that he would be dead before he could reach his sword, should Connor MacIntosh wish it so. Iain glowered at Nathaniel from the table behind his laird.

"We are in a village just north of here." That was common enough knowledge. "I have insisted my men pay for their accommodation," he added, and MacIntosh's brow rose, as if he were amused. "Tell me more of Fort Augustus."

"It's in Jacobite hands. That's all I know," Connor said. "I met a Fraser clansman in the hills while I was hunting."

Nathaniel kept his eyes on the laird. "Then I can only assume that the clans are massing, preparing for battle. Has the call gone out? Will you join Charles Stuart after all, or stay loyal to your king?"

"Not *my* king," Iain grumbled.

Mairi drew a sharp breath, but Connor caught her wrist, held her hand in his. Nathaniel watched her fingers curl over her husband's stronger ones until they were white. "I told you that I have no interest in this fight. I will keep my clan out of it if I can."

"If you can?" Nathaniel asked through tight lips.

"If I am attacked, I will fight. I have a home to defend, and a family. I will do what I must to keep them safe."

"What of your clansmen?" Nathaniel asked softly, nodding toward Iain.

"Some of them have kin in Charlie's army," Connor said

vaguely. He looked into his cup, and frowned. "Tell me, Captain, what would you do? If this was England, and you knew an enemy was coming, that your family was divided in its loyalties. What side would you take to protect what you love?"

"England had a Civil War a hundred years ago. My family home served as headquarters to a Royalist force. When they retreated, the Parliamentarians burned it to the ground," Nathaniel said.

Connor leaned forward, his elbows on his knees. "So which side did they support?"

Nathaniel smiled. "Both. One son fought for the king, the other was for Cromwell. Both were killed, and left only a child to inherit, and he did what he was told by the winning side. And when the second King Charles was restored to his throne, my ancestor pledged his loyalty to the Crown. He regained the family fortunes, the titles, and rebuilt everything. Like you, he did what he had to for his family."

"Many clans are divided now," Mairi said softly.

Connor looked at her briefly. "We will keep our folk together, and weather this, *gràdhach*."

Mairi met Nathaniel's eyes over her husband's head, and he read the fear in her expression, the question. He tightened his grip on his cup.

"Battle *will* come," Nathaniel said aloud. "Probably very soon."

"Is there no chance of peace, then?" Connor demanded.

"Will Charles Stuart surrender himself to the Duke of Cumberland, and swear allegiance to King George?" he asked. Mairi made a small sound of despair in her throat, and Connor frowned.

"Then it is inevitable," Connor said softly. "And after?"

"I suppose that depends on who wins," Nathaniel said. "Same as any battle. I am not willing to predict an outcome just yet. Are you?"

Connor set his cup down. "No. I only hope . . ." He didn't finish.

Mairi squeezed her husband's forearm, drew closer to him, her expression fierce, but not frightened. She sought to lend her husband her fragile strength, to reassure him with her touch. Whatever happened, Lady Mairi MacIntosh would not flee—she would stand by Connor and their people. He felt a thrill of awe in his breast at her bravery and her loyalty. He got to his feet. "I must go before it gets too late to travel safely," he said.

"It's already dark. I'll ride with you," Connor said, also rising. "It will provide safe passage."

Nathaniel hesitated, then nodded, remembering the bold anger on the faces he'd passed by earlier in the day.

He belted on his sword and waited as Connor bid his wife a whispered good-bye in Gaelic.

They rode in silence over the dark hills until Nathaniel heard the English pickets demand his identity as they reached the town, and called an answer.

"Captain, my family is very important to me," Connor MacIntosh said. "I have my doubts the battle will go well for the rebels. If it should go badly for the Scots—" He paused, his throat working, and Nathaniel nodded.

"I will do what I can for them," he said. "I don't believe in making war on women and children, MacIntosh."

"Aye."

He stood and watched as MacIntosh turned to ride away. "Come back again to Glen Dorian if you can, dine with us. You'll be welcome."

Would he? Nathaniel watched the Scot ride away, a tall shadow in the saddle. His own gut was tight with apprehension. The battle was coming, and he would be called to fight. As much as he'd come to admire the Scots, and to love the fierce beauty of the Highlands, he was a soldier. One day soon he would face men like Connor MacIntosh across the line of battle, and he would fight. He spurred his horse after the Scot.

"MacIntosh, what does *sláinte mhòr* mean?"

Connor drew his horse to a stop. "It means Health to Marion. It's a code, a secret name for Charles Stuart," he said softly. "Where the devil did you hear that?"

"At your hearth," Nathaniel said through tight lips. "Travel safely."

CHAPTER FIFTEEN

"**O**h for heaven's sake! It looks more like a fight in a hen house than a preparation to go to a dance!" Eleanor complained, coming into the dressing room where Devorguilla and Miss Carruthers were overseeing the readying of Megan and Alanna for the dance that evening. Upwards of a dozen gowns had been brought out for consideration, then discarded as "not quite right." They rolled across the room like a rising tide of froth and frills, and Eleanor used her stick to help her wade through the knee-deep flood.

"Perhaps if you add a sash of McNabb tartan," Eleanor suggested as Megan tried on yet another dress, this one creamy white with silk rosebuds at the bodice and hem. Megan's eyes lit, but Devorguilla frowned.

"Certainly not."

Alanna was already dressed in a pretty gown of coral silk that brought out the delicacy of her complexion. She was seated in front of the mirror while Devorguilla's maid pulled, twisted, and piled her auburn hair high atop her head. "She'll be taller than any of her partners, that's certain, and easy to find over the crowd," Eleanor quipped, settling into a chair to watch the commotion. Megan sent her sister a sympathetic look as a pin scraped her scalp and Alanna winced. Megan spun in place at her mother's command and allowed her gown to be considered from all angles.

"The gown is fine, but what fan to go with it, and which gloves?" Devorguilla fussed, circling Megan.

"And slippers, my lady," Miss Carruthers said. "I think the plain cream ones for Lady Alice, and the pink for Lady Margaret, to match the rosebuds on her gown. Perhaps she might also wear pink rosebuds in her hair. Shall I send someone out to pick some?"

"I'll go," Eleanor said, rising again. "I'll not have some ham-handed servant molesting my roses." She grinned at Megan. "Shall I bring the red ones, just to shock them?" she asked, and cackled at Devorguilla's gasp.

Devorguilla herself was dressed in a glamorous gold-colored satin, with silver lace at the bodice, sleeves, and hem, which suited her very well, made her look every inch the elegant and wealthy mother of two lovely and well-dowered daughters.

Alanna rose gingerly from the dressing table, her towering coiffure threaded through with ribbons, pearls and garnets, and Megan was pressed into the chair for her turn. She winced at the tug of the comb. Eleanor returned with a basket of rosebuds—pink ones—fragrant and still warm from the late-day sun. Megan buried her nose in one of the soft blooms. The maid deftly wove them into the artful nest of curls.

"Shall we go over the rules?" Devorguilla asked.

"A lady does not dance with the same partner more than twice, preferably once," Alanna said.

"Unless he is a gentleman we have hopes of," Devorguilla said. "Then it may be twice, and you may allow him to fetch you a cooling drink, or stroll around the perimeters of the room with him."

"Which gentlemen?" Megan asked.

Her mother held out a gloved hand, and Miss Carruthers put a sheaf of pages into it. "The Marquess of Merridew is the most important gentleman, of course. Lord Findlay is second—he has ten thousand a year, and two estates."

"Lord Findlay is nearly fifty!" Megan said, and earned a sharp look.

"Does that really matter when a he has such a fortune? Of course, Viscount Salisbury is a dear friend to the Prince Regent, and has an estate by the sea. He would be a fine catch for Alanna, perhaps, since he'll certainly be an earl eventually. The Earl of Markham is recently widowed. He didn't even know he wanted a new wife until he met you, Megan, but he is still in need of an heir. Can you imagine being the mother of future earls?"

"Not at all," Megan murmured. "Is there anyone fun coming? What of Miss Parkhill and her brother, or Thomas Fraser from Craigmile?"

Devorguilla sent her a pointed look. "If they do, you will ignore them. It would not do to give them the notion that they may hope, when there is no hope at all."

"Will Lord Rossington be in attendance?" Alanna asked, and Megan felt her heart flip in her breast. She shot her sister a silencing look.

"Ah, Rossington," Eleanor said with a sigh. "I'm sure he cuts a very fine figure in the country dances. It will be a pleasure to watch him—if he attends at all, of course."

"I am sure he will not," Megan said, though she hoped he would. She felt hot blood creep up her cheeks at the thought of seeing him again. She would refuse to dance with him, of course, if he asked. Nor would she acknowledge him with anything more than a regal and dismissive nod of her head as she swept past him.

"Now, if we work together, we shall easily provide just the right encouragement the gentlemen we favor will require in order to come to the point," Devorguilla continued. "Which gentleman will you have, Margaret?"

Megan could not imagine being married to any of the men her mother mentioned—and other than her fortune and her connections, there was no reason at all why they would want to marry her, either. They certainly could not love her if they knew nothing about her besides her worth in pounds sterling. "How will I know who will suit me? It is too soon to know if we might eventually love them," she said. It would be quite impossible to love any of them in fact, since her heart already belonged to Eachann.

Miss Carruthers trilled a dry, humorless laugh. "Love? Love has nothing to do with marriage in the aristocracy. A successful match is about convenience, connection, and cash. It will be most *convenient* if these noble gentlemen find a suitable marriage partner here in Scotland. Many gentlemen cannot abide the London Season. You have excellent *connections*, and a suitable dowry—*cash*. You are also presentable, in good health, and available. Those *facts* are enough to explain their interest in you. *Love* does not enter into it."

"Goodness," Alanna said, looking worried. "You make it

sound as if they were considering the purchase of a pair of coach horses."

Eleanor cackled. "Or a brood mare in Lord Markham's case. I daresay if you don't like him, there will be quite a crush of hopeful gentlemen at the dance tonight. You have become known as the Belles of Dundrummie—that's what they're calling you, all these English hunters. My maid heard it in the village. I daresay you'll be swept off your feet at this dance or perhaps the next, but either way, you'll be wedded and bedded and off to England before the snow flies."

Megan felt horror roll through her breast. Alanna paled.

"Which gentleman would you choose?" Alanna asked her aunt, her expression stricken.

Eleanor patted her hand. "That's the trouble, isn't it? It's a choice you have to live with forever. If you choose an old man, he might do you the favor of dying while you are still young enough to marry again, and you get to keep his money for yourself if there's no other heir. I've had three husbands. The first I married for money—the second one, too. My third husband was your uncle, and I married him for love, and came to live here." Her eyes grew misty. "He died after only a decade, which was not nearly enough time together. I could not bear to wed again after Jamie, and now I am far too old. Love does indeed matter, if you ask me."

"Really Eleanor, you should not be filling their heads with such talk," Devorguilla said. "Money goes a far way in making any man bearable."

"Well, then I would have chosen Rossington, myself," Eleanor said. "A handsome man, wouldn't you agree, Megan?"

"Handsome is as handsome does, my lady," Miss Carruthers said in rolling tones. "He is apparently not the marrying kind. I understand that he is much sought after, but refuses to be snared."

"Where did you hear that?" Alanna asked.

Eleanor laughed. "She's been listening to the servants' gossip. Apparently, the poor earl has been as beset as yourself, Megan—the innkeeper at the inn has been receiving floods of callers, and such a great number of scented notes of invitation for his noble guest that he hasn't room to store them all. He's been forced to lay in a supply of tea, fine French wines, and brandy for all the esteemed callers. When Rossington is out, which he invariably is, they insist upon waiting for him, and supping on fine fare. Mr. Fraser told our cook that if he doesn't go broke, he may just make a fortune. He doesn't know whether to be pleased as punch that the earl is here, or dismayed at the disruption. The villagers are taking odds on who Rossington will marry—that is, when they aren't speculating on Megan's choice."

"Me? I've given no one any cause to gossip!"

"Of course you haven't," Eleanor agreed. "You've been all that's proper, as you should be. But if you were to show Lord Rossington just the slightest favor tonight, I stand to win a small fortune."

"Aunt Eleanor!" Megan gasped.

Eleanor smiled smugly. "Shall we try inviting him for dinner again?"

Megan sniffed. "Absolutely not. I'd rather wed Lord Merridew!"

"Truly? Why, I think he is an excellent choice," Devorguilla said with a bright smile. "He is certain to be at the dance tonight. Shall I invite *him* to dinner?"

Megan felt her stomach lurch. "No! It was a foolish thing to say. I didn't mean it."

"Then who?" Devorguilla asked, staring at Megan. "Which gentleman will it be?"

"There must be one," Miss Caruthers prompted. The room fell silent, until the only sound was the ticking of the Ormolu clock on the mantel, and every eye was fixed on Megan's flushed face.

She shut her eyes. "Can we not just dance, and decide tomorrow?"

"A fine idea," Eleanor said. "Shall we go? It wouldn't do to be too late. All the best suitors might be gobbled up by other young ladies."

The maid placed gloves and fans into each lady's hands as they filed through the door, girding them for the tender battle ahead.

Megan regarded the fan balefully. She would have preferred a good, sharp dirk.

CHAPTER SIXTEEN

Surely the floor actually tilted as the Belles of Dundrummie entered the assembly rooms, and every gentleman in the place hurtled across the room toward them.

Alanna grabbed Megan's arm and drew a breath, scanning the faces, drowning in the cacophony of greetings, compliments, and requests for dances. Abandoned, the other ladies present glared daggers at the McNabb sisters, and flicked their fans open with a crack as sharp as a rifle shot, and whispered behind them, their eyes hard as bullets.

"What will we do?" Alanna whispered. "There must be a hundred gentlemen here."

Megan felt her stomach shrink. She wished she could bolt back out the door, but her mother and Miss Carruthers were standing firmly behind them, blocking any hope of escape. She took a breath and scanned the crowds. She'd gone to a cattle auction with her father once. It had been almost as noisy as this, with every bidder competing for one of the prize Glenlorne heifers. She knew now how the poor creatures felt.

"May I reserve the cotillion?" Lord Findlay asked, jostling his way to the front of the crowd.

"I shall take the Scotch Reel, if Lady Margaret is willing," Lord Salisbury cried above the din.

"May I fetch you a glass of sweet cider, my lady?" someone asked.

"Would she prefer punch?" another voice demanded.

"Or perhaps lemonade?"

Alanna was equally beset, equally tongue-tied.

"It won't do to hover in the doorway," Lady Eleanor said firmly, guiding her nieces through the crush, which parted obligingly when she rapped a few shins with her walking stick. They found chairs and sat, and Eleanor stood firmly in front of them, on guard, her fierce glare—and her walking stick ready—reminding the mill of desperate suitors that they were at a social event, and poor manners would not be tolerated. Eleanor arranged partners the first dance only—Merridew settled for Alanna when Salisbury claimed Megan for the opening reel.

Jane Parkhill sat down beside them. "Good evening. What a dreadful crush there is! I hadn't imagined that a country dance would be so dreadfully popular. I fear it will get quite hot in here before very long." She was already plying her fan as she searched the crowds.

Megan followed her gaze. "Who are you lo—"

But the room tilted yet again. This time feminine squeals filled the air, and satin gowns swirled and dancing slippers hissed on the polished floor as the ladies rushed toward the door.

Kit Rossington had arrived. Megan's breath stopped, and

she stared at him. He wore traditional English evening dress, exactly the same as most of the other gentlemen here—but surely his shoulders filled his coat to greater breadth, and the soft brocade of his waistcoat added a touch more dash than the plain ones of the other men. Was his hair longer, his face darker? He shone in the candlelight.

She didn't even realize she'd risen to her feet until Alanna caught her arm.

But by then, his gaze had come full circle around the room to her, and their eyes locked. The shock of recognition pierced her, and the instant memory of her body sprawled on his in the heather. It was a second or two, no more, and then the crush of females closed in and blocked her view, and Alanna tugged her back to her seat.

"What's wrong with you?" her sister said, and Megan swallowed and drew a ragged breath as her heart started beating again.

"Nothing," she managed. "I just wanted to see who had come in and caused such a fuss." She snapped open her fan and hid her hot cheeks behind it.

"He looks different," Alanna said softly.

"He looks like a Highlander," Eleanor said, looking as besotted as every other lady in the room. "All he needs is a kilt and a bonnet."

Megan's heart sighed, but she straightened her spine and plied her fan in rapid little beats. "Nonsense. He's as English as a man can be."

"Ah, but those eyes," Eleanor said. "He looks as if he's grown used to gazing out across the hills."

His eyes appeared to Megan to be fixed on the simpering

young lady before him, the daughter of an English marquess. His countenance was polite, but hardly conveyed joy. He did not smile as he made his bows, working his way into the room, avoiding entanglement with any one lady.

Megan realized she was holding her breath again, half hoping he would come to her. He was certainly moving in her direction. Then Edward Parkhill and Lord Merridew waylaid him, and he was forced to stop and speak to them.

Megan felt a fizzle of disappointment. The music began, and Salisbury bounded over to present his hand. Megan let him draw her onto the dance floor.

She felt Rossington's eyes upon her, but she dared not glance at him. She concentrated on counting the steps, making the turns and hops precisely, smiling vapidly at her partner all the while, though in truth his face did not even register in her mind. Her heart hammered in her chest, and she was aware only of Rossington.

She caught his eyes upon her as she turned, looking at her over the gaggle of ladies. Her heart threatened to burst from her chest.

The dance ended, and she dipped a curtsy, and swayed on her feet. "You look dreadfully flushed, Lady Margaret. Can I fetch you something to drink?" Salisbury asked kindly.

"Please," she managed. She needed air, space. When he stepped away, she hurried toward the door that led to the small balcony. It was against her mother's rules, leaving the well-lit and carefully chaperoned confines of the assembly room, but she slipped out into the velvet darkness anyway, and drew a long breath of cool air.

She wanted to go home—not just to Dundrummie, but

back to Glenlorne. She did not wish to be courted and haggled over, or persuaded into a marriage she did not want. If she were home at this very minute, she would pull the pins from her hair, cast off the frills and bows, and dive into the loch and swim. It would be—

"Are you quite all right?" a voice asked, and she turned to find Rossington standing beside her. For a moment her tongue tangled around her tonsils, making a reply impossible.

"Yes," she managed at last, aware that he was staring at her in the darkness. He was a silhouette against the night, his face in the shadows, invisible.

"Can I fetch your mother for you?"

"No!" she said quickly. Too quickly. "I'll be fine in a moment. It's just rather warm inside."

"I daresay there will be more than one attack of the vapors this evening," he said, and Megan bristled.

"I don't suffer from the vapors!"

"Good, because I haven't any smelling salts."

"Aren't your adoring admirers likely to miss you?"

"No more than yours, I imagine." He leaned on the railing and looked down into the market square below the inn. "I smell roses. Is there a garden nearby?"

"Oh, it's—um, my hair," she said, and pulled a rosebud out of her coiffure. "See? They're from Eleanor's garden."

He took the flower from her hand, his fingertips brushing hers for a moment, sending sparks flying up her arm. He held it to his nose. "It suits you."

She felt herself blushing, her cheeks hot, despite the cool of the evening.

"Has your finger healed?" she asked, and almost bit her

tongue in two. She did not want to think about the last time they'd met, or remind him of it.

"It has, and if I do have a scar, it will be a very small one, thanks to you."

They stood in silence for a moment. Another couple came out, and moved along the balcony. Kit took her arm and guided her farther from the door. "So has your mother proposed to anyone else? Which will be the lucky gentleman?"

"No one," she said softly. "I have no intention of marrying any of them. I-I love someone else, you see." He turned his head toward her, but said nothing. "He is not someone my mother would approve of, since he is a Scot, and not well-born. He has gone away to seek his fortune, and once he returns, we will marry. His name is Eachann."

"I see," he said. He was silent again, and she wondered why she had told him that, of all things.

"I am quite the opposite. I have no wish to marry at all," he said. "I came to escape hopeful females. Of course, I will eventually *have* to marry—"

"You'll need an heir."

"Precisely. I have a younger brother, but this is not the life I would wish upon anyone not raised to inherit a title."

She recalled he'd told her that he had come into his title unexpectedly. She wondered whom he would be if he had not become Rossington, if he'd taken up his army commission after all.

"So you will raise your son to expect to rule," she said.

"To understand how to do so, rather, and better than I."

She heard the regret in his voice again. "Love helps. A true passion," she said. Alec had thought he could not possibly be the laird that Glenlorne needed, but once he realized how much he loved the land and his people, he'd grown content. And with Caroline by his side—well, the Earl of Glenlorne was happy indeed.

"It has been difficult to love being an earl," he said. "In fact, the first peace I've felt since I inherited the title has been here in Scotland. I can certainly understand why you love this place and do not want to leave it, not for a fortune in English gold or a grand title."

"Yes," she murmured.

A cart clattered past in the darkness below them. "Something seems to be happening in the square below us."

She looked. "People are gathering for the Lugnasadh fair. It's the day after tomorrow."

"Lugnasadh?" he said, turning.

"It's a quarter day. Folk come and pay their rents, and it also marks the start of the harvest, and of autumn. There's bread and games and a fair."

"We have the same celebration in England. It's called Lammas there. The first grain is cut, loaves baked and blessed," he said. "Mostly it's an excuse to dance and drink ale and celebrate the change from summer to autumn."

She grinned. "There is always dancing and music."

"Will you attend that dance?" he asked. "It sounds a great deal more fun than this one."

She sighed. "It's for the common folk. There's no silk or evening clothes. The lasses tuck up their skirts and dance barefoot. The men wear plaids. 'Tis a grand night, and it lasts until dawn." Not that her mother would allow her to come. She would be stuck at Dundrummie, learning how to discuss the weather, or the fashions, or the price of tea. She would rather attend the fair. There would be bards and old folk sitting around fires, or at small tables, or cross-legged on the ground, telling stories. Megan grasped a fold of her silk gown and made a fist. One could hardly sit on the ground in silk.

"Margaret!" She spun at the sound of her mother's voice. "What are you doing out here in the dark? There are a dozen gentlemen or more waiting to dance with you. Come in at once."

Megan cast a glance at Rossington, but he had retreated into the shadow of the roof, all but invisible in his dark coat. Hiding from Devorguilla, was he? A sharp rebuke for his cowardice leaped to her tongue, but she left it unspoken. She could hardly blame him. Without a word she went inside.

Kit twirled the rosebud in his hand. Lady Megan McNabb was a puzzle. He had never met a lady he was so comfortable with. She was beautiful, desirable, and he had no intention of acting on his ridiculous lust for her. He crushed the flower in his hand, and the perfume rose up around him. He could not remain in Scotland much longer, and he tried to imagine Megan McNabb at a *ton* ball. It was easier to imagine her with her skirts tucked up, her feet bare, her head thrown back as she danced in the market square—with roses in her hair, of course. His chest tightened. He'd love to see her that way.

He tucked the remains of the rosebud into his pocket and went inside. Megan was flushed once again with the heat of the room, and the rigors of the dance. He waited until it was over, admired the graceful way she moved, the elegance of her slim figure, the way her smile flashed. When the music ended, he crossed to her and bowed.

"May I have the next dance?" he asked.

He read the wariness in her eyes, the surprise, but she nodded. He led her out.

"Will you be at the fair?" he asked.

She bit her lip, and glanced at him. "Yes," she said. "Will you?" The steps of the dance carried them away from each other, and Kit waited until their hands joined again, felt the pull of desire once again, and swallowed.

"I will," he said as he bowed as the set ended. He moved through the crowds to the door, ignoring the pleas of the ladies that he stay longer.

CHAPTER SEVENTEEN

"You are being foolish and stubborn, not to mention ungrateful, Margaret—and after all I have done for you," Devorguilla said to her daughter, who stood on the carpet before her, her hands clasped so tightly that her knuckles were white, her face mutinous. "Not that Lord Merridew would want you now if he could see that frown on your face. Still, I see no reason why you should not accept him at once. The marquess is a respectable gentleman, heir to a dukedom. You will be a duchess. Your sons will be marquesses and dukes. You will outrank the Countess of Somerson, even."

"But I don't love him!" Megan objected. She had been summoned out of her music lesson to attend Devorguilla in her sitting room, but far from being delighted to hear that the marquess had paid the countess a call that very morning and had formally asked for Megan's hand in marriage, she had been horrified.

Devorguilla set her teacup down and glared at her daughter. "Don't be ridiculous. You will be rich, and a healthy allowance is better than love. Think of the homes, the clothes, the jewels, the parties . . ."

Megan felt her lunch shifting in her belly. She was thinking of Merridew himself, of his greedy gaze, his penchant for killing things, his loud, grating voice.

She swallowed revulsion. She could not marry him, but she knew if she refused outright, then her mother would dig in her heels and insist. There would be no escape. She drew in a deep breath and forced a wan smile. "I will consider the match if you wish, but until Alec is consulted I cannot accept," she said. Surely Alec would refuse the match once he met Merridew. At the very least, he would allow her the opportunity to say no.

Devorguilla's chin came up, and her eyes glittered dangerously at the mention of her despised stepson's name. "I have informed Merridew of that. Once he has your answer—and he will have it tomorrow morning when he calls—he will ride directly to Glenlorne to see your brother. The wedding can take place within the month."

"Tomorrow morning? A *month*?" Megan squeaked. "But I don't want to marry him."

"Then name the man you prefer, and I will invite him to tea this afternoon. Is it Salisbury, or Lord Findlay, perhaps?"

No and no!

She shut her eyes, whispered Eachann's name in her mind, but it was Kit Rossington's face that appeared there. She felt a moment of panic. She couldn't remember exactly what Eachann looked like. She felt tears sting her eyes. "I can't decide so quickly. Perhaps if I had more time—a few weeks or months . . ."

"Months?" her mother said. "Lord Merridew will be gone by then, and the opportunity will be missed. Why delay? A marquess is just what we'd hoped for."

"I thought an earl was wanted," Megan murmured.

Devorguilla sent her a quelling look. "A marquess is even better. If his father is old or infirm, then you will be a duchess all the sooner. Being a marchioness for a short time will give you time to practice for the higher title."

Megan felt as if her chest would burst. She had done nothing but practice. She was sick of primping, sewing, dancing, walking with books on her head, learning the perfect simper, and having the accent corrected out of her speech lest she give her origins away. "Please, Mother, I cannot do this!"

Her mother rose to her feet, her eyes hard. "You can, and you will. Go upstairs at once and prepare yourself. Have Miss Carruthers choose a suitable morning gown, practice your curtsy, and learn to say "I will" without the brogue, is that clear?"

Megan fled. Surely there was something she could do, a way to get out of this. She could write to Alec, but Merridew would surely arrive before her letter. There had to be another way . . .

She looked out the window at the maids, picking flowers for tomorrow's Lugnasadh fair, laughing as they pushed roses and daisies and heather into their braids and curls.

Megan dared to smile. Perhaps there *was* a way.

Kit was building a table for the cottage in the morning sun, enjoying the sharp scent of new wood as he planed the surface smooth. His muscles were pleasantly tired, his mouth tasted like iron nails, and he had a fine sense of accomplishment. He'd finished fixing the shutters, and he'd laid in all the supplies and tools he'd require. Tomorrow he would be ready to begin working in earnest in the castle itself, seeking Mairi's treasure.

He heard a distant shout and looked up in alarm as a pair of coaches burst over the lip of the glen, airborne for a moment before they touched down, swaying and hurtling onward toward him, the horses running at a white-eyed gallop. They were racing dangerously, each coachman jockeying over the rough ground to be first. The vehicles swerved, changed direction, coming across the uneven ground toward him. Kit's heart lodged in his throat. There was surely going to be a disaster. The turf flew under the hooves of the matched pairs—one set of grays, one of chestnuts, and the horses' nostrils flared in panic, even as the drivers whipped them on.

The grays won the race, and pulled up almost at Kit's feet. The chestnuts were moments behind, but by then, the occupants of the first coach had dismounted and were whooping at the force of the wind even as they attempted to make their curtsies to him, their skirts and petticoats billowing around them.

Which ladies were these? Had he met them? He heard the chatter of English voices, a sound very much like geese being herded to market—and like hungry geese, they pressed in upon him, all gabbling for his attention at once.

The road exploded once more as three horsemen came down the steep slope—no, not horsemen—*women*, riding sidesaddle. One had her riding crop gripped in her teeth, another lost her stylish bonnet, and did not even bother to look behind her in her haste. Kit felt sheer terror grip him. What lady lost her bonnet without looking for it?

No one he knew—unless she had far more important matters on her mind. Like marriage.

He imagined this is how a fox felt, run to ground by baying hounds with nowhere to hide.

In horror he retreated, racing down the slope toward the causeway, with the pack on his heels. He didn't stop until he'd reached the inner door. This time, he prayed that it would indeed lock behind him, the way it had when he was here with Megan.

He slammed it shut and leaned up on it, and waited until they all went away.

He was besieged. These visits—invasions—would become a daily trial now they knew where to find him. He had faced the same at his London townhouse, almost as soon as he'd inherited the title. They'd been put off—eventually—by the unassailable Swift, but Swift was far away at Bellemont Park, and there seemed to be something in the Highland air, something that made these women all the more rapacious in their quest for his flesh—well, his hand, at least. In marriage.

He was trapped. Kit crept to the window and looked to see if they'd gone. To his dismay, they were taking refreshments on the grass in front of the cottage, and waiting for him.

He stared around at the destruction of the castle hall, looked up at the open sky above him, and wished he could fly.

CHAPTER EIGHTEEN

Megan slipped out of the kitchen door as the sun peeped over the horizon. The maids were already up, primping and making themselves pretty for the fair, and she hurried past them and out the door.

She picked up her skirts and all but ran toward Glen Dorian. She was taking a dreadful chance. What if Rossington laughed at her? She would find herself with no choice but to marry Lord Merridew. Even if she was able to rid herself of the marquess somehow, there were other suitors already lined up to take his place, and propose to her in their turn until she finally said yes to someone. She would not be able to wait for Eachann, and her heart would break.

The Earl of Rossington was in the precisely the same predicament.

Megan had seen the eager ladies at the dance, had heard the rumors in the village that Rossington was a prime catch, and would not be allowed to get away this time. He would not get the peace he wanted unless—she drew a sharp breath, felt her stomach flip—unless he was able to find a way to dissuade them.

A temporary way, of course. Something—or someone—close at hand and convenient.

Her.

She reached the edge of the glen with the first rays of the morning sun and stared at the cottage, wondered if he was inside. He had to be. She hurried down and knocked. There was no answer. She looked around the glen, saw the otters peering at her curiously. The sun stretched like a lazy cat across the walls of the castle, turning the gray stones to gold.

The castle—he must be there. She ran down the slope.

Soon, her mother would send the maid to wake her, and Miss Carruthers would arrive to begin the arduous task of preparing Lady Margaret McNabb to accept the marriage proposal of the Marquess of Merridew. Megan's heart climbed into her throat as she rushed across the causeway as if a thousand devils—along with one marquess, an English companion, and one angry dowager countess—were chasing her.

"Hello?" she called as she reached the castle, out of breath. "Lord Rossington?"

Her voice echoed through the ruined space. She hurried to the inner door. It swung open as she reached it, the hinges groaning a welcome—or a warning.

She didn't take the time to consider which it might be. "Hello?" she called again, but there was no answer. Buttery fingers of sunlight were creeping over the lip of the windowsill.

Then she saw him. He was curled against the wall, wrapped in his coat, his eyes shut.

She felt her heart stop beating, sure this time that the

curse had killed him. He lay unmoving, as the sun caressed his face, and glanced off his fair hair and the blond stubble on his jaw, making him look gilded.

Megan crouched beside him and stared at him. He had long eyelashes for a man, high, sculpted cheekbones, and a broad clear brow. His shirt was open at the neck, his cravat missing, and she stared at the line of his collarbone, the strong sinews in his neck, and suppressed a sigh. She let her eyes move back toward his face—and let out a cry of surprise when she realized his eyes were open, and he was staring at her. She fell backward and landed on her bottom.

"I thought you were dead," she managed. He sat up, tousled and muzzy with sleep.

"I thought I was too," he muttered. He ran a hand through his hair. "What time is it?"

"Just past dawn."

"Are they gone?" he asked.

"Who?" Megan asked, frowning.

He rose to his feet and looked out the window, then his eyes widened and he looked at her again. "Why are you here?"

She scrambled to her feet and advanced a step toward him. He retreated the same distance. She ran her hands over her skirt, her palms sweating. "You said you wished to go to the fair today. It's Lugnasadh."

He shut his eyes for a moment, his relief evident. "Oh, yes. I did—I do."

Megan couldn't resist a smile. "Lord Rossington, I have a proposition for you. Well, more of a proposal."

She saw disbelief bloom in his eyes, and panic stiffened his limbs, and he looked around for an escape.

"How is it the curse did not kill you in the night?" she asked.

"There is no curse, my lady—and the greater danger lay outside, not inside."

"You sound as if you were afraid you'd be ravished, my lord."

She watched his throat bob as he swallowed.

"Have you ever heard of handfasting?"

"It's a kind of betrothal, isn't it?" he asked, his voice thick.

"More a type of marriage—a temporary marriage, that is. Um, I wanted—" Nerves made her mouth dry, and her voice faltered. She took a breath and began again. "You see, Lugnasadh is a traditional time for contracts of all kinds, including handfasting, and I thought, that is, I hoped . . . um, I wanted to ask—" She was babbling. She took a breath. "I wanted to ask you to join with me in a handfasting." The last part came out in a rush, and she held his eyes, saw nothing register there for a moment.

She took another step toward him. "You see, I don't want to get married, not to Merridew, or anyone else—except Eachann Rennie, of course. But my mother is insisting I accept Lord Merridew, and I would rather not, but if I don't marry *him*, there are others, and I'll run out of time and excuses, and—"

She paused as he took a step toward her, frowning. "Are you asking for my protection?"

She felt her skin heat. She knew what that term meant, had been warned about it by Miss Carruthers. A mistress. "Not exactly. Well, not in *that* way. I just thought that since you are trying to escape from the same fate as I am—"

"A fate worse than death," he interrupted.

"If you would rather not be pursued, then you might consider entering into this—"

"Handfasting," he supplied when the word failed her. "It's a marriage, but not forever, is that correct?"

"A year and a day is the usual term," she said. "I suppose it would end when you return to England, or when Eachann comes home again. Until then, we would be as man and wife—almost." She felt her skin heat once more. "No one could expect you or I to marry until the year was over."

He folded his arms over his chest and rubbed his hand over his stubbled chin, considering. "And we would be married for that time?"

She raised her chin. "A match of convenience only," she said. "If we were to, um, that is, if there were any—children, then we would be required to stay together, permanently." She was making a dreadful mess of this.

"Eternity," he murmured.

"Yes. There couldn't be any, um—romantic entanglements."

"I see. But I would still be considered married, off the market, unavailable?"

"*We* would," Megan assured him. "Will you do it? I don't want to wed Merridew."

"I don't blame you," he said, and paced the floor. "So how is it accomplished? Do we simply shake hands and agree, or cut an X on our palms and exchange a blood oath?"

"We go to the fair, and stand with the other couples who wish to handfast today. We promise to stay together for a year and a day, take a sip of whisky to seal the pledge, and jump over a broom."

"That's all there is to it?"

"Aye," she said. "That's all."

"It seems far too easy. Are you sure this is binding?"

She glared at him. "Would you like to go and seek proper legal advice? Perhaps you'd like to talk it over with your admirers. No doubt they'll be back just as soon as they've breakfasted."

He glanced anxiously out the window. He straightened the collar of his shirt, and ran his hand through his hair. "Will I do as I am? I could stop at the inn, have Leslie shave me, change my clothes—"

"No, you'll do," Megan said quickly. By now, her mother probably had the whole household searching for her. Merridew was probably on his way to Dundrummie, flowers in hand, a ring in his pocket, ready to drop to one knee and—"We'd best hurry." She moved toward the door.

"Do we need a ring?" he asked, following. "I haven't one, I'm afraid."

"We just need strip of cloth to bind our hands together," she said. She stared at the portal, wondering if the castle would lock them in again. She realized she didn't have so much as a sash.

"Will this do?" he asked, and drew her handkerchief from his pocket. He'd washed the blood from it, and it had been laundered and ironed. She stared at it. "I've been meaning to return it to you."

"It will do."

He pulled on his coat, and ran his fingers through his hair, and they walked in silence, side by side, across the causeway, up the hill, and on toward the village to wed—in name only, and for just a year and a day.

Chapter Nineteen

The village market square, so empty days before, was crowded with people, animals, and goods for sale. Kit instinctively drew Megan closer to his side, and guided her through the crush. "Where do we go?" he asked.

She pointed. "There's a *seannachaidh*—he's a clan's tradition bearer. He keeps the stories of his clan, including records. In the old times, when there weren't always priests on hand to marry a couple, they would ask the *seannachaidh* to witness their handfasting, and if all went well, when a priest did eventually travel through, he could marry them in the eyes of the church—but the handfasting was lawful in the eyes of the clan, and that was enough."

"I see. Will this fellow—the *seannachaidh*—ask any questions?"

Megan skirted around a stack of cages containing chickens, and nearly tripped over a wooly sheep, which muttered a rude objection. Kit caught her arm to steady her, drew her against his side. For a moment he met her wide hazel eyes, felt the softness of her skin, the warmth of her hip against his and saw her lips part in surprise.

"He will ask—" Her eyes roamed over his face, settled on his mouth, and stayed there. He wanted to kiss her. His mouth watered with it. "He will ask if we wish to join together, and if we agree to remain so for a year and a day."

"Oh," he said, staring at her lush lips, speaking slowly, his mind moving slower still. "I meant will he ask to see a license, or some kind of paper that gives me permission to enter into this contract? Will your father object?"

"My father's dead," she said. "There's only my brother—"

A lass with a basket of flowers bumped into them, and broke the spell. They sprang apart, and started walking again.

"Buy a *Bonnach lunastain* for luck?" called a buxom woman with very few teeth. She held out a pair of loaves. Megan drew Kit to a stop.

"They bring good luck. I give you a *luinean* loaf—" She pointed. "And you give me a *luineag* like that one."

He examined the lumpy oaten bread. "And what do we do with it?"

The good wife behind the stall began to laugh, her bosom shaking. "You eat it, of course!"

Kit felt his skin color. "In England we have wedding cake."

Megan rolled her eyes and handed him a *luinean*. He placed the *luineag* in her hands, and gave the baker a few coins. "Good luck to you both," the baker said, pocketing the money. "Are you going to see old Duncan?"

Megan's smile wobbled. "We are."

"Then good luck to you indeed. May the year be a sweet one."

They walked on, until they found an old man lounging under a tree by the well in the center of the square. "Are you the *seannachaidh*?" Megan asked in Gaelic.

The gentleman glanced from her to Kit, then back again. He blew out a puff of smoke from his pipe. "The lass from the glen, isn't it? Have ye come to hear another tale?" he asked.

Kit saw Megan's eyes widen with recognition. "You!"

He grinned and sketched an exaggerated bow. "Duncan MacIntosh at your service. Did you find what you wanted in the old castle?"

Kit watched Megan blush. "I don't know."

The old man's eyes were canny. "What did you find there?"

"Him," she murmured. "I found him."

The old man turned to look at him, his pale eyes sharp amid the folds of his weathered skin. It felt as if the old man could see inside his skull, but Kit held his gaze.

"Rossington," he murmured.

"A Sassenach," Duncan replied. "Now what were you doing at Glen Dorian, I wonder?"

"We wish to handfast," Megan interrupted.

"Do ye now?"

"Yes," Megan said with conviction.

"You did tell me you had a true love when we met? Is this the man?"

Kit watched Megan's cheeks bloom with color. As long as he lived, he would never forget the way she blushed. It was like watching a rose bloom. He curled his hand against his side to keep from running his knuckles over her cheek, to see if her skin was as hot as it looked, or as cool as a rose petal.

Megan straightened her spine. "He—Lord Rossington—has agreed to keep me for a year and a day. Is that not enough?"

The old man squinted. "For me, aye. I need only that. And you agree?" he asked Kit.

"I do," he said firmly.

"Then tie your hands together," the *seannachaidh* said. Kit produced Megan's handkerchief, tied it into a loose knot, put it over his wrist, and held out his hand.

Megan put her hand into his, and he closed his grip over her fingertips, ice cold though the day was hot, and felt a pulse of awareness flow through him. She raised her eyes to his, and he slid the cloth over their joined hands. Duncan took a fold of his plaid and draped it over their hands. "Say the words," he commanded.

"What words?" Kit asked.

The old man rolled his eyes. "Your name, her name, the pledge you're making. You show him, lass."

She swallowed, and blushed again. "I Megan Catriona McNabb pledge to remain by your side for a year and a day. Will that do?"

Duncan scratched his head. "Well, it isn't very romantic, but aye, it will do." He turned to Kit. "And now you say the same."

"I, Christopher Nathaniel Alexander Linwood, Earl of Rossington, pledge to remain by your side for a year and a day."

The air grew thick and still, and the old man stared at Kit for a moment. "*Linwood* did ye say?"

Kit nodded. "My family name."

The old man gave him another soul-searing look. "Then it's begun," he murmured. "I never thought I'd live to see it."

"What does that mean?" Megan asked.

Duncan turned his eyes to her. "It means 'tis done," he said.

"You said begun," Megan said.

"So I did," he said, still staring at Kit. "I'm an old man, lass. You came to me to beg a tale. I'd say you found one after all, and the telling of it has just begun, and who knows how it will end?"

He turned and pulled a battered cup out of his pack, a once grand thing carved of horn and decorated with silver, now cracked and all but naked of metal. He poured a splash of whisky into it and held it out to Kit. He sipped, felt fire burn his throat, sear his limbs, draw the breath from his lungs. He watched Megan's eyes water as she sipped after him.

"Now kiss her," Duncan said.

Kit hesitated, and Megan looked at him in surprise, blushing again.

"Go on!" Duncan insisted. "I haven't got all day."

Kit reached for her, set his hands on her waist, drew her closer. Fear warred with something softer in her eyes, and she lowered her lashes as their lips met. He could feel the warmth of her breath as he brushed his lips against hers. He could taste the whisky, too, and it warmed him yet again, and he closed his own eyes, pulled her nearer, kissed her more firmly. She rose on her toes, pressed closer, kissed him back.

"There now, that'll do nicely," Duncan said, interrupting.

Kit didn't want to stop kissing her, but he pulled back reluctantly, and looked at the old man. "I haven't got a broom, just my staff. It will do to jump over, I think." He laid a gnarled root on the ground, nearly five feet in length. The topmost end was shiny from years of use, shaped to the old man's palm, and the bottom end was blackened by dirt.

With their hands still clasped Kit grinned at her. "Ready?"

She nodded, smiling back, her lips and cheeks pink from his kiss, her eyes bright. He counted to three, and they jumped. For better or worse, they were joined—and free.

"Megan McNabb! What are you *doing?*" a voice screeched, and Megan looked up to see her mother staring at her in horror. Her eyes were so wide, Megan feared they might pop out of their sockets, fall on the dusty ground, and roll away. Lord Merridew stood beside Devorguilla, his eyes narrowed on Kit like a rival dog. His lip curled back and he growled. Megan held tight to Kit's hand.

"We—that is, Lord Rossington and I—have agreed to handfast for a year and a day."

Devorguilla's face turned purple with fury. She reached out to grab her daughter's arm, her nails biting into Megan's flesh. "Oh no you will not, young lady! Stop this foolishness and get back to Dundrummie at once!"

Duncan held up a gnarled hand. "It's not a 'will not' anymore, missus. It's been done. I performed the ritual myself. He was willing and she was willing and—"

"Be quiet!" Devorguilla commanded. Duncan stepped back. She turned to Merridew. "This is not binding in any way, my lord. 'Tis just an old superstition, a silly Highland game, something fey to amuse the children."

Merridew continued to glare at Kit. "Lady Margaret is hardly a child, Countess. Nor is Rossington. I saw them kissing."

"They're old enough, aye, and they've agreed," Duncan added.

Devorguilla turned her ire on Kit. "How dare you, my lord? Is this the way an English gentleman behaves, taking a respectable earl's daughter, turning her into a strumpet at a village fair?"

"Badly done, Rossington," Merridew added. "Your brother would never have done such a thing."

Megan felt Kit tense beside her, and his hand tightened on hers. "I am not my brother, Merridew."

"Mother, I tried to tell you that I did not wish to marry Lord Merridew. You would not listen. I asked Kit—Lord Rossington—"

"He's a Linwood," Duncan murmured, grinning. "A Linwood! I never thought I'd see it come full circle, but it has, at long last. What did you call him, lass?" he asked Megan, but she was watching Jane Parkhill push through the crowd.

"Rossington? Lady Margaret?" Jane looked suspiciously at their clasped hands, her over-bright smile fading. "What's all this?"

"They've been joined together," Duncan said, but no one was listening.

"How dare you? You refused to marry her, and now *this?*" Devorguilla stepped forward and slapped Kit with all her might. Kit's head jerked sideways, and a bead of blood bloomed on his lip.

"Blackguard!" Merridew said, the only warning Kit had before the viscount's fist connected with his jaw.

"Married?" He heard Jane Parkhill squawk the word like an angry farmyard goose. "Married?" She advanced on Megan, her claws flexed, and her brother restrained her. "She said she was not in the least interested in marrying him. Edward," she wailed.

Edward's eyes bored into Megan's, condemning her with a scathing look. "She obviously lied," Edward said. "Damned Scots."

"Perhaps it was destined," Duncan said calmly. "These things happen, you know. Curses are placed and lifted and you never know how a tale will turn out until the ending of it," he told the crowd that was gathering to watch. The old *seannachaidh* was the only one still smiling. Everyone else was in varying states of fury and dismay.

Kit glared at Edward. "If we were in London, I'd call you out for that insult, Parkhill."

"Then do so," Parkhill said, thrusting his sister behind him, throwing out his chest.

Merridew pushed him aside. "Not until I'm done with him, Parkhill," Merridew said, rolling up his sleeves and advancing on Kit. "If he's still alive, then you have my blessing to kill him."

"Come along at once, Margaret," Devorguilla said, grabbing Megan's arm. "No harm has been done." She grabbed her daughter's arm and pulled hard, and Megan jerked forward, and stopped. She was still tethered to Kit by the knotted handkerchief. Everyone stared at the snowy linen, and fell silent. The crowd murmured, and wagers were made.

"As I said, the match is made," Duncan said happily. He looked at Jane and Edward. "Perhaps you two would like to join hands yourselves? You seem very keen to marry someone."

"He's my brother!" Jane bellowed, and the crowd murmured again, translating, and laughter broke out.

Kit stared around him. There was blood dripping from his lip, and he wanted a bath, a cold drink, and a way out of this nightmare. Merridew was yelling at Devorguilla, who was screeching at her daughter. Jane Parkhill was railing at her brother and shaking her fist at Megan, and Edward was threatening to murder him. And he, for better or worse, for a year and a day, was married. What the hell had he done?

He began by putting Megan safely behind him, slipping his hand out of the handkerchief. Then he turned and punched Edward Parkhill square in the center of his smug, ugly face. Parkhill fell backward, landing into the mud, taking Jane with him.

Jane screamed like a banshee. She picked up a handful of mud and flung it at Megan. Instead, she caught Devorguilla square in the chest. The dowager countess shrieked like a scalded alley cat.

Merridew swung his fist at Kit, but this time, Kit saw it coming and ducked. Merridew's punch connected with the jaw of a very large Highlander standing behind him. The man shook off the blow and advanced on the marquess, cursing in Gaelic, raising his own fist. Merridew's eyes rolled up in his head as he toppled into the mud beside Edward Parkhill.

Jane's next handful of mud caught the butcher's wife, and she picked up a stout stick and Jane fled, screaming, with the good wife hard on her heels. She tripped over a lamb, part of a flock being herded to market, sending the poor creatures fleeing into the crowd in panic. More folk went down shrieking.

Kit stared around him at the mayhem. Tables were overturned by the unruly sheep, chicken cages broke open, and feathers flew. Dogs barked, and the brawl began in earnest, fists and curses, chicken, sheep and feathers filled the air. Kit doubted anyone knew why they were fighting.

Duncan caught his sleeve, and Kit nearly punched him. He held off as the old man raised his hands. "Och, lad, I'm on your side. I think it would be best if you take your lass and slip away while you can, Linwood."

He looked at Megan, standing under the tree, regarding the mayhem in utter dismay. She was spattered with mud and dust, her gown ruined, if he was any judge of such things. Not as bad as Jane Parkhill's ruffled summer frock, but—

How the hell could he have been so stupid? Perhaps if he just untied the handkerchief, put Megan's hand back in her mother's grip, where it belonged, all would be well again. He reached for her and began to undo the knot.

He felt the old man's hand grip his. "Go on, take her home." His eyes were bright on Kit's, insistent.

Kit stopped thinking. With Megan's hand in his, he began to run. He tugged her down a narrow lane between the inn and a stable. She didn't let go. She ran with him.

He didn't stop until the village was behind them. Only then did he look back. A lone sheep was following them, trotting up the hill behind them like a bridesmaid. A cloud of dust rose in the air above the village as the melee continued. Megan's hand was still in his, and he looked at her. She stared back solemnly.

"That will be a Lugnasadh Fair that Dundrummie village will never forget," she said.

Kit couldn't help it. Despite the pain on his bruised jaw

and his split lip, he began to laugh. For a moment, Megan stared at him, and then she laughed as well. They stood on the hillside and laughed like loons until their sides hurt.

"Where will we go?" she panted. "I had thought it would be a simple matter of speaking the words, and then I could go home, and you could go home, and all would be well," she gasped. "But I think that's impossible now."

"I assume we'll have to stay together."

Her smile faded, and tears sprang into her eyes. "I hadn't thought of that," she said, and began to cry in earnest. "Oh, how horrible!" She pulled her fingers free, taking the handkerchief with her, and pressed it to her eyes. His hand felt cold without hers.

"Look, we needn't go any further with this. Surely the point is made. You could go home, if you wished. I'll take you," he said, wondering how else to comfort her.

"I can't! I'd be married off at once to Merridew," she wailed. "Or Miss Carruthers would make me marry *you* for real." She put her hands around her sides and sobbed.

Was he so horrible? Kit felt a withering sense of rejection.

"Who the devil is Miss Carruthers?" he demanded, but the question just made Megan cry all the harder.

Kit had no idea how to deal with crying females. He hated tears. He usually fled, let someone else handle things like this. He looked around for help, but only the ewe that had followed them out of the village stood by. She chewed on a patch of scrub and looked balefully at him, her yellow gaze putting the responsibility firmly on Kit's shoulders.

Megan was shaking. Not knowing what else to do, Kit put his arm around her, and patted her back awkwardly. When that didn't work, he pulled her into his arms and held her, let her cry on his chest, soaking his shirtfront. He found he didn't mind. He liked holding her. She was soft and warm, and her hair smelled like heather and roses—as well as mud. He kissed the top of her head, and she looked up at him, her rain-washed eyes meeting his. Her nose was swollen and red, her face blotchy. She was still beautiful, he thought, and took the handkerchief from her and wiped away the tears.

"Come on," he said, taking her hand. And they walked up the hill toward Glen Dorian together, with only a sheep to see them off.

CHAPTER TWENTY

"Your lip is bleeding," Megan said as they sat on the hillside outside the cottage, watching the otters. She had collapsed here in the soft heather and he had folded himself beside her, sitting close, but not touching her. He was staring down at the castle, his brow furrowed. There was a dreadful bruise on his jaw, slowly turning from red to purple. She held out the handkerchief, only to discover it was too thoroughly soaked by her tears to help the blood on his lip. It made her start weeping all over again.

"Really, it doesn't hurt at all," he said, putting a hand to his mouth, mistaking her reason for crying. "In fact, it's hardly bleeding at all."

"What will we do now?" she asked again.

He was silent for a moment. "I don't know. I doubt we'd be welcome to stay in the village," he said.

"Not after the fight," she agreed.

"The castle is not habitable, and the cottage—" He hesitated. "It's very small inside."

"How small?" she asked.

"A single box bed, a table, a pair of stools, a hearth, and a loft."

"Oh," she said.

"Perhaps I could speak to your mother, explain how things are, that we—I—have no intention of, um, consummating this match."

"You have the right to do so, you know," said a voice behind them, and Megan turned to find Eleanor standing on the hillside. Behind her Graves carried a heavy basket. He stopped at a safe distance, just out of hearing, his expression as stiff and unreadable as ever. He kept one hand on his hat against the wind, and his eyes fixed on the distant hills.

"Aunt Eleanor!" Megan got to her feet.

"Tears? On such a happy day?" Eleanor said, approaching slowly over the uneven ground. She handed Megan her own handkerchief. "Well, I won't say I'm surprised. When Jeannie came back from the fair and told me what had happened in the village, I went to see for myself. It must have been quite a ceremony. How bold of you, Megan! It's set your mother into a terrible fit." She looked positively gleeful.

"Is she very angry?" Megan asked.

Eleanor grinned. "Livid. She's locked your sisters in, says she won't let them out until the English lords she chooses for them come to fetch them. She's talking of taking Alanna to London for the fall Season instead of waiting for spring."

Megan felt guilt climb her spine. She hadn't thought that her actions would harm Alanna. "Oh no. I didn't think—I just didn't want to wed Lord Merridew."

Eleanor cackled. "Nor would I. No, you made a better choice. Rossington strikes me as a fine husband for you. When your mother calms herself, she'll realize that she's gotten what she really wanted all along—you're married to an English lord."

Kit stood silently behind her and Megan could feel him bristling. "Oh, but I've already explained to Lord Rossington that this is not a *real* marriage, only a handfasting. He kindly agreed to do it so I wouldn't have to marry the marquess."

Eleanor looked at him. "How very chivalrous of you, my lord."

Kit bowed without speaking, as elegant and sober as a knight receiving laurels for rescuing a damsel in distress. Megan's heart swelled a little. He really was kind, even with a split lip.

Eleanor observed him soberly. "Mind you, I daresay Glenlorne will have something to say about this match. He's likely to insist you marry her properly, in a church, at once, if not sooner."

"If no one else does, Alec is bound to consider what will happen when word of this handfasting business gets about— and they won't stop talking about it for some weeks, I daresay," Eleanor continued. "The village is a shambles, and I daresay this story will become a local legend to rival Mairi's tale. Before long, word of it will also go south to London with all those rejected lords and ladies, where it will be crouching in the grandest salons and ballrooms, waiting to pounce when you make your debut in the spring. It won't be just a tale then—it will be scandal."

Megan's chest tightened, and she put a hand against her heart, felt it pounding like a drum before a hanging. "But it's not like that at all! And anyway, I don't want to make my debut. I intend to remain here."

Eleanor smiled. "How willful the young are! Have you thought of Alanna? Devorguilla will still insist that she must go to London."

Megan's stomach dropped at the thought of her shy sister facing the scorn of the English *ton*. "Oh no."

"Oh yes. I thought I'd better come and see if you had entered into this match just to spite your mother, or for love, or simply for sheer lust. I'm sorry to see it is for another reason entirely." Megan felt her aunt's sharp eyes on her face, and knew she wouldn't miss the hot blood that filled her cheeks. "So, what will you do now, the two of you? You could put a brave face on it, see it as what's done is done, and consider yourselves properly wedded in the old tradition until you can get yourselves before a proper man of God—or at least a blacksmith."

Megan didn't dare look at Kit. She'd cry again if she did.

"Can one annul a handfasting?" Kit asked. "This is a mar—er, *match*—of convenience only."

Eleanor squinted at him. "On what grounds? You seem well enough suited."

"Not at all!" Kit said quickly. "I mean, I never intended to marry—"

He had the grace to stop when Megan turned to glare at him. He closed his mouth and shifted his stance, clasping his hands behind his back, and squaring his shoulders. He would have looked more fearsome without the bruises and bloodstains and the rip in his coat. He wasn't even wearing a cravat. He looked younger now, Megan thought, less English, and rather angry. "I believe we must consider this sensibly, my lady," he said to her in a stiff tone. "I think what's called for is a formal announcement of our *betrothal*," Kit said, stressing the word betrothal. "That's honorable enough. Then, after a time, we will simply agree not to marry after all, put it about that we have broken our engagement, and go our separate ways, with no harm done."

Megan felt a little of the tension seep from her shoulders. Surely that would be a suitable, honorable solution. She looked at her aunt, but Eleanor shook her head.

"Perhaps if you were in England that would work, my lord. Here, the only honorable thing is to go through with the contract you have made," Eleanor insisted.

"For the entire year and a day?" Kit said, his voice breaking slightly, his face reddening.

"Indeed," Eleanor said. "Now, do you intend to stay here in the glen?" she cast a glance at the cottage, and at the castle.

Megan followed her gaze, realized that it would be impossible. The whole situation was impossible. "We can't stay here," she murmured.

"And you can't come back to Dundrummie," Eleanor said. "I doubt Devorguilla will welcome you home—in fact, I'm sure she won't, and even if Dundrummie is my home and my castle, I enjoy my peace too much to insist she take you back. It will be some time before she and Alanna are ready to leave for London. There are letters to write, accommodations to see to, packing to be done—" She made a small sound of pity at the sight of Megan's renewed tears and reached out to tuck a strand of hair behind her niece's ear. "You could go and stay in Inverness or Edinburgh, or go to England, I suppose."

"England?" both Megan and Kit said together in horror.

Eleanor raised one gray brow. "Or there's the hunting

lodge at Dundrummie. You could stay there, Megan, with Jeannie as your chaperone."

"Oh, I see," Kit said enthusiastically. "And I would depart for England. Once the time has run out, then I—we—would both be safe—er—honorably free." Megan cast him another sharp look, but he kept his gaze on Eleanor. "Would that satisfy propriety, my lady?"

"English propriety, yes. The Scots won't like it, especially Glenlorne. No, for the time being, you'll have to stay here, at least give the impression that you are honoring the handfasting. You can sleep here in the glen, my lord, and Megan can stay at the lodge, with Jeannie to guard your virtue. At the end of the allotted time, you can easily part. If necessary, Jeannie will be able to swear—as will I—that there hasn't been the slightest hint of anything remotely romantic between you."

"Could it be sooner than a year and a day? I cannot be away from my lands as long as that," Kit said anxiously.

Eleanor frowned. "I left England some fifty years ago, because I fell in love with a Scot—so much passion! He was so different from the Englishmen I knew. I see I made the right decision."

Megan saw Kit color indignantly. "He's been very kind, aunt," she said quickly.

Eleanor's lips rippled, but she did not agree or disagree. "Now—I brought you a picnic. I daresay you'll need time to discuss this. I will take Graves and go and ask Jeannie to prepare the lodge, and send her up to fetch Megan at sunset. Will that do? She'll bring you back here again in the morning."

Megan looked at Kit, saw the frown on his face. He nodded at last, unable to think of another, better solution.

"Good." Eleanor beckoned Graves forward and he set the basket down.

"I'll serve, Graves," Megan said quickly as he bent to open it.

"As you wish, my lady. May I offer congratulations?"

"Not just yet, Graves, not just yet," Eleanor said. "Come along. We'd best get ourselves home. I daresay there's a mess to handle there, too."

Megan watched her aunt go down the hill, leaning on her walking stick, with Graves's hand under her elbow.

A mess to handle. And that's exactly what this was. She turned to look at Kit. He was standing a short distance away, staring out across the loch, his expression miserable. She supposed she owed him an apology.

She no longer had to fear being married off to a noble lord. She clasped her hands around her arms. She was damaged goods now, a wanton, willful wife to a man who did not want her. Yet not a wife at all. She felt her skin heat.

"I did not intend for this to be—" she began, and he looked at her over his shoulder, his eyes dark, angry, and her tongue stuck to her tonsils.

"You did not mean to trick me into marriage?" he asked, his tone cold.

She raised her chin. "I had no intention of marrying you at all!" she said.

"Yet here we are."

She tasted the bitterness of that. She stood a dozen feet from a stranger, a man she'd met not a fortnight before, and had disliked on sight. Now, for a year and a day they were stuck with each other. Surely, when Eachann came home, or if Rossington was called away to his earldom, she would be free again. She watched the wind blow his fair hair back from his tanned forehead. She could see the repairs he'd made to the cottage, the new bench that stood by the door. The work had made him broader, added muscle, and his coat looked just a bit tight across his shoulders now, where it had been flawlessly tailored before. Even with the sleeve torn, and stains marring his buff breeches, and blood on his shirt collar, he looked every inch an aristocrat. Her heart leaped in her chest, and she turned and carried the basket up to the bench by the cottage.

"Will you have something to eat?" she said. She hadn't had breakfast, and it was now nearly noon.

"What is there?" he asked as he came up the hill to her.

"There's chicken, cheese, cherries, a flask of wine, and one of whisky. There's bannock, as well—oh, and the *lunastain* cakes." She reached into her pocket and pulled out the crumbling loaf. He looked at it disdainfully. "Do you still have yours?" she asked.

He took his *luinean* out of his pocket and regarded it. "Is there some kind of magic spell attached? Does it bind us further if we eat them?"

She looked at them. "Perhaps we can feed them to the otters. Someone should enjoy the bread, if not the luck." She set her loaf aside, and refused to look at it, busying herself with getting out the rest of the meal.

She poured him a glass of wine, the ruby liquid sparkling in the sun. It was cool, and tasted good, and she broke off a bit of bannock and chewed it slowly. He picked at a bit of chicken.

"What did you intend to do today, my lord? That is, if I had not interrupted your day so rudely?"

He sent her a sharp glance, perhaps wondering if she was mocking him, and she held his gaze. He sipped his wine. "I suppose I would have worked in the castle, trying to clear some of the rubble—if I had not been beset with—"

"Go on," she said. "What were you going to say? Beset by ghosts, the curse, me?"

"Women," he said. "You are not the only one hounded by suitors you do not want, remember?"

"The very reason we entered into this, I think," she said, and looked around. "There's not a soul here now."

He looked almost surprised. "No, there isn't." He sounded relieved.

"Except me, of course," she said, and he looked at her sharply. She smiled, and knew this was the place to apologize, but she could not.

"I will be pleased to allow you to go about your own business," he said.

"What, here in the glen, every day, for the next year and a day?"

"And half a day," he murmured as he looked at the angle of the sun.

"Shall I cook and clean and sweep the cottage while you shift charred timbers?"

A frown creased his brow. "If you wish. Do you read? I have several books. Or if you like to sew—"

"I detest it," she said. "Sewing that is, not reading. I could help you."

He looked horrified. "What? Searching for—" He bit the

sentence off short. "A lady cannot clear rubble. It's too dangerous."

"Then I shall weed the garden by the wall. I thought I saw roses struggling to grow there when we were here last." She could have bitten her own tongue in two. Her skin heated at the mention of the day she'd fallen on him, lay atop of his body in the heather like a lover, imagining how it might feel to kiss him. Her breath caught in her throat. She supposed she knew that now, having kissed him at the handfasting. He'd tasted of whisky, and his mouth had been warm and sweet. She swallowed and turned away, looked for the wine, though she wanted water.

The sun came round to shine down on the bench, and after the meal, they sat in silence, watching the birds wheeling in the clear sky, bearing the curious stares of the otters who came out to sun themselves likewise on the rocks by the shore. She felt languid, sleepy, comfortable.

"What would you have been doing today?" he asked. "If we had not—spent it as we did?"

He could not even say it. *Handfasted.* She tightened her lips. "I would have been standing on a stool in my mother's parlor, being fitted for my wedding gown," she said.

"What color?" he asked.

"Whatever the color is in Lord Merridew's coat of arms, I suppose. I would not have had any choice in the matter. My mother would have chosen the style, the fabric, and the color. She has waited since the day I was born to see me as the bride she's always envisioned."

"It must have been a shock to see you in the village square, wearing a plain blue gown, your hand bound to mine with a handkerchief."

She felt guilt chill her. "I fear I've disappointed her dreadfully."

"Surely she would have been equally disappointed if you'd married your Eachann."

Eachann. She'd barely thought of him all day. His name sounded strange on Kit's lips, spoken aloud, here, between them.

"Yes, but I had intended to be more—careful—in convincing her."

"And your brother, what does he think of Eachann?"

Alec would tell her she could do better than Eachann Rennie. That's why he'd allowed Devorguilla to insist that the girls must have at least one Season in London, so they could see some of the world beyond the hills that marked the borders of Glenlorne, and then decide who they loved. If she and Eachann had asked to wed, he would have told them to wait a year, and see how they felt when Megan returned from London. But surely she knew her own heart better than Alec did. She loved Eachann.

"Alec?" she said, realizing Kit was waiting for a response. "Oh, he would insist I wait and think on my choice," she said truthfully.

"For a year and a day?" he asked.

She colored. "Aye. But I know my own hea—mind."

He smiled. "Your brother may be right. People change over time. It may be that your Eachann will return a different man than the one who left."

She gritted her teeth at the sound of her love's name on Rossington's lips. "Of course he won't. He will always love me, and I will always love him. Why should that change?"

He studied her. "You don't give up on what you want, do you?"

She tossed her head. "Never." Well, once she had imagined herself in love with a handsome cousin, and then realized how silly he was, and had fallen out of love just as quickly. She wondered now if it was possible that she would fall out of love with Eachann, too. It was just the faintest of doubts, but she put a hand to her heart to still it. "I love Eachann," she said aloud. "Have you never been in love?"

"I have found myself infatuated a time a two, but love? No. I have left that to my sister, and my younger brother. My sister's marriage is a battleground. My brother is newly wed. He chose his bride from a list my mother gave him, for her fortune and her father's title. He had decided to marry her before he'd even set eyes on her."

"Truly? What if she'd been ugly or bossy, or had a limp or crossed eyes? What if she didn't care for any of the things he did, or didn't like *him*? Did they fall in love when they met?"

Kit pursed his lips. "He was introduced to her at a ball, and they exchanged less than a dozen words. Still, he called upon her the next day, and spent the requisite fifteen minutes in her company. Then, the day after that, he asked her father for her hand, and was given permission to propose. My brother was determined to wed a fortune, you see, and Regina offered the best and the biggest. It hardly mattered what she looked like. She isn't a beauty, not like—" His eyes were on her face, but he looked away.

"And does it matter to you?" she asked. "Not what she looks like, but if there's love between you?"

For a moment he looked wistful. There was love in his

eyes as he scanned the glen, taking in the beauty of the hills and the loch. "I should like to have at least a sense of regard for the woman I marry. It is difficult in my position to expect to find love. How would I know if the lady's feelings for me were genuine, or if she simply wished to be a countess?"

"How *would* you know?"

"Not one of the debutantes, or any of the widows and ladies who have set their cap for me since I inherited my title, even bothered to glance at me before that. That's how I know. My brother used to be the one mobbed by debutantes and their matchmaking mamas."

"I can't believe that," she said without thinking. How could a woman not long to make Kit's acquaintance? He was the most handsome man she'd ever met, and kind and intriguing.

"Love is for poor folk, because they can't afford a better match," he said. "That's my mother's motto. I'm sure she has it embroidered on a pillow somewhere. Better to marry for money and hope to fall in love later than to marry for love and hope riches will follow."

"Would it not be best to have both? Before marrying, I mean?" she said. "Surely that is the only guarantee of happiness. Otherwise—" She shrugged. "And I think you should have something in common, as well. And an admiration for the other person."

He met her eyes with a wry smile. "Your Eachann must be quite a man."

She blinked. Was he? "Of course he is," she said quickly.

"My lady?" Jeannie Fraser stood at the corner of the cottage shyly. She dipped a curtsy when they turned to her.

"All is in readiness at the lodge. Lady Eleanor asked me to fetch you."

Kit rose as well. "I'll escort you both there and then come back," he said, and they walked in silence, over the hill, through the forest and along the river, and up to the back gate of the lodge. There he paused, and bowed.

"Goodnight, my lady," he said stiffly. "I suppose I shall see you tomorrow."

"Indeed." She curtsied. "Goodnight—" She paused, unsure what to call him in front of Jeannie. He was her husband. It seemed strange to call him "my lord" or "Rossington," yet she blushed at the idea of using his first name, though he'd given her permission once. "Goodnight, Kit," she said it softly. He met her eyes and then turned and left, and she watched him go before she climbed the steps and went into her new home.

CHAPTER TWENTY-ONE

Kit woke in the cottage the next morning as a shadow blocked the sun that streamed across his bed through the open window. He opened his eyes to find Megan McNabb leaning over the sill, peering in at him.

Or was she Megan Linwood now, or perhaps Lady Rossington? Like his mother ... Those frightening thoughts brought him fully awake, and he grabbed for the sheet, and pulled it up to his chin like a modest maiden.

"Good morning," she said.

"Good morning," he replied and stared at her. Silhouetted by the morning sun, her hair shone, and her cheeks were flushed. Was that from walking up from the lodge, or because she was surprised to find him lying in bed? She wasn't actually *looking* at him—she was staring fixedly at a point high above his head. It gave him the opportunity to look at her. She was quite fetching, perched on his windowsill like a sparrow, and in his half-awake state he wondered what she would do if he threw off the covers and invited her into bed.

It would be disastrous.

"I fear I may have arrived earlier than expected. I was coming down the path and noticed the window was open. I—I brought breakfast. I wasn't sure if you had arrangements for food. Jeannie told me you have a valet staying in the village," she babbled, her gaze averted, her cheeks flaming.

"Yes, Leslie," he said. "Yes." He didn't move. She really was quite mesmerizing to look at. His grandfather had hired an artist to paint the ceiling in the earl's apartments at Bellemont Park with a regiment of adoring angels. They stared down at the earl—him—as he lay in his bed, encouraging pure thoughts, good governance, and blessing the begetting of heirs. Megan might have descended straight off the plaster to Earth . . .

She cast a quick glance at him, and raised the basket to the sill. "Shall I leave the basket and go?"

He remembered his manners. What were the rules of proper behavior for a situation like this? "No," he said. "I mean, please come in."

By the time she had come around to the front of the cottage and opened the door, he was on his feet, wrapped in the sheet, only his bare feet visible. She glanced at them, and her lips parted in surprise, and she blushed all over again, no doubt guessing what lay beneath the linen, or in this case, what did not. She turned away at once and busied herself with unpacking the basket.

There was not an inch of private space in the tiny cottage. Should he send her out, make her wait on the bench, or ask her to stroll the grounds for a half-hour while he dressed, made himself decent and ready to face her? He needed to shave, to bathe, and to pass water. He frowned at her back. What time was it, anyway?

He carefully reached for his watch, and flipped it open. Leslie would not be here for at least an hour, and he could hardly wear the sheet until then. He frowned. Why had she come so damnably early? Of course, he was usually up long before now, dressed, ready for the day. But he hadn't slept well.

He grabbed his clothes in one arm, and strode toward the door. He awkwardly grabbed a bucket by the door too, all without meeting her eye. "I'll go and fetch some water." He hurried out before she could stop him.

The heather prickled his feet, and he hung on to his make-shift robe like an ancient Celtic king. All he needed was a crown, a brooch at his shoulder, and a queen by his side—he put a stop to that line of thinking right there, and glanced nervously back at the cottage. There was no sign of Megan.

He dropped his clothing and the bucket by the shore of the loch and rubbed the end of the sheet over his face. The surface of the water was placid, calm, and silent, and the hills and the castle reflected in the black depths. The sun on his back was warm and pleasant, though the breeze was crisp enough to remind him autumn and cooler days were not far off. Responsibility loomed at home.

But for now, he was here, free, and unencumbered. He took a deep breath, tossed aside the sheet, and dove into the loch.

The water chilled him instantly, and he swam for the sur-face and gasped for breath before diving again, swimming outward in strong, swift strokes, until his body grew accustomed to the cold water, the weightlessness, and the simple joy of floating.

He rolled over, floated on his back, stared up into the sky and watched the clouds. The glen was blissfully silent. There were no crowds of marriage-minded females, no brothers or fathers hoping to convince him to marry his wealth into their family. There was nothing and no one. Save Megan McNabb. He clasped his palms over his crotch and looked nervously at the cottage, but he could scarce see it from here. Still, he swam farther out, behind the castle, out of sight entirely.

Had she tricked him, or guaranteed everything he wanted—peace and quiet, and time to solve the mystery of Mairi's treasure? He'd been awake half the night trying to decide.

The only determination he'd made was that he would have to set some rules. Not that the setting of rules ever worked with his mother or his sister, but he would be firm with Megan. He would forbid her to so much as set one foot on the causeway. The castle would be completely off limits. She could remain at the cottage and read, or write, or sew, or go away and visit her family and friends. Just because they were handfasted there was really no reason why his life and his plans must be disrupted any further than they already had been. She had asked him to assist her, and he had.

By marrying her. *Temporarily.*

He remembered the way she looked with the dappled shade of the ancient trysting tree on her skin like a lace veil, the way she'd tasted when he kissed her, the trust in her eyes, the flare in the hazel depths of some emotion he did not wish to contemplate. That had kept him awake, too. He clenched

his fist in the water now, reliving the feeling of her hand in
his, the slight weight of the lace-edged handkerchief that
bound them together. And the kiss—yet again. Why couldn't
he forget kissing her? It had been a peck, a sip, and nothing
more. Despite the coldness of the water his body responded.
He rolled, dove deep, and swam for shore, banishing any
more thoughts of Megan McNabb—or Megan Linwood.
Which was it?

　　He would have to ask . . .

Chapter Twenty-Two

Megan leaned against the table as he left her, her cheeks burning. She had no idea he would be still abed when she arrived. Nor had she had any idea that a man might sleep—well, in nothing but a sheet. She felt her heart turn over in her chest. She would have left at once if he hadn't opened his eyes and looked up at her. How was it possible for a man to look so remarkably handsome clad in nothing but a sheet, his hair tousled, his eyes still full of sleep? His chest, before he yanked the sheet up to cover it, had been broad, sun-kissed, and naked. She blushed even now, the image refusing to leave her mind.

She wore a nightgown to bed, buttoned to the neck, her hair carefully braided, her robe near to hand. She concentrated on unpacking the basket—a loaf of bread, a pot of butter, some cheese, a pitcher of ale, apple jam, and some ham, but her hands shook. She wondered what it felt like to sleep entirely unclothed and nearly dropped a pot of cream.

She set it down carefully and crossed to the bed and ran her hand over the mattress. It was still warm from his body.

She picked up his pillow, held it to her nose, breathed in the scent of his hair, the faint fragrance of his soap, and felt her pulse race. She hugged it to her chest, tried to imagine the two of them, here, the way they'd been the day she'd landed on him, only without the barrier of clothing between them.

Then she made the mistake of looking out the window. Rossington was emerging from the loch, sleek and wet, his shoulders naked, his chest naked, his belly and—*oh my*—

She stood in the middle of the cottage and stared, clutching his pillow in a death grip.

She had seen men without shirts on, of course—hewing wood or hauling heavy stones, but she had never felt like this. Her belly trembled, her limbs felt slack and heavy. She knew she should look away, but she couldn't make her eyes obey.

He used the sheet to dry the water from his limbs, and dressed. She saw white buttocks as he drew on his breeches, and the broad muscles of his back and shoulders rippled as he shrugged into his shirt. He looked tall and fit. She watched until he turned, and began coming back up the hill, carrying the sheet over his arm now, fully dressed, every inch an English earl once more.

She tossed the pillow back on the bed and threw the blanket over it, tried to tidy it with shaking fingers.

"I assume you usually have servants to do that sort of thing," he said, obviously seeing how she was struggling with the simple task, and she spun, feeling guilt rise in her throat. He leaned in the doorway, and suddenly the cottage was very crowded, as if he took up all the space and all the air with it.

"I just thought—" What had she thought? "My, it's hot in here. Shall we go outside?"

He began to gather the food, and she helped, and their hands met on the loaf. She drew back as if he were on fire.

He looked at her oddly. "Is anything wrong?" he asked.

She shook her head, the power of speech gone, her whole body tingling from one simple, accidental touch. She picked up the basket and hurried outside. She sat on the very farthest edge of the bench, and tore the bread, handed him some.

"Thank you." He smeared it with jam, and bit into it, and looked as if he were eating ambrosia. Megan smoothed her palms over her skirt, and picked up a plum, and bit into it. She tasted the sweetness of the fruit, felt the burst of saliva in her mouth, and the warmth of the sun on her skin, the sudden cool rush of the breeze. But most of all, she was aware of Kit Rossington, seated by her side. Her skin buzzed. If she reached out her hand just the slightest bit, she'd be able to touch his, and bring it to her lips. Would he taste of the loch, the sweetness of clear water, with a tang of peat and heather? He was looking out over the loch, his eyes narrowed against the sun, crinkled at the corners. His hair was soft and fair, lighter than brown, darker than gold, and streaked with sunlight where the breeze lifted it back from his brow.

She forced herself to swallow the fruit, to take another bite. "What shall we do today?" she asked him.

He looked up at her. The contented look vanished. He looked startled for an instant before he schooled his features to calm. "We? I thought I would go and spend time in the castle, clear some of the rubble, perhaps."

"I can help," she said quickly, and saw panic in his eyes.

"You? No, I don't think so. It would be better—safer—if you were to remain here, perhaps. I mean it isn't strictly necessary that you stay here at the cottage. You might walk into the village, or visit friends, or your mother, perhaps."

She raised her chin. "I doubt either of us would be very welcome in the village at present, and my mother has sworn never to speak my name again."

"Which name, Margaret or Megan?" he asked, then put a hand to his brow. "Never mind. It doesn't matter." He got up and began to pace, his hands clasped behind his back, his eyes on the heather beneath his boots. "I believe we must set some rules if we are to—endure? tolerate?—each other's company."

"Endure?" she asked, feeling her temperature rising again for an entirely different reason. He glanced up at her as if surprised by her sharp tone.

"Perhaps that wasn't the right word. Get along, maybe?"

Megan folded her arms over her chest. "No, I believe *endure* was an excellent choice. What rules did you have in mind?"

He paused. "Well for one thing, you may not venture into the castle."

"Why?"

His skin flushed. "Why? Do you not recall what happened the last time you were there?"

She did indeed. She had fallen out a window, lain on top of him, touched him. He must have remembered that as well, for his skin flushed, and his mouth dropped open. "No, not *that*—that isn't what I was thinking of. I meant—" He ran his hand through his hair, and began pacing again. "I meant that it isn't safe. I would not wish you to suffer an injury."

"Such as a splinter?"

He looked at her balefully. "Yes," he said through tight

lips. "Look, I only got the splinter in the first place because you distracted me."

"I saved you." She couldn't resist teasing him. "I took the fearsome thing out, plucked it from your flesh, bound up the terrible wound."

He looked indignant. "I could have managed well enough alone. It wouldn't have happened in the first place if you hadn't been there."

"So you said. Are there other rules I will be expected to follow?"

He stopped pacing again. "Yes—well, no. Just that one. Otherwise, you are free to come and go as you wish."

"Just not to the castle."

"Precisely." He looked pleased as punch that she understood. Irritation sizzled through her veins.

"Or to the village, or Dundrummie." She got up and began to gather the remains of their breakfast. "I'll have you know I did not cook any of this food, my lord—and you saw the way I made your bed. It looked even more slept in after than before. I do not enjoy sewing, and I abhor watercolors, at least my own efforts. Shall I pick flowers and weave daisy chains all day?"

He looked affronted. "You should have thought of that before you came here yesterday. What would you be doing if you were at Dundrummie?"

"Planning a wedding," she said tartly. "And I don't doubt you'd be doing the same, if I hadn't interrupted Miss Parkhill's courtship.

He flushed and glanced over his shoulder at the castle, as if it were calling to him.

"Do you read? Have you a book to occupy you?" he asked.

"Just go," she said, dismissing him. "I shall find something to do. Laundry, perhaps, or baking bread, or I might busy myself with shearing a sheep or two."

"Oh, there's no need to do laundry," the daft man said. "Leslie will be coming soon. He'll see to that."

"But the baking and shearing are fine with you, my lord? No rules about those?" she quipped. He was growing flustered.

"I suppose you must do as you please. Look, given the circumstances in which we find ourselves, stop calling me 'my lord.' I think it would be best if we called one another by our Christian names—Megan."

Still simmering, she dipped a curtsy. "If that's your command—my lord."

He colored again. "It is." He waited, but she kept her lips stubbornly shut. "I'll bid you good day, then," he said, and turned on his heel. She watched as he made his way down the hill, across the causeway, and disappeared into the castle.

She hoped it fell on him.

CHAPTER TWENTY-THREE

Kit lifted another broken piece of wood and tossed it aside with a grunt. She was the most infuriating, annoying woman he'd ever met, and that included his mother and his sister.

Arabella would have taken his commands as a challenge to do exactly the opposite. His mother would have murmured, "Yes, of course, Christopher—whatever you wish. You are the earl, after all." And then she would have ignored his wishes entirely.

Would Megan do the same? If she did, he would get a sturdy lock for the castle door, or see if the old portcullis still worked. He rubbed a hand over his sweaty brow, and grinned at the idea. He may have yielded the sovereignty of all his other castles, but he intended to keep this one wholly for himself.

He looked up at the sun, now peering down at him through the hole in the roof. He'd been here several hours, and had managed to clear only a few feet. The staircase rose mockingly close on the other side of the fallen rubble.

He crossed to the window and sat down on the wide sill,

and looked at the room. Where would he hide a treasure if he didn't want anyone to find it? He rose and began tapping on the walls, but they were either solid or they crumbled under his hand, revealing noting. If the castle knew Mairi's secret, it was not going to give it up easily. There were plenty of niches and nooks and cracks, but the ones he'd examined were empty of anything but spiders.

Was there a strong room? If there was, he couldn't reach it. There was one wing of the castle that had all but caved in entirely, rooms still blocked. If that was where the treasure lay, he would have to tear down the whole bloody castle, stone by stone to get to it.

The wind moaned, as if it feared he might just do that.

He put his palm against the wall, and the stone radiated cold, despite the heat of the day. "I won't tear it down. I only want to know the secret," he murmured. "Where is the treasure?"

The wind whistled, then died away, and Kit went back to moving rubble.

"Did you have a good day?" Megan asked when he returned to the cottage as the sun was setting over the lip of the glen. He'd stayed at the castle until his stomach grumbled and his muscles ached, in hopes that she would be gone.

Instead she stood on the hillside, her hand shading her face against the glare of the sun and watched him come up the hill toward her. Oddly, he was glad to see her. His heart lifted at the sight of her.

He stopped a dozen feet from her, aware he wasn't fit

company for a lady in his current state. He needed a bath, or another swim. "There's much work to be done," he said. "And you? Did you shear sheep and bake bread after all?"

"I met your Mister Leslie. He had plenty of gossip about the village. The brawl lasted for three hours after we made our escape. He stayed firmly locked inside the inn, and watched it all from the window."

"All of it?" Kit felt his dignity shrivel. What must his valet think of him now?

"He said he wished he'd been part of it. Those who were not fighting are bragging that they were, and those who were there will dine out on the tale for some time to come."

"Is there much damage?" Kit asked.

"Well, Miss Parkhill is claiming a broken heart, but so are at least a half-dozen other ladies. Jane has declared you heartless, and is promising to write to your sister at once."

Kit felt his stomach curdle.

"And Lord Merridew? Has he recovered from the loss of you?"

"He retreated to his rented lodge in a fury. He was heard to say that he will not set foot anywhere near a female for the rest of his stay, unless it is one he may shoot on sight. I do hope he's referring to grouse and deer."

Kit quirked a smile. "I believe you are fortunate you do not have a rack of antlers or a fine pelt."

"Then you think I made a lucky escape?"

"Undoubtedly."

"I asked Mister Leslie to walk over to the lodge and advise Jeannie that you would be coming back with me for dinner. It was that or stale bread and cheese from this morning's meal.

You may return here to Glen Dorian after you've eaten—and bathed." Her nose wrinkled slightly.

"Kind of you," he said, moving away a little more.

"Not at all. Neither Mister Leslie nor myself cook. I can catch a fish, of course, and cook it over a campfire—at least I think I could, since I've seen it done. Or bannock—I could make that, but not proper food, though I have recently learned to plan a menu for a dinner party of twenty guests or more."

"A useful skill," he murmured, trying to imagine Megan crouched over a campfire roasting a plump trout on a stick—or twenty fish, if guests were expected.

"Shall we go?" she asked.

Kit offered his arm, and heard Megan's breath hitch as she hesitated for a moment before tucking her hand under his. Her blush rivaled the sunset. Did he smell so odious, or was it something else? He quite liked the way her arm felt, linked with his, and the gentle swish of her skirts against his boots, the way their steps fell into a rhythm, like horses, perfectly matched.

Chapter Twenty-Four

To Kit's surprise, there was a room all ready for him at the lodge, complete with a bath and the services of Mr. Leslie. His clothing had been hung in the wardrobe, and his shaving kit and toiletries were laid out on the dressing table.

He'd been expecting a washbowl in the corner of the kitchen.

The valet offered him a welcoming smile as Kit stood in the doorway, considering what all this meant. "Good evening, my lord. Lady Eleanor suggested you should keep a room here in the lodge. It's closer than the village, and far more private."

"Private?" Kit demanded, warning bells clattering in his head. He looked for a connecting door that might lead to Megan's chamber, but there wasn't one.

"Mister Fraser was rather insistent that I—we—well, you—vacate his inn at once."

Kit winced. "Was there much damage?"

Leslie nodded. "There was, I'm afraid. The brawlers helped themselves to the inn's supplies of brandy and French wine. Fortunately, Lady Eleanor Fraser was kind enough to offer space here, since you were now—"

"Did she indeed?" Kit murmured.

"Her ladyship is a very kind lady. I took the liberty of moving your things and my own here this afternoon. I hope that was acceptable. Are you married, my lord? One hears of these things, of course, being 'married over the anvil in Scotland,' and such, but I never dreamed—"

"No, I'm not married, Leslie," Kit snapped. "Don't be ridiculous."

Leslie's brow crumpled. "But Lady Eleanor seemed to think—" He swallowed. "Shall I pack everything again, my lord?"

Kit looked at the kettle of hot water waiting on the hearth. The room was rustic, but comfortable, and far more spacious than the little cottage. He could scarcely imagine the starchy Mr. Leslie making the hayloft into servants' quarters. Kit looked at the tub, and enticing tendrils of steam beckoned to him. There were fresh clothes laid out as well, and he could hardly go down to dinner the way he was. He began to unbutton his shirt. "I shall have a bath and dress for dinner—but after that, I intend to return to the glen to sleep, is that clear?"

"Perfectly, sir," Leslie said, smoothing his expression into the perfect flatness that told Kit his valet didn't understand the arrangements in the least. That made two of them, Kit thought, stepping into the bath.

He slid down into the hot water, and considered. Eleanor was concerned about appearances—if Kit's possessions, and his manservant, were still at the inn, then it would surely cause sharp-eyed folk to ask questions. Was he handfasted to Megan McNabb or wasn't he? He was—for the next three hundred and sixty-four days.

He picked up the soap and lathered his sore muscles, and the fragrance of heather filled the room. It was the way Megan smelled. He'd thought it was the wind in her hair, or the sun. He brought the cake to his nose, inhaled deeply, and pictured her standing in the glen, her hand shading her eyes, smiling at him. "Where did you get this soap?" he asked Leslie.

"Lady Eleanor was kind enough to supply it, my lord. She also had bed linens and a few other odds and ends sent over for your comfort."

"What odds and ends?" Kit demanded, looking up at the valet through the soap on his face.

"A full sized plaid, my lord. I believe it is the MacIntosh sett. It's quite popular hereabouts, and the wee maid downstairs assured me it is a very comfortable garment, and practical for walking the hills."

"A plaid?" Kit spluttered as Leslie poured a pitcher of water over his head to rinse away the soap. *The wee maid? What the devil was happening to the stiff, English Josiah Leslie?*

"Will you try the kilt, my lord?" Leslie asked, as Kit rubbed himself dry.

"Certainly not. I'll dress for dinner as I usually do," Kit growled, grabbing for his linen shirt, made by the finest London clothier, monogrammed at the cuff with his initials and crest, as proper and English as it was possible to get. He thought he detected the slightest hint of disappointment in the ripple of Leslie's lips, and he ignored it. When he was dressed as an English gentleman, Kit went downstairs to dinner.

The dining room was an extraordinary thing indeed, and Kit paused in the doorway. The plastered walls were hung from one end of the barrel-vaulted room to the other with antlers and hunting trophies. It made the room like more like a cave with roots growing inward, or the den of some ravenous animal—a wild, mythical creature. The table was quite ordinary, covered with a white cloth, set with fine china and silverware for two. The candlelight played over the points of sharp horns, the rough black beams of the ceiling, and the shining glass eyes of a stuffed wildcat that stood stiffly on the top of an elegant sideboard. The bare planks of the floor creaked as he entered the room. It looked very Scottish indeed, the preserve of a rough and ready Highland laird, a man at one with the hills and glens and lochs that surrounded him. *He'd* have worn a kilt to supper. Kit straightened his monogrammed cuffs, feeling overdressed.

"Good evening." He turned to see Megan in the doorway. She wore an elegant gown in coral muslin, her hair twisted up high on her head. She looked as English as he did. She indicated a seat at the table, a heavily carved chair, the remarkable arms and legs made of yet more antlers. "Will you sit down? Jeannie is ready to serve."

He assisted her into her chair, set to the right of his own. Her seat was a perfectly ordinary dining chair of fine polished mahogany with elegantly turned legs.

"It's a simple meal, I'm afraid—roast lamb with tatties—potatoes, that is—" She blushed, and sent him a watery smile.

"It sounds delicious," he said, and it turned out it was indeed. Perhaps the air and the hard physical work had made him hungry. He let Jeannie refill his plate when he'd finished, and couldn't recall when he'd taken more pleasure in a meal.

"What would you have had for your supper if you'd stayed in the glen?" she asked.

"Probably whatever was left over from breakfast. Or I might have caught a fish and cooked it over a campfire. This is far more—civilized," he said. Not to mention that he hadn't so much as tried cooking a fish since he and his brothers had done so when they were boys. It had been half raw, and Kit still bore a scar on his thumb to remind him of the experience.

"There's a lot to be said for civilization, I suppose," she said. "I'm sure a hot bath was more pleasant than a cold swim in the loch." She put a hand over her lips, her eyes widening, and Kit looked up at her in surprise. "I didn't mean to say that."

"You saw me? You watched me this morning?"

Her blush was fiery in the candlelight. "Quite by accident, I assure you. I saw something moving in the water, and merely looked—glanced, really—to see what it was. I thought it was an otter, you see." She fidgeted with the stem of her wine glass. "I mean, I wasn't really *watching*—besides, it was you who dropped his clothes in full view of the cottage window, and stood there stark naked."

He pictured her in the window, staring down at him as he stood on the shore of the loch, drawing a breath and bracing himself for the plunge into the icy water. He imagined her eyes roaming over his naked flesh, and felt desire flare.

Kit shifted in his chair, cleared his throat, and counted

to ten. "Do you swim?" he asked trying to keep the timbre of his voice even. "I don't imagine it's common among girls the way it is with boys—at least my sister never swam, though she used to hide in the bushes and watch us—her three brothers. At least she did until her governess caught her and boxed her ears." He was aware he was babbling. He'd begun to speak, hoping to ease the sudden tension that crackled in the air between them. Her hand lay on the tablecloth, inches from his own, and he had the oddest desire to clasp her fingers in his. He gripped the arms—antlers—of his chair instead. "I remember the poor governess arriving to find her wayward charge, then realizing what Arabella was looking at. We were as horrified as she was. Her eyes popped, she grew as red as a beet, and then she fainted dead away."

"I can imagine," Megan said, and blushed again. "I mean, I'm sure it was a dreadful shock to everyone involved."

Had she been shocked when she looked out the window that morning, spied on him, or had she felt—breathless, the way she was now, her eyes bright, her lips soft, slightly parted? His arousal rose higher still. He was as stiff as the damned antler under his palm.

"There's a loch at Glenlorne, too, and my sisters and I swam," she said. "It was too tempting on a hot day *not* to swim. We wore our shifts, of course, and the lads wore their long shirts."

"Lads?" he stared at her.

"The village children," she said.

"Eachann too?" The words were out of his mouth before he'd thought not to say them. She looked up at him sharply.

"Yes, I suppose so. I don't really remember."

"Then he wasn't your childhood sweetheart?" he asked.

"No. That came later. Just a few months ago, really. We danced together at the spring fair, then again at Midsummer. He began to wait for me, to walk me to and from the village when I went to listen to tales."

He laughed. "And let me guess—one fine evening he stopped and stole a kiss."

She sent him a look from under her lashes. "It was morning."

"Bold lad," Kit murmured.

Her eyes sharpened. "Did you never steal a kiss from a lass, my lord?"

She was flushed and pretty, her lips reddened by the wine. No wonder Eachann couldn't resist. He was having trouble resisting himself.

"It's Kit," he reminded her, his eyes fixed on her mouth. "And no, I never stole a kiss, for I was far too shy as a boy. My brothers got all the girls. I had to wait until a lass finally stole a kiss from me. Actually, she was a widow, a friend of my mother's." She gasped, and he looked up to meet her eyes. "Have I shocked you? I apologize. I wasn't thinking what I was saying."

"I don't know," she said slowly, and dropped her eyes to her hands. "Was it just a kiss?"

He grinned. "She taught me a number of things, as a matter of fact—discretion above all."

Her eyes widened. "Oh, I wasn't prying. It's just that I forget sometimes that I hardly know you. I can imagine—" She paused. "Actually, I can't."

"What can't you imagine?" he asked, leaning toward her, curious.

"I imagine that you've led a far different life than mine. Perhaps I am too used to listening to other people's stories, or I'm a busybody at heart. She twisted her napkin in her hands. "Perhaps we should change the subject."

"Then what shall we talk about?" It had been quite some time—well, never—since he'd shared anything so personal with anyone else. He pondered why he'd told Megan McNabb of all people. She made him think, and imagine—and do— the damnedest things. He wasn't himself with her. Or perhaps he was, more than ever before, and that was the most unsettling thought of all. He straightened in his chair, squared his shoulders.

"I am conversant on any number of topics more suited to polite company. Gardens, architecture, the weather, the price of corn . . ." It's what he spoke to his mother about, or the gentlemen at his club, or the females who cornered him and didn't really listen to a word that came out of his mouth. But Megan was listening. Her eyes were on his, interested and engaged. He pushed away the word "engaged" at once. "Perhaps we should set rules for conversation."

She pursed her lips. "More rules? All right then—honesty. I insist on that."

He swallowed. "Shall we limit our honesty to one true thing per meal?"

"Done."

He raised his glass in salute and touched it to hers.

"Tell me about England," she said.

"If you'll promise to tell me one of the tales you've collected."

He sat back to listen, captivated by the soft burr in her

voice, her facial expressions, the way she used her hands as she spoke, the contagious, hypnotic, delicious sound of her laughter.

The hours passed before he knew it, and Kit rose form the table realizing he'd never enjoyed a meal more than this one, and it wasn't the food or the wine.

It was Megan McNabb.

Kit dreamed he was swimming. Not alone, but with Megan, their arms and legs tangled together in the water, her dark hair floating around him like seaweed, her mouth on his, hot and sweet in the cold water.

He woke with a start, alone in his bed in the cottage. He gripped the sheets in his fist, expecting them to be as wet as the loch, but they were dry in the moonlight—and tented over his hips like a marquee. He rubbed a hand over his face, and rolled over, pressed his erection into the lumpy mattress, and willed it away as he buried his face in his pillow.

It was no use. The soft images of the dream clung. He could smell her perfumed soap on his own skin, remembered the way her mouth had tasted of whisky in his dream, just the way it had when he'd kissed her in the market square. He tossed and turned until dawn, then rose and dressed, lest she catch him in bed again. This time, he wouldn't be able to resist . . .

By the time the sun was up, he was halfway to Inverness.

CHAPTER TWENTY-FIVE

Megan was careful to arrive at Glen Dorian a full hour later than she'd come the morning before. She hoped that Kit was up, dressed, and ready to receive company. To her surprise, there was no answer when she knocked loudly on the door.

"Kit?" she called, but no one replied. She looked at the castle, and wondered if he was there already, working. He had come out dust-smudged and looking content yesterday. What did he find to do there all day? She pursed her lips, felt a small ball of resentment form in her chest. She'd never know, since he'd forbidden her from setting foot in the old castle. She sat on the bench and stared at the ruin, watched the otters and wondered if he'd come out to look for her, but he did not.

She opened the door and went into the cottage. It was tidy, but the bed was unmade. She crossed to remedy that, and as she moved the bedding, the scent of him surrounded her. She picked up his pillow and held it to her face again, remembered how he'd looked, lying in bed, staring up at her in the window yesterday. She tried to imagine him here, and dropped the pillow and turned away with a gasp at her wicked thoughts. She felt as if someone was watching her, and she spun, and cast a quick glance out the window at the loch—but there was no one there. She was entirely alone. She felt a fizzle of disappointment.

She rubbed her eyes, tried to gather her composure. She hadn't slept well, and that was surely the explanation for why she was so addled this morning. She'd been plagued with dreams of Kit swimming naked, then walking toward her up the hill, unclothed, the water glinting on his skin. In her dream, he'd taken her in his arms, kissed her, and she'd kissed him back. She woke with her heart pounding, her body hot and restless. It was Eachann, she told herself—the man in her dreams—but he'd never kissed her like that. No one had. She touched a hand to her lips and cursed her too-vivid imagination. It wasn't like that, in her experience. Kissing Eachann had been more a mashing together of mouths, and a somewhat breathless crush of one body to another. The kisses they'd shared were pleasant, but they had hardly evoked the kind of unsettling desire she'd imagined in her dream.

She backed out of the cottage, took a deep gulp of fresh air, and sanity. She hurried down the path to the lodge. Safer there today, where she could nap, or write, or plan just how she was going to face Kit when she saw him at supper, without blushing, or making a ninny of herself by throwing herself into his arms to see if it was true, that kisses were indeed more akin to fire than air.

CHAPTER TWENTY-SIX

Angus Grant's Inverness office was dark, smoky, low ceilinged, and filled with untidy stacks of paper and decanters of whisky. Kit tapped his fingers on his knee as he waited for the solicitor to appear. His clerk had told Kit that his master was having breakfast, it being very early in the day, but that his lordship could come in and wait, and the clerk would give him tea, then go on to Mr. Grant's home and fetch the man himself.

A half hour later, the clerk flung open the door yet again, and Mr. Grant hurried through it. "Good morning, my lord, I trust all is well?"

"Quite well, thank you," Kit said. "I have some questions."

Grant's eyes widened as he took his seat and leaned across the desk. "About Glen Dorian? Has anything of an unusual nature, shall we say, occurred there?"

Kit ignored the cryptic remark. "In a manner of speaking. It appears to be a prime location for sheep and cattle. I was wondering why there are no tenants in the glen."

Grant sat back. "Well, there were once, of course, but that

was long ago. The people who lived there—MacIntoshes, they were—removed."

"Removed?"

"They were driven out after the battle of Culloden, declared traitors. Their cottages were razed, the castle burned, their cattle and sheep taken."

Kit recalled the tales of the government forces marching through the Highlands after the battle, looking for Jacobites, plundering, raping, and destroying all in their path. He wondered if Nathaniel Linwood had been part of that. "I understand, but why did they not return?"

"I daresay there was no one *to* return. Most of the men of Glen Dorian were arrested, many transported—or worse. Lady Mairi MacIntosh took to the hills with the folk she could save when they burned the castle. She swore she'd come back to wait for her husband's return, and so she did, but there was really nothing left to return to. There were no sheep, no cattle, no folk."

"Does no one else graze their stock there? There are farms nearby."

Grant brightened. "Oh, aye, there are indeed. Some do, but it's seen as cursed land. In truth, I'd say you're most fortunate in that, my lord."

"How so?" Kit asked, frowning.

"So many landowners have the opposite problem. They've got too many tenants, and they wish to be rid of them, so there's more land for the lucrative raising of livestock for meat and wool. In my opinion, it does the poor wretches good to turn them off the land. It forces them to shift for themselves, make new lives. Who's to say they won't find a better life elsewhere?"

"Where do they go?" Kit asked.

Grant chuckled. "Who knows? The land being better used for other things is the point."

Kit imagined city slums crowded with destitute families. He frowned and Grant tutted. "It's not so tragic. Many landowners are modernizing. Some fools cleave to the old ways out of some misplaced loyalty to the old clan way of life, but I can see you're a man of modern thinking, an English lord, instead of a Scottish laird." He laughed at his own joke, but Kit remained sober. "My point is that there are possibilities to make a fortune here." He took a sheet of paper out of the desk drawer and leaned across the desk. "I could assist in drawing up a plan . . ."

Kit rose to his feet. The low ceiling was suddenly oppressive, the room airless. "I'll consider it," he said, and turned to go without bidding the man of affairs good morning, or waiting for his farewell.

He rode back to the glen deep in thought. When he had inherited his father's titles and lands, he'd received some of the same advice from his managers in England, too. He could tear down Shearwater and build a factory instead. Or if he were to revoke the leases of the tenant farms on his lands at Coalfax Castle, he could increase sheep production and ship more wool. Those men promised the same thing as Grant had—another fortune for him, and certain destitution for the people who had lived on the land for generations. Instead, Kit had built new houses at Shearwater, added hardier new breeds of sheep, and encouraged his steward to try new crops. So far, he had indeed realized another fortune. At Coalfax, he funded a weaver's collective, providing looms and raw

materials—wool from Shearwater and his other estates—
and invited new tenants with weaving skills to come and live
there, rather than throwing folk off the land.

But this was Scotland. He knew nothing of how a clan
would feel if he brought in new folk, introduced new ways of
doing things. It could be a disaster. Even if he intended to go
back to England—especially since he intended to do so—he
needed advice.

One thing was certain. He intended to leave Glen Dorian
better than he found it.

CHAPTER TWENTY-SEVEN

Kit didn't come to the lodge for supper. Megan waited in her room, dressed and ready, yet not wishing to appear eager when he arrived to bathe and change, but the clock ticked on, and her stomach grumbled, and he did not appear.

She went down to the kitchen, where Jeannie was waiting with Leslie. They looked up at her hopefully. "Has his lordship not arrived yet, Mister Leslie?"

"No, my lady, and it's growing quite dark," the manservant said, despite the fact it was still light. He rubbed his hands together anxiously. "If I may be so bold as to ask, are there wolves in these mountains?"

Megan's heart clenched. There may not be wolves, but there were other things. What if Kit had fallen, or something had fallen on him? Again the old worry filled her, the thought that even now he might be lying in the castle, watching the sky darken above him, his leg or his arm trapped, or bleeding, or his leg broken.

"I'm sure he's just lost track of the time. Jeannie, pack up some food, and I'll take it up to him. I'll just go up and change my gown and come back."

She hurried upstairs, wondering if she'd need bandages, or a sharp knife. She decided to take both, stuffing a sheet into a bag to tear up if it was necessary to bind a wound or staunch bleeding, and a knife to cut the cloth. Her heart was pounding when she returned downstairs and found the basket ready and waiting.

By the time she'd arrived at the glen, she was imagining the worst, and praying that he would live until she arrived. She recalled with a twinge of guilt that she'd wished him ill after he'd so rudely rejected her mother's proposal at Dundrummie—more than ill. And if there was the curse . . . She picked up her skirts and moved faster. Highland tales were full of ghosts and curses and ill-wishings. Surely some must come true. She stopped dead in her tracks as she reached the edge of the glen.

He was sitting on the grass in front of the cottage, staring down at the loch, lost in thought, the setting sun lighting his face, turning it to bronze, his hair to burnished copper. She paused with her hand on her heart, so relieved her knees nearly gave way. Then she switched the basket to her opposite arm and carried on toward him. She wanted to fall into his arms, tell him she's been worried, afraid.

She frowned. If he was unhurt, why hadn't he bothered to come for supper? She felt the sharp pinch of anger. He was avoiding her. She was tempted to melt back into the trees and go back to the lodge and let him go hungry.

But he turned his head and saw her standing there. For a moment they stared at one another. Then he rose and began to come down the slope toward her.

"Leslie and Jeannie were most concerned when you didn't come for supper. They imagined something dreadful must have happened to you."

He took the basket from her. "You weren't worried?" he asked.

She sent him a level look. "Of course not. I assumed you were avoiding me. If that's the case, I'll not interrupt. I've brought the food—Jeannie insisted—and I'll go."

"No, stay. Please stay. This basket is heavy enough that I assume there's enough food for at least two."

Megan followed him up the slope, and he stopped on the hillside in front of the cottage, and opened the basket. He found the sheet she'd brought for bandages, and looked at her. She felt her face heat at her own foolish fears. She snatched it from his hand and spread it over the grass. "Jeannie thought it would be a fine night for a picnic."

"Jeannie does a great deal of thinking," he said. "What did she pack for supper?"

"Ham," Megan said, and watched as he unwrapped the pot. "Chicken," she amended, seeing the contents.

They ate in silence. Megan was too anxious to eat very much. She pretended to nibble, all the while watching him to see if he was indeed injured, looking for signs of a bandage under his shirt, an awkward movement, a wince of pain, but he simply looked lost in his own thoughts.

"What are you thinking about?" she asked at last, and he turned to look at her, his eyes widening as if surprised to see her there.

"Hmm? Oh, I was wondering what people do here. Does Eleanor have tenants?"

"Yes, of course. She raises Highland cattle. They're in the hills now, fattening up. In a few weeks, before the frost, they'll come down and go to market."

"And are there farms?"

"Yes, of course."

"And what do people grow? What crops, what livestock, how do they live?" he fired at her and she drew back.

"They raise cows, and sheep, and grow oats and barley. They fish, too. Is that so different from what folk do in England?"

"No, not at all. I just wondered . . ."

"I've heard tales that they used to make whisky here in the glen," she said. "Eleanor told me."

"Whisky?" He looked at her.

"Yes, whisky. The oldest folk remember it, and they make it sound as if there was no finer drink on earth, or heaven, for that matter."

"Why did they stop?"

She looked across the glen. "The most fanciful tales say the heart went out of the people after the forty-five, and their tears made the whisky bitter. More sensible folk say the government taxed the making of whisky, and since many couldn't pay, they took their kettles deep into the hills, became smugglers, then they died out."

"What does your brother do at Glenlorne?" Kit asked.

"Alec? Oh I suppose he's a rare creature, a laird determined to protect and provide for his people. He's given them hope and opportunities."

He turned to look at her. "But if there are opportunities here, then why do young men like your Eachann have to leave?"

She bristled. "He'll come back."

"Then what?" he asked, biting into a mouthful of bread.

"Then we'll build a house, and live in it."

"And after that?" he insisted. "What will your children do, and their children, and all the children of Clan McNabb for that matter?"

She bit her lip. "Well, I suppose they will be free to do whatever they wish to do. They will remember the old ways, the stories, and the traditions—I'll see to that—but we want them to know the new ways as well. Alec feels that way too. He's building new cottages, a school, and adding more cattle, new breeds of sheep. He's offered to send the brightest lads to school in Edinburgh, so they can learn to be doctors, or to build bridges and roads. He's determined to keep the clan intact, or give those who wish to go a helping hand, let them know they're always, always welcome to come home again. I will do likewise—my children will learn to care for the land, the people, and each other."

"But what if your brother's heir decides that his land is better suited to livestock than people, and the cottages and tenant farms are in the way? What then?"

"Alec? Never!"

"What about Eleanor? What of Dundrummie after she's gone?"

Megan frowned. "So many questions! I don't know. I don't know who will inherit her land. Someone will."

He studied her. "Someone like Eachann, perhaps?"

"No, not like Eachann. Eachann took ship for India. He wants to become a trader. If he's successful, he intends to ask Alec to invest in another venture, a bigger one, and let him lead it."

"How could your brother say no if Eachann is married to you?"

She felt her skin heat. She hadn't thought of that. She recalled now how long and often Eachann had spoken of his plans, his travels, and Alec's money. She'd been the one who talked of a house and babies. It gave her an uneasy feeling.

"How indeed?" she chirped, and began to clear away the remains of their meal. "I'd best be getting back. It's getting dark earlier, now that autumn is coming closer."

"I'll walk you back." He rose, offered her his hand, and pulled her up. She felt lightning sing through her veins at his touch, and she found herself standing inches from him, nearly nose to nose. Her hand still clasped in his.

"Oh," she said.

His gaze fell to her mouth, and he drew a sharp breath. Her heart leaped in anticipation as he leaned in and lowered his lips to hers.

Megan shut her eyes, concentrated on the buzz of desire that coursed through her at the simple, gentle kiss. After a moment, he pulled her into his arms, and slanted his mouth over hers. Her body melted into his, her breasts pressed to his chest, her belly against his.

He was the second man she'd ever kissed, if she counted Eachann. Perhaps that didn't count at all—this kiss was completely different. She felt hot all over, and cold, and drunk, and infinitely aware of the feeling of his lips on hers. His lips were mobile, insistent. He drew her lower lip into his mouth and she stayed still, allowed it, and he gently explored the inside of her lip. He kissed her mouth, her cheek, moved along her jaw to the pulse point at the base of her neck, and kissed her there too. Her heart was beating like a trapped bird. When he found her lips again, she sighed and kissed him back, inexpertly. He nipped at her lips, slipped his tongue inside her mouth to spar with hers. The intimacy was stunning, unbelievable, delicious. Her knees weakened and she slid her arms around his neck, and pressed closer still.

He let her go so suddenly that she almost fell, and he steadied her. "Forgive me," he said, his eyes on hers, his breath ragged. "I don't know what came over me."

"No harm done," she managed. "I wasn't thinking."

He stepped back a little. "Honesty, remember? What *were* you thinking?"

She let her eyes drop to the open collar of his shirt, stared at the vee of golden skin. "Um, I was thinking it was a very nice kiss," she said. "What were *you* thinking?"

"That I'd never enjoyed a kiss so thoroughly."

Her mouth watered to do it again, but he sighed and turned away. "I don't think we should, though," he said, answering her unspoken desire.

"No," she agreed, though there was nothing she wanted more. "It was only a kiss, of course. I think that it would be perfectly within the rules."

"What rules?" he asked.

"The rules of handfasting."

He gave her a slow grin that made her heart pirouette in her chest. "I daresay the rules allow far more than a kiss, but we'd best leave it at that, and see that it doesn't happen again, just to be on the safe side."

"What if it does?" she whispered. They were still inches away from each other, and she raised her hands to the lapel of his coat, and his hands found her waist, rested there.

"Then I will apologize profusely," he said, and lowered his mouth to hers once again, even as she rose on her toes to meet him halfway.

Chapter Twenty-Eight

He walked her home, his hand under her arm in the twilight. It was a simple, polite, careful touch, and nothing more, but she was aware of him, the rub of his shoulder against hers, the careful way he guided her past roots and rocks that poked through the path, as if she was the most precious thing on earth. At the gate, he'd stepped back, let her go, and smiled at her, the light in his eyes intimate, devastating, and she'd wanted to kiss him again. He gave her a half-smile and bowed, taking her hand instead. He kissed her fingertips in a courtly gesture. "Goodnight, Megan," he said softly.

She resisted the urge to curtsy, to hold tight to his hand and not let him go. She'd clasped her hands together instead. "Goodnight, Kit."

He waited until she reached the door, and went inside. She felt his eyes on her back. The second the latch clicked behind her, she raced upstairs, threw back the curtains on the nearest window, and watched him go, his strides long and sure, his hands clasped behind his back. Her heart hammered against her ribs, and her lips tingled. Sweet, he'd tasted sweet, and as long as she lived, she wouldn't forget that, no matter how old she grew, or how much she loved Eachann. Was that wrong? She laid the back of her hand against her lips. It most certainly was.

Kit walked slowly through the twilight, back to the glen, and the cottage. He wouldn't sleep tonight. He had thinking to do. Oh, not about Megan, or kissing her, or the overpowering desire he felt for her, but other, more important things. Unfortunately, he could not seem to tear his thoughts away from the way she felt in his arms, the soft sounds she made when he kissed her, half surprise, half desire.

He should not have done it. In England, a kiss like that— *kisses* like that, for they'd stood there in each other's arms for quite some time—would be tantamount to a clear declaration of a gentleman's intent, if not an actual proposal. He'd find himself forced to marry Megan McNabb in earnest if he wasn't careful. He stopped walking, watched a hawk on the wing, hunting for a last meal before night came. Would it be so bad to have Megan for a wife?

He pictured his mother's reaction, her shock veiled, yet visible in every disapproving line of her body, and the purse of her lips. She was the only woman he knew who could purse her lips and smile at the same time. Arabella would laugh— she'd bray like a horse—and his brother would regard him with the familiar look of bafflement and pity, as if Kit was somehow letting the family down, disappointing their father's hopes, yet could not precisely understand how. He simply was not his father, or his older brother.

For the first time since he'd inherited the title, Megan made him feel as if he was worthy after all—worthy of attention, of conversation, and of kissing. Had any other woman ever kissed him the way she had, freely, without expectation of reward? Megan was the first honest person he'd met in a very long time. But then, he reminded himself, she didn't want him as a husband, any more than he wanted her as a wife. Still . . .

He paused on the edge of the glen and looked out at the soft light that fell over the hills, the loch, the old castle. He felt for an instant that he belonged here, or wanted to belong here at least. He *wished* he belonged here, with Megan. But she'd given her heart to someone else, and her future was decided, and there was no place for Kit when the year and a day came to an end. How would they part when the year was done—with a kiss? He groaned and walked up the hill to the cottage.

Inside, he lit a lamp, and took out Nathaniel's journal. He needed something else to think about besides kissing Megan McNabb.

CHAPTER TWENTY-NINE

Glen Dorian, April 16, 1746

"Ruairidh's gone," Mairi said to Connor, hurrying up the hill toward him as he spoke with a clansman in the dawn light.

Connor's eyes darkened he gripped her shoulders. "Did he go with Iain to Nairn, to join the prince?"

Mairi felt tears sting her eyes, and her belly tightened with fear. "How could he have? No, Ruairidh was here last night. Iain left yesterday morning, long before."

"I might as well tell you that Donal and Alain have gone as well, laird, against your orders," the clansman said, his face grim. "And there are others, too. They have kin among the MacIntoshes of Moy, and they left to join them. They want to fight for Charlie Stuart. Word has come that they're gathering at Culloden Moor."

"Connor, Ruairidh's just a child!" Mairi cried. "He's too young to go to war. We have to do something!"

Connor muttered under his breath, and she saw the worry in his eyes, the way he looked anxiously around the glen. "I'll go after him, find him before anything happens—the others, too, if I can persuade them to come back. How long ago did Ruairidh go?"

Mairi wrung her hands. "I don't know—Sometime in the night. His bed was empty this morning, his pack gone." She began to cry again.

He wiped away her tears with the pad of his thumb. "I'll find him, *Mo chroi*." He put his hand to her cheek. "You stay here and take care of things, hmm?"

She closed her hand on his for a moment, and gave him a watery smile. "Will you take food with you?"

He nodded. "Ruairidh will be hungry. You can pack it while I get my horse ready, but hurry."

He led her back down the hill to the castle, and the clansman followed. "Is there anything I can do, laird?" he asked, and Mairi watched Connor nod, his face grim.

"Keep watch while I'm gone, Fionn," he said. "Help Mairi keep everyone safe."

Mairi followed him down the hill toward the castle, felt the icy wind cut through her woolen gown and her plaid shawl and chill her very bones, and feared what would come of this day.

CHAPTER THIRTY

Megan changed her gown three times the next morning, trying to find something that was alluring, yet not too alluring, and pretty, yet sober. She settled on a green muslin walking dress with long sleeves and ribbon trim. Her heart thumped at the prospect of seeing Kit again.

It thumped a little less when he didn't come out of the cottage to meet her.

It stopped dead in her chest and fell into the pit of her stomach when she realized he wasn't in the cottage, or standing on the shore of the loch, or coming over the edge of the glen. He wasn't here. She stared at the castle, and wondered if he was inside, busy, and if he'd really mind if she crossed the causeway to find him. She wasn't prying—she simply wished to bid him a good day, to look in his eyes, and see if the kiss had affected him as much as it had her. That's all—nothing more.

She would sit and wait for him, she decided. She went into the cottage and sat down at the table, and stared across the surface of the wood. The minutes ticked slowly past, and still

Kit didn't return. Megan sighed and paced the floor—bare earth, carefully swept—had Kit swept it? The bed was made, too, after a fashion. It made her smile that he hadn't done any better than she had with that task. She glanced at the shelf, noted the cup and plate and pot, and paused. There was a stack of books there, and she took the top one down to look at it.

A piece of paper fluttered loose and fell to her feet like the first yellow leaf of autumn as she opened the cover. She bent to retrieve it. It was a letter—but who would be writing to Kit here? Perhaps one of the hopefully ladies had penned a billet-doux to tell him of her love, to plead with him to kiss *her*. Megan's lips rippled. He wasn't allowed to kiss anyone else, not for a year and a day. The idea pleased her somehow. She glanced at the letter. She'd never received a love letter, not even from Eachann.

She frowned. The letter wasn't addressed to Kit. It was addressed to someone named Connor MacIntosh at the Inverness Gaol. The hair on the back of her neck rose. "Now why would you have this?" she wondered aloud, asking the air. Had he found it in the old castle, where it had lain lost and forgotten for over seventy years? Curious, Megan opened the worn folds and sat down to read it.

CHAPTER THIRTY-ONE

Glen Dorian, April 16, 1746

Mairi MacIntosh stared out the window of her bedroom, looking out across the glen to the road that ran through the gap between two hills—the road that would bring Connor and Ruairidh back safely. It was almost dark, and her heart was lodged in her throat, fearing the worst. She tried to concentrate on her sewing—a tiny shirt for the baby she carried, a baby that not even Connor knew about yet. She would tell him tonight, when everyone was home and safe and life was normal again. The fine linen dropped from her nerveless fingers as a horse and rider burst through the pass.

Connor! She put a hand to her heart, felt it pounding against her ribs. But the horse was black, not Connor's dun-colored garron. She saw a red coat, and a cry of fear escaped her lips, but as the rider drew closer still, she saw the flutter of MacIntosh plaid flying out behind like a sail in the wind. There were two people on the horse.

She picked up her skirts and rushed down the stairs, not knowing what to do first. The folk in the hall stared at her, dread in their eyes. "Morag, set the table," she called. "Annie, heat some water."

She threw open the door and hurried into the courtyard as Nathaniel Linwood pulled his foaming horse to a stop. She read bad news in his eyes before he even spoke. She curled a hand against her belly, felt her knees weaken, feared the worst. She leaned against the wall, and forced herself to look at the body in the saddle behind him.

"Ruairidh!" she cried, rushing forward to catch her brother as he tumbled off the horse, exhausted. Tears and dirt smeared his face, and there was blood on his shirt. He began crying anew when he saw her, throwing himself into her arms.

"He's not hurt," Nathaniel said, as she looked at her brother in horror, rubbed at the blood and dirt on his face "He's just frightened."

"They took Connor," the boy sobbed, and Mairi met Nathaniel's eyes. He nodded.

Mairi felt the sky fall on her, suck the breath from her lungs, and she stared up at him, unable to speak.

"I'm sorry. I could not stop it. If I'd tried, they'd have taken the boy as well. They took him off with some other prisoners. He'll be in Inverness Gaol. I'll go and get him, bring him home."

"They fell on him with swords," Ruairidh said. "He was bleeding. They were all bleeding."

She looked at her brother, saw the fear in his eyes. In the span of hours, he'd aged a decade beyond his thirteen years.

Nathaniel wheeled his horse, and made ready to go. She caught his bridle, and the horse's eyes rolled in fear. "Wait," she said, "I'll come with you, tell them—" But he shook his head.

"The rebels lost the battle, Mairi. It was quick and brutal, a rout. It's no place for you now." He rubbed a hand over his eyes, and she read weariness in every line of his body. "I'll bring him back, I swear it."

She stepped back. She had no choice. She stood silently, feeling fear curl through her limbs like smoke, chill her to the bone. Nathaniel gazed at her for an instant longer as if he wished to say something, but looked away, let his eyes flick over Ruairidh, and closed his mouth. He set his spurs to his horse and was gone.

Chapter Thirty-Two

Megan could scarcely see the path that led through the glen beyond the blur of angry tears. She had no idea where she was going—anywhere away from the glen, and the castle, and *him*. It didn't matter.

She heard a shout, and hands caught her shoulders, stopping her.

"Hold on, lass, where are you off to in such a tearing hurry? You nearly ran me over!" Duncan MacIntosh said, letting her go, righting himself with the help of his stick—the very stick Megan and Kit had leaped over at their handfasting. "Och, no wonder you didn't see me. You've been crying."

"I most certainly have not!" Megan said, swiping at her cheeks.

"Yes you have. There have been enough tears shed in this glen if you ask me. In truth, there never used to be a loch here at all until—"

"I'm not in the mood for a tale today," Megan interrupted.

"Ah, there's been a lover's quarrel has there? I've all the

time in the world to hear your tale instead, and it's a lovely day, though it's sure to rain later."

"There isn't a cloud in the sky," Megan said, glancing up.

"I rely on my bones to tell me when bad weather is coming. You wait and see. There's going to be a fearsome storm."

"There will indeed," Megan murmured, and Duncan's white brows flew skyward.

"We're not talking about the weather now, are we? Tell me, what's your braw Sassenach done?"

"Do you know why he's here?" Megan demanded.

Duncan rubbed his chin. "Well, I know he's bought Glen Dorian, and he's handfasted with you, and all in just three short weeks of arriving. 'Tis a captivating place right enough—"

"There's a treasure!" she said.

He gave her a sweet-eyed look. "Of course there is. It's a very likely thing to happen when two young people fall in love. I trust you'll be staying together then—you have my congratulations."

Megan's jaw dropped. "You think that I'm—Oh, no, I'm certainly not with child!"

"Yet," the old man teased, winking at her.

"*Ever*," she said fiercely. "He had an old letter, written by Mairi to her husband, Connor, after the battle. It mentions a treasure that's hidden in Glen Dorian Castle. *That's* why Lord Rossington is here."

The old man's eyes sharpened. "A letter?"

"She entrusted it to someone named Linwood to deliver, and he kept it—*he kept it!*"

Duncan frowned and held up a gnarled hand. "Now don't

work yourself into a lather, lass. Nathaniel Linwood was a good man as I recall him." He moved over to sit on the boulder, and patted the other half of the makeshift bench. "Sit down, lass, and I'll tell you what I know. My old bones don't keep me upright the way they used to." He took out his pipe and put it into his mouth, unlit, and pondered the hills and the heather for a long moment. "I've lived here in Glen Dorian all my life. I was born here, in the castle itself, and I daresay I'll die here when the time comes, and that won't be long now."

"Were you here when Mairi lived?" Megan asked.

"Aye, of course I was. My father was Connor MacIntosh's *seannachaidh*, and his father served Connor's father before him, and so on. I was raised to be the next MacIntosh tradition bearer, but the line will end with me." He pointed at her with the stem of his pipe. "It is my sacred duty, as you know, to see the old tales are told, and passed on. Now what did the letter say?"

She told him, and watched as his eyes filled with sadness.

"I daresay she wrote the letter in the days after Culloden. Connor left here the day of the battle to find his brother—the Ruairidh she mentions. He was Mairi's wee brother in truth, but Connor made the lad his brother as well when he married her. Ruairidh had been forbidden to set foot out of the glen, but he ran off to see the great battle, thinking it would be an adventure. He wanted to see Charlie Stuart in the flesh, watch the clansmen rout the English, send them south with their tails a 'twixt their legs. He said later that there were a number of boys there that day, all hiding in the heather on the edge of the moor, watching the men gather. Young Archie Fraser was only nine, there to watch his father, the chief of the Frasers, lead his men out. Archie told the tale often, for it was the last time he saw his father's face. If the chief had known the boy was there, he would have thrashed him and sent him home to his mother where he belonged. As it was, the lad wished for the rest of his life he hadn't been at Culloden Moor that day. He saw things no boy should see, including his father's death, and Connor's wee brother Ruairidh was right beside him."

"Did Connor find him and bring him home?" she asked.

"Aye, he found him, but he wasn't the one to bring Ruairidh back to Glen Dorian. The battle had ended, and the clans had lost. Those who still lived fled from the field, including the lads who'd been hiding in the heather. Ruairidh got caught in the retreat. He saw Connor, all right, but just as a soldier in a red coat slashed him across the back with his saber. He watched the laird fall to his knees, bloodied, but alive. It was then that Ruairidh himself was snatched up by a soldier."

Megan gasped, and he shot her a look. "Aye, and you'd be even more surprised to know it was Captain Nathaniel Linwood who caught him up. Do you recognize the name? He's your own Rossington's ancestor, lass. I knew it when he gave me his name at the handfasting. He's come back so the tale can end at last. Captain Linwood saved Ruairidh MacIntosh's life that day, and after, too."

"What happened to Connor?" Megan asked.

Duncan sighed and gnawed on his pipe. "He was taken away to Inverness Gaol with all the other prisoners in their hundreds. Nathaniel couldn't stop it, though he tried. They wanted the boy, too, and Nathaniel had to choose, or lose both. He took Ruairidh home to Mairi, promised her he'd bring Connor back as well."

He stopped talking, and Megan stared at him. "Then what?" she asked.

He squinted at her. "He didn't come back—Connor, I mean. When Linwood came back to the glen, it was to warn Mairi that the redcoats were marching on her, looking to steal and destroy and burn. She had to flee. My mother went with Mairi, up into the hills, with me just wee a child in her arms. Mairi gathered as many clanspeople as she could, led them to safety. The rest were lost, killed, or arrested, like Connor himself. We found a cave in the hills—a corrie that Mairi knew—and hid ourselves there, in fear for our lives, and for the lives of our men." He stared down the hill at the castle. "We looked down the glen and watched as the soldiers took what they wanted, then set fire to our cottages and the castle, and drove off our cattle. They left nothing."

Megan watched his eyes grow misty as he relived that day, seeing it. "Mairi hoped, dreamed. She was sure that Connor would return to her. My mother was just as certain that my father wasn't coming home again. It was she who told me all the tales she could remember, the ones she'd heard my father tell over and over again. The rest of Clan MacIntosh's stories are lost, lass, gone with Connor, my father, and Mairi. I had to start again. I am the *seannachaidh*, responsible for keeping the clan history, you see, and telling it, like I am now. I never thought I'd learn the end of Mairi's story, but you're here, and you're Linwood. How it will end, I haven't a clue."

"Do you know where the treasure is?" Megan asked.

Duncan shook his head. "No. Mairi never spoke of it that

I know of. In fact, I've not heard of it until today. She only told the clan that all would be well again when Connor came home. Over and over she said that, every day, never giving up hope."

Megan felt sorrow sink into her bones. "Then it is lost forever."

He looked at her. "Is it? It seems that man of yours—another Linwood—intends to find it."

"Steal it, you mean," Megan replied. "And he's not my man."

Duncan chuckled. "Not your man? I handfasted the pair of you, lass, remember? I know what I saw—I thought you were in love. I've seen that look before in a pair of Linwood eyes."

Megan felt her skin flush. "You're mistaken. It was a matter of expedience, and convenience, and—" She couldn't find the word she wanted.

"Kindness?" Duncan asked, chewing his pipe. "Honor? The Linwoods all seem to be kind, honorable men, despite the fact they're English. Brave, too. The captain certainly was all those things, even when he might have been hanged by his own side for his kindness, or had his throat cut by ours. He took a terrible risk. I was just a child, but I remember him coming to that cave—" He pointed off into the highest hills at the end of the glen. "He brought us food, blankets, medicine, news . . ."

"What happened?"

"Hmm?" Duncan focused on her. "He kept us alive through the winter, but he stopped coming after a time. I think he fell in love with her, but she could not love him back while her heart belonged to Connor. But now he's returned."

Megan frowned, wondering if the old *seannachaidh* was addled, or confused. "No, Duncan, it's not Nathaniel. He's dead. It's Kit who's here now—*Christopher* Linwood—and he's not here for kindness' sake."

He smiled at her gently as if he thought she was the daft one. "Is he not? I thought you fancied yourself a *seannachaidh*, lass. D'you not understand how tales work? They need an ending—a happy one is best, if that's possible, or at least a hopeful one. Things in this world come full circle, back to where they began. Wrongs can be righted, secrets revealed, if you can wait long enough."

He rose to his feet and tucked his pipe away into his coat. "Well, I must be off. Come and tell me when you find it."

"The treasure?" Megan asked.

"Och, no—the ending to the tale, lass, the ending. That's what's important. You'd best go too, find shelter before the storm hits."

Megan looked up again at the clear blue sky. When she turned back to argue about the weather, Duncan MacIntosh was gone.

Chapter Thirty-Three

She blew into the castle like an ill wind.

Kit looked up from where he was shifting the last beam that blocked the staircase. Megan came across the room, her eyes blazing, her determined steps ringing on the stone floor. He felt his heart leap at the sight of her, then fall flat at the anger in her expression.

He descended the steps toward her.

"I came to tell you that I'm leaving—tomorrow, in fact."

So soon? His chest clenched, and he swallowed. Had the kiss upset her so much? "I see," he said carefully. She was staring at the floor between his feet.

"I want to end our—agreement. I intend to go home to Glenlorne and wait for Eachann."

"And you'll want to marry right away," he said, keeping his tone flat, though jealousy churned in his belly.

"Yes."

The wind caught the shutter behind him and blew it against the wall with a boom that filled the whole castle. Megan cried out, and he stepped toward her, but stopped short of taking her into his arms. "Just the wind," he murmured, but she cried out again—and so did he—as the rain followed, a sudden unexpected downpour. Water descended as if it had been poured from a bucket, coming in a torrent through the broken roof. The heavy drops bounced and sizzled on the floor like musket balls. He grabbed her hand and pulled her toward the steps, sheltered from the deluge by the overhanging floor above. "Come on—we'll be soaked if we stay here. The roof appears to be intact upstairs."

She looked up the long stone staircase and hesitated. "Is it safe?"

"I don't know—I haven't been up there yet, but the floor looks sound enough from here. I don't think the fire made it beyond the stairs—there's another wing, I think, or at least a few rooms that might have been spared when the roof of the hall fell in."

A crash of thunder echoed off the stones, and she flattened herself against the wall and looked up at the lead gray sky. The rain fell on her upturned face, and Kit grabbed his pack and pulled her upwards. "Come on," he said. "We'll shelter here until the rain stops—it's too far to go all the way back to the cottage. Do these showers last long?"

She followed him. "I don't know. It was a fair day when I left the lodge, but the autumn weather in the Highlands can be unpredictable."

He paused on the top step, and they looked down a narrow passageway, dark as pitch. Part way along, a door stood open, the room beyond illuminated with thin gray storm light. "Wait here until I'm sure it's safe," he said, but she refused to let go of his hand.

"Who'll keep you safe?" she asked. Kit saw fear in her eyes, though she was doing her best to hide it. Her chin was high, her back stiff with determination. Her hair was wet, and water shone on her pale face, and he resisted the urge to brush away the lock of sodden hair. It would only lead to a desire to kiss her, and then—he turned away.

"We'll go slowly," he said, meaning walking on the ancient wooden planks of the floor, of course.

The boards felt solid enough. They moved forward until they came to the open door, and stood on the threshold. "It's a bedroom," he said.

"I can see that," she murmured.

A carved bed stood against one wall, once vast and regal, though worm-eaten and cracked by age and weather now. The mattress had long since been picked apart by birds and other nesting creatures, who had stolen the straw and the feathers and left only the torn canvas shell. The blankets and the linens were gone. The window shutter hung wide open, but the roof was intact. Kit drew a breath and crossed the room to pull the shutter closed. The wind fought for control, and he was instantly soaked, but finally closed the latch.

"It's dark," she murmured, and bent to look at the fire-place, then at him. "There's plenty of wood downstairs. We might as well light a fire and be warm."

While he went down to gather what wood he could, Megan gathered scraps of old cloth and dry moss. Together they watched the smoke curl as the flame opened one bright eye, fed it small pieces of wood until it grew strong, demanded bigger fuel.

Megan rose and prowled the room, her hands wrapped around her wet gown.

"Look at this," she crouched to open the lid of a carved wooden chest, and Kit held his breath.

The box contained a few moldering garments, and a length of age-darkened plaid that was stiff and dirty. Kit gingerly lifted the plaid and peered beneath it.

"No treasure, I take it," she said tartly and he turned to look at her.

"I found the letter Mairi wrote, in the cottage," she said. "That's why you're here, isn't it, in Scotland?"

Was there any point in denying it? "Yes. I found the letter in England, among my great-uncle's things," he murmured, his stomach tensing at the disdain in her eyes. "It was in his journal." He stopped, not sure what else to say.

"And have you found it yet?" she demanded. "Or did *he* steal it all those years ago?"

She was beautiful, even angry, filled with indignation, but he felt his own anger flare. "Nathaniel didn't even know what was in that letter. It was still sealed when I found it. I was the one who opened it."

She made a sound of disbelief, and got up and went to the window. She stared out at the rain through a long narrow crack in the shutter with her arms folded across her chest. "He loved her, you know," she said with her back to him. "Nathaniel loved Mairi, I mean." The silver light lit her cheeks, the long white length of her swan's neck, the slim curves of her figure. The wet muslin of her gown was sticking to her legs, and he could see the long, lean shape of them. He tried not to look, but he couldn't help it. His eyes refused to budge.

He felt hot blood fill his face as she turned suddenly, her eyes sharp, but she didn't seem to have noticed he'd been staring. "Duncan MacIntosh told me," she said. "He was here then, just a wee bairn, but he remembers Nathaniel Linwood. He said he was a good man, kind and brave."

"I hope so," Kit said. He heard the wood crackle behind him, looked to see the flames licking the edge of the timbers, wondered if Nathaniel had ever stood here, in this room, staring at Mairi just this way. "I never met my great-uncle myself. He died just as I was being born. I can imagine he must have loved her, though, especially if she was like—" He clamped his lips shut on the thought he hadn't meant to speak aloud, but Megan turned to look at him, her brows raised, waiting.

"Like what?"

He was trapped now. He met her eyes, foundered in the hazel depths. "Like you," he said softly. "If she was like you."

"Me?" she asked. The colors in her eyes changed from russet to gold, before her lashes swept down, and a blush bloomed over her face.

He took a step toward her. "I suppose Nathaniel knew Mairi somewhat longer than you and I have known one another, but it seems to me that she must have been fierce, loyal, stubborn, and brave like you—especially given the situation she faced. She was willing to protect what she loved, and she never gave up." He stopped when he reached her side. She had to look up to meet his eyes because he was taller than she, stronger, broader. He felt acutely the differences between his male body and her female one. He read uncertainty in her eyes before she looked away again, back out the window, but she didn't move from his side, or flinch at his nearness.

"I—she—would have been lost without Nathaniel—or so Duncan says. But she couldn't love him back," she murmured, flustered.

"Perhaps that's why he never married. He couldn't forget her." He was close enough to feel the heat of her body, smell the soft sweet scent of her soap. "But her heart was already given to someone else. Like yours."

She turned her head, and her face was inches from his. "Mine?"

"Eachann," he said, and the word came out rough and cold.

She looked away. "Oh, yes," she said it as if she'd forgotten Eachann Rennie existed. But he did exist. Kit put his hand on her arm, and even that simple touch was erotic, stirring.

"I will let you go, Megan."

"Like Nathaniel did with Mairi?"

Kit swallowed. Would his great-uncle have left if Mairi had given him a choice, or would he have stayed, knowing there would always be a ghost between them? "I suppose so," he said. "Why did you come today? You could have just gone, left a note for me in the cottage."

Her chin rose. "I wanted to thank you. No, I wanted to ask you—beg you—not to tear this castle down."

He frowned. "Tear it down? I have no intention of tearing it down."

"Then what will you do now? Will you go home to England?" she asked. "You can't stay here forever. You said so yourself. You have responsibilities."

He gazed out at the glen, let his eyes move over the rain-wet hills, shrouded in mist and the yellow light of the storm.

Even in bad weather, he loved it here, felt at home here, but she was quite right. He couldn't stay. Without Megan it would be . . . He pushed the feeling of loss away. "Yes, I suppose I will go back to England."

"Then I wish you well." She stood on her toes, put her hands on his shoulders, and kissed him on the cheek.

He should have left it there, or offered his hand for her to shake, or bowed and walked away, but it was still raining, and there was nowhere to walk away to, not without getting soaked. He didn't want to say good-bye to her in the rain—or in the sun for that matter. So he did the only thing he could think of.

He turned his head and kissed her properly.

Her lips melted under his, fitting perfectly to his. He tasted the sweetness of the rain, smelled heather. When he remembered Scotland, he would think of the scent of Megan's hair, the softness of her skin, the colors of her eyes, the quirk of her smile, and the unbearable delight of kissing her. He didn't want to stop kissing her, couldn't. He trailed soft butterfly kisses over her mouth, her chin, her cheeks, and she tilted her head to grant him better access, and he took it, though he knew he should not. She sighed, and he returned to her mouth, and this time her lips parted for him, and his tongue tentatively touched hers, brushing over the delicacy of the inside of her lower lip, before finding her tongue. Her arms crept around his neck, tangled in his hair, and she pressed nearer still, her body joined to his from knee to breast. He looked down at her.

Her eyes were shut, her face soft and sweet and rosy, and he shut his own eyes, reveling in the feeling of Megan in his arms, the rightness of it—and the wrong of it, too. He knew that, somewhere in the back of his mind, but it was a small thing compared to his need for her. Her tongue sought his, and he let her taste him, felt desire stir, a longing for more. He angled his head, deepened the kiss. Had a kiss ever felt like this before? He couldn't remember, didn't want to think about anything but her. Her soft moan went straight to his groin like a lightning strike.

Kit forced himself to pull back—back as far as only kissing her cheek, and her eyelids and her forehead instead of her mouth. "We really should stop," he said, his lips pressed against her temple. She opened her eyes. They were wide and dark and soft with her own need. It didn't help the situation. He was instantly hard and ready.

"I—suppose we should." Her voice was smoky and regretful.

"Not that I want to." He couldn't seem to let go of her.

She fixed her gaze on his chin, and her fingertip began to draw distracting little circles on his shirtfront. "We could—well, I mean we have the *right* to do this, Kit, if we both want to. We are pledged for a year and a day, and that includes the nights, too."

"But it's scarcely past noon," he said stupidly and shook his head. "I mean, do you understand what you're asking? What about Eac—"

She put her finger against his lips before he could speak his rival's name. There was fierce determination in her eyes as she looked at him. There was longing, too. "I don't want to think about anyone else now. Just you and me. And since it's still raining and we can't leave . . ." She let the thought trail off.

He kissed her fingertip, held her hand in his, mesmerized by the sensual way her fingernails curled against his palm. "We don't have to—um—we could sit and talk, or just sit without talking, if you prefer." The look in her eyes told him she wasn't interested in either of those activities. "Or—" He swallowed.

"Yes," she whispered. "That." She pressed closer still, and her hip brushed his erection, making him crazy. He tried to force his wits into line, to concentrate.

"That? Yes?" he parroted as his wits abandoned him. They weren't truly gone, just residing in his damned cock. She moved her hips again, a sinuous swirl that made him grit his teeth and hiss.

"Kiss me again," she said, and he let his eyes fall to her lush mouth, soft and expectant, and he kissed her ear instead, nibbled on the lobe.

"I won't be able to stop if I start kissing you again," he babbled, though he'd already started. She had the softest skin, and he found the sensitive pulse point beneath her ear, and nibbled.

"Good," she said on a moan.

"But I will if you want me to, Megan—if you change your mind—I swear it." Honor was everything. Or was it love? He couldn't remember.

"Stop talking," she whispered, and rose on her toes to kiss his eyelids the way he'd kissed hers, then his cheeks and his nose. She stopped and looked at him, a deep blush rising over her cheeks. "Oh. I suppose you'll have to talk, at least to tell me what to do." She said it as if she expected a tutorial in the matter, a lesson. Of course she would—she'd been taught how to dance, how to address a duchess, and how to plan a dinner party for twenty guests. And now . . .

He couldn't help it. He threw back his head and laughed. "You're doing just fine, sweetheart," he said. He leaned closer to whisper in her ear. "Tell me what you like."

"I like—oh . . ." She sighed as he ran his mouth along the length of her neck. "Oh, I like that," she murmured.

Kit smiled against her collarbone. He concentrated on learning the delicate curves there, kissed the throbbing pulse. He ran his hands over her back, felt the indent of her waist, the flare of her hips, and the sweet swell of her bottom through her thin wet gown. She shivered and pressed nearer.

"Are you cold?" he asked.

"I'm on fire," she replied, and put her hands on his buttocks too, following him touch for touch, learning by copying. It was erotic, teasing, delicious. Kit imagined the pleasures of the game without the impediment of clothes. He wanted her naked, her skin against his, their bodies twined, joined.

"We really should take off our wet clothes," he said. Had he shocked her? He took off his coat, tossed it onto the post of the ancient bed, and immediately felt her hands on the buttons of his shirt. Not shocked, then.

"You'll have to help me—my gown buttons up the back," she said simply, and he reached over her shoulders, trying to ignore the tickle of her nails on his chest as she unfastened his shirt, opened it, let her eyes fall on his naked flesh. He seemed to have forgotten how buttons worked, and his fingers felt clumsy and slow on the ridiculously small pearls that closed her gown.

She slid her palms across his chest and over his shoulders, sliding the fine linen out of her way. He watched her eyes travel over him, fall on the muscles of his chest, the flat nipples, the small scars and marks of an active childhood. Had she looked at Eachann this way, naked, unclothed? She slid her arms around his ribs and pressed her cheek to his chest, and he held her there. "I can hear your heart beating," she said, and laid a kiss on his skin.

He worked at her buttons, wanting her as naked as he was. His hands shook, but somehow he managed . . . one, then two, then three. He felt the soft silk of her chemise beneath, the lacey, feminine edge of her undergarments, and felt frustration that so many layers of clothing barred him from touching her.

He fought three more buttons, and wondered how many more of the bloody things there were. It was open halfway down her back. For now, it was enough. She shut her eyes as he slid the muslin off her shoulders, down her arms, exposing the soft smooth skin of her shoulders, kissing every inch as the fabric retreated before his questing lips. He undid the ribbon that held her chemise closed, and cupped the weight of her breasts in his hands, naked, soft, and warm. She gasped and dug her nails into his shoulders.

Was she alarmed, frightened? He looked at her, but her eyes were heavy lidded, her mouth soft with desire. "How beautiful you are," he murmured, and rolled his thumb over her nipples, watched her flush, heard her sigh, felt her hands flutter on his shoulders. She stepped back, and he frowned. Now she would ask him to stop, he thought.

But she didn't say a word. She wriggled out of her gown,

let it fall at her feet, tossed the chemise and the stays away, too, until she was standing in a froth of silk and muslin and lace. Through it was cold, she didn't cover herself. She stood naked before him, wearing only her stockings, tied up under her knees with blue ribbons, and let him look at her. She was perfect. He stared like a ninny. She wasn't at all like the angels that graced the ceiling of his great houses—she was better by far. Could an artist capture such beauty, do it justice? Perhaps it was the Highland light, and the silver mist of the rain, the golden glow of the fire.

"What happens now?" she asked softly.

The room was cold, and he held out a hand to her. "Come by the fire," Kit said. "No, wait—" He opened his pack and took out the length of plaid Leslie had given him and suggested he wear. He'd carried it for days, thinking it might do to keep the sun off at some point. Now, he folded it and laid it in front of the fire. He knelt on the edge and held out his hand again. "Come here, sweetheart."

She came forward and stood before him. He set his hands on her waist, kissed her belly and her hipbones. He untied her garters, let her lean on him as he slipped her stockings off and tossed them aside.

She dropped to her knees too, put her arms around him, brought her mouth to his. Her skin on his was warm, soft, and he explored the lines of her back as he kissed her. Her hands roamed over him, too, tangling in his hair, smoothing over the muscles of his back, dipping into the waistband of his breeches. She paused only a moment before slipping inside to caress his buttocks the way he was touching hers. He gasped and gritted his teeth against the rush of lust.

Slowly he lay back, drawing her down with him, pressing the length of her body against his.

"You're still wearing your boots, my lord," she said softly. "And your—inexpressibles? We call them breeks here, but Miss Carruthers said we are never to mention any garment a gentleman wears below his waist." She giggled nervously. "Though I don't suppose it matters in this moment, does it?"

"Kit," he reminded her. He reached to unbutton his flies, one handed, while kissing her. Would she be shocked by the sight of a naked man? She'd seen the village lads swimming, he recalled, and probably Eachann, too. Had she—and he—ever . . .?

Her fingers skimmed across his chest and pinched his nipples, making him gasp.

He gave up on the buttons and shoved his breeches off his hips. They caught on his damned boots. He wasn't usually this awkward, or this clumsy, but then his sexual encounters were usually brief, and did not engage his emotions. This time, when he wanted to be perfect—the kind of lover Megan would never forget, he was tangled in his clothes and tugging on his boots like an idiotic schoolboy with his first lass.

Finally he was naked, and he looked back to find her lying on his plaid, her head resting on her elbow, watching him, her expression languid. "You're a beautiful man," she said softly.

"Are you sure you wish to—um, continue?" he said.

"Do all Englishmen talk this much?"

"Only the nervous ones," he murmured. "Do Scottish lasses always ask so many questions?"

"When it suits us," she said, a naked goddess in the firelight. Her hair had come loose, or perhaps she had taken it down while he fumbled with his clothes. It lay over her shoulder in glorious, silken waves. For a long moment he stayed where he was, leaning against the ragged post of the Laird of Glen Dorian's ancient bed, gazing at the delectable sight of Megan spread out on the MacIntosh plaid with the fire reflecting in her eyes. He wanted to memorize this moment, so he'd always remember it, on other rainy days, far from here, and—

"Isn't it chilly standing so far from the fire?" she asked.

Who exactly was seducing whom? he wondered.

"Yes," he said.

He came to her, dropping down beside her, cupping her face in his hand. "I just thought it would be best to go slowly."

She looked up at him. "Are you a virgin, Kit?"

He gaped at her in surprise. "Me? No, of course not. I just wanted this to be perfect for you, since I assumed you were—are—might be, a virgin."

She swallowed. "I am. If you're nervous, then I'm twice as nervous."

"I doubt that," Kit said. "I suppose I am a virgin when it comes to bedding a virgin. I've never—I mean, I assumed my wife would be untouched when I eventually married, but—"

She stopped his babbling with a kiss. The firelight played over her perfect breasts, crested in rosebuds, her skin as golden as cream in the firelight. She put her arms around him, drew him down until he lay full length against her.

He looked down at her face, saw the desire clear in her eyes as she looked at him. She moaned softly as he cupped her breast in his hand, moved his hips against hers. Rubbing, teasing, raising the level of desire, and pleasure, and need.

He was lost in the silk of her skin, the scent of her hair, the warmth of her flesh, the soft sounds she made. Her mouth tasted like honey. Her curves fit perfectly with his angles. Wherever he touched her body, she touched his—running her fingernails over his nipples, letting her hand wander over every inch of his body, exploring. If he sighed, she lingered. He was on fire, his control crumbling—and he was a man famous for his control in bed. As a rule, Kit gave pleasure before he took it. He was quick and considerate. But then, he had never had a lover like Megan. She broke all the rules. She squeezed his buttocks again, and he arched against her. Heaven help him if she reached around and found—he shouted when her hand closed on his erection, and clamped his hand over hers.

"Don't move," he managed, and counted to ten.

"It's soft," she said.

"It most certainly is not," he countered. He gritted his teeth and let her explore until he couldn't stand it a moment longer. He disengaged her hand and leaned over and to kiss her breasts, her taut belly, her hip. She drew a sharp breath as he kissed the hollow below her navel and blew on the dark curls between her legs. He laid his hand there, and her fingers fluttered over his, her eyes widening. He dipped his fingers between, and this time it was Megan who shouted.

He grinned and she looked at him in surprise. "That's—" she began, then faltered as he moved his fingers, stroked her, made her cry out again. "Heaven," she managed. He left his hand where it was, teasing her, and pressed himself beside her and kissed her, drew her nipples into his mouth until she moaned, rolled her hips restively, enjoying what he was doing.

She arched her back, and gripped his shoulders, her fingers talons, her cries small and sweet and frantic as her need rose.

He caught her cry in his mouth as she bucked against his hand as she found her release.

He shifted, positioning himself between her thighs. "Will it hurt?" she asked, still breathless.

"I think it might," he muttered, lost to everything but the need to be inside her. He rubbed against her, entered a scant inch, and gritted his teeth against the desire to thrust deeper. "I'll go as slowly as I—"

Megan tilted her hips, shifted deliciously, and he cried out again, just as she did, unable to keep himself from burying himself in her body. She gasped, her eyes wide. He wanted to move carefully, with grace and control, but she wrapped her ankles around his hips when he tried to withdraw, urging him forward instead of back. She threw her head back, the firelight playing over the taut muscles in her neck, the sweet, lush softness of her mouth. "Oh," she said, as if she'd discovered something marvelous, something she hadn't expected, more precious than jewels or gold.

Treasure, he thought.

She was tight and hot and sweet, and he was lost when she moved, circling her hips restlessly, drawing her nails over his skin, pleading for more. He obliged. He thrust into her again, filling her, withdrawing and filling her again, holding on until she cried out again, though it almost killed him. He waited until he felt her body ripple around his, and let his release burst over him, intense and powerful. The room dissolved. The whole world dissolved, until it was just Kit and Megan, their bodies melting into pleasure.

When it was over, he lay down and pulled her into his arms, cradling her against his side, drawing the plaid over them. He didn't want to let her go. She snuggled against his shoulder, and he stroked her hair.

"Was that perfect?" she asked. "I mean, I imagine if it wasn't, I must assume it was very close."

"It was perfect," he said, smiling against her hair, and meant it. He lay beside her and listened to the rain, and they slept.

M egan woke with a scream as the wind blew the shutter back against the wall with a crash, and wind and rain blew into the room. The fire shifted and danced in the maelstrom, and shadows filled the room, flapping above them.

Kit got up and forced the panel shut again, and latched it, sealing out the weather—stark naked, gasping at the icy needles of rain on his flesh.

He turned to find her watching him, lying on her stomach, her slim ankles crossed behind her, her lips curved into a half-smile.

"You're a bonny man, Christopher Linwood." He felt his cock stir hopefully at her bold appraisal, especially when she rolled over and opened the plaid for him. "Come back and get warm," she said.

He lay down again, and pulled her into his arms, and they stared up at the cobwebs that clung to the beams above them. "D'you suppose Mairi and Connor ever lay here like this on a rainy afternoon?" she asked.

He stroked her arm and smiled at the idea. "I'm sure it

was a grand castle in those days—a proper place to make love to a lady."

She kissed his cheek. "It still is."

What else could he do but turn his head, capture her mouth with his, and start all over again?

CHAPTER THIRTY-FOUR

It was dark when they woke again, the fire a low glow in the hearth, the room cold.

Megan watched as Kit rose and added wood to the fire, lit a lantern in his pack and set it on the chest.

He peered out through the crack in the shutters. "The rain is coming down sideways. I can't see a thing," he said. "I think the storm is getting worse." He looked worried.

"We'd better get dressed." He reached for her gown and petticoat and handed them to her, and she turned away to put them on, suddenly shy.

"I need help with the buttons," she said, and waited as he fumbled with the tiny fastenings, as if they'd done this a thousand times, were old and married and familiar with each other. Every inch of her body was aware of him behind her, and she wanted nothing more than to turn and drag him back to the rumpled MacIntosh plaid by the fire.

"Do I look respectable?" she asked, smoothing her hand over the irreparable wrinkles of her gown. He smiled.

"Your hair is tangled, your lips are red and swollen, and

you look like a woman who had just been bedded, and very well bedded at that, if I do say so. How do I look?"

She let her eyes roam over his tousled hair, his rumpled shirt and dust-stained breeches, and her heart flipped in her chest. He had never looked better—except of course when he had stood before her, naked, ready, his eyes telling her she was beautiful and desirable. She felt hot blood rising in her cheeks. "We should go, I think."

He took the lantern and escorted her down the stairs, holding her hand. Only for safety's sake, she told herself, gripping tightly, not wanting to let him go. The rain was noisier in the hall, an angry hiss and sizzle. It was cold away from the sanctuary of the fire, too.

He paused on the stairs and held up the lantern, and Megan followed his gaze.

Below them, the hall looked more like the loch than dry land. Debris floated in water deep enough to lap against the third step. He surveyed the damage, his face grim in the light, and Megan felt her chest close with dread. Rain still poured in through the roof, an icy waterfall. By morning—she swallowed. If floodwaters could wash away sturdy bridges like kindling, what would happen to the ruins of Glen Dorian?

With an oath he turned and pulled her back upstairs. "What are you doing?" she asked.

"Rescuing you," he said, bringing her back to the bedroom. He bent to add more wood to the fire. It blazed back to life.

She folded her arms across her chest, trying not to be afraid of the rising water, the fearsome thunder. "It feels more like you're kidnapping me. Do you mean to keep me here for the whole rest of the year and a day, make me your love slave?" The fey quip died on her lips as he turned, his face worried.

"There's no point in both of us going out in the storm. You'll be safe here for now. I'll go to the lodge, get a cart or a coach or a plow horse, even, and come back and get you."

Megan felt her stomach tighten with dread, and she watched a bolt of lightning invade the room like a sword. The shutter shivered.

"Eleanor and Jeannie will be beside themselves with worry," she said. She pictured the maid running across the park to Dundrummie to report that Megan had not come home. Would they assume Megan had been washed away in the flooding, or imagine her here, amid the ruins of Glen Dorian, wrapped naked in a plaid on the floor in Kit's arms? "I'll come with you," she said.

He shook his head. "Be sensible—you haven't even got a cloak, and the causeway might be flooded. I'd rather you stayed here," he said.

"But—" she argued, but he was turning to go, pulling the collar of his rumpled coat closer around his neck, scant protection against the raging storm. "If it comes to it, you'll be safe and dry here for the night."

Megan's heart quivered. "Alone?"

He touched her cheek. "There's no curse, sweetheart. There's more to fear outside these walls than inside, especially tonight."

She looked into his eyes, saw the determination to keep her safe, and felt cherished. He was being chivalrous, kind, and brave, like Nathaniel. Megan gathered the plaid from the floor and wrapped it around him. "It will help keep you dry—at least a little."

He took her icy hands in his and kissed her, a lingering kiss, and she felt a moment's fear that it was a farewell kiss, that she'd never see him again. She clutched tighter and he forced a smile.

"Stay by the fire, sweetheart. I'll be back as quickly as I can," he promised.

She followed him to the top of the stairs and watched him descend, holding the lantern high. He sloshed across the floor, the water nearly to his knees. He picked his way carefully around floating timbers, choosing his steps carefully, and was gone.

She went back upstairs and peered through the shutters, watched the lantern move across the half-flooded causeway, over the path that led into the woods, and disappear into the dark. She was completely alone. The storm crashed around her, battered at the walls, shrieking and wailing like a living thing, full of rage and sorrow.

Megan went back to the bedroom and crouched by the fire, her arms clasped tightly around her body. Her teeth chattered, but her shivers had nothing to do with the cold.

"*Keep him safe,*" she whispered to the air. "*Bring him back to me.*"

She closed her eyes and thought of Kit's mouth on hers, the firelight in his eyes as he loved her, his smile. Was that all it took to fall in love with a man? She had thought she loved Eachann, but she hadn't felt this way with him. His kisses didn't set her on fire. She loved Eachann's charm and his humor and because she'd known him all her life—but she loved her brother for the same reasons. It was different with Kit. He was kind, and charming and funny as well, but there was more. She loved him the way a woman loves a man, desired him, felt the twining of her soul with his. Her heart leaped in anticipation when she saw him, and when he wasn't with her, she could scarcely think of anything or anyone else.

The storm pounded on the shutter, demanding to be let in, and her throat closed with fear—not for herself, for Kit, somewhere out in the deluge. What if he was washed away into the river, or lightning struck him, or a flash flood carried him away? He wasn't a Highlander, wasn't used to such dangers. He might slip and hit his head, or—a million terrible thoughts went through her mind, and she got up, paced the floor of Mairi's bedroom, knowing Mairi must have done the same, waiting and worrying, her heart aching for the man she loved.

Megan went to the window and unlatched the shutter, throwing back the panel to look out across the loch, into the dark hills, his name on her lips, her eyes scanning the darkness for him. How long had he been gone? The rain soaked her hair, drove into her like needles, and she felt panic welling in her breast. If something happened to him, if he didn't come back—she hadn't told him she loved him.

A gust of wind wrenched the shutter from her hands, tearing her fingernails, whipping her hair around her face in sodden, stinging tentacles, laughing at her puny attempts to wrench the panel back again. The fire danced in the maelstrom, as the wind swept in to torment the flames. They writhed, throwing shadows against the walls and the ceiling, forming shapes—monstrous things that made her heart climb her throat.

Thunder rattled the stone walls, shook the very floor beneath her feet, and Megan watched the bolt of lightning illuminate the glen in an otherworldly glow for an instant. Sounds filled the room, noises that came from beyond the dark doorway. She stared at the portal, heard footsteps on the stairs, hobnailed boots ringing on the stone, voices sounding a warning that came too late. Megan's heart stopped, she backed up against the wall, dug her nails into the stone wall behind her. *Hide.* The whisper filled her mind. But there was nowhere to go.

The fire guttered pitifully, all but vanquished by the wind, and Megan swiped a hand across her face, slicked the rain off her icy skin. She was being foolish. She grabbed a stick and tore a scrap of canvas from the mattress and wrapped it tightly around the end. She thrust it into the fire, waited for the flames to catch hold of the makeshift torch. When it flared, she rose, forced herself to go to the dark doorway. "Hello?" she called, but the stones snatched the word, drew it into the walls, held it.

The stairs were empty. Another burst of lightning lit up the hall below, shattered and wet. There was no one there, only shadows. Megan's ears pricked. She heard singing, a sad lament, the words broken by tears, and gasps of anguish. And she could hear bagpipes, far away, calling out from the hills, playing a slow and sorrowful *Ceol Mor*. Her flesh crept, and she backed away from the edge of the stairs. Surely it was the wind playing tricks on her, just the wind, but her torch guttered and shook in her hands, making the shadows shift, giving them room to draw nearer. Surely they *were* moving closer now, coming for her. She backed away, moving along the hall, the rough edges of the stone walls catching at her skirts. Cobwebs snatched at her hair, caressed her face with ghostly fingers, and she swatted them away, felt them tangle around her fingers as the wind whispered in her ear. She turned and fled, but the shadows followed her, lurching along the corridor behind her, chasing her, driving her—

"No!" she murmured as the flame of her torch began to flicker and dwindle. For a moment, the wind toyed with the fragile tongue of fire. Then she felt one last breath of warmth before the torch was snuffed into darkness. She shook it, but it was no use. She dropped it, and put out a hand to find the wall. The icy darkness seeped out of the ragged stone and into her bones, claiming her, drawing her in to the very walls of this place.

"Who's there?" she whispered in Gaelic, and turned her head. "I'm not afraid!" But she was. Her heart pounded in her chest, and she could barely breathe. Her eyes were wide in the dark, but blind. Was something moving, watching, waiting for her? Something brushed by her cheek like a breath, or a faint caress, clung, and she swiped at it, pulling it away. It was just a cobweb, only that, and she drew a gasp of breath, tempted to laugh at her ridiculous fear, but it came out as a gurgle of fear. She rubbed her hand along her skirt, raised her chin, told herself again there was nothing to be afraid of, that she was equal to the dark, better, and her own foolish imagination was all that plagued her. She would go back to the bedchamber, add more wood to the fire and simply wait. Surely the storm would blow itself out soon. The night could not last forever. She put her hand on the wall, took one step forward, then another.

Surely she hadn't come far from the bedchamber. She would come around a corner, and see the glow of the fire, and all would be well. She could laugh then. She drew a breath and took another cautious step into the dark, shivering, wanting the light and heat of the fire more than she'd ever desired anything in her life.

Too late, Megan heard the floor crack under her feet, and the exclamation of the breaking wood shot up through the soles of her shoes, filling her belly with stronger, fiercer, sharper terror.

She sprang for the wall, fought for a handhold among the stones, but it was too late. The ancient boards surrendered at last, and Megan dropped into the darkness.

CHAPTER THIRTY-FIVE

The door of the lodge opened at Kit's pounding knock, but it wasn't a worried Jeannie Fraser who greeted him. It was a tall gentleman Kit didn't know, his face as forbidding as the weather outside.

"I'm Rossington," he muttered through cold lips. "I need blankets and a cart, or at least a horse—" he began, but the man's nostrils flared as he reached out to grab the sodden MacIntosh plaid wrapped around Kit's throat.

"Where the hell is my sister?" he demanded.

"Alec, let him go," someone else insisted—an English voice, gentle and female. She was drowned out by others as they rushed toward Kit—by Jeannie's frantic sobs, and Eleanor's strident questions, and even Leslie, who began flapping around Kit like a demented crow, predicting illness and death if Kit did not get dry and warm and properly dressed at once. Kit put him off, and stood where he was, dripping on the floor, blinking at the candlelight.

"I need warm blankets, oil cloth," he said again. "Some whisky, too, I think."

Jeannie shrieked in dismay.

"What's happened?" Alec McNabb's voice cut through the female cacophony. "Is Megan—" Kit saw his brows crumple with dread.

Kit was ice cold, soaked to the skin, and shedding water on the flagstone floor. "I take it you're Glenlorne," Kit said. "She's at Glen Dorian, safe. She came to the castle and it began to rain, and we thought we could wait out the storm, but it got worse. I came to—"

"You left her there? In that cursed place?" Jeannie cried.

"She's safe," Kit said again. His body ached, and he rubbed a wet hand over his even wetter face. His skin was as cold as a death mask. "She has a warm fire, and it's dry. Look, I promised I'd come back with a cart," he felt forced to insist yet again. Is there something close by? Lady Eleanor—?"

Her eyes were dark with worry. "The road to the glen is bound to be flooded. No vehicle is going to get through there tonight. How did you come?"

Kit felt panic warm him momentarily. "Through the woods. Is there a horse perhaps? If I don't get back soon, the causeway might flood, and then I'll need a boat." He remembered the fear in her eyes the last time she was trapped in the castle. She'd jumped out the window. Surely she wouldn't do that this time. He wouldn't be there to catch her. He felt panic squeeze his chest. He had to get back to her. He should never have left her.

"I'll get my coat," Alec McNabb said. "Caro, get him something dry to wear. Jeannie, fetch some blankets and wrap them well."

"I'll get the whisky," Eleanor said, "and I'm coming with you.

Kit shook his head. "It's not a fit night for anyone who doesn't need to be out," he said. "I would prefer you all wait here."

"I shall certainly wait here, my lord, and heat some water," Leslie said. "If you'll come upstairs, my lord, I will assist you into dry clothes."

"No time," Kit said, unwrapping the sodden plaid. "Just wring this out, if you would, Leslie." He tossed it to his valet, who recoiled at the icy weight of it.

Eleanor grinned. "A MacIntosh plaid. You looked like a proper Highlander coming through that door. A length of plaid has many uses." Kit's mouth rippled as he pictured the last use the plaid had served, as bed and blanket. He pictured Megan lying on the length of tartan, her hand extended to him, her lips curved into an alluring smile, her lovely body warm and naked. The image was enough to lift the exhaustion creeping up through the soles of Kit's boots, though it did nothing at all to stem his worry. He needed to get back to Megan.

"Dry clothes? Here? You *live* here?" Alec McNabb demanded.

Kit squared his shoulders. "I do not."

"Yet your clothes are here, your valet is in residence, and you have entered into a—a—"

"Handfasting," Eleanor provided.

Kit watched Alec McNabb color, his brows lowering. "You did not have my permission, Rossington."

Kit glared back. "It was a private arrangement, Glenlorne."

Glenlorne's eyes flared dangerously, and he came toward Kit. "If you have harmed one hair on her head, or de—de—"

"Debauched her?" Eleanor offered.

Alec continued to glare at Kit. "If he has, I'll kill him." Kit watched the woman he assumed was Glenlorne's countess clutch at his arm. She regarded Kit with cool speculation.

Kit held his ground, read the question in every set of eyes staring at him. What could he say? He had indeed debauched her, but that was between himself and Megan, or so he'd thought. He glanced at the door that led to the kitchen, half expecting the absent but long anticipated Eachann Rennie to stride out of the kitchen and help Glenlorne kill Kit for his audacity. *Will you take the cleaver or the knife, my lord?* The way Glenlorne's fists were clenching and unclenching, Kit knew the earl would prefer to strangle Kit with his bare hands. It was obvious Alec McNabb loved his sister. Her whole family did, and Eachann loved her most of all, and she loved him.

Kit swallowed. When Eachann did appear, would he be as angry as Glenlorne? What if Rennie rejected the woman he professed to love, and broke her heart?

Kit felt his heart swell, a small warm place opening in his frozen breast. He'd marry Megan McNabb himself, Kit decided, make her his wife without any question of convenience or time limitations.

He stood dripping on the floor, considering the matter, and realized to his amazement that he *liked* the idea—more than that, even. He had avoided the very notion of marrying for so long, and at last he knew why. It had never been right before, and he had never found the perfect woman. Until Megan. If it hadn't been exactly honorable to *debauch* her without the blessing of family and clergy, and he suspected Duncan MacIntosh didn't count in Glenlorne's eyes, it was most certainly the first thing in his life that had felt *right*. If he married Megan McNabb—if she'd have him, of course—it would be because he loved her, and not out of duty, or for honor's sake, or anything else.

But what if Eachann returned, and she still wanted him instead of Kit?

Kit shifted his feet, his boots squelching. He wouldn't stand in her way. He'd kiss her cheek—just her cheek—wish her well, and go home. He'd probably never marry at all if he couldn't have Megan, just like Nathaniel. He wouldn't be the first Linwood to leave his heart in the Highlands.

But for now, he was in love, and where there was love, there was always hope. He stood there dripping on the floor, considering that.

"What are you grinning at?" Glenlorne demanded.

"It's the curse of Glen Dorian," Jeannie said in a loud whisper, staring at him in horror. "They say it drives men mad." She screamed as thunder crashed above the lodge, rattling the windows, making the antlers that lined the walls shiver.

Kit didn't reply. He took the plaid back from Leslie and wrung it out himself, on the floor of the hall, since the flagstones were already wet. "There is no curse," he said through gritted teeth. He tossed the wet wool back over his shoulders, and glared at each member of the assembled company in turn, ending with Glenlorne. "I'm going," he said. "She's probably afraid, and I am going to get her."

He turned on his heel without waiting for a reply and walked out the door into the storm.

Glenlorne caught up with him before he'd even reached the edge of the woods. "My wife is pregnant," the laird said over the roar of the storm.

"Congratulations," Kit said, as the rain drove into his face.

"She should be home, with her feet up, drinking one of Muira's goat milk and honey possets, not here, worried half to death about Megan."

"Eleanor will take care of her," Kit said absently, his mind on Megan. Had the fire been enough to keep her warm? She was no doubt hungry, and—he wondered if the activities of the afternoon had an effect on a woman. He felt marvelous, but perhaps it was different for a virg—

He stopped walking. "Pregnant," he muttered.

"What?" Glenlorne shouted.

Kit didn't answer. What if she was? The idea filled him with a dozen emotions, including joy, and he grinned again.

"I wish you'd stop that," Glenlorne said. "This is hardly a matter for mirth. In fact, when I get Megan back to Dundrummie, I intend to wring your neck. Then I'm going to thrash her within an inch of her life, and after that, I'll lock her in the highest tower I can find."

"No, you won't," Kit said, stepping in front of Alec. "Under Scottish tradition, or law, or by the power invested in Duncan MacIntosh, Megan is my wife." *Wife.* He liked the sound of that, and his chest swelled as he stood up to Glenlorne.

Megan's brother stared back at him for a moment and

stayed silent. Lightning lit up a furious scowl. Kit waited until the laird looked away first, rubbing the water from his face with one hand as he began to walk again. "Come on," Glenlorne said "I think we'd best hear what Megan has to say before I punch you senseless."

CHAPTER THIRTY-SIX

Megan landed hard on something solid that cut off her scream. She curled into a ball and held her hands over her head as things crashed around her in the darkness, and waited for the whole castle to come tumbling down on top of her. She felt something sharp pierce her shoulder, drawing another scream from her. She lay still, panting in pain and terror until everything stopped moving. Only then did she dare to raise her head and looked around There was a hole in the corner, high up, a narrow crevice of gray storm light, but it illuminated nothing.

She reached out a hand, searching the empty air around her. The floor was dry here at least. She drew back as another explosion boomed around her, but it was only thunder, and the walls stayed where they were, solid, silent, and stead-fast. The flash of lightning that followed barely penetrated the darkness, and only served to make the shattered timbers around her leap like talons, then retreat.

She could hear the sound of her own harsh breathing echoing around her. "Hello?"

The word echoed, mocked her.

Her arm hurt, and she reached up with trembling fingers and felt the slick heat of blood. Her stomach rolled, and she fought back panic and fear. "Just a splinter," she whispered. "A small cut, and nothing worse."

"Nothing worse," the echo agreed. The sound of the rain mixed with the patter of falling dust, little pieces sucked down into the new abyss her fall had created, but she considered herself fortunate—no great stones or roof timbers fell.

Megan stretched out her hand again, felt a solid stone floor beneath her.

She drew a deep breath and shifted carefully, sitting up. She blinked, trying to see, but it was too dark. *Like death.* She shook the thought away, and pushed herself onto her knees.

She screamed as the floor moved, felt the crack forming under her palm. This time, it happened slowly—the floor beneath her tipped inward, and once more she was falling. She clawed for something to hold on to, but it was no use. The flagstone slid out of her grasp, and she was falling again. It didn't take so long to land this time, or so she thought, but she landed in water, and the icy plunge stole the breath from her lungs. She thrashed, kicking, trying to swim, found something solid under one foot and pushed upward, felt it shift, slip away from under her, then come back again, bashing against her leg. She fought for a foothold, slipped farther. She cried out at the sudden grip on her ankle, a crushing, grinding grab that dragged her downward. She gasped, and tried to draw her leg up, but wouldn't come. It was stuck fast.

She could hear the rush of water, a cascade in the darkness, and an ominous boom as things she couldn't see shifted nearby, floated past her. She felt the coldness of the water creeping higher, soaking her gown. She looked up at the gray hole, and it seemed as bright as the sun in her terror. Inside the hole, all was darkness, and movement, and icy cold. She gritted her teeth and tugged her leg again, but her foot was wedged in. She gasped at the pain.

Her sodden gown began to lift and float around her, the muslin brushing and fluttering against her legs like a fish—or an eel. She shut her eyes, stifled the scream that rose in her throat. She hated eels. The water rose slowly from her thighs to her waist, then up to her chest. Megan realized there was a greater peril than eels. Her skin was instantly chilled, and she tried again to free her foot, and pain raced along her leg like fire.

She took a breath and ducked into the water, face down, her hair wound around her throat like seaweed, choking her. She reached for the place where her foot was caught, but it was wedged between two immoveable objects, barrels, perhaps, since they were wooden and slightly round. She scrabbled at them, pushed, kicked at them with her free leg, but they held on to her without mercy.

Her lungs burned, and she rose above the water, higher still now, and sucked in a long breath, and tried not to give in to panic. The water was up to her armpits now. She kicked harder at the barrels with her other foot, screaming curses at them, loudly refusing to die here, but they heartlessly refused to budge. At least the cold of the water numbed the pain in her arm, and she felt her heart kick with panic—everything was becoming numb, as cold and devoid of feeling as if she were already a corpse.

"Kit!" she screamed, feeling tears on her face, oddly hot against the ice of her skin. She hadn't told him she loved him. Why hadn't she told him?

"Kit?" she screamed again, staring upward as the water rose higher still, reached her chin, filled her ears.

But he had gone for help, and she was all alone.

She drew another breath, and choked as water filled her mouth.

CHAPTER THIRTY-SEVEN

Kit heaved a sigh of relief when they cleared the woods and Glen Dorian came into view, ravaged by rain and mist. The castle still stood, a grizzled sentinel against the storm, rising black and bony from the leaden sheen of the loch. A narrow strip of causeway stood out—barely—above the rising waters.

"She's in *there*?" Glenlorne growled.

Kit scanned the side of the castle as they crossed the loch, searching for the window of Mairi's bedchamber, hoping to see the faint glow of firelight inside, and know that all was well, but the room was dark, and the shutter was open, banging against the stone wall in the wind, drumming a steady death march. His stomach rolled, and he hurried forward. Glenlorne kept pace with him.

"Megan was taught to stay out of places like this—there's an old tower at Glenlorne, crumbling where it stands, but I daresay it's in better shape than this place. How could you let her go in there?" Alec lectured as they crossed the courtyard.

"Does anyone truly 'let' Megan do anything? I haven't

known her long, but I got the impression that once Megan decides what she wants, no one could change her mind."

"And are the females in your own family any different, Rossington?"

"Not in the least," Kit said. The inner door stood wide open. He was certain he'd closed it when he'd left earlier. He entered the dark hall and held up the lantern. There was water on the floor, and he waded through it. "Be careful—there's rubble under the water," he warned Glenlorne, like a host offering advice to a guest in his home. When had he begun to think of Glenlorne as his, or as home, or anything else?

Since it contained Megan.

"Megan?" he shouted, moving toward the stairs. It was dark at the top, and he carried the lantern high as he took them two at a time, his boots sloshing water.

"There's something up here that's intact?" Glenlorne asked from behind him, raising his own light to look.

Kit hurried down the hall to the bedchamber. It was cold and dark, the fire down to a single gleaming eye amid the ashes. "Megan?" he called.

"It's a bedroom," Glenlorne said.

"It's where I left her," Kit said, feeling panic rise in his throat.

Glenlorne went and picked something up from the floor near the fireplace. He held it up, his brows rising into his hairline. Megan's silk stocking gleamed like a ghost.

"Is this hers?" Alec McNabb demanded, his eyes glowing in the lantern light, indignant and angry.

Kit snatched the stocking from his hand and stuffed it into his pocket. "Yes." Glenlorne's fist connected with his jaw, turned his head sideways, and Kit saw stars. He stumbled, but held up his hands, palms open as Megan's brother came at him again.

"We need to find her," he said, wiping a hand over his split lip. "Once we do, and she's safe, we can—discuss—this matter further." He waited until the fury shifted in the other man's eyes.

"Don't think we won't, Rossington. I intend to—"

A howl filled the air, and the hair on the back of Kit's neck rose with it. "What the devil was that?" Glenlorne whispered. "It sounded like bagpipes—or singing."

Kit listened for it to come again. "It's not bagpipes, it's a curse." He hurried out of the room.

"I thought you said there was no curse on Glen Dorian."

"There isn't. It wasn't the castle—that was Megan cursing," Kit said. He moved down the hall and only just in time saw the hole in the floor. His heart climbed into his throat. He held out an arm to warn Glenlorne back, heard the boards groan under their feet.

"Megan?" he shouted. He could hear the rush of water.

"I'm here! Hurry!"

Kit swung the lantern, trying to illuminate the space below him. He saw broken beams, but she wasn't under them. He saw a jumble of furniture, but she wasn't there either. Then he saw the hole in the floor, the malicious glint of rising water in the lantern light, and his heart stopped beating when Megan's white face appeared in the dark pool of water, shining and wet, her eyes wide.

"The water—" she managed, gulping some. "I'm stuck. Hurry—"

He didn't need a second warning. Without taking his eyes off her face, Kit thrust the lantern at Alec and lowered himself over the edge of the broken floor and jumped. He leaned over the edge of the pit that held Megan. "Give me your hand, sweetheart."

She shook her head. "I can't, I'm stuck. My foot is wedged . . ." She managed, trying to breathe and talk at the same time. "The water is coming up—"

He tossed aside the plaid and dropped into the water next to her, instantly felt the cold chill his limbs. She must be freezing. "Kit," she gasped, her hands reaching for him, icy talons, "I—"

He didn't hear the rest. He took a breath and dove under the water.

Her foot was caught between two massive barrels, and he tugged, felt her tense, knew he was hurting her. He couldn't see anything, was working blind. He braced himself and kicked at the barrel, but it refused to move. He needed light, time, and he didn't have either. His lungs threatened to burst as he pushed on the obstruction that held her fast.

Above him, a lantern appeared and he knew Glenlorne had arrived. Mere seconds had passed, but it felt like hours. He looked up at the yellow light wavering through the water, but it was enough. He saw the plank that wedged the barrel in place, and he kicked at it, dislodged it, and the barrel floated free.

Glenlorne pulled her out, was holding her when Kit emerged. Megan was shivering and coughing, trying to talk and to cry as she held her brother. Kit found one of the blankets, wrapped her in it and sat back on his heels.

Her hand on his arm was icy, as she left the circle of her brother's arms to come to him. He opened his arms and folded her against his chest. Her eyes were wide and wet and luminous as she looked up at him. "You came back," she whispered. "You came back to me."

CHAPTER THIRTY-EIGHT

Alec wrapped her in blankets, but she wanted the MacIntosh plaid—their plaid, and Kit. It was damp still, but he put it by her side, his eyes never leaving her face. His own face was white and tense, as if he'd been very afraid, and was still worried. She put her hand on his cheek—her pale, wrinkled, icy hand—and he set a quick kiss on her palm as Alec prowled the room, searching for a way out.

"Looks like it was a chapel once," her brother said, holding up the lantern to reveal a crucifix, leaning at a rakish angle against broken benches. "There's no way out. I'll have to climb up and pull you up, one at a time," he pronounced. Megan noted the annoyance in her brother's expression as he glowered at Kit, hating the fact that she lay in his arms. Kit's arms tightened protectively, and she almost smiled at the silent debate going on between the two men above her head.

"I can't climb, Alec," she said.

"Nonsense. You used to climb trees like a squirrel," he said, and she felt her cheeks flush with hot blood.

"My ankle," she murmured through gritted teeth. It hurt

like the devil now, and so did her arm, and she was tired. So very, very tired. "I mean, I will try," she said.

"I believe the hall is probably just a few feet that way—" Kit said. "A handful of men could clear the timbers that are blocking the door to this room, but it's more than you and I can manage. We'll need help, tools."

Megan felt frustration bloom in her chest as her bother stood mutinously before her.

"One of us has to go and get help, Alec," she said. "Would you mind if I waited here?"

He glowered at her. "I think Rossington should go," he said. "It isn't proper to leave you here alone with him."

Megan wondered if marriage had made her brother daft. "If can't climb, Alec, then I'm certainly in no condition to—" The words stuck in her throat at the look of indignation on Alec's face.

He glared at Kit. "I haven't forgotten our 'discussion,' Rossington. We will continue it as soon as Megan's safe, is that clear? Boost me up."

She watched as Kit helped her bother to climb out the way they'd come, and he peered down from the ceiling one last time before he left. "I'll be back *soon*."

Kit was by her side again, kneeling on the floor, fussing with the makeshift bed of blankets, making her comfortable. She was cold, in pain, and hungry—but none of that mattered. Kit was here by her side, and all was well. "I need to check your injuries," he said apologetically as he shifted the blankets aside, but didn't move them any lower than necessary. She kept her eyes on his as he looked at her shoulder. She saw the muscle in his cheek twitch at the sight of the cut, the slight furrow between his brows.

"Is it bad?" she asked.

"It's just a splinter," he replied.

"Then you'll know what to do," she said, and turned her head away as he pulled the shard of wood from her arm. She stifled a cry of pain, felt the blood spurt. He began to unbutton his shirt, and she looked at him in surprise, staring at his naked chest.

"It needs a bandage," he said, and took the fine linen in his hands and tore it.

"Haven't you got a handkerchief?" she asked.

"Handkerchiefs lead to trouble," he quipped. He poured whisky over the wound, his eyes sympathetic as he did so, knowing how much it stung. He bound the injury carefully, his fingers gentle, then he held the flask to her lips, made her drink. His arm under her shoulders, and the sound of his heart under her ear, were nearly as warming as the spirit.

He turned to her ankle, lifting her gown with a murmured apology for the impropriety, and probed gently. She resisted the urge to scream.

"I don't think it's broken but it needs to be wrapped tightly in something cold and wet," he said, and tore another strip from his shirt, and went to the edge of the hole in the floor to wet it. He glanced back at her. "The water's receding," he said.

"Has it stopped raining?" she asked. She listened for a moment, heard nothing.

He was staring into the hole. "I suppose it has," he murmured distractedly. She stared at him, his chest naked, his fair hair water-darkened and tousled.

Her lover, her hero.

Her heart did a slow turn in her chest. She also noted

his swollen lip. Someone had punched him, hard. He wet the cloth and carried it back to wind it around her injured ankle, resting her leg on his knee. She gritted her teeth, both at the pain and the cold of the cloth.

"What did Alec mean by 'our discussion'?" she asked.

He raised his hand to his injured mouth, as if he'd forgotten it. "He found your stocking in the bedchamber upstairs, I'm afraid, and assumed—"

"Oh," Megan said. "Oh!" Her face flamed, and she tried to sit up. She gasped as her injuries objected. Alec *knew*? It was a wonder he'd left her here at all. Not that he'd had a choice. "Oh," she said again.

"I'm afraid so," he said, sighing.

Indignation flared. "What, do you regret it so soon?"

He regarded her in her cocoon of blankets, the long bare length of her leg on his lap. His eyes were filled with an emotion that put out the flames of indignation at once, and made her want to sigh. "Regret it? Never." He lowered his head and kissed her—one quick, unsatisfying peck. "But that doesn't mean it should happen again." She considered. Had he ended that sentence with hope, or was it fear? She felt bitterness fill her mouth.

"It won't, if—" She stopped. There was a fearsome clunk, a hollow, sonorous sound from under the floor, and he turned to look down the hole, holding the lantern above the dark space.

"It's the barrels—they're floating," he said. Then he got to his feet and went to peer into the hole again, taking the lantern "It means they're empty," he said. "Or at least some of them are. There are more, lined up along the walls. Those ones aren't going anywhere."

She felt a moment's annoyance that his attention had been so easily drawn away from her. "Why is that so unusual? The ale in them might have leaked out, or the water—or the fish they once held, or the salt beef, for that matter. It might have been eaten and the barrels forgotten."

He turned to her, his gray eyes bright. "But why would the barrels be here, under the chapel? Isn't that where they bury bodies?" he asked.

She blinked at him. "There's a small burial ground on the mainland, down the glen from Mairi's cottage, where the village used to stand. They would have taken the dead there."

"Even a laird?" Kit asked.

She shrugged, and winced at the pain it caused. She had almost been fit for burying herself, if he might remember. She had no wish to discuss the truly dead now.

"Then it's a storeroom?" he asked.

She shifted, the pain of her injuries biting into her with sharp little teeth. "Is that where you imagine the treasure is hidden?" she asked tartly. "Why don't you go and see?" she said, knowing that he wanted to.

"Will you be all right?" the daft man had the nerve to ask.

"Go," she said. She wanted him by her side, holding her, but this was why he'd come to Scotland. He had no intention of staying, or of making love to her again. She felt her skin heat. Had she made a terrible mistake?

Dawn had come, and the narrow crack high above the floor offered a few pallid streams of kitten-weak sunlight to see by. She watched as he lowered himself carefully into the hole, taking the lantern, and Megan's heart pounded as she heard the splash. "Are you all right? What do you see?" she called, unable to resist curiosity.

"The water's almost gone. There are at least a dozen barrels here, maybe more," he said. "Most of them are heavy, so they must be full."

"What's in them?" she asked.

She heard him laugh. "What is it?" she asked again, and forced herself to sit up, to gingerly move closer to the edge of the hole, inch by careful inch.

"It's whisky," he said. "And it's the finest I've ever had." He gave a whoop of laughter.

"It must have lain there for over seventy years," Megan said. "Is that all?"

"There's a tomb here, made of stone. A knight, his effigy carved on the lid. Sir Alasdair MacIntosh, he is—or was."

Megan's skin tingled. "Is that the treasure?" she whispered.

"There's weapons here on the floor beside him—a sword with jewels on the hilt, a shield. There's a dirk as well."

He brought them up to her, climbing out of the hole grinning, his eyes glowing. The weapons rang on the stone floor, the gems winking coldly. Megan's heart fell as she stared at them . *Now he'd go, leave forever.* Her chest tightened.

He held out the sword to her, like a knight presenting his honor to a lady. The ruby in the hilt glinted like a drop of blood. "Magnificent," he murmured, his eyes on the blade, turning it in his hands, ignoring the fact that he was wet, and shirtless. "A few hundred years old, I think. It must have been a fine blade."

She didn't touch it. "There are tales of Scottish knights

who fought in the Hundred Year's War with the French," she said. "Perhaps Alasdair MacIntosh came home a hero."

He looked at her with keen interest, then frowned, noticing her pallor. He set the sword aside at once, and laid the back of his hand against her cheek, checking for fever.

Her brave knight. Megan sighed, then frowned. No, he wasn't. He didn't belong to her at all.

"Are you in pain?" he asked, and wrapped the blankets carefully around her.

"Yes," she said. Of course she was. She had only just realized that she loved him, and now—now he'd take his sword and go, the prize won, the fair maid forgotten. She lowered her eyes, fought back tears.

"Take some whisky for the pain," he said, raising the flask Alec had left, but he'd emptied it on her wounded arm. He grinned at her. "No matter—I'll just go and get more," he went back to the hole in the floor and climbed down.

She heard a shout. "Kit? What is it? What's the matter?" she cried. Was he hurt?

"It's an otter," he muttered. "Just an otter. It moved in the corner, its eyes shining in the lantern light. It startled me."

An otter? Megan frowned. How did an otter come to be in the crypt of Glen Dorian Castle? She felt her stomach clench. "But that means—"

"Indeed—there's another way out," Kit said, his voice distant. She heard the sound of things moving, water splashing, then silence.

"Kit?" she said. He didn't answer. She pushed the plaid away and began to move toward the hole on her bottom, her eyes on the dark void, suddenly afraid. Her ankle objected, and her shoulder screamed in agony, but she ignored the pain. If she had to, she'd go down the hole, find him, save him. She peered over the edge into the darkness, saw nothing but the shadowy stone face of Sir Alasdair MacIntosh staring back at her. There was no sign of Kit. Fear rose like the water had done.

She almost screamed when something shot out of the hole and landed on the floor at her feet. It was just a box. Kit followed, pulling himself up over the edge of the stone, as agile and sleek as an otter. There was mud in his hair, weeds, too.

"I'm here," he said. She almost collapsed with relief. He grinned at her, his gray eyes alight. "There's a tunnel that goes out to the loch. It's how the otters got in, where they make their den. It's probably been there for years, a hiding place, and a way out. I found this, in a niche in the wall."

Even muddy, Kit made Megan's heart tumble in her rib cage, and she began to raise her hand to wipe away a smear of dirt on his cheek, wanting to touch him, but he was staring at the box, and didn't notice her gesture. She lowered her hand to the folds of the plaid and waited while he worked at the latch, his attention all for that now. Hot blood rushed her cheeks, and she cursed the treasure, if that's what it was.

"It won't open," he said, working at the lid of the box. He sat back and regarded it, his brow furrowed. The box was small, a hands breadth wide, and perhaps four times as long. Although it was scratched and muddy, inlaid gems glittered in the morning light that peered into Glen Dorian's chapel.

"It's a jewelry box," she said. "Or a trinket box, perhaps."

"Jewels?" he said, his voice eager. So eager it made her head ache, along with everything else.

"Is there whisky in the flask?" she asked.

He came to her at once, held Alec's flask to her lips. The McNabb crest glinted, a warning of the burn of seventy-year-old whisky. It stung her tongue, and slid down her throat like liquid fire. It exploded when it reached her belly, warming her everywhere at once. The tang of smoke and peat filled her head.

"Oh my," she said, putting a hand to her throat.

"Feeling better?" He grinned, and she nodded. "That's the treasure, I think. The whisky is probably worth a fortune," he said. "Or it might be the jewel in the sword. He looked extraordinarily pleased with himself as he looked at her. Despite everything, she felt her heart quicken yet again. "You have mud, just there—" she said, reaching out again to touch his cheek. This time he caught her hand as she rubbed at the mud, turned her palm over and laid a kiss there.

"You've been very brave, Megan," he said, as if he were speaking to a child. But she wasn't a child—she was a grown woman, and she was in love. She lowered her eyes before the whisky made her incautious, and she said something she'd regret.

"And you have your treasure now," she said. She felt exhaustion catching up to her, her bones melting into the blankets. She reached for the plaid, pulled it closer. "I want to sleep." In fact, she wanted a lot of things—food, a bath, sleep, and him. She was afraid he wouldn't be here when she woke again, and she looked around the ruined chapel, felt the weight of the castle's curse and shivered.

"Sleep, then. I'll keep you warm." He lay down beside her, and settled her gently against his chest, held her in his arms.

"Am I hurting you?" he asked, and she laid her head on his chest, pressed closer, felt the beat of his heart and the warmth of his skin. *Yes*, she thought. *You'll leave me, and that will hurt, and I will forever wonder—*

"No," she said. "You're not hurting me." She was being foolish. She curled her fingers against his chest, and he caught her hand in his, rubbed his thumb over her knuckles. She began to drift into sleep, safe in his arms. He began to talk. She could hear the rumble of his voice, but her mind wanted rest, not conversation. She was warm again, and exactly where she wanted to be. She closed her eyes and sighed.

"Megan, we need to discuss what will happen if—by chance—you are . . . I mean, the natural consequences of our—well, it could result in—um, if there is a child, then we . . ." A soft sigh made Kit glance down at Megan's dark head, her soft hair a tangled skein of silk across his naked flesh. Her eyes were closed, and he realized that she hadn't heard a word he'd said. Her long lashes lay over bruised cheeks and she was soft and warm in his arms, fast asleep. He felt his heart swell, thinking himself the most fortunate man in the kingdom. He stroked a lock of hair back from her face and swallowed, thinking of what might have happened— *would* have happened—if it had taken him just a few minutes longer to reach her.

But he had been there in time, and she was safe. He kissed the top of her head, let her battered body draw strength and warmth from his. "If there is a child I will marry you if you'll have me," he whispered, even though he knew she couldn't hear him. "And we will make more children, and I will love you always. I will keep you safe, and do my best to make you happy."

The only reply was the softest, daintiest snore. He glanced at the items he'd pulled from the muddy crypt—a sword, a flask of whisky, and the box. It was remarkable, and far more than he'd expected to find.

But the real treasure, Lady Megan McNabb, lay in his arms, asleep, her body curled against his as if she had always belonged there. He couldn't imagine she didn't.

Since the rain had stopped, and dawn was coming up pink and rosy over the horizon, Lady Eleanor insisted on returning to Glen Dorian with the rescue party. In the interest of expediency, Alec took the men nearest to hand, including Graves, Leslie, and Lady Eleanor's gardener, since he had the key to the shed that held the shovels and axes they'd need. Alec tried to forbid her from leaving Dundrummie, of course, but she was old enough to ignore him, which Caroline, as his wife, could not do. Eleanor climbed into the cart with Jeannie as the laird of Glenlorne blathered at her, insisting on having his way. He didn't get it. "Megan will need a woman," she said, ignoring the earl, and nodding to the gardener, who drove the cart. "Go on, Robbie, fast as you can." Alec was left to follow on his own horse, exchanging his fine stallion for a sturdy garron, like his ancestors rode, a creature far more likely to manage the mud and water without fuss.

They got stuck twice, and discovered water had covered the causeway like a thin sheet of glass. It was only inches deep, but Eleanor had to pat Jeannie on the back as she gibbered in terror. By the time they arrived at the castle's once formidable gate, the impeccable Graves was muddy to his knees, Leslie was on the verge of tears, and the gardener was grinning at the pair of them, and muttering unkindly in Gaelic that adversity existed solely to prove that Scotsmen were superior to Englishmen in every way.

Eleanor handed Graves the blankets she'd brought, and the basket filled with food, and a few medical supplies like smelling salts, clean handkerchiefs, and whisky. Alec helped her down and set her stick in her hand, and she waved away his hand under her elbow as she walked into the ruins of the ancient home of the MacIntoshes of Glen Dorian. She paused beside Alec and regarded the destruction soberly. It must have been magnificent once.

She stood in the hall, leaning on her cane, watching the men as they worried away at the burned and broken tangle of timber, and then asked Jeannie to help her upstairs, so she might see the scene of the accident for herself. As Alec had described it, poor Megan had cashed through the floor, and it was a miracle she hadn't been killed. He blamed Rossington, of course, even as he described how the English earl had saved Megan.

Eleanor peered carefully down the hole and grinned at the sight below her.

On the floor below, in a cocoon of blankets, her niece lay asleep on the naked chest of Lord Christopher Rossington, looking as content as if she were in a much more luxurious bed, though Eleanor couldn't think of a grander place to sleep than draped across such a muscular, manly chest. Rossington's eyes opened as she stared at him. For a moment he looked startled.

"Are you surprised to see me?" she asked him, her voice echoing through the space below.

"Not at all, my lady. In fact, I am used to seeing angels staring down at me in my bed," he murmured, and Eleanor chuckled.

"I have no doubt you are indeed, my lord. I fear I have been away from England so long that I had quite forgotten the arrogance of English lords. Quite refreshing."

"Have you come to rescue us?" Kit asked.

"Me? Heavens, no. Glenlorne is downstairs with a troop of stalwart fellows. You'll be out of there eventually, I suppose. Graves is putting in a fine effort, but Your Mister Leslie is bemoaning his deepest fear—that you're stuck in there with nothing suitable to wear. I see he's quite correct in that," she let her eyes wander over the earl's naked chest once more, covered only by Megan. "May I assume you simply don't care what Glenlorne will think when he comes through that door?" She watched him color, but he didn't move away from Megan. His arm tightened gently on her shoulder.

"I'm wearing his shirt, aunt," Megan said, opening her eyes at last and squinting up at her visitor. "He used it to bandage my shoulder and my ankle."

"And you decided to keep him warm instead, did you?" Eleanor asked.

Megan sat up gingerly and stared at her aunt. "Are you shocked?"

Eleanor grinned. "Not at all. Delighted. I always thought

you were a resourceful lass, Megan. I brought you a bite of breakfast. Shall I have Jeannie lower the basket?"

"Good morning, my lady. We've been dreadfully worried about you," Jeannie said, poking her head over the edge of the hole. "This is all the doing of Mairi's curse, I'd say. The sooner we're out of here, the better."

"Just lower the basket, Jeannie," Eleanor insisted, despairing that the girl hadn't a single romantic bone in her body. She helped her maid tie a shawl around the handle of the basket and lower it through the hole to Rossington, who caught it with a nod of thanks.

"I'd invite you to join us if it were possible, Lady Eleanor," he said graciously.

"Not at all, dear boy. Give Megan a full tot of the whisky for the pain. The trip back in the cart will be bumpy and rather uncomfortable. I think I'll go and see what progress is being made below."

"Dundrummie?" Megan said, looking at her aunt. "I expected to go back to the lodge."

"What, and shock poor Alec?" Eleanor said. "You've given him gray hair already with this handfasting, and he still has two other sisters to see married and settled yet. He is insisting that if Rossington's belongings and his valet are in residence at the lodge, then you must return to the bosom of your family at Dundrummie. What have you to say to that, Rossington?"

Did she detect a hint of sorrow on the earl's handsome face? There certainly was disappointment in Megan's eyes. To Eleanor's dismay, Rossington bowed as if they were meeting in a drawing room, as if he were fully clothed, and not bound to Eleanor's niece by anything more than the torn scraps of his fine linen shirt. Was he aware that the carefully embroidered monogram was emblazoned across her wounded shoulder like a brand? She hoped Alec took note of that.

"It will be as Glenlorne wishes," Rossington said, his voice flat, carefully devoid of any hint of emotion. He turned to Megan. "You will be more comfortable there."

"Fiddlesticks," Eleanor murmured, and rose to go downstairs, taking Jeannie with her. Was there no hope at all to make these two see sense? Marriage wasn't a bad thing, when it was with the right person. In fact, it was the making of a person, and their happiness. It had taken her three husbands to discover that, but she had, and she hoped that Rossington and Megan were not too daft to see that they had stumbled on the very thing that she had spent her life looking for. They were made for each other. She looked around at the crumbling stones, the broken timbers, the open roof and sighed. If the old place hadn't already burned down, the polite, over-careful, and damped-down passion in their eyes would set Glen Dorian aflame all over again with just a single spark.

"I should do what I can from this side," Kit said as Eleanor and Jeannie disappeared, and crossed to the blocked doorway of the chapel. "It will make the work go faster. He moved a timber aside, using his frustration to shift the heavy weight.

Megan simply stared at him, her eyes huge and soft with sleep, her face sober. She was beautiful. He imagined waking up next to her this way every morning. He could not swallow the lump in his throat. "You'll be comfortable at Dundrummie," he said.

She picked at the edge of the plaid. "Will you stay at the lodge?"

He considered, then shook his head. There would be reminders of her there—not that there wouldn't be at the cottage. He would see her everywhere, he realized. Even places she'd never been. "I will stay in the cottage."

"It will soon be too cold to stay there. Winter can come early in the Highlands. Will you go home then, to England?"

Kit felt his stomach drop to his feet. "I suppose I must. There are things to see to—the harvest, for one."

She lowered her eyes before he could read the emotion there. She simply nodded.

"Will you come to London with your sister in the spring?" he asked.

She shrugged, and grimaced at the pain it caused her, and her fingers dropped the plaid and fluttered over the bandage. "For now I'll go home to Glenlorne," she said, not divulging any further plans.

"To wait for—" She stopped him with a look, her eyes flying to his, the pain there acute.

"Don't say it, Kit. Not now."

"Will he mind, Megan?"

She plucked at the edge of the plaid. "It doesn't matter," she said on a whisper of sound.

What did that mean? He didn't get a chance to ask.

A mighty crash shook the room as the final timber shifted. Kit wrapped Megan in his arms as the debris fell with a crash. Light streamed into the chapel, and Kit looked up at the opening. Glenlorne stood in the swirling dust, scowling at the sight before him, his sister in Kit's naked arms. Graves remained stoically dignified, and bowed, despite the muck staining his shirtfront, face and trousers. Kit had no doubt that Graves, if asked even now, could manage to rustle up a proper tea from somewhere, just like his own butler, Swift Josiah Leslie sobbed while Jeannie patted his back, and Eleanor leaned on her stick and grinned.

Megan peered out at her brother from the safety of Kit's arms. She knew by the look in Alec's eyes, there was going to be hell to pay.

CHAPTER THIRTY-NINE

Glen Dorian, late April 1746

"They won't release him."

Mairi stared at Nathaniel in horror.

"At least not yet. I'll do what I can, tell them what I know, but for now, the gaol is full, and they're still hunting down rebels."

"Connor didn't fight," Mairi said softly. "No one saw him fight. He only went to fetch my brother, just a child. No one can fault him for that." She'd said the same thing over and over in her mind, at night as she paced the floor, longing for Connor, hoping that everything might still turn out for the best. She paced the hall now, her hands clasping and unclasping, afraid now her worst fear had been spoken aloud. None of the men who had fought for the prince had returned. Their women watched the road into the glen too, waited, as she did, but hope faded as the hours and days passed.

Nathaniel didn't reply, and she stopped pacing to look at him. He looked tired and grim, and her heart clenched again. She wanted to see hope in his eyes, certainty, but there wasn't any. "Will you take me to him?" she asked. "I want to see him, to tell him—" She swallowed.

He shook his head. "It's too dangerous, Mairi. They are taking revenge on everyone—women as well, especially women." She felt her cheeks flush with indignation, understanding what he meant. "Stay here in the glen for now." He came forward and put his hand on her arm. "I swear I will do my best to get him freed."

"Can I write to him?" she asked. "Just so he knows—" She swallowed as tears stung the back of her eyes. She would not cry, or mourn him yet.

Nathaniel nodded, and waited while she wrote the letter, her hand shaking, her tears falling on the paper. She wrote quickly, knowing there wasn't much time. She sealed it, and brought the parchment to her lips, kissed it, and sent up a prayer for her beloved.

Nathaniel tucked it into his pocket and picked up his hat. "I'll get it to him, Mairi, and I'll tell him—"

Mairi wrapped her arms around her body, and suppressed a shiver. Tell him what? There was so much to say. That she loved him, that she was carrying his child, that she was afraid without him? "Tell him that I am waiting for him to come home."

CHAPTER FORTY

Megan sat in the salon of Dundrummie Castle, staring out the window. The first frost had come early, hard on the heels of the storm, which had washed away the last vestiges of summer in one night. The frost lay on the faded roses and empty stalks of the garden in sharp lacy spikes. The sun was tentative, shivering behind the branches of the apple trees. Their fruit harvested, their job done for another season, the leaves had turned to gold and brown, like aged brass.

She shifted gingerly on the window seat and sighed. Her leg was elevated on a pile of cushions, her ankle wrapped in better bandages than Kit's shirt. It still throbbed after two days of rest, but it was healing.

A hasty note had been sent to Devorguilla, who had taken Alanna away to Edinburgh for some finer, fancier gowns. Eleanor said the dowager countess wished to keep Alanna away from Megan, lest Alanna too should pick up the taint of disobedience. As if it were catching. Megan missed her sister, and longed to talk to her, to tell her everything. Would Alanna understand?

Alanna had a new confidante now. Jane Parkhill, still indignant over the loss of Rossington, with the hunting season quite ruined for her, had accompanied the McNabb ladies to Edinburgh. Megan wondered if her mother would hurry back when she heard of Megan's injuries, but there hadn't been any word.

Miss Carruthers was keeping Sorcha busy with lessons. Her youngest sister's eyes had glowed when Megan told her of the adventure she'd had at Glen Dorian—in secret, of course, since Miss Carruthers did not approve. Megan hadn't said a word about the treasure. That was Kit's tale to tell.

She glanced out the window again. Beyond the orchard stood the lodge, invisible from here, and beyond that lay the wood, and the path that led upward to Glen Dorian. Was he there? He hadn't come to see her. She scanned the orchard for signs of him, watched the door, waited for Graves to announce him. No one even mentioned his name, as if he no longer existed, was part of the past. She twisted her handkerchief in her hands, fought tears.

At Glen Dorian, Kit had carried her out to the cart, cradled against his chest, and set her gently aboard. He'd stepped back, letting Eleanor and Jeannie fuss over her. He'd stood in the courtyard of the castle as they departed, his eyes on hers, until they'd lost sight of one another. She had not seen him since. She glanced again at the path between the trees, hoping, but there was no one there.

"How are you feeling?" Caroline said, coming into the salon, followed by Graves, who was bringing yet another pot of tea.

"I'm well, thank you, Caro." Her sister-in-law sat down on the settee. They waited for Graves to pour the tea and depart.

"How is—Alec?" Megan asked, too much of a coward to ask after Kit, afraid to hear he had left for England, and was lost to her forever. "He hasn't said a word to me since—" She bit her lip. She wanted to cry, and not because of her brother's neglect.

"I asked Alec to wait a day or two before he spoke to you," Caroline said.

"Oh, but I'm well enough for visitors," Megan said quickly.

Caroline picked up her teacup. "I know you are. I didn't ask him to wait because of your injuries. He's rather angry at the moment. He needed a day or two to think everything through. He was rather surprised to find you in Lord Rossington's arms, wrapped in a MacIntosh plaid—or so he described the scene to me."

"Would it have been better if it was a McNabb plaid?" Megan asked, raising her chin. "How did he find out? Did Mother write to him, or Eleanor, perhaps? I mean, how did you know about the—"

"Handfasting?" Caroline supplied calmly when Megan faltered. "We didn't know about that until we arrived, and we came because there was other news we didn't want to put into a letter. Something rather sensitive."

Megan burst into a smile, her heart lifting for the first time in two days. "You're expecting!" she cried, delighted.

Caroline blushed to the roots of her red hair. "Why yes, but that's not—"

But Megan hobbled across to hug her sister-in-law. "How wonderful. I suppose Alanna knows, and Mother, and Eleanor. Am I the last one?"

"Actually no one else knows yet, save Alec of course."

Megan frowned. "Then what brought you here?"

Caroline met her eyes. "Eachann Rennie."

Megan felt her throat dry to dust. "Eachann?" His name sounded strange, felt strange on her lips. She hadn't even thought of him since—she felt her skin heat.

"He came home last week, to see his father, and paid a call on Alec while he was there."

Megan kept her expression flat. They'd told no one about their plans, their hopes for the future. Now Eachann had come back, formally asked for her hand, and she—what would she do?

"He's married, Megan."

She met Caroline's gaze. "Married? Eachann? To someone else? A woman?" she babbled daftly.

"Her name is Grace."

"Grace?"

"She seems very nice. Her father owns an inn in Glasgow, and a half-interest in a shipping venture. Eachann met her while he was waiting for passage on an outbound ship."

"How—nice," Megan managed, still stunned.

"He explained to Alec that you and he had made an agreement before he left. He wanted to release you from your promise to marry him."

"Alec didn't hurt him, did he?" Megan asked.

Caroline pursed her lips. "He had to be convinced not to

beat him to a bloody pulp. That's why we came. Alec feared your heart would be broken by the news. Is it?"

Megan looked at her fingertips. "No. I realized some time ago that Eachann and I wouldn't suit."

"About the time Lord Rossington arrived?"

Megan met her sister-in-law's eyes. "Has *he* said anything?"

"Not to me."

Megan's heart sank. "Has he—" She swallowed. "Has he gone back to England?"

"I don't think so. He looked like he needed a long rest and a bath when last I saw him. That was the night he appeared in the storm. He looked more like a wild Highlander than any English gentleman I know."

"But he *is* English, Caro. He's got estates, and responsibilities, and the harvest to see to."

"What will you do?" Caroline asked. "Will you go to England with him?"

Megan felt her face fill with hot blood. "He has not asked me to. Our handfasting was never meant to last for a year and a day. It was simply a match of convenience, until—well, don't they have such arrangements in England?"

Caroline reached out and squeezed Megan's hand. "Of course. It's just that whatever side of the border one is on, these things never turn out to be convenient at all."

"I can see that," Megan murmured.

"Megan, Alec *can* insist that Rossington marry you properly. He's been pacing the floor muttering something about a stocking."

Megan's blush renewed itself, all the way to her toes. Her

ankle throbbed. "No! Oh, Caroline, Alec mustn't say anything. Kit—Lord Rossington—has no desire to be married at all. I won't force him."

Caroline sighed. "Then how will this end?"

Megan looked out the window again, across the orchard, but the path was still empty. "I suppose like all stories, we shall have to wait and see."

CHAPTER FORTY-ONE

Glen Dorian, May 1746

Nathaniel carried sorry news for the Lady of Glen Dorian. He had tried to deliver her letter and see Connor MacIntosh, but every trick he tried, from bribery to asserting his rank and family connections, had failed. No one had any news, just strict orders not to let anyone in to see the prisoners. He heard a rumor that Connor MacIntosh had been among a consignment of prisoners sent south for trial in England. He'd sent a letter to his brother Robert, the Earl of Rossington, pleading for his intervention, but had received no reply. Now, he would have to tell Connor's wife all of this, the woman who sat in the window every day and watched for her husband's return, the innocent wife of an innocent man.

The army wanted to make an example of the rebels, intent on crushing them utterly and forever. They were calling it the pacification of the Highlands, but it was a fey name for a dark and brutal deed. It had already begun—homes burned, cattle driven off, women raped, men murdered in cold blood. They hadn't reached Glen Dorian yet, but it would be only a matter of days. Connor MacIntosh's name was on a list of traitors, and there would be no mercy for Mairi, or the boy, or for any of the folk of the glen. Nathaniel felt sick.

"What news?" Ruairidh asked, catching the reins of Nathaniel's horse as he rode into the courtyard of the castle.

Nathaniel didn't have the heart to smile and lie. "Is your sister here?" he asked, dismounting, but she appeared in the doorway, her face tight with hope, which faded to dread at the sight of him. Her cheeks paled, and she put a hand to her mouth. He didn't soften the news.

"You have to go, Mairi, leave Glen Dorian. Is there a place you can hide?"

"Go? Hide?" she asked, swaying. He wondered when she had last eaten or slept. "But Connor must see to it, give the order. Is he coming?"

He climbed the steps to her, put his hand under her elbow to steady her. "Lad, go get her a drink of water," he told Ruairidh, and waited until the boy ran off to do so.

She met his eyes. "I'm all right," she insisted, her eyes dry. "Connor—"

Nathaniel shook his head, his mouth filling with bitterness. He couldn't tell her, couldn't say the words. "They are still holding the prisoners, questioning them," he said instead, and she sagged with relief.

"But he's well?" she asked, searching his face. "He got my letter?"

"He's well," Nathaniel said, repeating her words.

Ruairidh raced back toward them, the cup in his hands bouncing on the stone paving of the courtyard. "Soldiers! Mairi, there's soldiers coming!" he screamed, his eyes wide, filled with terror. Nathaniel had almost forgotten that the boy had seen the battle, knew what would happen next, even if his sister did not. She blinked at the boy, uncomprehending.

"Are they bringing Connor home?" she asked, and the boy stared at Nathaniel, suddenly looking younger than his thirteen years. Much younger. He looked from the boy to Mairi.

"No," Nathaniel said. "They aren't here to talk. They're here for revenge, to destroy. You have to go. They'll take everything, rape the women, burn and murder and pillage. Is there a safe place you can go?"

Mairi turned white. "There's a corrie—a cave—up in the hills near the waterfall."

"Is it far?" Nathaniel asked.

"Four or five miles," Ruairidh said.

Too far. The troops would be here before the hour was out, lusting for blood and plunder and Mairi, lovely, gentle Mairi—he couldn't let that happen, wouldn't.

She surprised him by moving first. "They'll come to the castle first. Ruairidh, go and get Fionn, tell him to go to the village, send them out now. Tell them to take what they can, but they must be gone within the hour, is that clear? They're to go to the corrie, leave no trail for the soldiers to follow."

"Yes Mairi," the boy said, and set off across the causeway.

"You've got to go too," Nathaniel said, his heart pounding in his breast. "Get on my horse."

She picked up her skirts and hurried into the castle instead. "There's something I must do first," she said. She opened cupboards and rushed to the kitchen, yelling orders. Folk began to scream, to panic, and he watched her calm them. She handed out loaves of bread and blankets and lengths of plaid as they passed her, giving orders in a soft voice, her face placid, though her hands shook. He took a box of candles off the shelf, and handed it to a woman who took it, and spit on his boots, muttering a curse on Gaelic.

"She doesn't know, doesn't understand," Mairi said. "Her husband is gone, too, and she's sure he's dead."

He probably was, Nathaniel thought.

Once her people had left, Mairi turned and raced up the steps. "You've got to come now, Mairi—there's no time!" he said, but she kept going. He followed, found her in the bedroom, kneeling before a chest, looking for something.

Through the window he could see the troop marching across the glen, their red coats glowing against the green of the hills, the drum still too far away to hear. An officer rode with them, and Nathaniel sent up a prayer that he outranked the man. Mairi wouldn't get out now, not without being seen. If he put her on his horse, they'd intercept him, take her, and—

He grabbed her arm. "Is there a place you can hide?" he demanded roughly. There was a scrap of cloth in her hands, white and soft, and she looked up at him in fear. "Go there, Mairi, Go now. I'll try to send them away."

She took a box from the chest, tucked it under her arm, and left the room with a single backward look. He followed her down the stairs. He could hear the drums now, which meant they were crossing the causeway. "Hide," he said through tight lips, reaching for the hilt of his sword. This time she didn't hesitate, she hurried through the kitchen. He watched saw her run through the garden to the edge of the loch. She disappeared behind the rocks on the shore, and he heard the sound of English shouts, and hobnailed boots on the stone floor of the hall.

He grabbed a half-empty pot of ale and walked out of the kitchen. Three soldiers turned their bayonets on him, then stopped at the sight of his uniform. "What the devil are you doing here?" the captain leading them demanded.

Nathaniel forced a sly smile. "Same as you, I assume. Looking for a bit of goods to sell on."

The man relaxed. "Is there anyone here?"

Nathaniel shrugged. "It was empty when I got here, and that was hours ago."

"Where's your company?" the captain demanded.

"I got lost in the hills," Nathaniel said, drinking deeply. He feigned a drunken grin. "Easy enough to do. Fortunately I found this place."

"Damned dangerous. You're lucky you didn't get your throat cut. These hills are a nest of bloodthirsty rebels. We killed three of them this morning. Hanged 'em outside one of those hovels they call cottages. Pigs live better."

The captain jerked his head and watched his soldiers scatter, begin to search. Nathaniel heard the breaking of china, the crash and splinter of furniture. They came back with a few trinkets, bottles of ale, pewter plates. "Load it all up," the captain ordered. "Any gold, jewels, plate?" he asked Nathaniel.

He felt bitterness fill his mouth. He forced himself to smile, and turned out his empty pocket. "Not a farthing. They must have taken it with them. Even the ale is sour."

The officer squinted at him, then cast a suspicious look around. "No women, no children, no old people?"

Nathaniel glanced at the soldiers prowling through the garden, his heart in his throat. He put his hand on his sword, and held his breath, waiting for the shout of discovery, expecting to hear Mairi's screams as they dragged her inside. But the soldiers came back alone. "No one," they reported.

Nathaniel met the captain's eyes. "No one at all," he agreed.

The captain spat on the floor. "The bastards must have been warned." He turned to his men. "All right, take what you have, then burn it, Sergeant. Leave nothing for the Jacobite scum to come back to."

CHAPTER FORTY-TWO

Alec was seated in Eleanor's study at Dundrummie castle, and Kit's first thought was that the Earl of Glenlorne was far too big for such a small and ladylike desk.

He waited while Glenlorne's eyes roved over him, assessing him now he was dressed properly. His linen was crisp and white, his excellently tailored coat a sober shade of dark blue, his breeches buff, and his boots polished to a gloss. He took off his beaver hat and tucked it under his arm as he bowed. Leslie had assured him he looked precisely as an English earl should look, but Glenlorne's dark expression told Kit that he was not going to be so easily impressed.

"You wished to see me," Glenlorne said crisply, folding his hands on the surface of the desk, his fingers laced together as if he were imagining them around Kit's throat. Kit sat down, though he hadn't been offered a chair. "I trust you are unscathed by the events at the castle?"

He wouldn't say unscathed, exactly. He'd slept poorly for the last two nights, having agreed at Glenlorne's insistence that he would wait that long before coming to call at Dundrummie to "discuss things." Alec needed time to think everything through, he said. Kit was here at last, and once this was settled, he would sleep for a week—hopefully with Megan.

"I wish to ask for Megan's hand in marriage," he said without responding to the earl's question. He watched Glenlorne's face redden dangerously.

"Are you doing this because honor demands it?" he asked.

Kit raised his chin. "In part. She'll be a countess."

"I doubt she cares about that."

"Because I'm not a Scot?" Kit asked.

"In part," Glenlorne parroted. "Have you heard of Eachann Rennie?"

Kit felt his throat tighten. "I have."

"Then you'll know she cares nothing for titles. Megan is the most romantic and sentimental of my sisters. Alanna is sensible, and considers matters with her head. I know she'll make a good match. But Megan follows her heart, and it's not always right. Eachann is not the first man she's fancied herself in love with. She loves her homeland with a far more steadfast passion. I doubt she'd be happy in England."

Kit swallowed. Did Glenlorne expect him to declare his love for Megan here and now? He hadn't even told her yet, and he wouldn't if she still loved Eachann.

"I would do my best, of course, to make her happy, but if she loves Eachann, and you are amenable to that match, then—"

"Eachann has Grace," Glenlorne said.

Grace? What did that mean? Was it some deep Scottish quality, perhaps, or was grace simply the blessing of Megan's love?

"Megan will never be a typical countess," Glenlorne went on. "Not an English one at any rate. No doubt Devorguilla will approve of you."

Kit's eyebrows rose at that pronouncement. "Does her approval have a bearing on our conversation?" he asked. "I had thought this was between you, me, and Megan."

"It is, but her entire family will become involved. Tell me, if you wished to marry Megan, then why the handfasting?"

Kit leaned forward. "Neither of us wanted to marry at all. She wished to wait for Eachann to return, and I didn't wish to wed." Glenlorne looked baffled. "If you met my sister, Arabella, you'd understand. She is the most unhappily married person in all of England, save for her husband, of course. I must admit the Dowager Countess of Glenlorne did propose, and I said no."

Glenlorne's eyes popped. "Devorguilla wanted to marry you?"

"She wanted me to marry Megan. We had only just met, and her hair was—" He raised his hands above his head, trying to describe the high and ridiculous coiffure Megan had sported the night they met. "I didn't know her, you see. How wonderful she was with her hair down her back, walking over the hills as she does . . . that fire in her eyes . . . those incredible eyes of hers . . ." He realized he was babbling, and Glenlorne was staring at him in astonishment. "Of course, if she prefers to marry—elsewhere—for love, then I shall not stand in her way," he said again.

"I think I shall need to speak to Megan," Glenlorne muttered. "Or my wife. None of this makes any sense to me."

"It's simple. I will withdraw my offer, leave for England at once if Megan's heart is engaged elsewhere, grace notwithstanding." He took an envelope from his pocket, pushed it across the desk. "My wedding present to her, whether she chooses to marry me or not, is Glen Dorian."

"You're giving her a ruin?"

Kit smiled and took a flask from his pocket and offered it to Glenlorne. "I'm giving her a treasure," he said.

CHAPTER FORTY-THREE

In the hills above Glen Dorian, January 1747

Nathaniel climbed the side of the mountain and whistled softly. Ruairidh popped out of the heather, taller now, but leaner too, more hollow eyed. He smiled warily. A younger boy came shyly out from behind him. "Duncan, is it?" Nathaniel said, ruffling the child's dark hair, and gave him a bit of sugar. He popped it into his mouth and ran to tell his mother.

"How is she?" Nathaniel asked Ruairidh.

"Not the same since she lost the babe. Have you brought news?"

He handed the boy the pack he carried, filled with oats, bacon, dried beef, and what flour he'd been able to find. "No," he said. "There's no word of Connor."

The boy's face fell.

The boy blamed himself, Nathaniel knew that. If not for him, Connor would have been at Glen Dorian on the day of the battle. Nathaniel knew now they still would have come for him, not caring if he was a Jacobite or not. They would have arrested him or hung him in the courtyard while they killed his people around him, raped his wife before his eyes. It had happened all over the Highlands, was still happening. People were starving, dying.

Nathaniel walked up the slope with Ruairidh, toward the hidden corrie that held the tattered remnants of the Glen Dorian MacIntoshes—less than two dozen people, and fewer every day, though Mairi did her best to keep them together, warm, fed, and hopeful. They left anyway, slipping away, sure they'd find something better somewhere else, knowing there was nothing left for them here. They accepted what Mairi refused to believe. Connor MacIntosh was gone, almost certainly dead. He'd simply disappeared. Nathaniel knew now that he wasn't in England. His name was not on the rolls of those tried or executed or transported.

For Mairi's sake, and without much hope, Nathaniel had even gone to search the fearsome prison ships that lay at anchor off Inverness, filled with prisoners who overflowed from the overcrowded gaol. You could smell the hulks from land, the stench of decay, death, and despair. He was glad for once that he didn't find Connor. A guard told him they cast the bodies of the dead out of the holds every day or two, burned the putrid corpses, not bothering to record the names. Nathaniel couldn't imagine the proud, educated, gentle MacIntosh suffering such a fate, nor could he imagine telling Mairi that he had.

And so he kept searching for Connor. It became an obsession. Now, nearly ten months later, there was still no word, and each time he came to the corrie, bringing what supplies he could, he watched the hope in her eyes grow fainter and fainter. He braced himself to see it again now, to feel it hit him like the lash of a whip, knowing he must disappoint her.

She gave him a faint smile of thanks as Ruairidh dropped the pack at her feet. She was thinner now, and strands of gray wove through her dark braid.

"How kind of you to come," she said, as she always did, as if she were still the Lady of Glen Dorian, inviting him into her castle. He looked around at the hollow faces that crouched by the fire, and wondered how they were going to survive the rest of the winter, how he was going to find enough food to help feed them all. Ruairidh and the other lads set snares, trapped rabbits when they could, or grouse. He'd brought three chickens for eggs in the fall, and a ewe to give milk, but they were gone now, eaten. Mairi was always the last to eat.

"Two men left last week, and didn't come back," Ruairidh told him. "They said they were going across the sea."

Mairi laid a hand on her brother's shoulder. "They might still decide to come back again," she said. "Will you eat?" she asked Nathaniel, holding out a bowl of thin soup.

"No," he said. "I have to go back before I'm missed." It's what they said to each other every time he came.

"Is there news?" she asked breathlessly.

He stared at her in the firelight, beautiful and brave for the sake of Connor's people. He still saw determination in her eyes, and weariness as well. Would it be kinder to tell her what he feared, or leave her to hope? Would hope keep her warm through the winter? He opened his mouth, then shut it again. "No," he said, and left her.

CHAPTER FORTY-FOUR

Kit sat on the bench outside the cottage, and stared down at the castle. Autumn had turned the glen from green to brown and gold and russet, the colors of Megan's eyes. It would be four days tomorrow since the storm, and two days since his meeting with Glenlorne. Alec had insisted that Kit wait until Megan had recovered before he made his proposal—and Glenlorne would inform him when that time came. Kit was beginning to suspect the earl was hoping Kit would change his mind and leave. He folded his arms over his chest and watched an eagle circling the glen. He would wait for as long as it took.

"So what will you do with all that whisky?" Alec McNabb asked, and Kit looked up to find him standing beside him, his eyes on the bird as well. His expression gave nothing away.

"Sell it, I suppose. But look there, where the village used to be—" Kit pointed. "I thought I'd make more. Build a proper distillery, there by the stream."

Glenlorne sat down on the bench and stretched his long legs out before him and looked across the glen. "Aye," he said, as if he could see it.

"And there's space for cattle. I understand there used to be cattle here—fine fat herds that made the MacIntoshes of Glen Dorian rich."

"So the story goes," Glenlorne said. "Can you do all that from England?"

Kit sent him a sharp look. "I'll need a good steward, of course, a man who knows whisky making."

"And someone who knows cows," Glenlorne added.

"Does—Eachann Rennie—have any skills in those directions?"

Alec rubbed his jaw. "I doubt it. Last I heard, the lad wanted to be a shipbuilder, in Glasgow. His father's pleased."

Kit looked around the glen and wondered if Megan would like living in Glasgow, being married to a shipbuilder.

"Beautiful place, this glen. The castle isn't ever going to be habitable again, though," Alec said.

"No, but the cottage could be enlarged—or I'd build a house here, on the hill."

"It would have an excellent view," Glenlorne said. "Would you take the castle down?"

Kit laughed. "Duncan MacIntosh was here yesterday to ask me the same thing. He wanted to see the sword Megan and I found in the crypt. He declared it to be the legendary sword of Alasdair MacIntosh, who fought in France with the Maid of Orleans before he came home to build this castle. Duncan swore Glen Dorian would fall down of its own accord if the sword wasn't returned to the knight's tomb at once. Duncan has hopes, you see, that the glen will be restored to its former glory—especially since he tasted the whisky." He took a flask from his pocket, and passed it to Glenlorne. "It's a fine thing indeed after seventy years."

Alec sipped, then sipped again, and rolled his eyes with pleasure. "It is indeed. What's that?" he said, pointing to Nathaniel's journal, which sat on the bench beside Kit.

"My great-uncle's journal. He was here, fought at the battle of Culloden. He knew Mairi MacIntosh, saw the castle burned. Duncan says Nathaniel was quite in love with the lady."

"Love?" Glenlorne said. "What happened?"

Kit shrugged. "He returned to England eventually. He asked her to go with him. Her clan had left the glen, scattered, but Mairi was determined to wait for Connor to return. Nathaniel built this cottage for her, but he could not stay, not if she didn't want him."

"And how did the story end?" Glenlorne asked.

"I don't know," Kit murmured, thinking of Megan, his fist clenched against his knee as he tried to stem the tide of longing.

"Megan knows a good many stories. Perhaps she knows the end of this one," Glenlorne said, rising to his feet. "I think you should ask her."

CHAPTER FORTY-FIVE

Glen Dorian, May 1747

Mairi stood with her eyes shaded against the sun, watching Nathaniel climb up the side of the waterfall, her slim figure wrapped in a threadbare cloak.

"Where's Ruairidh?" he asked when he reached her.

"He left," she said, her tone flat. He watched her scan the hills, as if looking for the boy, the way she looked for Connor. "He said there was no life here, no chance of happiness, no hope. He believes Connor must be dead, you see, and he—" She dashed away tears with the back of a work reddened hand. "He thinks I'm foolish for staying."

There was almost no one left now, a handful of folk—fewer than a dozen—all weak and nervous from more than a year in hiding. He clasped her hand, ran his thumb over her fingers, felt her grip him back for an instant. "It's safe enough to come down now, Mairi," he said.

"Connor?" she whispered, her eyes widening. For an instant she was the pretty woman he'd met over a year ago when she welcomed him to her hearth.

His mouth tightened, this time with jealousy as much as

regret. "No," he said. "Mairi, there's no trace of him. He's disappeared. He isn't coming back."

"Is he dead?" she asked, her voice a thread of sound. "Do you know for certain that he's dead?" He wondered if she hoped for that as much as for his return, an ending, a certainty, permission to move forward with her own life.

Nathaniel shifted. "No. I don't think there is a way to know that. But I'm sure of one thing—you can't stay here." He squeezed her hand tighter. "Come with me. Marry me," he said.

She looked at him in surprise, her eyes wide and blue as the sky, and for a moment he thought she might say yes, but then she closed her eyes, and shook her head. "You're a kind man, a good man. If not for you—" She swallowed tears. "If not for you, we would not have survived, but it wasn't for me, not ever for me. I did this for Connor. He told me to keep the clan safe, and I must do that. I will wait for him until he returns, or until I know for certain he's dead."

Nathaniel felt his heart cave in. "You can't live up here. Come down, back to Glen Dorian."

"To the castle?" she asked.

He shook his head quickly. "To the village, perhaps—Dundrummie village."

She sighed. "I belong in the glen, Nathaniel."

He studied her face, beautiful and stubborn, and considered tossing her over his shoulder, carrying her away, but knew she'd hate him for it.

"Then I will build you a cottage in the glen."

She searched his face, and put a hand to his cheek, a brief, gentle touch. "Thank you. And then, you must go, and not come back again."

"Promise you'll send for me if you need me," he said, and she smiled again.

"Of course."

But he knew she would not.

CHAPTER FORTY-SIX

Even sitting quietly in a shaft of sunlight by the window, dressed in a plain blue gown, her hair in one long silken plait over her shoulder, Megan McNabb took his breath away. He steeled himself for the devastating moment when she would look up and see him here, in the doorway, and he would feel electricity course through him.

"Good morning," Kit said, stuck where he was, as if he was glued to the floor. Her head rose, and she bloomed like a rose—her eyes widened, her cheeks flushed pink, and her lips parted in surprise.

"Oh!" she popped to her feet, and he rushed forward.

"Your foot—don't get up!"

"It's much better," she said, still standing to show him, wobbling a little, her eyes were on his, whisky warm. He was drawn to her as if he were on a string. He stopped just short of touching her.

"Hello," he said.

"Hello," she replied.

He was staring at her, and she was staring back. "I—"

He stopped. The declaration of love hovered on his lips, his proposal, but surely it was too soon. He remembered the box under his arm, and he held it out. "I brought this."

She glanced at it. "The box from the crypt," she said. Her voice dropped an octave as her smile faded. "The treasure."

She made no move to take it, or touch it. "Have you come to tell me what's in it?"

He shifted his stance. "I don't actually know. I haven't opened it yet. I thought you—we—might do it together."

He followed her gaze to the inlaid box. The colored bits of wood had faded, but the gems, the mother-of-pearl flowers, their delicate stems and leaves made of gold, were s still exotic.

"All right." She sat down on the settee, and he took the chair beside her. He set the box on the table. She bit her lip as he reached for the delicate latch, and opened it. The lid popped up with a click, and they glanced at one another, holding their breath.

He began to draw out the contents. "A stone bottle," he said, and set it down. The next item was folded in a scrap of plaid, tied with ribbon. He unwrapped it as she leaned forward to see. He could smell the heather-sweet scent of her hair.

"It's a baby's gown," she said, picking up the fine linen, yellowed now. "But it's not finished."

A small item fell out, and he picked it up from the floor. It was a small gold ring with a heart-shaped ruby.

"Is this treasure?" he asked.

She looked at him solemnly. "To Mairi it was."

He picked up the bottle and opened the stopper. A sheaf

of furled paper hid inside, and he drew it out. There were two pages, rolled together, tied with faded blue ribbon.

She took them from his hand and unrolled the outermost page. They were in Gaelic. "What is it?" he asked, leaning forward, his shoulder brushing hers.

"It's a letter. It's in the same hand as the one you found in your great-uncle's journal." Her eyes scanned the words.

He felt his heart beat faster. "Then it was written by Mairi."

Glen Dorian, 1778

My Dearest Beloved,

It has been more than thirty years since my eyes beheld you, though it feels like only yesterday. I still wake in the night and reach for you, and feel sorrow that you are not there beside me, where you belong. At better moments, I smile at the memories we had time to make, and feel bitter at the hours, months, long years that were stolen from us. We would have grown old together, you and I, here in this glen, watched our children grow, and their children.

I have waited for you, hoped, lived a life of longing. I am the last one left in the glen now—everyone you knew has died or gone, and I cannot find fault with that.

Even now I am waiting for you to come walking over the edge of the glen, your smile broad, your arms wide. I long for that so much it hurts. The pain is unbearable, made worse by not knowing what happened to you, if you are alive, and unable to return to me, or dead. I would know if you were dead, would I not? Or is it just that you are alive forever in my heart, and my mind, and part of my soul, and I cannot let you go?

I am leaving this last letter in the place we used to meet before we were wed, our trysting place you called it. If I am not here, I trust you will go there first, to see our treasure is safe—it is, after all these years, and I hope you will find this letter. I leave it with my wedding ring, in case you have no coin for bread and meat. I also leave you word of my greatest sorrow. I was with child when you left, Connor—our son, but he was born too early, high in the hills, and could not live. If you are in heaven, I hope our bairn is with you, as I will someday be. Until then, I remain

    Your own loving Mairi

Kit wiped away Megan's tears with the pad of his thumb, moved over to sit beside her and hold her close as she sobbed. She lifted her head at last and looked at him.

"Please tell me the other letter is his reply, that he came back to her."

Kit unrolled the second bit of paper, crinkled and yellowed and begrimed and scanned it. "It's a recipe, by the looks of it," he said. "It's in Gaelic, though."

She took it from him and scanned it, and he watched her cheeks flush. "It's whisky," she said in amazement. "The MacIntosh recipe for making whisky."

Kit laughed out loud. "That's the treasure! Not the sword, or the box, or the casks of whisky—the recipe," Kit said. "Nathaniel's journal said Connor was an educated man. He probably wrote out the recipe that had been passed down through generations of MacIntoshes, knowing it would be lost or changed if he didn't. He must have known that no matter what the future, as long as his clan had this recipe, all would be well."

Megan blinked at him, her color rising. "All will be well? I suppose you'll sell the whisky we—you—found in the castle?" she said sharply.

"It's worth a fortune," he confirmed. "Nineteen fortunes, in fact, one for each barrel."

She folded her arms over her chest. "I thought you counted twenty barrels," she said. "Will you keep one for yourself?"

He sobered, remembering why he had come. He looked at her, studied her sweet face, read the question in her eyes, felt longing wash over him.

"It's meant to be a gift," he said carefully.

"For whom?" she demanded.

"For a bride," he said.

"What bride?" she shot back.

"Mine, hopefully," he said.

"You're getting *married?*" She looked horrified.

"I—I hope to." He wasn't doing this very well, he decided. He stared at her mutely, trying to form the feelings in his heart into sensible words.

She got to her feet, began to pace. "I see. Shall I come to the wedding, wish you well?"

He rose as well, followed her, not daring to touch her, but ready to catch her if she stumbled. She turned to face him so suddenly she almost did. He gripped her arms, and they stood almost nose-to-nose. "I do hope you will be there," he said. "That is, if you aren't marrying Ea—anyone else."

Her eyes fell to his mouth. "Eachann has Grace," she whispered, and his mouth watered to kiss her.

"I know," he said. "But I wanted to ask you anyway." He met her lips with a gentle brush. "I don't want to wait a year and a day, or another minute. I want to marry you, if you'll have me." He kissed her again, more firmly this time. She softened in his arms, kissed him back. "Of course, if you're in love with Eachann and his bloody state of grace, I will go at once, and wish you well." He stepped back to prove he could, and would. "You may keep the whiskey, of course, and Glen Dorian—as a wedding present."

"A wedding present? Don't you want it?" she asked, taking a step toward him. He stepped backward.

"Not without you."

"Yes," she said.

"Yes? You'll take the castle?"

She came closer still. He backed up until he hit the settee. "Yes, but there are conditions," she said, putting her arms around her neck, pressing her lips to his, a proper kiss, her body against his, her lips parting on a sigh, her tongue meeting his. He kissed her back, wanted more when she pulled away.

"What are the conditions?" he asked. "That I stay away forever, leave you in peace?"

She smiled. "Quite the opposite. I insist that you *stay* forever, never leave me. I love you, Christopher Linwood. Not for convenience, or for a year and a day. Not because of a castle, or a fortune in whisky. I'd live in a hut with you."

He stared into her eyes. "That could be a problem. I own five—six—rather grand homes. Of course, we may have to live in a hut, since they're all full at the moment—"

She blinked at him, and he realized he was babbling. "I love you," he said, and felt something stiff and unyielding melt in his heart. "I love you." He pulled her close and kissed her again. "I love you. Wait—what about Eachann? What will you tell him?"

She gave him a slow smile. "Not a thing. He's happily married to Grace now. He has thrown me over, and I am a free woman—well, after a year and a day."

Kit felt a shock run through him. "Thrown you over? Shall I call him out and shoot him?"

She sent him a sharp look of irritation. "Stop talking and kiss me."

EPILOGUE

On a perfect blue and gold autumn day, when the hills shimmered with color, and the sun glowed like a ripe red apple, the meadow of Glen Dorian was filled with people. There were MacIntoshes, Frasers, McNabbs, and a Linwood—earls, ladies, and farmers. The joyful trill of the pipes echoed off the hills, and the shadow of the old castle loomed over the celebration of the wedding of Lady Megan McNabb and the English Earl of Rossington. The tables groaned with food and fall flowers, and the finest whisky anyone present had ever tasted.

Duncan MacIntosh helped the local churchman perform the marriage, which was held in the chapel of Glen Dorian Castle, where the last wedding celebrated was the union of Laird Connor MacIntosh, who took the lovely Mairi Fraser to wife in the autumn of 1745, seventy-two years earlier.

After the vows were said, villagers and crofters, clansmen and kin had greeted the Earl and Countess of Rossington on the meadow by the loch, and the cask of whisky was tapped and poured out, making everyone all the merrier. There were a score or more of toasts to the loveliness of the bride, though she had married a Sassenach and would live part of the year in England. Her new husband promised they would be back in Scotland often, and was forgiven for stealing away the prettiest lass in all the Highlands, since it was obvious by the love in both her eyes and his he could not have done otherwise.

And far away on the hill, above the cottage, where the land rose high enough to overlook the whole glen at once, from the road at one end to the misty waterfall far away at the other, a wistful shadow passed over the grass, hovered there for a moment watching, and moved on at last.

You've read about what happens in Autumn,
but have you seen what the summer winds brought?
Read on for an excerpt from

ONCE UPON A HIGHLAND SUMMER,

available now!

An Excerpt from

ONCE UPON A HIGHLAND SUMMER

"Angus MacNabb!"

Was there no peace in his own grave?

He'd been tormented enough in life. He squeezed his eyes shut and tried to ignore the soft voice calling him, drawing him, pulling him back into the world, even knowing she was the one and only person who could.

"MacNabb, I know you can hear me. Stop being stubborn and come out. We wouldn't be here if it wasn't for your foolish curse, and you're going to help me fix it."

"Stubborn!" Angus snapped, unable to resist the goad. "Isn't that a case of the pot calling the kettle—" He stopped and stared. Georgiana stood shimmering in the air before him.

He blinked, wondering if he was seeing a ghost, then recalled that he was.

Even dead, Georgiana had the power to steal his breath away—if he'd had any breath to steal. She tilted her head and smiled at him, just the way he remembered. It had been nearly sixty years since he'd seen that smile, but he'd never forgotten it. It smoked through him now like life itself, filled him with passion and pain.

Georgiana Forrester, the late Countess of Somerson, raised her eyebrows as if she was waiting for him to finish his comment, but he didn't. How could he speak while her eyes roamed over the plaid he'd been buried in? He'd looked his best when they'd laid him out, and he straightened his shoulders proudly now, and pushed the laird's bonnet back on his brow.

"That's a fine gown ye're wearing. You still look like a lass." His lass.

Georgiana looked down at the silver satin with a moue of distaste. "I detest this gown. I married Somerson in it, and they chose it for my burial. The only good thing I can say about it is that it still fit perfectly after all those years. I don't know how they found it. I ordered my maid to burn it."

MacNabb frowned, and one of the eagle feathers in his bonnet fell over his eye. The three feathers proclaimed him laird of his clan, chief over every rock, tussock of grass, and starving child as far as the eye could see from the crumbling tower of old Glenlorne Castle, where they stood now. It had been their trysting place until—. The old, familiar anger flared.

"Somerson!" he spat the name, filling it with sixty years of hatred. "Only a cheap fool would bury his wife in her wedding gown."

Georgiana's chin came up. "You said you liked it. Besides, the day of my marriage and the day of my burial were equally sorrowful. I think it was a most appropriate choice."

MacNabb sighed, and a breeze moved restively through

the treetops beyond the tower's crumbling walls. "Aye, well, that's not why we're here, is it, to debate our grave clothes?"

He looked around the tower, open to the sky now, the roof long gone. The rotting stones of the windows framed a view of the glen, the loch, and the new castle of Glenlorne at the opposite end of the valley. The new keep, already over a hundred and fifty years old, looked near as decrepit as this tower, older by four centuries. He sighed again.

If he turned and looked away to the east, he'd be able to see Georgiana's uncle's cottage, Lullach Grange, but he kept his back to it. He'd spent sixty years watching the empty house for her candle in the window, the signal that she'd meet him here, at the tower, but that light had gone out when their families tore them apart forever. The familiar bitterness of loss filled him again, still, and he turned to glare at her.

"What do you want of me, woman?" he asked gruffly.

Her eyes remained soft, unafraid. "You cursed us, Angus."

"I had cause enough!"

She shook her head, her smile wistful. "We were in love, and they would not let us marry, but your curse has echoed through two generations of both our families. It must end. I want my granddaughter to know the kind of happiness we shared, Angus."

"Was it happiness? It made the rest of our lives unbearable. Well, mine anyway. I canna speak for you, of course." There wasn't a day he hadn't thought of her. Her name had been the last word on his lips.

She looked down at her hand, where her wedding band had once sat. The family heirloom now graced the hand of the present countess. It was another ring she missed, the one

Angus had given her to seal their love, a promise ring with a small ruby. "Neither of us had joy in our marriages." She waved her hand to indicate the tower. "The last true happiness I felt was here, that last night, in your arms."

Angus could see the place she meant right through her transparent body, the sheltered spot where they'd lain together, wrapped in his plaid, alternately making love and whispering about the future, pledging themselves to each other. His hands coiled, aching to touch her. *Could* they touch? He didn't know, but to reach for her and close his arms on empty air yet again would be too much to bear.

"Ye've come at a bad time, *gràdhach*," he said, the Gaelic term for "beloved" slipping off his tongue. He could have bitten that tongue in two when she smiled sweetly at him. "My son just died, and my clan's left leaderless. My daughter-in-law is trying to sell out to Engl—"

"Not leaderless. You have a grandson, don't you?"

"I do. But Alec left Glenlorne years ago, swearing he'd never return. Mayhap it's better he doesn't."

"You don't believe that."

"What's left for him to come home to?" he asked, his mouth twisting bitterly.

She floated over to stand beside him. "There's the land, Angus. And there's love. Love can rebuild anything."

He stared at her, saw the foolish hope in her eyes. That look, that hope had made him fall in love with her, made him believe anything was possible. He shut his eyes against the feeling stirring in his breast. "Ye can't truly think I believe in *love*, do ye?"

She reached out a hand, laying it on his arm. He couldn't

feel it, but light flared where their shadows touched, glowed. "You did once—an Englishman's daughter and a Scot—who would have imagined it in those terrible times? It was almost impossible."

"It *was* impossible."

She laughed, and the sound echoed through the tower, startling a bird to flight. It flapped into the night with a frightened cry. Georgiana ignored it. "It was only impossible for them, not for us. I doubt we'd be here now, together in this place again, if our love had died too."

No, his love for her had never died. Not even here, on the other side of death. He loved her still, yet what point was there in that? Was it to be an eternity of pain instead of a mere lifetime? "What has any of this to do with Alec?" he demanded. Was it his imagination, or could he smell her perfume?

"My granddaughter's name is Caroline." Her voice was soft, fond, gentle.

"Caroline? You want to match her to my grandson? How can you be sure they'd even suit? Wouldn't the current Earl of Somerson object to a match with a penniless Scots laird o' nothing?"

"Leave him to me. We need only bring my Caroline and your Alec together, remind them, perhaps, of—" She cast a meaningful look at their trysting place.

"Has she any money?" he asked ruthlessly, trying to ignore the tender memory. "He needs to marry a lass with a bloody fortune if he's to save this place!"

She dismissed his concern with a wave of her hand. "She has a respectable dowry, of course, but that hardly matters.

They'll find a way, but not because of money—love, Angus, love." The sound of the word swirled in the air around him. It softened his heart.

"I'm not against trying, *gràdhach*, but we can't force them to fall in love, or be sure it'll last."

She smiled sweetly and sighed, and the white heather growing under the walls shivered restively. "'Tis almost summer, Angus. Remember how easy it was to be in love in the summer? All we need do is bring them here. The rest will take care of itself."

Angus frowned, still dubious that anything to do with love or marriage could ever be that simple.

Beyond the sanctuary of the tower, belligerent clouds covered the moon, and thunder muttered a dark warning.

A storm was about to descend on the peaceful valley of Glenlorne.

CHAPTER ONE

"I'll have your decision now, if you please."

Lady Caroline Forrester stared at the carpet in her half-brother's study. It was like everything else in his London mansion—expensive, elegant, and chosen solely to proclaim his consequence as the Earl of Somerson. She fixed her eyes on the blue swirls and arabesques knotted into the rug and wondered what distant land it came from, and if she could go there herself rather than make the choice Somerson demanded.

"Come now," he said impatiently. "You have two suitors to choose from. Viscount Speed has two thousand pounds a year, and will inherit his father's earldom."

"In Ireland," Caroline whispered under her breath. Speed also had oily, perpetually damp skin and a lisp, and was only interested in her because her dowry would make him rich. At least for a short while, until he spent her money as he'd spent his own fortune on mistresses, whist, and horses.

"And Lord Mandeville has a fine estate on the border with Wales. His mother lives there, so she would be company for you."

Mandeville spent no time at all at his country estate for that exact reason. Caroline had been in London only a month, but she'd heard the gossip. Lady Mandeville went through highborn companions the way Charlotte—Somerson's countess—devoured cream cakes at tea. Lady Mandeville was famous for her bad temper, her sharp tongue, and her dogs. She raised dozens, perhaps even hundreds, of yappy, snappy, unpleasant little creatures that behaved just like their mistress, if the whispered stories were to be believed. The lady unfortunate enough to become Lord Mandeville's wife would serve as the old lady's companion until one of them died, with no possibility of quitting the post to take a more pleasant job.

"So which gentleman will you have?" Somerson demanded, pacing the room, his posture stiff, his hands clasped behind his back, his face sober. Caroline had laughed when he'd first told her the two men had offered for her hand. But it wasn't a joke. Her half-brother truly expected her to pick one of the odious suitors he'd selected for her and tie herself to that man for life.

He looked down his hooked nose at her, a trait inherited from their father, along with his pale, bulging eyes. Caroline resembled her mother, the late earl's second wife, which was probably why Somerson couldn't stand the sight of her. As a young man he'd objected to his father's new bride most strenuously, because she was too young, too pretty, and the daughter of a mere baronet without fortune or high connections. He'd even objected to the new countess's red hair. Caroline raised a hand to smooth a wayward russet curl behind her ear. Speed had red hair—orange, really—and spindly pinkish eyelashes.

Caroline thought of her niece Lottie, who was upstairs having her wedding dress fitted, arguing with her mother over what shade of ribbon would best suit the flowers in the bouquet. She was marrying William Rutherford, Viscount Mears—*Caroline's* William, the man she'd known all her life, the eldest son and heir of the Earl of Halliwell, a neighbor and dear friend of her parents. It had always been expected she'd wed one of Halliwell's sons, but Sinjon, the earl's younger son, had left home to join the army and go to war rather than propose to Caroline. And now William, who even Caroline thought would make an offer for her hand, had instead chosen Lottie's hand. Caroline shut her eyes. It was beginning to feel like a curse. Not that it mattered now. William had made his choice. Still, a wedding should be a happy thing, the bride as joyful as Lottie, the future ripe with the possibilities of love and happiness.

Caroline didn't even *like* her suitors—well, they weren't really *her* suitors—they were courting her dowry, and a connection to Somerson. They needed her money, but they didn't need her.

"Is it truly such a difficult choice? You are twenty-two years old. Time is of the essence." Somerson said coldly. "Surely one gentleman stands out in your esteem. Do you find Speed handsomer, or perhaps Mandeville's conversation is more enjoyable?"

No and no!

She looked up at her half-brother, a man twenty-four years her senior, and one of the most powerful earls in the realm, ready to plead her case, but saw at once that was pointless. He'd married the daughter of an equally powerful earl, had nine children, and seemed happy enough with his wife, though Charlotte was a virago, a gossip, and a glutton. She weighed eighteen stone, and was never without a plate of sweetmeats close to hand.

Speed was the male version of Charlotte. Somerson was just like Mandeville, obsessed with his own importance.

No, there would be no point in arguing, or refusing. Somerson had decided, even if she had not, could not. Caroline's stomach turned over, and she closed her mouth. Her half-brother's face was hard, and without the slightest bit of sympathy. She was simply a matter he wanted settled as quickly and quietly as possible. Caroline was an unwanted burden now her mother was dead. She knew he'd choose for her if she refused to do so, and it was impossible to say which gentleman would be worse. She shifted her feet, which made him stop pacing to regard her like a bird of prey.

"Caroline?" he prompted.

The curling vines in the carpet threatened to rise up and choke her, though her own misery was already doing the job well enough.

She forced a smile. "I promised Lottie I'd help her choose a gown for her wedding trip. There really has been so much to do for *her* nuptials that I have not had a moment to think about my own," she said as lightly as possible, twisting the ruby ring, her mother's legacy, on her finger.

"It's been two days," Somerson admonished. "How much time could it possibly take to make such a simple choice?"

Caroline shut her eyes. It was hardly simple. She'd been a sentimental child, and had grown up to be a young woman with starry-eyed ideas of what romance and marriage ought to be. She'd always thought she'd know the moment she set eyes on the man she wanted to marry. She'd feel a surge of love that would warm her from her toes to her crown, and angels would sing. She felt only horror when she looked at Mandeville and Speed. Her skin crawled and crows croaked a warning.

Flee.

The idea whispered in her ear.

She swallowed, and met Somerson's eyes, steeling her courage to refuse, but the ice in his expression chilled her. She had been raised to be obedient, even when the yoke chafed. "Tomorrow—I'll give you my decision tomorrow."

His eyes narrowed as if he suspected a trick. She widened her smile till it hurt. "At breakfast, is that clear?" he said at last.

"Perfectly," she murmured. "May I go?"

But he'd already turned away, as if he had more important things to think about and she'd taken up too much of his time. She curtsied to his back and left the study.

Upstairs, Charlotte was shrieking at the modiste, berating the poor woman because the lace wasn't sitting properly at Lottie's bosom. Caroline felt sorry for the dressmaker—it was past midnight, and this was the third time Charlotte had changed her mind about her daughter's wedding gown. Caroline had no doubt Charlotte would let her half-sister-in-law get married wearing a burlap sack if it got the matter done faster, and got Caroline packed off, out of sight and out of mind forevermore.

A distant door slammed, and a maid rushed down the steps, nearly colliding with Caroline.

The poor girl was flushed, and she nearly tripped trying to curtsy and run at the same time. "Oh, excuse me, my lady—

more treacle tarts are needed upstairs at once." She bolted down the kitchen hallway like a frightened rabbit.

Caroline set her hand on the banister. She lifted her foot, held it over the first step, and stopped.

There was another loud objection upstairs, and Lottie burst into noisy tears.

Caroline stepped back. She should go up to help soothe her niece, or go to bed and think about her choice, but there was no point in that. She could never bring herself to pick Speed or Mandeville.

Flee.

She turned, wondering if someone had spoken, but there was no one there, just the modiste's cloak and bonnet, hanging on a peg beside the front door.

Flee.

Caroline grabbed the cloak and swung it over her shoulders, and clapped the bonnet onto her head. The brass door latch was cold under her palm. Her heart pounded. Another shriek of rage echoed down the stairs, and she opened the door and stepped out, shutting it behind her, cutting off the dreadful sound. For a moment she stood on the front step, looking up and down the dark street, wondering which way to go. It was yet another choice—and one she couldn't wait until morning to make. Taking a breath, she pulled the hood close to her face and turned right.

She hurried away from the lights of Somerson House, moving into the shadows. If anyone bothered to look for her tonight, they'd find her gone. If not, then even Somerson would understand her choice when he sat down for breakfast tomorrow.

Want more?
Check out this sneak peek at

WHAT A LADY MOST DESIRES,

the next fabulous romance from Lecia Cornwall

An Excerpt from

WHAT A LADY MOST DESIRES

The Duchess of Richmond's Ball, Brussels, June 15, 1815

He was the only man in the world who had the power to stop her breath just by walking into a room.

Even now, when she hadn't set eyes on him for over a year, the familiar dizzy sensation stopped her in her tracks on the grand staircase that led down to the Duchess's ballroom.

It wasn't that he was the handsomest man here. There were many officers present, from five different armies, all equally resplendent in their dress tunics. At least half of them had fair hair that shone just as brightly as his did under the light of the inestimable number of candles that lit the room. Many were as tall, or taller, and had shoulders that were just as broad as his.

It wasn't high rank or exalted title that marked him out, or that he was both a diplomat and a cavalry officer. Rather it was his quiet confidence that compelled people to look at him, to take note of Major Lord Stephen Ives, and mark him as unusual, as if his good opinion mattered, carried weight. To look in the gray depths his eyes and be found wanting was a harsh blow indeed, as Lady Delphine St. James well knew.

They had met the major in London at another ball, over a year ago, and she had spent just a few minutes in his company, but it had been enough. What she had read in his eyes that night had changed her forever. From that moment, he was the one she measured all other gentleman against, and she found every one of them wanting by comparison.

Even now, after all the months that had passed, Stephen Ives still had the power to make her breath catch in her throat, weaken her knees, and make her heart race. He had made it clear that he did not feel the same, and she desired above all things to know why. If she could choose one dance partner tonight, one man to escort her to supper, it would be—

"You," she whispered to the air, her eyes fixed on his back.

He turned as if she'd shouted the word. He looked up to where she was standing on the stairs, and she felt a thrill run through her body as their eyes met. She read surprise, then a moment of dismay before he smoothed his features to a flat expression and nodded a brief acknowledgement. The thrill in her breast fizzled and died. Nothing had changed, then. He liked her no better now.

Still, she smiled sweetly at him, though he did not smile back, or show any sign of moving from where he stood. The crowd took up every inch of space between her place on the staircase and his position on the edge of the dance floor. It would be quite impossible to cut through the crush to reach his side.

Impossible was not a word Lady Delphine St. James endured.

"Excuse me," she said, pushing past a Dutch officer exchanging pleasantries with a lady in blue silk. "Your pardon," she murmured, squeezing by a red-coated lieutenant, keeping her eyes on Stephen Ives all the while. He was watching her, his expression unreadable, probably hoping she was heading somewhere else.

She made a quick curtsy to the Duchess of Richmond, her hostess, at the bottom of the steps. "Good evening, Your Grace," she said breathlessly. The duchess merely nodded. If she found Delphine's haste unseemly, she did not remark on it. There were other, more important guests to see to. Delphine glanced up to see if Stephen had moved. He hadn't. That was a good sign, wasn't it? She picked up her skirt and hurried on.

Someone stepped into her path, forcing her to stop.

"Why Lady Delphine—what an unexpected pleasure."

She almost cursed aloud. The gentleman bowed, and she gazed at Stephen over his bent shoulder before he rose again and blocked her view of her quarry.

Her withering glare turned to surprise. "Oh, it's you, Captain Lord Rothdale." He was a friend of her brother's, or rather a compatriot in Sebastian's debauchery.

"Captain Lord Rothdale? Is that any way to greet an old and dear friend?" He preened, showing off his Royal Dragoons uniform, making the gold braid glitter in the candlelight. "You promised to call me Peter when we met at your father's home in London. Don't let the uniform scare you away. I may be one of the heroes, but I am still as tame as a house cat, I assure you."

He smiled at his own joke and picked up her hand, though she hadn't offered it, and brought it to his lips. For a moment she wondered if he intended to lick it, cat-like. The intensity of his eyes on her bodice reminded her of an animal far more dangerous than a mere tabby. "How may I be of service this evening, Darling Dilly? You appear to lack a dancing partner."

Her jaw tightened at the sound of her family nickname on his lips, and she tried to withdraw her hand from his. He refused to let go. Instead he tightened his grip, leaned closer still, and she could smell rum on his breath. The glitter in his eyes had more to do with the amount of the spirit he'd consumed than the pleasure of her company. He had arrived foxed then, since the duchess was serving champagne, not rum, which made his condition all the more shocking.

She tried again to free her hand, but he gave her a teasing smile and held on. She felt her cheeks heat, and a scathing insult came to mind, but this was hardly the place. Rothdale stepped closer still.

"Dance with me, Dilly. Or better yet, come out to the terrace, and I'll whisper lavish compliments in your ear. Rumor has it we'll be off to battle come sun-up. Don't you want to give me a proper send off?"

She did indeed, but not the kind he hoped for. She felt a flare of anger. "Please excuse me, Captain," she said in her tartest tone, emphasizing his military title to remind him where he was, and who he was. She swept a cold glance over the uniform he was dishonoring by such boorish behavior, but he didn't move. He laughed.

"Now don't be like that. I'd like to know you better. I had no opportunity to enjoy your company in London. You were always out when I called." He had the audacity to run his fingertip down the exposed length of her bare arm, from the edge of her short puffed sleeve to the top of her lace glove.

Delphine enjoyed flirting as much as the next lady—in fact, she was a renowned charmer, but not like this, not here. She tried again to pluck her hand free, but still he would not let go. She drew a breath, stiffened her spine. She was going to have to make a scene after all. She clenched her free hand around her fan, ready to deal him a crushing blow with it even as she opened her mouth to rebuke him for his boorish behavior.

"Lady Delphine, I believe this is our dance."

Stephen Ives was standing next to her, and her breath stopped yet again. She shut her mouth with an audible snap.

He bowed and held out his hand, waiting for her to take it. Rothdale released her fingers as if they were on fire, obviously surprised to see the major. His handsome face reddened with displeasure.

Delphine clasped Stephen's hand like a lifeline and let him lead her away.

The music began—a waltz. Stephen set his hand on her waist and swept her onto the floor. She should thank him, but he was staring over her shoulder at Rothdale as the captain disappeared into the crowd.

"Do you know Captain Lord Rothdale? He's a friend of my brother's. He is not—that is, he and I are not—" She realized she was babbling.

His eyes remained on Rothdale. "We are in the same regiment."

Oh. Delphine felt like a ninny. He didn't add to his terse comment, or offer any pleasantries. He had rescued her from

a boor at a ball, but it appeared it was now entirely up to her
to change the subject, to charm him if she could, to make him
like her.

She had the advantage of being at a summer party in a
room filled with flowers and candles, and she was in his arms,
waltzing. She wasn't about to waste such an opportunity
talking about anyone else. The room was warm, but the glow
she felt had much more to do with being held in Stephen's
arms. She could smell his shaving soap, the wool of his tunic,
the heady fragrance of flowers as they whirled past the open
windows.

"Goodness you dance well," she tried again.

"I spent six months in Vienna. They invented the waltz."

She felt her cheeks heat. Where was her famous charm
and glib tongue now when she needed them most? "Ah, yes.
You were at the peace conference, part of the embassy. I have
heard stories, of course, about all the glittering parties with
the kings and queens of Europe, the Tsar of Russia, the Em-
peror of Austria . . ." He looked slightly bored. She swallowed.
He was a diplomat, and most unlikely to want to gossip or
repeat salacious stories about crowned heads or anyone else.
"Was the congress successful?" she asked.

His hand tensed momentarily on hers. "Unfortunately
not, or we would not be here awaiting yet another battle with
Napoleon."

"Will it come soon?"

He met her eyes at last, as if assessing the seriousness of
her question. There were many in Brussels who doubted the
battle would come at all, but she was the sister-in-law of a
colonel and knew better. She kept her eyes on his.

"Within hours, I hear. The French crossed the Belgian frontier this morning," he said at last.

She stumbled slightly, and he caught her against his body and guided her expertly into the next step. Her breath stopped again as her breasts momentarily pressed against the hard muscles of his chest. It was thrilling, like flying.

He set her down, utterly unaffected, and changed the subject. "How is it you are here in Brussels, my lady, especially now with the London Season in full bloom at home?" She did not miss the slight edge of disdain in his tone. He was making it clear that he thought her the same vain and silly creature he'd known in London, a woman who lived for pleasure and flattery, all sharp wit and flirtation, and no substance. She felt her cheeks heat.

"I came to Brussels with my sister, Eleanor, and her husband, Colonel Lord Fairlie. Meg Temberlay is with us as well. We are lodging at a villa on the outskirts of the city. It is to be a hospital, if necessary. We know that the battle is coming, of course—there are hundreds of men camped in our orchard, and even in the rose garden—but within *hours?*"

His eyes lit with interest at last. "Meg? Is Nicholas here?" he said, referring to Meg's husband, a mutual friend, Major Lord Nicholas Temberlay. Delphine felt a flare of annoyance as he scanned the crowds, looking for them, forgetting her, even though he didn't miss a step.

"Nicholas is not in the city, my lord, and we've had no real news of him, only that he is on reconnaissance. What exactly does that mean? Meg is beside herself with worry."

He swung his gaze back to her. Had he expected her to prattle about the heat of the evening, or the number of guests present, or some other banality? His look of surprise told her that was exactly what he expected from her. He brushed a glance over her gown, her face, the flowers in her hair before meeting her eyes and looking at her—*really* looking at her, gauging the depths of her interest, her intelligence. It was the way he'd looked at her before, that night long ago, before—

"It could mean many things," he said in reply to her question.

"*Is* there reason to worry? Surely Wellington will crush the French . . ." She stopped when his eyes darkened, her breath hitching for an entirely different reason now. She felt a shiver run up her spine. She tightened her grip on his hand for a brief instant.

"I do hope so, but the outcome of a battle is never certain," he said.

"Will you—will you fight?"

"Yes," he replied.

"Then you are not here in a diplomatic role?"

He scanned the ballroom again, his expression flat, whatever emotions he might be feeling closed to her. "I will ride with my regiment when the order comes."

Delphine understood a little better the terrible worry her friend Meg and her sister Eleanor felt, having men they loved in battle. Bitterness filled her mouth, and lowered her gaze to his chest.

"The Royal Dragoons," she murmured, staring at his tunic. She bit her lip. What should a lady say to a man riding off to war? This moment might be the last chance she had to speak with him, to tell him—what? That she adored him, admired him, wished he would sweep her out into the

June night and kiss her? She'd allow it. She'd kiss him back. Would she know then what she'd done wrong, all those months ago?

She looked up at him hopefully. "Major Lord Ives, I—" she began, but a soldier entered and crossed the room to Lord Wellington, his spurs and boot heels ringing above the music and the laughter of gay ladies, and the tinkle of champagne glasses. Conversation stopped, dancers faltered, and everyone watched as the soldier bowed and handed the duke a note. Wellington rose to his feet at once, his expression carefully blank, and nodded to his adjutants. The Duke of Richmond led his esteemed guest to a private room and shut the door behind them. She felt Stephen tense as a buzz of speculation rose to hover over the ballroom like a black cloud.

"Is it bad?" she whispered.

"Possibly," he said through stiff lips. "May I return you to your sister, Lady Delphine?"

She felt panic well in her breast at the thought of losing him now, or tomorrow, in battle.

She forced a teasing smile. "But the music has not ended."

He colored slightly. "No, but—"

The door of the study opened again, and a grim faced cavalry officer held up his hand for silence. The music faltered and died. "Gentlemen, finish your dances, take leave of your partners and return to your units at once." Dismayed cries rose from the ladies, and Stephen looked around, taking note of the officers in his own regiment. She saw the eager light in his eyes, knew he was already on duty, and she was all but forgotten. Still he kept his hand under her elbow protectively as he caught the arm of a passing adjutant. "What news?"

The young soldier glanced at her and bowed before replying. "Napoleon crossed the frontier at Charleroi. Wellington plans to engage him south of here."

Delphine put a hand to her throat. It was suddenly real and frightening—all the weeks of watching troops gather in preparation for a battle that seemed like it would never come, or at worst, would happen somewhere else, somewhere far away. Weeks of rolling bandages they were sure would never be needed, of flirting and dancing and picnicking with handsome officers, laughing at their bravado and the brave boasts of the daring adventures they'd have when Napoleon appeared at last. Now he was here, just south of the city. Delphine looked around her at the keen faces of the men, the tears in the ladies' eyes. Despair made her sway. Stephen took her arm more firmly, and tucked it under his own.

"Come, I'll escort you back to Lady Fairlie," he said gently.

She felt the hard muscles under his tunic, warm and alive. She wondered again just what to say when she may never see him again, and he might—she closed her eyes, leaned against him for a moment.

He squeezed her hand, and smiled faintly, offering courage. Yet the depths of his gray eyes remained cool, and there was a shadow of something else there, resignation, perhaps, or sorrow. That scared her most of all.

"My lord, what—" she began, but they had reached Eleanor's side, and he turned his attention to her. Her sister was white faced, her lips drawn into a thin line. It did nothing to soothe Delphine to see an experienced officer's wife like Eleanor, a woman who had been through many battles before, looking so grim.

"Ellie." She took her sister's hand. It was ice cold inside her glove.

Eleanor's grip was like iron. "Fairlie has gone to muster his men. He says we must go at once. We're to return to the villa, keep the horses harnessed, and go north to Antwerp and home to England if it goes badly." She looked at Stephen. Though her eyes were dry, they were huge, filled with worry. "*Will* it go badly do you think, my lord?"

"We have an excellent commander, Lady Fairlie, and excellent officers under him, Colonel Fairlie among them," he said gently. "We can hope for the best outcome, I think."

"And yet, Napoleon's officers are every bit as fine as ours. I've heard Fairlie say so," Eleanor said.

Stephen didn't reply to that. "If I may, I think Colonel Fairlie's advice was sound. You must leave at once if things go badly." He turned to Delphine and met her eyes, as if he expected *she* would be the brave one, would be the one get her sister to safety, instead of the other way around. "Come ladies, I'll see you to your carriage. The streets will be filled with troops moving up, and it may take you some time to reach home, so it's best to leave now." He took Eleanor's arm, and Delphine walked next to her sister as Stephen pressed through the crowds, seeing them safely through the crush.

Outside, the yard was in chaos. Torches lit the faces of panicked horses, their eyes rolling white as yelling coachmen tried to force their way to the door to pick up their passengers. Stephen stayed close to them, protecting them from the mayhem as they waited for Colonel Fairlie's coach to arrive.

And who would keep him safe, Delphine wondered? He was still wearing dancing pumps. He could not fight in dancing pumps. He'd need to find his boots. She felt hysterical laughter bubble up in her throat. The other officers nearby also wore their formal footwear. No, they could not fight like that, so they must stay. But they were leaving, going to war. Fear formed a hard knot in her throat, and she tried to swallow, couldn't. She watched a grinning officer mount his horse, stilling the beast's panic as it capered anxiously in the crush. He reached down and hauled a lady up to perch on his stirrup, held her close, the satin of her gown shimmering. Her arms went around his neck, and their lips met in a long, passionate kiss.

Such behavior would have been unacceptable at any other ball, on any other night, but it was right in this moment, with battle looming. Delphine wondered how many of the men here would die tomorrow. She looked at Stephen, so alive, strong and vital. The torchlight shone on his fair hair, lit his eyes, flared over his shoulders, made his scarlet tunic glow. He looked back at her as if he expected her to speak. Her lips parted, and she stepped closer, but the coach pulled up, and he turned to help Eleanor into it before taking Delphine's hand. "Goodnight, my lady, and thank you for the dance," he said with cool politeness. "Remember, if things go awry tomorrow—"

She didn't want to think about that. She threw herself into his arms to stop the words, and kissed him. He caught her, and for moment he was stiff, his posture indignant, but she stood on her toes and pressed her lips to his, praying he would come back alive.

Then his arms wrapped around her and he kissed her back. She felt the sudden desperation in him, the need. He deepened the kiss, and she opened to his urging, let his tongue sweep in. He tasted of champagne, smelled of fine wool and leather—like a soldier on his way to battle. She pressed closer still, and he kissed her with all the passion she had dreamed of.

"Delphine St. James!" her sister cried. "What are you doing? Get into this coach immediately!"

Stephen released her at once, his gaze hot and surprised for an instant. He bowed stiffly, the proper diplomat once more, the officer, the gentleman. "Good-bye, my lady," he said, and took her hand in his, and squeezed it, a thank you, perhaps—or forgiveness for her forward behavior. Her heart throbbed in her chest, and she was on the verge of tears.

"You will come back," she whispered, making it a command.

His eyes swept over her. "English daisies," he murmured, looking at the flowers in her hair. "I used to pick them when I was a boy, carry them to my mother, my sister, even the cook."

She plucked one loose and held it out to him. "Take this one for luck."

He stared at the small pink blossom for a moment before he closed his hand over it. "Thank you."

He helped her into the coach before she could say another word, his eyes on hers as the vehicle lurched forward.

She fought with the latch, lowered the window, and leaned out so she could watch him walk away. "I will see you again," she said softly. "You will be safe." The shadows swallowed him.

Suddenly it hardly mattered now if he admired her or not. She only wanted him to live.

ABOUT THE AUTHOR

Lecia Cornwall lives and writes in Calgary, Canada, in the beautiful foothills of the Canadian Rockies, with five cats, two teenagers, a crazy chocolate Lab, and one very patient husband. She's hard at work on her next book.

Visit her online at www.leciacornwall.com.

Visit www.AuthorTracker.com for exclusive information on your favorite HarperCollins authors.

Give in to your impulses . . .
Read on for a sneak peek at six brand-new
e-book original tales of romance
from Avon Books.
Available now wherever e-books are sold.

CATCHING CAMERON
A Love and Football Novel
By Julie Brannagh

DARING MISS DANVERS
The Wallflower Wedding Series
By Vivienne Lorret

WOO'D IN HASTE
By Sabrina Darby

BAD GIRLS DON'T MARRY MARINES
By Codi Gary

VARIOUS STATES OF
UNDRESS: CAROLINA
By Laura Simcox

WED AT LEISURE
By Sabrina Darby

An Excerpt from
CATCHING CAMERON
A Love and Football Novel

by Julie Brannagh

Sexy football player Zach Anderson and sports
reporter Cameron Ondine find that their past
has come back to haunt them—and maybe even
ignite a few sparks—in the third installment
of Julie Brannagh's irresistible new series.

Zach Anderson was in New York City again, and he wasn't happy about it. He wasn't big on crowds as a rule, except for the ones that spent Sunday afternoons six months a year cheering for him while he flattened yet another offensive lineman on his way to the guy's quarterback. He also wasn't big on having four people fussing over his hair, spraying him down with whatever it was that simulated sweat, and trying to convince him that nobody would ever know he was wearing bronzer in the resulting photos.

Then again, he was making eight figures for a national Under Armour campaign with two days' work; maybe he shouldn't bitch. The worst injury he might sustain here would be some kind of muscle pull while running away from the multiple women hanging out at the photo shoot who had already made it clear they'd be interested in spending more time with him.

He was all dolled up in UA's latest. Of course, he typically didn't wear workout clothes that were tailored and/or ironed before he pulled them on. The photo shoot was now in its second hour, and he was wondering how many damn pictures of him they actually needed. But there were worse things than being a pro football player who looked like the cover model on a workout magazine, was followed around by large numbers of hot young women, and got paid for it all.

"Gorgeous," the photographer shouted to him. "Okay, Zach. I need pensive. Thoughtful. Sensitive."

Zach shook his head briefly. "You're shitting me."

Zach's agent, Jason, shoved himself off the back wall of the room and moved into Zach's line of vision. Jason had been with him since Zach signed his first NFL contract. He was also a few years older than Zach, which came in handy. He took the long view in his professional and personal life, and encouraged Zach to do so as well.

"Come on, man. Think about the poor polar bears starving to death because they can't find enough food at the North Pole. How about the NFL jumping up to eighteen games in the regular season? If that's not enough, *Sports Illustrated*'s discontinuing the swimsuit issue could make a grown man cry." Even the photographer snorted at that last one. "You can do it."

Eighteen games a season would piss Zach off more than anything else, but he gazed in the direction the photographer's assistant indicated, thought about how long it would take him to get across town to his appointment when this was over, and listened to the camera's rapid clicking once more.

"Are you sure you want to keep playing football?" the photographer called out. "The camera loves you."

"Thanks," Zach muttered. Shit. How embarrassing. If any of his four younger sisters were here right now, they'd be in hysterics.

Cameron smiled into the camera for the last time today. "Thanks for watching. I'm Cameron Ondine, and I'll see you next week on *NFL Confidential*." She waited until the floor director gave her the signal that the camera was off and stood up to stretch. Today's guest had been a twenty-five-year-old quarterback who'd just signed a five-year contract with Baltimore's team for seventy-five million dollars. Fifty million of it was guaranteed. His agent hovered just off-camera, but not close enough to prevent the guy in question from asking Cameron to accompany him to his hotel suite and "hook up."

Cameron wished she were surprised about such invitations, but they happened with depressing frequency. The network wanted her to play up what she had to offer—fresh-faced, wholesome beauty, a body she worked ninety minutes a day to maintain, and a personality that proved she wasn't just another dumb blonde. She loved her job, but she didn't love the fact that some of these guys thought sleeping with her was part of the deal her employers offered when she interviewed them.

An Excerpt from
DARING MISS DANVERS
The Wallflower Wedding Series
by Vivienne Lorret

Oliver Goswick, Viscount Rathburn, needs money, but only marriage to a proper miss will release his inheritance. There's just one solution: a mock courtship with a trusted friend.

Miss Emma Danvers knows nothing good can come of Rathburn's scheme. Still, entranced by the inexplicable hammering he causes in her heart, she agrees to play his betrothed despite her heart's warning. It's all fun and games . . . until someone falls in love!

"Shall we shake hands to seal our bargain?"

Not wanting to appear as if she lacked confidence, Emma thrust out her hand and straightened her shoulders.

Rathbun chuckled, the sound low enough and near enough that she could feel it vibrating in her ears more than she could hear it. His amused gaze teased her before it traveled down her neck, over the curve of her shoulder and down the length of her arm. He took her gloveless hand. His flesh was warm and callused in places that made it impossible to ignore the unapologetic maleness of him.

She should have known this couldn't be a simple handshake, not with him. He wasn't like anyone else. So, why should this be any different?

He looked down at their joined hands, turning hers this way and that, seeing the contrast no doubt. His was large and tanned, his nails clean but short, leaving the very tips of his fingers exposed. Hers was small and slender, her skin creamy, her nails delicately rounded as was proper. Yet, when she looked at her hand covered by his, she felt anything but proper.

She tried to pull away, but he kept it and moved a step closer.

"I know a better way," he murmured and before she knew his intention, he tilted up her chin and bent his head.

His mouth brushed hers in a very brief kiss. So brief, in fact, she almost didn't get a sense that it had occurred at all. *Almost.*

However, she did get an impression of his lips. They were warm and softer than they appeared, but that was not to say they were soft. No, they were the perfect combination of softness while remaining firm. In addition, the flavor he left behind was intriguing. Not sweet like liquor or salty like toothpowder, but something in between, something ... spicy. Pleasantly herbaceous, like a combination of pepper and rosemary with a mysterious flavor underneath that reminded her ... *of the first sip of steaming chocolate on a chilly morning.* The flavor of it warmed her through. She licked her lips to be certain, but made the mistake of looking up at him.

He was staring at her lips, his brow furrowed.

The fireflies vanished from his eyes as his dark pupils expanded. The fingers that were curled beneath her chin spread out and stole around to the base of her neck. He lowered his head again, but this time he did not simply brush his lips over hers. Instead, he tasted her, flicking his tongue over the same path hers had taken.

A small, foreign sound purred in her throat. This wasn't supposed to be happening. Kissing Rathburn was wrong on so many levels. They weren't truly engaged. In fact, they were acquaintances only through her brother. They could barely stand each other. The door to the study was closed—*highly improper.* Her parents or one of the servants could walk in any minute. She should be pushing him away, not encouraging him by parting her lips and allowing his tongue entrance. She should not curl her hands over his shoulders, or discover that there was no padding in his coat. And she most definitely should not be on the verge of leaning into him—

There was a knock at the door. They split apart with a sudden jump, but the sound had come from the hall. Someone was at the front of the house.

She looked at Rathbun, watching the buttons of his waistcoat move up and down as he caught his breath. When he looked away from the door and back to her, she could see the dampness of their kiss on his lips. *Her kiss.*

He grinned and waggled his brows as if they were two criminals who'd made a lucky escape. "Not quite as buttoned-up as I thought." He licked his lips, ignoring her look of disapproval. "Mmm . . . jasmine tea. And sweet, too. I would have thought you'd prefer a more sedate China black with lemon. Then again, I never would have thought such a proper miss would have such a lush, tempting mouth either."

She pressed her lips together to blot away the remains of their kiss. "Have you no shame? It's bad enough that it happened. Must you speak of it?"

He chuckled and stroked the pad of his thumb over his bottom lip as his gaze dipped, again, to her mouth. "You're right, of course. This will have to be our secret. After all, what would happen if my grandmother discovered that beneath a façade of modesty and decorum lived a warm-blooded temptress with the taste of sweet jasmine on her lips?"

An Excerpt from
WOO'D IN HASTE
by Sabrina Darby

Miss Bianca Mansfield is ready for her
debut. If only her older sister didn't insist
on marrying first. She's doomed to wait
to find love. Until she meets . . . him.

For Lucian Dorlingsley, Viscount Asquith,
recently returned from an extended tour
abroad, it is love at first sight. He's determined
to meet Bianca, even if it means masquerading
as a tutor to her young half-brother.

A man's life can change in an instant. Lucian Dorlingsley, Viscount Asquith, heir to the Earl of Finleigh, had heard this aphorism many times, but until that particular August morning, he had never experienced such a profound moment. Not once in his sheltered childhood at his familial estate. Or during the more arduous years at Harrow and Cambridge. Not even during the long continental tour from which he had just returned.

Yet here, in the sleepy town of Watersham, where he was stopping briefly with the Colburns on his way home, his life had been rocked down to its very essence.

"I'm in love, Reggie!" He paced the length of the veranda where they were enjoying an al fresco luncheon. The sky beyond was a cerulean blue and the weather, for once, that rare balance of very English sunshine (and he had now seen enough of the world to know that sunshine had different qualities in different places) tempered by a delicate breeze. In other words, the perfect day to fall in love.

His friend, the younger brother of the Duke of Orland, looked at him doubtfully, a cautious smirk on his lips.

"Who is she, then? A Parisian dancer from the Opera? An Italian nymph? What paragon did you meet on your travels who has you so bound up in a paroxysm of amorous emotion?"

Reggie saw the world as one large jest, and on most occasions that was one of his charms. In fact, his boisterous manner was what made him so easy to be around; often Luc could simply follow him about and be amused without having to put himself forward in any way. It was also, at this moment, the one thing Luc did not need. Not about a matter so serious.

"No, nothing so cliché as all that. I saw her here, in the village this morning. I stopped by the apothecary, and there she was."

"And did you pledge your undying love to her?"

Luc shook his head, ignoring Reggie's exaggerations and persistent humor in the face of confessional honesty. An honesty that he had with few others, including his sisters. But Reggie had been the foremost companion of his youth, his roommate at Harrow and later at Cambridge. At least for the one year that Reggie had attended before he decided the pretense at study was a waste of his time. He'd been gallivanting about London ever since. "I could hardly approach her."

"I shall never understand how such a giant as yourself can be one of the most painfully shy men that I know. One would think a Grand Tour would cure you of that."

Europe had cured him, in many ways. Out of the shadow of his gregarious father, away from the judgments of his usual society, he had been able to be more himself. But now he was back in England, and . . . this was not just any woman.

"Miss Mansfield, they called her," said Luc. "Do you know her? Can she be mine?" Not that he had ever thought twice about marriage before this point. He was still young and most of his friends unattached. Yet the idea of such beauty being his . . . His own Botticelli. He looked expectantly at Reggie, but his friend's usually round, smiling face looked aghast.

"What? Is she promised to someone already? Are you in love with her, Reggie? Or is Peter? Have I lost my heart to some untouchable?"

"Untouchable, perhaps," Reggie choked out, taking a moment to twirl the long hair that fell over his forehead in sandy curls. "I didn't realize Kate was back from Brighton. But listen, Luc, this one— Forget about her. She may have been a success in London these last two seasons, but everyone in these parts knows her for the brat that she is."

Brat? Luc couldn't reconcile that word with the image that still lingered in his mind. Honey blonde hair framing a rosy-cheeked countenance. Eyes as blue as today's perfect sky. A paragon of quiet English beauty, in fact.

"She seemed quite well liked. She had a charming smile and manner. Brat seems like an unfair epithet."

"Not for Kate, but oh! Perhaps it was Bianca. Your Venus, was she fair or dark?"

An Excerpt from
BAD GIRLS DON'T MARRY MARINES
by Codi Gary

When hard-edged Valerie Willis suddenly
finds herself face-to-face with former flame
Justin Silverton, she knows her tough image
won't be enough to protect her heart.

It's been ten years since Justin kissed Val, but he's
never moved on. So when a twist of fate brings
him the chance to finally win her over during a
singles mixer, Justin's all in. Because the bad girl
who stole his heart is just too good to let go . . .

"So, why is your dad making you come down here and participate in a giant singles mixer?" Justin asked, stealing her attention away from the white slip of paper.

"He calls it good press. Guess he figures I need help finding a man," she said, wishing she hadn't answered him quite so candidly. "I don't, though. Need help, I mean."

Why are you stammering? Bending over the counter, she started filling in the blanks, hoping he couldn't see the obvious blush warming her cheeks.

"If it makes you feel any better, I never thought you needed any help in that department," he said, his voice dropping to a low whisper.

Val could feel the desk clerk's eyes on her and muttered, "Stop it."

"What? It's a compliment."

"You're just messing around to get a rise out of me."

"How is me being honest messing with you?"

"Because . . ." How did she not have a comeback to put him in his place? She always knew what to say. It was one of her strengths, but he had the ability to turn her into a stumbling, stuttering simpleton. "Because I said so."

His chuckle was a deep rumble, and her insides squeezed

in on themselves, making her cross her legs as a tingling started between them. Quickly, she handed the paper back to the desk clerk and turned to face Justin with what she hoped was a cold, hard stare.

"I don't like to be made fun of."

He seemed genuinely surprised as the desk clerk said, "Alright, Miss Willis, here is your room key and your itinerary bag. I hope you enjoy your stay in True Love and that you have a blast at the festival."

Val took the bag and key from the woman, resisting the urge to make a face. "Thank you."

Spinning away from Justin, she walked back out to her truck, only to hear him exit behind her.

"Hey!" His hand circled her arm gently, and he turned her toward him, but on the slick ground, she lost her balance. Falling against him, her face got buried in the puff of his jacket, and she wondered if the fates were trying to pull some weird *Serendipity* crap on her.

She tried to right herself, but he'd wrapped an arm around her waist and was using the other gloved hand to lift her chin, raising her gaze to meet his.

"I wasn't making fun of you. I was being serious. You're a beautiful woman. You just say the word and a dozen guys will line up to have you."

Whether it was his tone or the expression on his face, she didn't know, but her mouth suddenly seemed too dry. Words failed her, but then, who needed words when a pair of warm lips were suddenly covering hers?

As Justin kissed her, his tongue pushing past her lips, she could only hold on tight while her body turned to molten lava and the blood thundered in her ears.

Impatient honking and a loud voice yelling, "Hey, love-birds, get a room," broke through the drumbeat her heart was pounding out, and she whispered, "We shouldn't do this."

His lips touched hers lightly once more, and he whispered back, "You mean here or—"

The guy in the truck honked again and Val pulled away. "I mean, I'm not here for . . . for that."

Justin crossed his arms over his chest. "That's too bad."

Again a blast of honking ensued, and Val shot the driver a nasty look and a worse gesture before turning away from Justin and reaching for her car door. Looking over her shoulder at him, she couldn't stop herself from asking, "About the guys lined up . . ."

"Yeah?"

"I take it you're one of them?" She already knew the answer, but the small piece of her ego that had been smashed by Cole's designer shoes needed to hear it aloud.

He stepped forward and helped her into the car, grinning. "What do you think?"

She didn't answer before she closed the door and started her truck.

Why did you have to ask him that?

Because she was a glutton for torture and punishment.

An Excerpt from
VARIOUS STATES OF UNDRESS: CAROLINA

by Laura Simcox

What happens when the president's
daughter and her sexy Secret Service agent
find themselves snowbound? A little cabin
fever, some serious forbidden attraction,
and Various States of Undress . . .

Alarm coursed through Jake's blood the second his lips were on hers, but he ignored it. They'd already crossed the line, hadn't they? Hell, they'd probably crossed the line the minute they'd walked into the cabin yesterday, if he was being honest with himself. Not that he wanted to be honest right now. He just wanted more. More softness. More of her lips, which were brushing gently against his—opening, inviting.

Her fresh scent enveloped him when she wrapped her arms tighter, and he groaned, splaying his fingers across her slender back. This was wrong. No matter how safe it seemed, it would come back to haunt him. He knew that. But as his lips angled across hers and his tongue slid into her sweet mouth, the heat he found inside was intoxicating. He sank into her, returning her kisses, drawing her closer. Getting lost in her arms.

Trailing kisses across her cheeks and down her slender neck, he threaded one hand through her hair and cupped the back of her head as he bent forward, capturing her mouth again.

She let out a soft moan, and her warm hands drifted to the side of his face. She kissed him feverishly, and then her lips broke free and settled in the crook of his jaw. She whispered his name. "Jake. Jake, I want—"

"Carolina," he answered in a rush of breath. His eyes closed, and he dragged his hand from her back to caress the side of her breast. Even though she wore a couple of layers, he could tell that one of those layers wasn't a bra. His jaw tightened as he imagined her naked breasts. He wanted to taste them—and he could. Because she would let him.

Desire crashed through him, rushing straight down, making him swell in an instant. He opened his eyes and looked into hers, which were half-lidded with lust. Her head was still pillowed in his palm.

"Touch me," she said. "Please."

Instinctively, he shook his head. "I can't."

"You can." She settled her fingers over his, pushing them around her breast.

"I can," he admitted. He stared at her open mouth, aching to take it again. "But I won't."

She blinked. "We've already crossed the line, you know."

"Not completely." He let out a slow breath, lifted her back into a kneeling position, and let his hands slide away from her body.

"Far enough."

It was nowhere near far enough, but Jake couldn't think about that right now. Clearing his throat, he stood up and offered her a hand. She stared at it, not moving.

"Carolina . . ."

"Why can't we just enjoy each other?" She tilted her chin and stared up at him.

He shoved his hand into his pocket and turned away to walk into the kitchen. Once he was behind a counter, he adjusted the front of his jeans and reached for the coffee-pot. Annoyance began to seep in, killing his lust. Good. He needed the distraction of being irritated, because she *knew* the answer to her own question. He shouldn't have to spell it out.

"Why, Jake?"

He poured himself a mug and took a sip, buying time. Part of his job description was to reason with his protectees, but usually that meant explaining why, for security reasons, certain entrances, exits, and safety measures had to be used. It didn't mean reasoning with a daughter of the President of the United States . . . who wanted to sleep with him. Especially since he'd just given her every indication that he wanted the same thing.

"Your life depends on it, that's why."

An Excerpt from
WED AT LEISURE
by Sabrina Darby

In all of Sussex—scratch that—in all of England, there is no prettier Kate than Kate Mansfield, and Peter Colburn, heir to the Duke of Orland, has known that since the age of 15. But since she comes with a temper and a haughtiness to match, he's hidden his regard behind ruthless teasing. When his brother tries to enlist him in a campaign to help his friend marry Kate's younger sister, Bianca, he agrees, finally having the very excuse he needs to approach Kate not as a combatant, but as a lover.

1810

Kate ran through the thicket, gasping, her face hot with suppressed tears. The governess would chide her for the stains and small abrasions to her dress once she returned to the house. But those admonitions were nothing compared to her mother's continued disdain.

The scent of moist earth and the sound of rushing water meant that she was close, that soon she could let go. Finally, she broke through the cluster of trees and bushes and made it to the water's edge, where she dropped down to her knees, clutched at clumps of grass with her fists, threw her head back, and wailed.

"Ahem."

Kate clamped her mouth shut and looked toward the familiar voice, embarrassment flushing her body. How humiliating.

The Earl of Bonhill sat under a tree, a book open on his lap, his trousers rolled up and his legs dangling into the stream that, a mile off, fed into the river, and that farther upstream offered her father a perfect spot for angling. The same stream that marked the boundary between the Colburns' ducal seat and the Mansfields' more modest estate. Here, however, titles hardly mattered. What did matter was that Peter had gotten there first and taken the best spot. And was now witnessing Kate in tears.

She hadn't even known he was back from Harrow.

She scrambled to her feet, glaring at him, as anger was the only possible refuge from humiliation, and headed back to the thicket.

"You don't have to run," he said, the crunch of his footsteps on the fallen leaves growing louder as he came nearer. "I'll go."

For some reason that made her more upset, and she stopped, whirling around to face him. He was 16, she knew. Four years her elder.

"It doesn't matter if you do. It's already ruined." She wouldn't be able to indulge in tears the same way anymore.

"Then maybe I can help."

"How?"

He shrugged. "Why don't you tell me why you're crying?"

"I'm not crying."

"Not anymore."

"I'm—" She shut her mouth. It wasn't worth arguing. After all, she *had* been crying.

"That's right. The fearsome Kate Mansfield makes other people cry, but she'd never be caught with such lowering emotions herself."

He was mocking her. Or needling her. Or . . .

"Just because you're an earl doesn't mean you get to be cruel."

"Someone didn't do what you want? Didn't let you have

your way?"

Frustration welled up inside her. Why was he saying such things? Of course, it was just what everyone else echoed. Everyone but her mother.

"You don't know anything about me," she said hotly, tears once again burning her eyelids.

"Then why don't you tell me?"

And for some reason she did.

About her mother, who hated her, who said she was ugly because she was so dark, who criticized everything Kate ever did, while little Bianca could do no wrong. About how no one ever paid her attention unless she did something terrible.

"So you do it on purpose, then. All the fits and tantrums we hear about—you do that for attention."

She flushed with mortification for the hundredth time that hour. She'd never thought about her reputation in the community. At twelve, her world barely existed beyond Hopford Manor. And then there was this suggestion he was making, and she wasn't certain if it was a good thing or bad. But she knew one thing, she didn't *need* attention, and his intimating that she craved it made her seem terribly weak.

"As if I'd care what anyone thinks. Especially you. Look at you. A spotted maypole!"

He flushed, which made those *spots* redden even more. There weren't all that many, but anyone would be conscious of having such flawed skin. Kate's was not. Not that one would know from the many admonishments her mother imparted about good care for one's complexion.

"You're a spoiled child, Kate Mansfield," he pronounced, picking up his book from the ground. "Maybe someday you'll grow out of it."

She watched him leave in angry frustration, hands curled into fists. It didn't matter that he was an earl and heir to a duchy, or that previously she had thought him nice and handsome and had even imagined growing up, falling in love with him, and becoming a duchess. From now on she'd stay as far away from him as possible.